KNITORIOUS MURDER MYSTERIES BOOKS 7-9

A Knitorious Murder Mysteries Collection

REAGAN DAVIS

COPYRIGHT

Sign up for Reagan Davis' email list to be notified of new releases: https://landing.mailerlite.com/webforms/landing/b9p8h1

ISBN: 978-1-990228-04-9 (ebook)

ISBN: 978-1-990228-12-4 (print)

CONTENTS

SINS & NEEDLES

REST IN FLEECE

LIFE CRAFTER DEATH

A Knitorious Murder Mystery Book 7

Sins & Needles

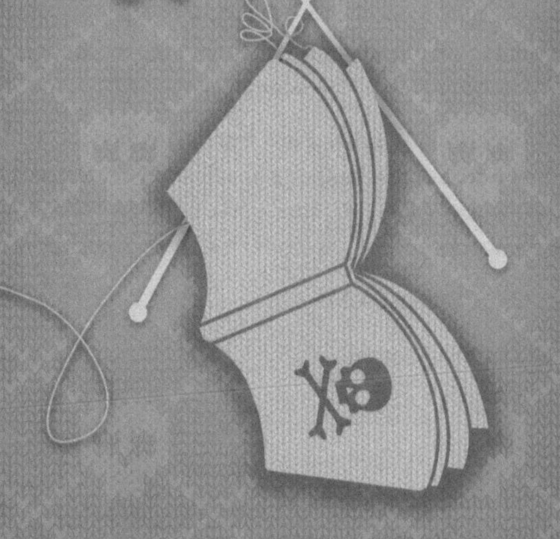

REAGAN DAVIS

COPYRIGHT

Sign up for Reagan Davis' email list to be notified of new releases: www.ReaganDavis.com

ISBN: 978-1-7772359-7-0 (ebook)

ISBN: 978-1-7772359-6-3 (print)

FOREWORD

Dear Reader,

Despite several layers of editing and proofreading, occasionally a typo or grammar mistake is so stubborn that it manages to thwart my editing efforts and camouflage itself amongst the words in the book.

If you encounter one of these obstinate typos or errors in this book, please let me know by contacting me at Hello@ReaganDavis.com.

Hopefully, together we can exterminate the annoying pests.

Thank you!

Reagan Davis

CHAPTER 1

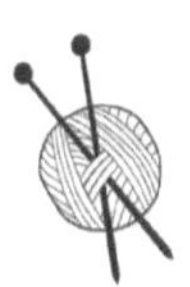

Wednesday, April 14th

"I can't believe Claire Rivera will be here, in person! At our humble, little yarn store!" Marla claps her hands in front of her chin in delight. Her short, spikey pixie cut and brilliant blue eyes remind me of an excited elf.

My corgi, Sophie, jolts awake at the sound of Marla's clap, then realizing there's nothing to see here, lowers her head and resumes her nap.

Marla works part-time at my yarn store, Knitorious. Claire Rivera is her favourite author. Besides being the world-famous author of the hugely popular Familia series of books, Claire is also an avid needle felter and fellow fibre enthusiast. She's in town this week to attend Harmony Lake's annual Between the Covers Book Fair.

In honour of Claire's attendance at the book fair, our local Charity Knitting Guild needle felted miniature versions of the characters and settings from Claire's famous book series. They're selling the miniatures during the book fair and donating the proceeds to ABC Life Literacy Canada, a nonprofit organization that supports community-based literacy programs.

Claire learned about the charity knitters' initiative when an anonymous fan—me! I'm the anonymous fan—sent her a link to an article on The Front Page, Harmony Lake's online newspaper. She emailed me, asking if she could visit Knitorious after-hours to view the display in person. I replied, telling her I'm closing the store early today for a special reveal for the charity knitters who crafted the display, and suggested that she would be welcome to attend. She accepted my invitation. To protect her privacy, and prevent mass disappointment if she doesn't show up, I haven't told the charity knitters that Claire is attending. The only people who know are me, Connie, Marla, my best friend, April, and my boyfriend, Eric.

"How's that?" I ask, after placing the last character into the display.

"Oh, Megan, it's perfect!" Marla replies, her blue eyes sparkling. "Claire Rivera will love it!"

Until this week, I never noticed how often we refer to famous people by their first and last names as if it's one name.

"I certainly hope so," Connie interjects. "As a needle felter, Claire Rivera should appreciate the time and effort that went into this exhibit."

Needle felting is the process of repeatedly stabbing animal fibre with a barbed needle to manipulate the fibre into 3D sculptures. Each miniature character and object in our display took hours of work and thousands of stabs.

Connie is my other part-time employee and surrogate mother. Connie and I met when Adam, Hannah, and I first moved to Harmony Lake almost seventeen years ago. We became instant friends, and soon after, we became family. I lost my mum just after Hannah's first birthday, and Hannah was born when I was just twenty-one. So, when Connie and I met, I was a young, recently married, new mum who was grieving. I'd wandered into Knitorious to buy yarn because I had knitted through my entire yarn stash while knitting through my grief during Hannah's naps. Connie welcomed us, nurtured us, and filled the mother and grandmother-shaped holes in our hearts. At almost seventy-one years young, she's the most beautiful, smart, and sophisticated woman I know. Connie is the original owner of Knitorious. I started working for her part-time about six years ago. Last year, she decided it was time to retire and move out of the apartment above the store. She moved into a new condo with her boyfriend, Archie, and I took over as owner of Knitorious. So, now I own Knitorious, and Connie works for me part-time. We've come full circle.

"According to the Harmony Lake rumour mill, Claire Rivera has been in town for over a week already," Marla informs us, smoothing her salt-and-pepper pixie cut. "Rumour has it she and her assistant are staying in a rental cottage on the lake, and she's writing the next *Familia* book."

Most of that is probably true. The Harmony Lake

rumour mill's remarkable accuracy rate is matched only by their speed and dedication.

"Has anyone seen her around town?" I ask.

"Not that I've heard," Marla responds, "but apparently, she's reclusive when she's working."

"Claire Rivera isn't the only celebrity in Harmony Lake this week," Connie reminds us. "I heard that Jules Janssen and her entourage booked an entire floor at King of the Hill."

Jules Janssen is an award-winning, A-list Hollywood actor. She's attending the Between the Covers Book Fair to sign copies of her autobiography, *Pretending to be Real: My Life as an Optical Delusion.*

King of the Hill is one of the two ski resorts in the Harmony Hills mountains. The mountains border our cozy town to the north, and the lake borders us to the south. Harmony Lake is a tiny patch of small-town paradise nestled snugly between a lake and a mountain range. The mountains keep us busy with tourists during the winter months, and the lake ensures we're overrun with tourists in the summer months.

"Why would she need an entire floor?" I wonder out loud.

Marla counts on her fingers and replies, "Her manager, her agent, her publicist, her security team, her glam squad…"

"I get it," I say, nodding. "It takes a team of people for Jules Janssen to go anywhere." Great, now I'm referring to people by their first and last names too.

"This will be our biggest, most successful book fair ever. We've never had three celebrities before," Marla observes. "And none of them would be here if it weren't for you, Megan. I can't tell you how thankful the book club is."

"It was nothing," I reply. "I just made one phone call."

The book club worried the annual book fair would be a bust because Harmony Lake has had some less-than-positive publicity over the past year, thanks to a sudden surge in mysterious deaths. It scared the organizers that book lovers might skip Between the Covers in favour of book fairs hosted by towns with lower murder rates.

The organizing committee embraced the negative publicity and made murder mysteries and crime thrillers this year's book fair theme. To help make the book fair a success, I asked my father, famous mystery author Mitchell Monroe, to attend as a guest author and maybe do a reading and sign some books. My father, who loves to be the centre of attention everywhere he goes, graciously accepted the invitation. He and my stepmother, Zoe, are scheduled to arrive in Harmony Lake tomorrow.

I doubt he'll be as excited as Marla about two other celebrities; Mitchell likes to be the most famous person in whatever room he occupies.

"Well, because of your phone call, the other two celebrities came to us!" Marla sounds amazed. "First, Claire Rivera contacted us because she heard we scheduled Mitchell Monroe to attend, then Jules Janssen contacted us and asked if we could fit her in as a guest author. Can you imagine? A celebrity worried *we* might turn *them* away!"

"I'm looking forward to seeing Mitchell and Zoe again," Connie says, changing the subject. "I hope we're able to spend some quality time together between book fair engagements."

"We're having a family dinner on Saturday night," I remind her. "And I'm sure Mitchell and Zoe will make time for you. I think they come to Harmony Lake as much to visit you and Archie as they do to visit me and Hannah."

Hannah is my daughter. She's nineteen years old and attends university four and a half hours away in Toronto. Mitchell and Zoe are stopping in Toronto to visit Hannah on their way here. They're staying in Toronto overnight, then driving to Harmony Lake tomorrow morning.

"Well, I'm carrying around a few copies of the celebrity authors' books and a pen, so if I bump into them around town, I can ask them to sign them for me."

"That sounds heavy," I respond. "If I bump into one of them, I guess I'll have to ask them to sign my e-reader," I joke.

While we tidy the store to prepare for the big needle-felting-reveal party and celebrity-author guest star, we gossip about the rumoured plot of Claire Rivera's next *Familia* book and the outlandish tabloid magazine stories about Jules Janssen's love life. Our conversation ends when the bell over the door jingles, and a customer enters the store.

"Hi, there," I greet the customer, smiling.

She acknowledges me with a tight-lipped smile. Sophie rushes from her bed to the door to greet the new arrival, but the customer either ignores or doesn't notice the corgi pacing at her feet trying to get her attention. Sophie finally gives up and jumps on the sofa in the cozy knitting area to lick her wounded pride.

She doesn't look familiar. But with her dark sunglasses and baseball cap pulled down over her eyes, it's hard to tell. She might be a tourist in town for the book fair.

I busy myself pushing a broom around the back half of the store, aware of the mystery shopper lingering nearby. She sneaks glances at me as she slowly wanders toward me. When I feel her gaze on me, I turn and she looks away. She pets the yarn like she's shopping for canned goods, not squishy, fluffy yarn. I don't think she's a fibre artist.

"Can I help you find anything?" I ask when she's about a metre away from me.

"Are you Megan Monroe?" The mystery shopper asks.

"I was. Once upon a time," I reply. "No one has called me that for over twenty years. Do we know each other?"

"I'm sorry." The mystery shopper shakes her head. "I wasn't sure. I couldn't find any information about you online. You're Mitchell Monroe's daughter, right?"

Great. She's a Mitchell Monroe fan. I bet she's here to ask me to help her meet my dad.

"Yes, Mitchell Monroe is my dad, but my name is Megan Martel," I explain. "Listen, if you're hoping to meet Mitchell, he's scheduled to read from his latest book..."

The mystery shopper waves her hands, interrupting me mid-sentence. "I'm not a fan," she elaborates. Then she chuckles. "I'm sorry, that sounded rude. I mean, I *am* a fan, I've read several of your father's books, but that's not why I'm here. I'm here to ask you a favour."

This piques my interest.

"What kind of favour?" I ask.

The mystery shopper takes off her sunglasses and baseball cap. She shakes out her thick, glossy, auburn hair and flashes me an impossibly white, toothy smile.

"You're Jules Janssen," I say, shocked and maybe a bit starstruck.

She nods. "Is there somewhere private where we can talk?" she asks, checking behind both shoulders for potential interlopers.

Why would an A-list celebrity look for information about me online? What kind of favour could she possibly want me to do for her? There's only one way to find out.

"Sure," I reply, "follow me." I jerk my head toward the back room.

CHAPTER 2

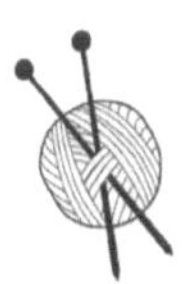

I GESTURE for Jules to go first, and as she steps in front of me, a finger taps my shoulder.

"Is that Jules Janssen?" Connie mouths, exaggerating her silent words to ensure I understand her.

"Yes," I mouth, nodding.

"What does she want?" Connie mouths, concern creasing her forehead and the corners of her blue eyes.

I shrug. "I don't know," I mouth. Then in my normal volume, I add, "Why don't you join us? I'm sure Marla can cope by herself for a few minutes."

Connie nods in agreement and slips past me into the back room.

Marla is busy making adjustments to the front display window and didn't seem to notice our incognito guest. I guess Jules's disguise works. I tell Marla that Connie and I will be back in a few minutes, and tell her to holler if she needs us.

Jules introduces herself to Connie, and I invite them

to have a seat at the table in the kitchenette area. I offer Jules a tea or coffee, which she declines, and join them at the small table.

"I understand Claire Rivera is planning to visit your store this evening," Jules says.

"Where did you hear that?" I ask, neither confirming nor denying her statement.

"Irrelevant," Jules responds, waving away my comment. "I've been trying to meet with Claire for months. She won't take my calls or answer my emails. She's a hard person to get in touch with. I've resorted to following her to book fairs and book signings to get some face time with her."

"OK," I acknowledge with a one-shoulder shrug. "What does it have to do with me?"

"I'm hoping you'll give Claire a gift for me," Jules explains, unzipping her backpack and pulling out a gift bag with tissue paper artfully sticking out of the top.

"What is it?" I ask.

Jules Janssen might be famous, but I don't know her, and I'm not comfortable acting as a liaison between her and Claire. Especially if Claire has made it clear that she doesn't want to talk to Jules, and if I don't know what I'm passing along to Claire on Jules's behalf.

"Just a few small tokens," Jules replies. "I'll show you." She pulls the tissue paper out of the bag and places it on the table. "A copy of my autobiography, signed of course." She places the book on top of the tissue paper, flattening it, then she pulls out another book. "A popular needle felting book, signed by the author, with a personal inscription for Claire." She places the needle-felting book on top of her autobiography. "I had to pull a few strings to get this," she says, smiling and tapping the felting book. Jules reaches into the bag once more and pulls out a small felted sheep. "I needle felted this sheep myself. I learned how to needle felt to show Claire that I'm the perfect actor to play Mama in the film adaptations of the Familia book series."

The Familia book series tells the story of a modern-day organized crime family and their matriarch, Mama. Mama is a complex, interesting character. She's a loving mother, PTA member, and moral compass, but she's also a ruthless mob boss who will stop at nothing to protect her family and their interests. She's also a needle felter, and her needle felting acts as a plot device to show the reader how Mama feels; the more aggressively she stabs her current project, the angrier she is.

"I wasn't aware the Familia series is being made into a film," Connie says, excited at the prospect.

"It's not," Jules confirms, looking at Connie, "but I plan to change that." Jules looks at me. "I was born to play Mama," Jules insists. "I know Claire has said publicly that she'll never allow the books to be made into movies, but I know if I talk to her, I could change her mind."

"And you're hoping these gifts will convince her to talk to you?" I deduce.

Jules nods enthusiastically. "Exactly!" Her smile shows more teeth than I think I have in my entire mouth. "When she reads my autobiography, and this note I wrote to her,"—Jules opens the cover of the needle-felting book to reveal an envelope addressed to Claire in cursive handwriting—"I know she'll see I can help her bring *Familia* to life and introduce the series to a whole new audience."

I feel like she's trying to sell me something. This is definitely a practiced sales pitch.

I sigh. "If I see her," I disclaim, "I'll give Claire the gift bag, but I can't guarantee she'll contact you, or that she'll even open it."

"That's all I ask," Jules says, then she places her hand on top of mine. "Thank you, Megan! I appreciate it."

"No worries." I smile and drag my hand out from under hers.

"Also," Jules adds, lowering her chin and looking up at me coyly from beneath her long, well-maintained lash extensions. "I was hoping you could put in a kind word for me. Maybe you could say something like, I think Jules would be perfect for the role of Mama."

I don't like being manipulated.

"Jules," I say, sitting up a little straighter in my chair, "I'm happy to give the gift bag to Claire on your behalf, *if* I see her, but that's all I can do. Besides, I don't even know Claire, so my opinion won't mean anything to her."

"That's not what I hear," Jules responds matter-of-factly. "I'm told Claire and your father used to be very close. I'm sure it's not a coincidence that she's attending this book fair and visiting your store. I mean, you must be friends, otherwise why would an author as famous as Claire Rivera attend a book fair in this hick little town?" She chuckles, ignorant to the casual insult she just made.

I'm offended, and judging by the way Connie is smoothing her silver, chin-length bob with her chin held high, I'm not the only one.

Connie opens her mouth to speak, but I speak first, hoping to stop her from saying something she might regret. Connie is fiercely protective of the people she loves and of our sweet, tight-knit community. I think Jules Janssen just lost a fan.

"Like I said," I stand up, "I'll pass along the gift to Claire if I see her. If not, I'll leave it at the front desk at your hotel." Following my lead, Connie and Jules also stand up.

Connie opens the door that separates the back room from the store. "It was lovely to meet you, Ms. Janssen. I hope you enjoy your stay in our hick little town," she says in an over-the-top, saccharine-like voice with a fake smile plastered on her face.

"It was lovely to meet you, too, Connie," Jules responds, seemingly oblivious to Connie's intended sarcasm. "Here," she says, thrusting a business card at me. "This is my private number. Call or text me if Claire says anything at all about my gift, a potential movie, anything."

I take the card and smile. Jules gathers her auburn tresses and twists them into a bun, which she covers with her baseball cap. Then she dons her sunglasses and tugs the brim of the cap to shield her face. She hoists her backpack onto her shoulders.

"Have a nice day," I say.

Jules walks briskly toward the front of the store with her head down.

I gesture for Connie to exit the back room ahead of me, but she closes the door, places her hands on her slim hips, and quirks an eyebrow.

"Claire Rivera used to be close to your father?" Connie asks. "Neither you nor Mitchell have mentioned this before."

"Actually," I say, securing Jules's business card to the side of the fridge with a magnet, "we told you. We just didn't use Claire's name." I resume my seat at the table in the kitchenette.

"I'm listening, my dear," Connie says, taking the seat across from me.

"Remember about ten years ago when my dad's author assistant resigned out of nowhere, then became an overnight sensation with a book series that my dad swears was his idea?"

Connie nods, then gasps when the realization hits her. "You don't mean Claire Rivera is the assistant who stole Mitchell's idea?"

I nod. "That's what my dad says. He swears the Familia series was his idea. He hadn't written any books, but the series was in the development stage, and he had made extensive notes when Claire quit. Then less than a year later, out of nowhere, she hit the best-seller lists with the first *Familia* book."

"Why didn't Mitchell do something?" Connie asks. "Couldn't he have sued her or something?"

"He considered it," I admit, "but he didn't want to give her any more oxygen, as he likes to say. He believes there's no such thing as bad publicity, and he didn't want to help make Claire's series more popular than it already was. Also, he didn't want to appear bitter, like he resented his former assistant's success. He confronted her privately, but she denied it. So, he did nothing. He kept writing his books and moved on with his life."

"Does Claire know you own Knitorious?" Connie asks. "Is she coming tonight intentionally to see you, or will she be shocked you're here?"

I shrug and shake my head. "I don't know. I've been asking myself the same questions. She emailed me at the store email address, but when I replied, I signed the email, Megan Martel. She knows my dad is attending the book fair. Back in the day, before my father accused her of plagiarism, she knew I lived in Harmony Lake. Claire and I were never close, but we were friendly. We haven't spoken since she resigned as my dad's author assistant."

"It sounds like tonight might be more interesting than we were expecting," Connie observes.

We stop talking when someone knocks on the door. Marla opens the door enough to peek her head in.

"I'm sorry to interrupt, ladies."

"You're not interrupting anything, Marla," I assure her.

"Megan and I were just talking about the book fair," Connie adds.

"Would one of you mind standing on the sidewalk and telling me if the book fair banner in the display window is straight and centred?" Marla asks.

"Of course," I reply, standing up.

"Megan, you take the sidewalk, and I'll help Marla in the window," Connie instructs.

Stepping onto the sidewalk, I squint into the midday sun. I should've grabbed my sunglasses. I position myself on the curb and use one hand as a visor to keep the sun out of my eyes as I squint at the store window.

I use my free hand to point to my left. "To the left," I shout, even though they can't hear me.

Marla and Connie nod, then move the banner to the left.

"Stop," I shout, holding up my hand in a stop motion. They stop, and I give them a thumbs-up.

I point to the right, then jerk my thumb upward. The right side needs to move up a little. Marla complies, and I wave when she raises it enough. Then I give them another thumbs-up.

I'm about to go inside when something catches my eye. In the blur of my peripheral vision, something moves around the corner, in the laneway that leads to the parking lot, behind the store. I check for traffic, then step backward, off the curb, and onto Water Street. I crane my neck and squint, trying to peek around the corner. It's Jules Janssen. The back of her baseball cap and backpack are facing me. She's not alone. A younger, well-dressed, bald man stands in front of her. They're stance is intimate and friendly, and they're in each other's personal space. He's smiling and laughing. He's handsome. His hand moves to her butt, further convincing me they're more than friends. He stoops down and kisses her. Yup, definitely more than friends.

If someone told me this morning that I'd catch A-list celebrity Jules Janssen canoodling with a tall, handsome stranger in the alley beside my store, I would have said they were crazy, but here we are.

CHAPTER 3

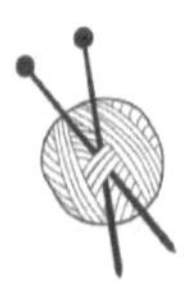

Marla and Connie go home to freshen up before they meet their favourite author, and I sit down at the harvest table near the back of the store and work on a miniature, needle-felted Sophie. It's for my daughter, Hannah. I plan to turn it into a key chain and give it to her when she comes home for the summer in a couple of weeks.

Stabbing is oddly satisfying; nothing relieves stress like stabbing something over-and-over with a sharp, barbed needle.

The bell over the door jingles, bringing me back to reality.

"Megastar, where are you?"

My best friend, April, likes to call me nicknames that are puns of my name. Today, I'm Megastar.

"I'm here," I say on my way to the counter.

April places a large, white confectionery box on the counter, and we have a tight hug. Then she squats down to greet Sophie, who's acting like she might explode if April doesn't acknowledge her right now.

"The needle-felting display looks amazing," she says.

"Thank you," I respond. "We worked hard on it. There are a lot of bandaged fingers in Harmony Lake this week because of this display," I tease, referring to all the crafters who accidentally stabbed themselves instead of the fibre.

"Are you ready for Claire Rivera's visit?" April asks, using Claire's first and last name.

I nod. "As ready as we can be. I'm waiting until the last minute to put out the finger food." I point to the confectionery box with the Artsy Tartsy logo on the lid. "What's this?"

April and her wife, Tamara, own the local bakery, Artsy Tartsy. Tamara is a talented pastry chef, and her creations are famous around here.

"A little something for your event," April replies.

She opens the box to reveal cookies shaped like stacks of book spines. Tamara used icing to make the book spines look like the Familia series of books. She captured the colours, titles, and even the font with perfection.

"Oh, April!" I gasp in disbelief at the artistry. "Please tell T she's outdone herself. These are beautiful!" I resist the urge to pick one up.

T is what we call Tamara.

"She wanted to do something special," April explains. "We'll be selling these, along with other bookish treats, during the book fair."

"These will take centre stage on the table," I declare, carrying the box to the harvest table.

I tidy my needle-felting supplies and head to the kitchenette in search of a platter to display the cookies.

"Has Claire confirmed she's still coming?" April asks, following me into the kitchenette.

I shake my head. "No, but she hasn't backed out, either, so I assume she'll be here."

"Do you think it will be weird?" she asks. "Because of her history with your dad? I can be here if it'll help," she offers.

"That's sweet." I smile. "But I know you and T are working all hours baking for the book fair. I'll be fine on my own. Besides, Connie knows about Claire and Mitchell's history, so if I need support, she'll have my back."

I find the platter I'm looking for; it's in the cabinet above the fridge. Seeing me struggle on my tippy toes, my tall best friend reaches above the fridge with little effort and retrieves it for me.

"Thank you for helping your short friend," I joke.

April and I are opposites in more than height. Where she's tall and willowy, I'm short and curvy. Where she has straight, blonde hair, I have long, curly, brown hair. April has blue eyes and a year-round tan, whereas I have hazel eyes and fair skin.

"What you lack in height, you make up for in personality, Megapop," April reassures me. "Anyway, you're in good company. T is friends with the chef at King of the Hill, and he said Jules Janssen is shorter in person than on the big screen. She's about your height. Good things come in small packages."

"He's right," I agree. "She is my height. I didn't realize it until you mentioned it."

"How do you know how tall Jules Janssen is?" April asks, her eyes narrow.

"I met her today," I reply. "She came to the store incognito."

"Spill!" April demands.

While we plate the bookish cookies, then plate and arrange the rest of the food, I tell April about my discussion with Jules, the gifts she wants me to give to Claire, and her cozy conversation with the unknown man in the alley beside Knitorious.

"If Jules's plan works, and Claire agrees to talk to her because of you, you'll be able to say you're the reason they made the *Familia* books into movies," April theorizes. "Maybe they'll include your name in the credits."

"As what?" I ask. "Artist liaison? Mutual acquaintance? Small-town hick?"

April stops plating finger sandwiches and looks at me. "Small-town hick?"

I tell April about Jules's offhand remark about Harmony Lake, and I think Jules just lost another fan.

We finish plating the cheese and crackers, and the bell over the door jingles. Connie, Marla, and a handful of charity knitters enter the store together.

"I have to go," April whispers. She stands up and pushes in her chair. "Text me if you need anything. I can be here in less than five minutes. Two if it's for drama."

I nod. "I will."

April gives me a smile and says hi and bye to everyone on her way out.

After the last charity knitter arrives, I lock the door and replace the OPEN sign with the CLOSED FOR A PRIVATE FUNCTION sign we hardly ever have occasion to use.

I make the rounds, greeting each person and thanking them for coming. Then, while everyone exchanges compliments, admiring the display and each other's needle-felting prowess, I slip into the kitchen to make tea and coffee.

While putting coffee and tea condiments on a tray, a dull thud at the back door gets my attention. Not a knock, more like a kick.

"Hello?" I say through the closed door.

"Hello?" a woman's voice replies, sounding strained. "A little help?"

"Oh, my goodness!" I say when I open the door to a young, blonde, full-figured woman who's buckling under the weight of a cardboard box. "Let me help," I insist. "You've really got your hands full."

"Careful, it's heavy." The mystery woman grunts as we ease the box from her arms to mine. "Thank you," she says with a heavy sigh. "As much as I love books, they're heavy when you pack lots of them in the same box." She chuckles.

I place the box on the table in the kitchenette. "I

didn't order any books," I say, confused and wondering if she's delivering them to the wrong store.

"Claire brought them for the needle felters who made the *Familia* display," she explains. "They're signed. We weren't sure how many to bring, and we probably brought too many."

"Oh," I say, struck with comprehension. "You're with Claire!" I smile. "Hi! I'm Megan Martel. It's nice to meet you." I extend my hand.

"Dina Langley," she responds, shaking my hand. "Claire Rivera's assistant."

"Will Claire be joining us, or are you here on her behalf?" I ask, pouring water from the kettle to the teapot.

"Claire's in the car. She's finishing a call. She'll be right in," Dina replies. "I hope it's all right to use the back door. I don't think I could carry that box around to the front."

"Of course," I assure her. "I'm glad I was nearby to hear you knock—er, kick."

I pick up the tray of tea and condiments to carry them to the harvest table in the store, with the finger food.

"Let me take that for you," Dina suggests. She's already taking the tray from me before she finishes her sentence. "I'm dying to see the display." Her smile is genuine and warm.

"Oh, do you needle felt?" I ask, letting go of the tray.

"No." She shakes her head. "But I've watched Claire do it, and I admire the creativity and skill. The little forest animals are my favourite. I think they're adorable."

A sharp rap at the back door brings an abrupt end to our conversation. On my way to open it, I tell Dina where to put the tray, thank her for her help, and tell her to help herself to the refreshments.

I take a deep breath and brace myself to see Claire for the first time in a decade. For the first time since she betrayed my father.

"Megan." Claire's smile is warm but cautious. "Do you remember me? Claire Rivera? I was Mitche..."

"Of course, I remember you, Claire!" I smile and she pulls me into an awkward hug. "You look the same as you did ten years ago. Why haven't you aged?" I ask when I pull away.

It must be the dimples; For whatever reason, dimples make people look younger. At thirty-five, Claire is six years younger than me, but she doesn't look a day over twenty-five. It helps she has ageless features; her large brown eyes, round face, and dimpled cheeks suggest youth. She styles her brown hair the same, just below her shoulders with bangs. Claire Rivera looks exactly as I remember.

"I was about to ask you the same question," she replies. "You're radiant."

"Thank you," I say.

"How's Hannah?" she asks.

I pull my phone from my pocket and open the camera roll. "You might regret asking that," I tease.

Claire and I spend a few minutes getting caught up. She moved to the West Coast after she resigned as my father's assistant, and she never married because *Familia* takes up most of her life. I sense a hint of resentment in her voice when she talks about how much of her life she devotes to her book series. I show her more pictures of Hannah than she needs to see and tell her about the divorce. Our interaction is less awkward than I expected, and I sense Claire feels the same way; our mutual relief is palpable.

"I'm sad I won't see Hannah while I'm here," Claire says. "But I'm glad she's doing well at university."

Behind Claire's back, Connie pops her head into the room and arches her brows, giving me a look that asks if everything is OK. I smile at her and subtly nod.

"I hope we can get together and catch up while you're in town," I say, "but I think you should make an appearance in the store before the charity knitters accuse me of keeping you to myself."

"Of course," Claire says. "Where's Dina?" She looks around the small room. "We'll need her to carry the books." She points at the box on the table.

"I'll carry the books," I offer.

When Claire enters the room, the collective gasp from the charity knitters sounds like we're deflating a giant air mattress in the store. Within seconds, Claire's fans surround her, clamouring to be next to introduce themselves and shake her hand.

I place the books near the door, so each guest can take one when they leave. When I stand up, I notice the top of Dina's head near the floor, behind the sofa, and in front of the display window.

"Are you OK?" I ask, approaching her.

"We're fine!" Dina flashes me a wide grin and looks up at me from the floor where she sits cross-legged with Sophie's head resting in her lap. "I'm not antisocial," she explains. "I just love dogs. And this one is so sweet that I can't stop rubbing her."

"Yes, she is," I agree. "Her name is Sophie, and she's allowed on the furniture. It might be more comfortable for you than the hardwood floor." I gesture to the two sofas in the cozy knitting area.

"I should socialize with the humans," Dina says. Then she looks at Sophie. "I'm sorry, Sophie, I have to do people things. I'll rub you again before I leave."

I extend my hand to help her up, and she accepts it.

"Nice unicorns," I say, pointing to the pink and purple unicorn bandage on Dina's index finger.

"Thanks," she laughs. "The first aid kit at our rental cottage has an eclectic collection of supplies. The only bandage options are unicorns or jack-o'-lanterns, and since it's April, I went with the unicorns." She shrugs.

"If it's serious, there's a walk-in medical clinic over…"

"It's not," Dina interrupts, flicking her wrist. "It's a paper cut. Occupational hazard in my job."

Through the display window, I spy the handsome, well-dressed, bald man who was kissing Jules Janssen earlier. He is pacing on the sidewalk across the street.

Noticing my distraction, Dina asks me what's wrong.

"That man," I say, nodding toward the display window. "Have you seen him before?"

Dina's eyes follow my gaze. "Brooks?" she asks. "The bald guy in the expensive suit?"

"You know him?" I ask.

She nods. "His name is Brooks Wiley. He's Claire's literary agent."

"Really?" I ask, wondering if he's the reason Jules knew about Claire's visit to Knitorious today.

Why would Brooks Wiley sneak around town, making out with Jules Janssen, someone his client is trying to avoid?

Duh! Why wouldn't he? She's Jules Janssen, recipient of Hollywood's most-beautiful-person-in-the-world-award.

"Why do you ask?"

I shake my head. "No reason," I reply. "He was hanging around outside earlier, and I've never seen him before. Tourists don't dress like that or look so intense."

"That's just Brooks," she assesses flippantly. "He's made of expensive Italian suits and smoldering intensity."

"Brooks is welcome to come in," I offer. "He doesn't have to wait for you and Claire outside."

"I don't think he's waiting for us," she says. "I don't know why he's there. Trust me, if he wanted to come in, he would."

Her last sentence sounds ominous.

I can't tell if Dina likes Brooks Wiley, but something about him makes me cautious, like I need to be hyper-aware of my surroundings when he's around.

CHAPTER 4

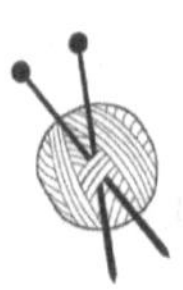

CLAIRE INSPECTS THE NEEDLE-FELTING DISPLAY, strolling from item to item with her hands clasped behind her back, smiling and dispensing generic compliments as she saunters past each piece of the exhibit. She reminds me of the parent volunteers who judged the science fair exhibits when Hannah was in elementary school.

A few paces behind her, Dina pets each miniature person, place, and animal. She marvels at the accuracy of each tiny character and setting from the books.

"There's even a miniature Mama needle felting in her easy chair!" she proclaims with awe.

With unbridled enthusiasm, Dina asks who made each item, then compliments their workmanship.

While everyone is busy hovering around the exhibit, waiting their turn for Claire and Dina to compliment their creative talent, Connie and I slip away to the kitchenette to refresh the tea and coffee and fill the water pitcher.

"Is it me, or does Claire Rivera seem... I don't

know"—Connie tosses her hand in the air—"indifferent to the exhibit?"

"It's not you," I assure her, plugging in the kettle. "I noticed it too. She's kind of standoffish."

"And she has touched nothing! My dear, have you ever encountered a fibre artist who doesn't squish the fibre?"

I shake my head. "I noticed that too," I concur. "Maybe she keeps her hands clasped behind her back to avoid touching it. Maybe she's afraid she'll break something, or doesn't want to touch it without buying it?" I venture a guess at some unlikely reasons to explain Claire's apparent apathy toward the craft she claims to love.

When we emerge from the kitchenette, Claire's inspection of the exhibit is over, and several knitters are milling around the harvest table, *oohing* and *aahing* over the bookish cookies from Artsy Tartsy. Dina is in the thick of it, taking selfies with the cookies and crafters.

Where's Claire? I scan the store and find her near the counter, looking disinterested as she thumbs through a book of knitting patterns, licking the tip of her thumb and index finger before each page turn.

I place a bookish cookie on a plate, grab a napkin, and join her.

"Our local pastry chef made these in your honour," I say, placing the plate and napkin on the counter.

"How clever," she comments, looking at the cookie and smiling.

"Would you mind if I took a photo of you holding the cookie?" I ask. "She's a dear friend, and it would mean a lot to her to have a picture of you with one of her creations."

"Of course!" Claire uses the napkin to pick up the cookie and holds it next to her cheek. She smiles and raises her eyebrows, moving her eyeballs toward the cookie without turning her head.

"Perfect," I say, snapping two photos. "Thank you, Claire."

"No problem," she says, then looks at her watch. "We should get going."

Claire stares at Dina until Dina makes eye contact with her. Claire winks and smiles at Dina before she resumes thumbing through the book, licking her thumb and index finger before turning the page.

Was that a wink, or a wink? Is Dina more than Claire's author assistant?

"Claire," I whisper. "Are you and Dina a couple?"

"What?" she asks, her face scrunched up with confusion. "No! Why would you ask that?"

"I'm sorry," I atone. "It's the wink. I couldn't tell if it was a friendly wink or a flirty wink," I explain. "It's none of my business. Please don't feel compelled to answer me. If you are a couple, Dina is super nice, and I hope you're happy."

Claire laughs and closes the pattern book, pushing it aside. "Dina and I aren't a couple, Megan," she informs me. "Our relationship is purely professional. She's my assistant, nothing more. We're barely friends, for goodness' sake. The wink is how I signal to Dina that I want to leave in five minutes."

"Ohhh," I respond. "That's smart."

Claire continues to chuckle under her breath and points toward the harvest table. "I'm going to say goodbye and thank everyone," she says.

I do a headcount of the felters. Twelve. I remove twelve books, then carry the box to the back room, place it on the floor near the back door, and place Jules's gift bag on top.

Standing in the doorway to the back room, I listen as Marla, on behalf of the book club and the charity knitters, thanks Claire and Dina for attending the book fair and gracing us with their presence at Knitorious this afternoon. Accompanied by applause, Claire and Dina retreat to the back room.

"What's this?" Claire asks, nodding at Jules's gift on top of the book box.

"It's a gift for you from Jules Janssen," I start. "I'm sorry. I'm not comfortable with this, and I understand if you don't want to accept it. Jules asked me to give it to you on her behalf."

Claire rolls her eyes, then looks at Dina, and they both laugh, shaking their heads.

"Unbelievable," Claire says, then she touches my arm. "Megan, I'm sorry Jules put you in the middle like this. She's been harassing me for months to sell her the movie rights to *Familia*."

"She mentioned that," I say.

"Well, she's wasting her time," Claire asserts. "The only way *Familia* will become a movie or TV series is over my dead body." She looks at Dina and points to the box and gift bag. "Take these to the car, Dina. I'll meet you there."

Dina nods, and stoops to pick up the box.

"It was nice to meet you, Dina," I say, holding the door open for her.

"You too, Megan," she smiles. "Maybe we'll see each other at the book fair."

"Megan, before I leave, can I ask you something?" Claire asks, scanning the room to make sure we're alone.

"Does Mitchell still hate me?"

That's a big question, and not one I'm qualified to answer.

"To be honest, Claire, I'm not sure how my dad feels about you. He hasn't mentioned you in years."

"That could mean anything," she surmises. "Maybe he hates me more than ever, maybe he's forgiven me."

I purse my lips into a tight line and shrug. I don't know what to say. "Your guess is as good as mine."

"I want you to know that I didn't steal *Familia* from Mitchell. I didn't know what he was working on when I resigned. I never had access to his works-in-progress. And I would never hurt him. Your father is a brilliant, creative author, and I learned so much from him. He's my mentor. I left because I felt it was time for me to stretch my creative wings. I was afraid if I didn't do it then, I never would. But I swear to you, I plagiarized nothing of Mitchell's."

"OK." I hope she's not looking to me for forgiveness because it's not my place to offer it.

"Do you think you could arrange a meeting between Mitchell and me while we're both in Harmony Lake?" Claire asks.

"*Ooof*," I sigh. "I'm not sure, Claire," I reply, shaking my head. "I can ask him, but I don't know if he'll be open to it. What do you want from him?"

"Nothing," she replies. "I want to explain why I left and assure him I didn't steal his idea. I don't expect us to be friends, but it would be nice if we weren't enemies. I'm ready to write the next chapter of my life, and I'd like this chapter to end with no loose ends." She reaches into her pocket and produces a business card. "Contact me if Mitchell agrees." She hands me the card. "This has my contact information and Dina's. Be sure to contact me. Dina is my assistant, and I keep my professional and personal lives separate."

"OK," I respond. "I'll tell my dad you want to bury the hatchet." I add Claire's card to the fridge, under the same magnet as Jules's card.

"I hope Mitchell wants to bury the hatchet too," Claire says, opening the back door. She chuckles. "I just hope he doesn't want to bury it in my head."

CHAPTER 5

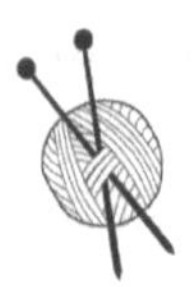

THURSDAY, April 15th

Hannah: Grandma and Grandpa just left. They said to tell you they'll be in Harmony Lake by dinner. Followed by an old-man emoji, old-woman emoji, and car emoji.

Me: OK. Thanks. Good luck on your exam! Followed by a shamrock emoji and heart emoji.

Hannah: And Grandpa said to tell Dad the books will be delivered to his office today. Followed by a book emoji, heart emoji and several cardboard-box emojis.

Adam: Thanks, Princess! Good luck with your exam. Followed by a crossed-fingers emoji and a one-hundred-percent emoji.

"Are you going to text Mitchell and tell him the books arrived?" Adam asks after he hits send on his text to the chez Martel group chat with him, Hannah, and me.

"There's no point. He and Zoe turn off their phones when they're in the car." I shrug. "I texted the person who sent them from the publisher and told her they arrived."

Adam is my ex-husband. He's also the mayor of Harmony Lake and our town's only lawyer. After twenty years of marriage, we finalized our divorce last year. As far as divorces go, ours was as amicable as it gets. We worked hard to keep our family intact, and we always put our daughter first. Some days are easier than others, but we've redefined our relationship and remain friends. We love each other, but not how married people should; we aren't a couple anymore, but Adam and I will always be family.

We met in university when I was eighteen years old. We got married when I was twenty, and I became pregnant with Hannah a few months later. Adam was an ambitious workaholic who spent most of his time climbing the corporate ladder to senior partner, at a law firm in the city. I focused on raising Hannah and immersing myself in the community. Our marriage didn't have a dramatic ending. It fizzled out. Neither of us noticed until it was too late; one day we realized the only thing we had left in common was Hannah. After a few failed attempts to rekindle our connection, we decided it would be best for everyone to end our marriage.

"Why did your father have his books delivered to *my* office, anyway?" Adam asks. "Why didn't he send them to Knitorious since you're hosting his book signing?"

"He worried the delivery person would leave them in the parking lot, and Connie and I would have to lug them into the store," I explain. "He figured you'd transfer them from your office and do the lugging for us. I didn't know the books were being delivered to your office until after he shipped them. Otherwise, I would have asked him to send them here."

Adam's short, dark hair is coiffed into place and doesn't move when he shakes his head. "He did it to get under my skin, Meg. Mitchell's always trying to antagonize me." He hoists another box of books onto the harvest table. "He's trying to get a reaction out of me. To goad me into freaking out so I'll look crazy." Adam shakes his head again. "I won't give him the satisfaction."

"Who's trying to get a reaction out of you?" Eric asks, the sleeves of his shirt stretching under the pressure of his biceps as he heaves two more boxes onto the crowded table.

Adam tells Eric his theory that my father's mission in life is strategizing covert ways to torment him.

Eric is my boyfriend. He's also our local police chief and my tenant. He lives in the apartment above Knitorious, though we're renovating my house so he can move in with me. Living together is a big step for me, so Eric is moving in slowly. He stays at his apartment about fifty percent of the time and at chez Martel the other fifty percent. Chez Martel is what we call my house.

"Brace yourself, dude, Mitchell hates all his sons-in-law," Adam warns Eric. "But he hates me the most," he adds, sounding almost proud of his position as the least-liked son-in-law.

By all his sons-in-law, Adam is referring to himself, and my sister's current and former husbands.

"Adam, stop scaring him," I say, referring to Eric. "You're being dramatic. My dad is always cordial and courteous to you."

"That's part of his strategy, Meg," Adam argues, furrowing his thick brows over his blue eyes. "He manifests his hatred passive-aggressively so I can't confront him without looking paranoid." He looks at Eric. "Guess how many times Mitchell has killed me?" The look on Eric's face is blank, and he blinks. "Go on, guess," Adam urges.

"Mitchell killed you?" Eric asks, confusion clouding his handsome, chiseled face.

"Nineteen times," Adam replies, over-enunciating each syllable. "He always revives me so he can kill me again." The look of concerned confusion on Eric's face deepens. "You know Mitchell's Shark Attack book series?" Adam asks.

"I love those books," Eric replies, his concerned expression replaced by a more enthusiastic one. "I've read the entire series. It's one reason I wanted to be a cop." Comprehension flashes in his brown eyes. "Wait!" he says, pointing at Adam. "Are you *The Shark*?"

Adam nods and smiles, looking proud of his self-appointed status as my father's favourite murder victim.

Mitchell Monroe's most popular book series is the Shark Attack series. The good guy is a cop named Rock Granite who devotes his life to apprehending a lawyer named Alan Mandell, a serial killer known as The

Shark. In each book, Rock hunts The Shark. At the end, when Rock is about to capture him, The Shark fakes his own death; there's never a body. In the next book, The Shark, miraculously resurrected, kills again, Rock hunts him again, and he fakes his death again. Lather, rinse, repeat. Adam believes The Shark, Alan Mandell, is him, Adam Martel. My father insists it's a coincidence and says Adam shouldn't flatter himself.

I roll my eyes. "Don't listen to him," I tell Eric. "He's worried Mitchell will hate you more, and you'll replace him as most-hated son-in-law."

Instead of laughing at my attempt to make light of the situation, Eric looks worried. He furrows his brow, and his brown eyes dart back and forth between me and Adam.

"I'm joking," I assure him. "Mitchell will love you."

"You'll know in a few months," Adam warns. "If he hates you, Mitchell will write you into his next book and kill you."

Thanks for your support, Adam.

"Let's get the last few boxes from your car," Eric says, nudging Adam and changing the subject.

"You can hide at my condo until he leaves town," Adam mumbles to Eric as they leave the store. "I've got your back, dude."

"That won't be necessary," I call after them.

Yes, my ex-husband and boyfriend are friends. Good friends. Eric was new in town and didn't have any friends here. Despite living in Harmony Lake most of his adult life, Adam didn't have many relationships here because he'd spent all his time at his office in the city. They bonded over a mutual love of golf and Buffalo wings and became buddies. Is it weird to watch my boyfriend and ex-husband hang out? Yes, but no weirder than the friendship I have with Adam's new partner.

Our modern, non-traditional family is one example of the many families of choice in our quirky little town.

My dad sent too many books to display in the store. Adam clears yarn from the yarn shelves to make room to display some of them. Eric rearranges the storage room to accommodate the rest of the books and the displaced yarn. I erect an easel in the window to display the poster board of my Dad's picture, his latest book, and the time and date details of his appearance this Sunday.

I wrestle with the large, awkward cardboard poster while trying not to step on Sophie, who is napping in the sunny window. Connie is heading toward Knitorious, walking as fast as she can without breaking into a run.

Something's wrong. She's walking like she's on a mission. I lay the poster against the easel, sidestep the sleeping corgi, and squeeze out of the window. I rush to the door, open it, and with Sophie awake and now in tow, jog toward her, meeting her in front of the local deli.

"What's wrong?" I ask.

"Haven't you heard the news, my dear?" Connie asks, hooking her arm through mine and leading me toward Knitorious.

"What news?" I ask.

"Look at any of Claire Rivera's social media accounts," she instructs.

I pat my hip pockets. No phone. "My phone is in the store," I say, as we arrive at Knitorious. I open the door and make a beeline for the counter with my gaze locked on my phone. I unlock my phone, open the first social media app I see, and navigate to Claire's account. "Wow!" I gasp, bringing my hand to my mouth.

"What is it?" Adam asks from the bulky-yarn section where he's shelving *Shark Attack: Between A Rock and A Shark Place*, my dad's latest book.

"Claire Rivera is ending the Familia series," I reply.

Claire's social media post is short and to the point. It reads, "The next installment in the Familia series will be the last. It's time for me, Mama, and the rest of the *Familia* to turn the page and start a new chapter. Thank you, dear readers, for ten wonderful years!"

"Why?" he asks, joining Connie and me at the counter. I hand him my phone so he can read Claire's social media post. "That's too bad," Adam says. "I love that series. I've read all the books."

"Think about the publicity her announcement will bring to the Between the Covers Book Fair," Connie adds. "People will flock here! They'll want to see Claire and get her to sign their books before she retires."

"She didn't say she's retiring," I point out.

Yesterday when she left, Claire told me she was ready to write the next chapter of her life and wanted to end this chapter with no loose ends. This must be what she meant.

We discuss the possibility that Claire's post is a

publicity stunt, or that she's retiring the series in its current form but will continue it another way, like a spin-off series featuring another character, or a prequel series when my phone rings.

"It's Rick," I tell Connie and Adam. Rick Ransan is a local property investor. He owns a few lakeside rental cottages, including the one Claire Rivera and Dina Langley rented for their stay in Harmony Lake.

"Hello?"

"Megan? It's Rick. I'm trying to get in touch with Eric, but he's not answering my calls or texts." Besides a telltale echo that tells me Rick is calling from his car, there's a sense of urgency in his voice.

"He's here," I say. "Hang on, Rick, I'll get him for you."

I hustle to the storage room where Eric is shelving books and yarn.

"Rick is trying to reach you," I tell him. "It sounds important."

Eric pats his pockets. "My phone must be in the car."

I hand him my phone, and he puts it on speaker. I close the storage room door.

"Hey, Rick. It's Eric. What's up?"

"There's a problem at one of my rental cottages," Rick explains. "Someone locked themselves in the den. Her friend says the woman in the den isn't answering her phone and isn't answering when she knocks on the door."

"Did you call 9-1-1?" Eric asks.

"No," Rick replies. "The woman locked in the den is

Claire Rivera. She was very specific when she rented the cottage that privacy is her biggest priority. I don't want to cause a big scene if she's having a nap or something. I'm on my way there with the spare key. Maybe you could meet me there. You know, just in case? Her friend sounds worried."

Eric nods, even though Rick can't see him.

"I'm on my way. Tell Megan the address. She'll text it to me in the car."

"If I get there before you, should I use my key to unlock the den door?" Rick asks.

"You won't get there before me," Eric says with confidence, then hands me the phone.

"Hang on, Rick." I put the call on hold.

"I'm sorry, babe, I have to deal with this. I'll be back as soon as I can to help you finish getting the store ready for your dad's book signing." He runs a hand through his short, brown hair.

"It's fine," I assure him. "Drive safe, please." I stand on my tippy toes and kiss him. "Let me know how it goes." I open the storage-room door.

"It's probably nothing," he says, hugging me and kissing the top of my head. "I'll be back before your dad and Zoe arrive. I want to make a good first impression."

"Stop worrying about that," I say.

Eric disappears out the back door, and I text him the address Rick gives me, then I look around, taking in the empty room. My eyes land on the business cards I stuck to the fridge yesterday. I take a photo of each card with my phone, then rip them up into tiny pieces, and drop the pieces in the recycling bin. I wouldn't want to be the reason some crazed fan gets hold of Jules Janssen's or Claire Rivera's contact information.

A WALL of warmth hits me when I open the door to Artsy Tartsy. The bakery always smells like warm, doughy bread and comfort.

"Hey, Megapop!" April greets me from behind the counter. "Are you here to pick up your strawberry dream cake?" she asks.

I ordered a strawberry dream cake for dessert tonight. It's one of my dad and Zoe's favourite desserts.

I nod. "Yes, but will it keep until tomorrow? Dad and Zoe called, and they won't be here until tomorrow."

"It'll be fine. Keep it in the fridge," April replies. "Are Mitchell and Zoe all right?" There's a hint of concern in her voice.

"They're fine," I assure her. "My dad had a sudden surge of inspiration. They followed his muse off the highway to the nearest Wi-Fi signal so he could capture his ideas before they disappear. They don't like to drive at night, so they'll finish the drive to Harmony Lake tomorrow morning. Zoe said they found a hotel two hours south of here."

This is typical of my father. Adam likes to say Mitchell exists in his own time zone, MST: Mitchell Standard Time. He often shows up a day early or a day late. Time is something my father is not a slave to. Time and cell phones. He only turns on his phone when it's convenient for him, and he never turns it on when he's in the car because, according to him, some of his best ideas come to him when he's driving, and a ringing cell phone would scare away his muse.

"So, Eric gets to stay nervous about meeting your dad until tomorrow," April points out.

"I haven't told him yet. He went to work. Something came up," I respond. "I don't know why he's so anxious." I shrug. "It must be because he's a fan of the Shark Attack series," I theorize.

"I think it's more than that, Megnolia," April says, as she boxes my cake. "He wants your dad to like him because he loves you. As far as Eric is concerned, he's meeting his future father-in-law. It wouldn't surprise me if Eric asks Mitchell for your hand in marriage," she teases. At least, I hope she's teasing.

"Whoa!" I raise my hands in a stop motion. "Settle down. I haven't even wrapped my head around moving in together yet. Anyway, who asks the bride's father for permission to propose nowadays? This isn't a Jane Austen novel." We laugh.

Eric wants us to get married, and so do I. Someday. There's no rush, and certainly no need for him to ask my father for permission. Some traditions are best left in the past.

I spy some fresh eclairs in the display. Adam and Connie's favourite. "Can you give me a few eclairs?" I ask, changing the subject. "Adam and Connie were amazing today. They helped me rearrange the store for Mitchell's book signing. The least I can do is thank them with treats."

While April boxes the eclairs, my phone rings.

"Eric," I tell her as I accept the call. "Hello?"

"Hey, babe. I'm sorry I haven't come back to help you at the store."

"It's OK," I assure him. "Police business is more important than a book signing."

Brief pause, followed by a sigh. "I don't think I'll make it home in time for dinner with your dad and Zoe. I'm sorry. Hopefully he understands."

"You won't miss dinner," I tell him. "They checked into a hotel for the night. They won't get here until tomorrow."

"Good." Another sigh, but this one is a sigh of relief. "This situation is more complicated than I expected. I'll be here for a while."

"Did you get into the den?" I ask. "Is she OK?"

"Yes, we got in, but she's not OK." Brief pause while Eric inhales a deep breath, then blows it out. "Claire Rivera is dead."

CHAPTER 6

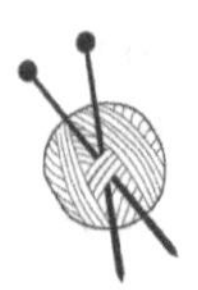

"PARDON?" I ask, hoping I misheard him.

I didn't mishear him. Claire Rivera is dead.

"It's not public knowledge yet," Eric explains. "We still have to notify her family."

Another customer enters the bakery, so I wander to the back of the store.

"I understand," I whisper. "Does it look suspicious?"

"No, but we have to treat it as suspicious until the coroner determines otherwise," he reminds me. "I have to go. The coroner just got here. I love you."

"I love you too."

We end the call, and I stare at April as she serves her customer. She knows something is wrong just by looking at me. I don't need to say anything. April is my best friend. She can gauge my mood from what I say, what I don't say, my body language, the look on my face—heck, sometimes April knows how I feel before I know how I feel.

I can tell she's rushing through the transaction. She hands her customer their box of mini lemon pudding cakes, then hurries from behind the counter, beating her customer to the door. She holds the door for her customer, wishes them a good day, then locks it, and turns the sign from OPEN to CLOSED.

"What happened, Megabuck?"

Still in shock, I sit at one of the small bistro tables. April sits across from me.

"You can't say anything," I warn her. "It's a secret."

"Of course," April says. "You know I won't tell anyone."

I look around, despite knowing we're alone, except for Tamara, but she's in the kitchen and can't hear us. "Claire Rivera is dead," I whisper.

"What?" April asks, confused, like I broke into a foreign language mid-sentence.

I shrug. "I know. Unbelievable. Eric is there. He sounded just as shocked as we are."

"How?" she asks.

I shrug again. "I dunno, but he said it doesn't look suspicious."

Starting from Rick's urgent call to Eric about Claire locking herself in the den, I tell April everything.

"Her assistant must be beside herself," April says.

"I hadn't thought about Dina." A wave of guilt washes over me.

"Maybe you should go there and make sure she's OK," April suggests. "And I should go with you to make sure you're OK."

"We can't just show up at a crime scene," I argue. "No matter how tempted we are."

April shrugs one shoulder. "You've done it before," she points out.

"Because I was the person who found the body," I remind her. "This is different." Despite this, I'm searching for a reason to go there. "Without Claire, Dina is all alone." Found a reason!

"And she's not from here," April adds. "She doesn't know anyone in Harmony Lake, except for you."

"And she's a guest in our town," I continue. "We're a tight-knit, caring community. It would be neighbourly to check on her."

"Yes, it would," April agrees.

I remember the business card Claire gave me with her and Dina's contact information.

"I think I might have her cell number." I unlock my cell phone. "I can text her and offer to go there if she needs support," I propose as a compromise.

"Do it," April urges.

Me: Hi Dina. It's Megan Martel. Are you OK? I hear there's a commotion at your cottage.

Within seconds, three dots appear on the screen, showing that Dina is typing a response. The three dots disappear, and my phone rings.

"It's her," I hiss.

"Answer it," April prompts.

I answer the call, and Dina is in hysterics. Her sobs make it difficult to understand what she's saying. I'm able to determine she's not allowed to go inside the cottage, but she's not allowed to leave. The police asked her a lot of questions but wouldn't answer the questions she asked them. Claire's family wants to talk to her, but the police asked her not to talk to them yet. They won't let her see Claire, and the police said she needs to find somewhere else to stay tonight.

"Oh, Dina, I'm so sorry," I say. My heart breaks for her. I know how scary it is to be at a death scene. "Is there anything I can do?"

"Ca-an you co-me he-re? Puh-lees? I do-n't kn-ow a-ny-one." She punctuates each syllable with the sharp intake of breath that accompanies hysterical sobbing.

"Of course," I say. "I'll be there as soon as I can."

I end the call, and April is already behind the counter boxing cookies.

"For the first responders," she explains. "And I'll bring a case of water too."

"I'll ask Connie to watch the store, and look after Sophie," I say. "Pick you up in ten minutes?"

My compact SUV is a tight fit as I steer it along the long, winding, gravel driveway at the cottage. The emergency vehicles parked along the edges make the already narrow driveway even narrower. It's like driving through an obstacle course. About halfway up, I parallel park between two police cruisers, and we walk the rest of the way. April carries the cookies, and I carry the case of water.

If, like Rick said, privacy was Claire's priority, she chose the right cottage. We can't even see the cottage from where we parked. Thickets of century-old trees line both sides of the driveway and cottage, and the driveway is disguised as an unassumed road. If I didn't have GPS, I doubt I would've found the place.

At the top of the driveway, a uniformed officer stands guard.

"Uh-oh," April mutters. "Will he let us pass?"

"I think so," I reply. "I know him. He has a crush on Hannah. You offer cookies, I'll try to get us past him."

She nods in acknowledgement.

"Hi, Lucas," I say as we approach the young officer.

"Hi, Megan." He smiles. "That looks heavy. Let me help you." He jogs over and relieves me of the case of water.

"Thank you," I say, smiling. "We brought them for you and the other responders. If you have to stay at your post, I can deliver them," I offer.

"Cookie?" April smiles and opens the confectionery box.

Lucas takes a shortbread cookie and tells me he'll call someone to pick up the case of water because he has to stay at his post. I take a few bottles out of the case and thank him. April and I continue walking; he doesn't stop us.

"Megan!" Dina is waving her hand above her head and running toward us. "It's so nice to see a familiar face." She throws herself into my arms.

We sway and I rub circles in her back while Dina squeezes me like a lifebuoy and cries. Meanwhile, April reaches into my tote bag and finds the portable tissue case. When I pull away from Dina, I introduce her to

April. I hand Dina a bottle of water, and April offers her a tissue.

Dina leads us to the Muskoka chairs that surround the fire pit beside the cottage. She sniffles and places her hand over mine. The skin around her red, swollen eyes is puffy and blotchy.

"Claire is dead," she says.

"I'm sorry," I respond, not letting on that I already know.

"She was my best friend." Dina breaks into a loud sob as she finishes her sentence.

This isn't what Claire said. I'm sure she said Dina was just her assistant, and they were barely friends. Maybe Claire misled me about their relationship to protect her privacy. When Claire gave me her business card, she said she keeps her professional and private lives separate. And Rick mentioned that privacy was her biggest priority when choosing rental accommodation.

I suppose it's possible Dina's interpretation of their relationship differs from Claire's. Regardless of how close their friendship was, they spent a lot of time together, even staying in the same cottage.

"I'm so happy you're here," Dina says when she composes herself. "Thank you both for coming." She looks at April, then back to me. "How did you get my number?" she asks.

"Claire gave me her card," I explain. "It has contact information for both of you."

She nods. "I'm glad she did."

An officer comes over and asks Dina if he can speak

with her. She excuses herself, takes a couple of tissues for the road, and steps away with him.

"I heard you were here!" Eric says, walking toward us. He bends down and kisses the top of my head. "Why are you here?" he rubs my shoulders.

"Dina asked me to come," I reply.

"Why?" he asks, looking confused.

I shrug. "I'm the only person she knows in Harmony Lake, and it's scary to be at a crime scene alone. Also, I brought you a couple of sandwiches since you're working late. They're in my car."

April offers Eric a cookie, and he chooses oatmeal chocolate chip—I knew he would—and I give him a bottle of water. His phone dings.

"Claire's agent is here," he says. "I need to talk to him. I'll see you later."

April gives him the box of cookies and instructs him to share them with his colleagues.

"Oooh, who's the mysterious-looking, handsome guy?" April asks, using her chin to point behind me.

I turn to see who she's referring to.

"Brooks Wiley," I say, watching Eric introduce himself to the well-dressed man. "He's Claire's literary agent." I look at April and smirk. She smirks back. We lean toward each other, meeting halfway. "I saw him making out with Jules Janssen," I whisper.

"Really?" she asks, craning her neck and peering around me to look at him. "I can see it. They're both beautiful."

"I can't stay here tonight," Dina announces, marching back to the fire pit with the officer she was talking to. "Not that I want to stay here, but I don't have anywhere else to go."

I'm about to assure her that April and I will help her find a room at a local hotel, when Brooks comes charging toward us with Eric close behind.

"Dina, what happened?" Brooks demands, then jerks his thumb behind him, toward Eric. "Is he telling the truth? Is Claire dead?"

Brooks's accent is a cross between British and Caribbean. It's beautiful and melodic, like he's speaking in cursive. The accent adds to the intensity of his charisma. I can see why Jules Janssen is attracted to him, but he still makes me anxious. When he's around, his chaotic energy makes me hyper-aware of my surroundings, and a small knot forms in my stomach.

Dina nods, her eyes welling up with tears again. "It's true," she mutters. "I didn't tell you on the phone because I didn't want you to drive here upset."

I stand up so Brooks can have my Muskoka chair. "Dina, if you need me, I'll be under that tree"—I point to a nearby sugar maple—"calling around to find you a room for tonight."

Dina nods and mouths, "Thank you."

"I'll go with you," April declares, standing up. "We can divide and conquer."

Three phone calls later, neither April nor I have any luck finding a room for Dina. The motel and two local resorts are booked because the book fair starts tomorrow. I'm about to call Rick Ransan and ask if he or any of his property-investor friends have somewhere for Dina to stay when she rushes over with Brooks and a uniformed police officer by her side, her blonde hair bobbing as she walks.

"Brooks found a room for me," she declares.

"I'm staying at King of the Hill," he explains in his hypnotic accent. "The manager said he can squeeze her in for one night. But she has to check out by 11 a.m., because they're fully booked for the book fair."

That's a relief, I was considering inviting her to stay at chez Martel.

"Now that you're sorted, April and I should get going," I say. "Dina, if you need anything, call me."

"Can one of you drive me to the hotel?" Dina asks, looking back and forth between me and Brooks. "Claire and I drove here together in her car. It doesn't feel right to drive it now... without her here."

"I can't leave yet. The police need to talk to me," Brooks explains, looking at me.

"I want to get out of here as soon as possible. I'd rather not wait for him," Dina says. "I understand if it's out of your way…"

"It's not out of our way," I interrupt.

"Of course, we'll drive you," April adds.

"Can you wait a few minutes?" Dina asks. She points to the officer standing just behind her. "He's going to escort me inside to pack an overnight bag."

I nod. "We're parked about halfway down the driveway," I tell her. "We'll meet you in the car."

Dina and the officer turn and head toward the cottage.

Eric walks April and me to the car so he can collect the sandwiches I brought for him.

The officer who accompanied Dina into the cottage walks her to the car. Besides an overnight bag, she has a box of tissues. The drive to King of the Hill is quiet. Dina sits in the back seat, crying into a tissue, and I check on her regularly in the rearview mirror.

April and I escort Dina inside the hotel and wait while she checks in. When she has a room number and a cardkey, we walk her to the elevator and hug her goodbye.

"Thank you, Megan." Dina touches my hand. "Thank you, April." She touches April's hand. "I'm so grateful I met you."

For the first time today, Dina smiles.

CHAPTER 7

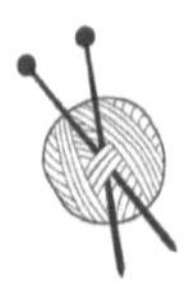

"HEY, HANDSOME." I place my needle-felting stuff on the coffee table and turn off the TV. "You're home earlier than I expected."

"I'm home earlier than I expected too," Eric responds, dropping himself onto the sofa next to me. "We've done everything we can for today. The cottage is off the grid. There's no electricity, so we'd have to bring in generators and lights. The propane-fueled lights inside are too dim to work at night. When the sun went down, we called it a day." Sophie jumps onto the sofa and rests her front paws on his lap. Eric rubs her instinctively. She's trained us well.

I cozy up to him and put my head on his chest. "Do you want to talk about it?" I offer, hoping he'll say yes.

"Claire was alone in a locked room. The door was locked from the inside," he discloses.

"Do you know how she died?" I ask.

"It looks like she fell on her needle," he replies.

I cringe and point to my felting needle on the coffee table. "Her felting needle?" I clarify.

I feel him nod.

Felting needles have small barbs that catch the scales of the fibre and force them together. The more you stab, the more solid and felt-like the fibre becomes. The needles are super sharp, and because of the barbs, if you stab yourself, it hurts more than a regular needle. It hurts more when you pull the needle out than it does going in.

"Did she hit an artery or something?" I ask.

"That's the thing," he says. "It didn't look like a fatal wound. But she was alone in the room. There's no other explanation. The door was locked from the inside. We found the key on the desk with her cell phone. Her cell phone was turned off. Something about her death doesn't feel right."

"Uh-oh," I tease, "my intuition is rubbing off on you."

"We found her by the door," he explains. "Her body blocked the door from opening all the way. I think she was trying to escape by picking the lock with the felting needle."

"Why would she pick the lock?" I ask. "The key was in the room with her."

This is the strangest accidental death I've heard of.

"The coroner and I asked the same question," he says. "The coroner thinks Claire could have been confused in her last moments. He's hesitant to declare her death an accident. After we rolled her onto her back and he looked her over, the coroner hinted that the cause of death might not be the puncture wound. He said he'll run a few tests and tell me more tomorrow."

"Did Dina shed any light on what happened?"

Eric shrugs and sighs. "She says Claire went into the den to work. She said it's common for Claire to lock the door and turn off her phone when she's working. According to Dina, Claire likes to work in silence, uninterrupted. Dina says she went down to the lake and sat on the dock. She said she read, then talked to her parents on the phone. She was on the phone with her parents for about an hour. Her cell phone records and her parents' statements verify she's telling the truth.

"Also, there's an excellent view of the dock from the neighbouring cottage. The family staying there said they saw Dina sitting on the dock. Dina says when she returned to the cottage, Claire was still in the den. She says she texted to ask Claire what she wanted for dinner, but Claire didn't answer. Dina assumed Claire's phone was off because she was still working. She waited a while longer, then knocked on the door. When Claire didn't answer, Dina said she panicked and pounded on the door, screaming Claire's name. When Claire still didn't answer, she called Rick. She said she had a feeling Claire was in trouble."

"You've done everything you can do until you hear from the coroner," I assure him.

"We secured the crime scene, and I assigned officers to guard it, just in case."

Crime scene. He called it a crime scene. Subconsciously, Eric believes Claire's death was murder. I hope he's wrong.

CHAPTER 8

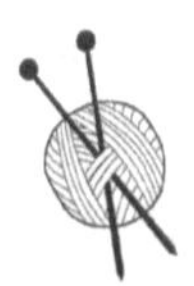

Friday, April 16th

"I can't believe Sherlock Holmes is standing in my store," I gush, accepting the maple pecan latte he offers me. "Thank you." The cape makes Eric's broad shoulders appear even broader. If capes ever come back in style, he's all set.

To commemorate the first day of the book fair, attendees, and almost everyone else in town, are dressed up as their favourite literary character.

"Who are you supposed to be?" Sherlock Holmes asks, putting his pretend pipe in his mouth.

"I'm the Paperbag Princess," I say, as if it should be obvious. "You know, from the Robert Munsch book?"

Eric shrugs his caped shoulders. "Never heard of it."

I look at my costume; a paper yard waste bag with holes cut out for my head and arms, and a tiara. It screams Paperbag Princess.

"Seriously?" I'm incredulous. "It was one of Hannah's favourite books when she was little. We read it to her every night at bedtime for at least two years. It's about a princess who uses her wits to save herself and the prince from the fire-breathing dragon."

"Then it's the perfect costume for you," he says, redeeming himself and giving me a kiss that makes the butterflies in my tummy flutter.

"You look pretty handsome, Sherlock."

"Thank you," he says, straightening his deerstalker cap. "What is Sophie supposed to be?" he asks, nodding at the costumed corgi. "Snakes don't have antennae."

"She's not a snake," I say, disappointed. "She's The Very Hungry Caterpillar." Eric shakes his head. "From the Eric Carle book?" I hint.

"Another kids' book?" he assumes.

"A classic in children's literature," I correct him. "I must've read it to Hannah at least a thousand times."

"Have you heard from your dad?" he asks. "What time are you expecting them?"

"We talked this morning," I reply. "He said they'll arrive after lunch."

"Did you tell him about Claire?"

I shake my head. "I decided against it. They still have a two-hour drive ahead of them, and it's best if they aren't emotional."

"Good call," Eric agrees.

"Have you heard from the coroner yet?" I ask.

He shakes his head and puts his magnifying glass—which I assume is part of his costume—in his pocket. "It's still early. I'm sure he'll be in touch today. I'll be back to welcome your dad and Zoe." He straightens my tiara and kisses me goodbye.

"ARE THEY HERE YET?" The Mad Hatter asks, charging through the front door.

I shake my head. "They're two minutes away," I reply. "They pulled over when they got off the highway and Zoe texted me." After which, I texted everyone else to assemble at Knitorious ASAP.

Adam looks relieved. He slides the pocket watch from his vest pocket and checks the time. He slips the watch back into his pocket and straightens the chain attached to it. "This get-up is warmer than it looks." He takes a handkerchief from his pocket, lifts his velour top hat, and wipes his brow. His dark hair sticks to his forehead.

Adam is a very tall Mad Hatter. The top hat creates the illusion that he's several inches taller than his six feet.

Madame Defarge straightens my ill-fitting headpiece. "Keep your chin up, my dear, or your tiara will slip."

Excellent advice for life in general, not just when I'm wearing a literal tiara.

I smile. "Thank you, Connie."

"Madame Defarge, right?" Eric asks Connie. "The knitter from, A Tale of Two Cities?"

"Well deduced, Sherlock," Connie praises him.

"Elementary," he says with a smile. "See, I read. I just don't read kids' books," he mumbles at me with a wink.

Nancy Drew jumps up from the sofa in the cozy

sitting area. "They just pulled into the parking lot!" she announces. "I'll open the back door, so they don't have to walk around to the front."

"Thanks, April!" I say.

On her way to the back door, she puts on her fake glasses, smooths the plaid skirt that matches her plaid hair band, and straightens the sleeves of her cardigan. The cardigan, part of a twinset, is draped over her shoulders with the sleeves tied in front of her chest.

"There's my little bean!" My dad comes toward me with his arms open wide.

"Bean?" Eric mumbles.

"Short for jelly bean," Adam explains to him in hushed tones. "I don't know why."

My dad has an air of distinction about him. It might be the full head of thick silver hair, or the sport jacket-turtleneck combo that has become his trademark uniform, or a combination of both. He's not a tall man. He's only a few inches taller than me, but I swear every time we see each other he's a little shorter than I remember.

"Hi, Dad!" We hug and sway. He kisses my cheek. "How was your drive?" I ask as we pull apart. Looking into his hazel eyes always unnerves me at first, because they're so similar to mine.

"Longer than necessary," Zoe interjects, nudging her husband out of the way and coming in for a hug. "You know your father, Megan. One of his superpowers is taking a short drive and making it long," she jokes.

I wouldn't call the five-hour drive from Toronto to Harmony Lake short, but it's all relative, I guess.

Zoe holds my shoulders and appraises me at arm's length. Her blue eyes inspect me, and her short, blonde curls bob when she nods with approval.

"You look wonderful, Megan," Zoe comments, still looking me up and down. "I suppose we can thank Sherlock for that?"

Blushing, I introduce Eric to Mitchell and Zoe Monroe. Mitchell nods and extends his hand for Eric to shake.

"It's a pleasure to meet you, sir," Eric says, his anxiety palpable.

"Likewise," Mitchell acknowledges before moving along to hug Connie.

"You must call him Mitchell," Zoe says to Eric, engulfing him in a friendly hug. "Calling him 'sir' will go to his head, and that's the last thing we need." She winks and we laugh. "And you'll call me Zoe."

"Nice to meet you, Zoe," Eric says.

Zoe moves on to hug Adam.

Mitchell greets everyone, including Sophie, before he greets Adam. They are cool but cordial to each other.

"Before I forget, Bean, this is for you." Mitchell hands me a thick, letter-size, sealed envelope.

"Thank you, Dad," I say, knowing it's a signed copy of his latest book.

He personally delivers a signed copy of the manuscript for each book he writes to my sister and me. He seals the manuscript in an envelope and signs the seal. My sister and I think it's a personal superstition. I display them in a bookcase. Books aren't small, and

Mitchell is a prolific writer, so over the years, we've installed additional bookcases to house them.

"Keep it safe," Mitchell warns with his eyebrows raised.

"I will," I assure him, slipping it under the counter and placing it in my bag.

After everyone greets one another, and I serve refreshments, we sit around the harvest table. When Mitchell and Zoe arrived, Connie locked the door and turned the sign from OPEN to CLOSED. Business would've been dead today, anyway, with the book fair opening, and this isn't a conversation we want to have with customers browsing nearby.

My father marvels at the bookish cookies Tamara made for his Shark Attack book series, and Zoe takes photos of the cookies and of her and Mitchell posing with them.

I'm about to break the news to them about Claire's death. The five of us—me, Eric, April, Connie, and Adam—decided it was best to tell them as soon as they arrived to ensure they didn't hear it from someone else.

Eric says Claire's death will become public knowledge at noon when her family and publisher release a joint statement to the press. It's after 11 a.m., so I'm sure the Harmony Lake rumour mill is on the job, news of her death has somehow leaked, and is already spreading throughout the community.

"Dad," I say, placing my hand on his. He places his other hand on top of mine. "You know they scheduled Claire Rivera to attend the book fair this year, right?"

"I'm aware," he says, sounding agitated. "I noticed

when we were driving through town that there are more posters promoting Claire's attendance at the book fair than my attendance. The posters refer to her as the guest of honour. I thought *I* was the guest of honour. There can only be *one* guest of honour, Bean. Is it me or Claire Rivera?"

Here we go. Mitchell doesn't like to share the spotlight. While I'm sure the news of Claire's death will shock and sadden him, I'm worried part of him will resent her death eclipsing his appearance at the event.

"Actually, Dad, I think the posters refer to her as *a* guest of honour." I shake my head and force myself to stay on task. "Regardless, there's been a development regarding Claire's attendance..."

"Oh, I already know about it, Bean." He waves his hand as if it's old news.

"You do?" I ask, squeezing my brows together. "What did you hear?"

Mitchell shrugs. "I heard the same thing as everyone else. Claire Rivera is ending her book series," he says. "I'm not surprised. Writing the same characters book after book isn't for everyone," he justifies. "But her decision to announce it at a book fair we're both attending is uncouth and shows the lengths she'll go to ensure she's the centre of attention."

I inhale deeply. Under the table, Eric gives my knee a reassuring squeeze.

"There's more, Dad," I say as I exhale. "Claire died yesterday."

Zoe gasps and places a hand on her husband's shoulder. "Mitchell, did you hear that?" she whispers.

He nods without breaking eye contact with me. His eyes fill with moisture. "She was too young." His voice catches on the last word. "Are you sure?" His voice is just above a whisper.

I nod. "We're sure. Her family is issuing a statement at noon."

"What happened?" he asks. He looks at Eric. "You're the police chief, what happened?"

"The cause of Claire's death hasn't been released," Eric says in his cop voice.

The lunacy of this situation strikes me. Here we are, seven people sitting around a table, five of us dressed as literary characters, with a corgi under the table dressed as a caterpillar. Having a serious conversation about a tragic death. If it wasn't so sad, it would be laughable.

"Was it an accident?" Mitchell probes. Eric purses his lips into a tight line, then opens his mouth to say something, but Mitchell beats him to it. "It was her nut allergy, wasn't it?"

"Umm... nut allergy?" I ask. "Claire had a nut allergy?" This is the first I've heard of it.

Mitchell gives me an exaggerated nod. "She did," he confirms. "When she worked for me, I would tell her to be more diligent about her allergy before it killed her."

"What do you mean diligent?" Eric asks.

"She was lackadaisical about carrying her EpiPen with her." Mitchell looks at his wife. "Wasn't she, Zoe?"

Zoe nods in agreement. "When Mitchell would attend events, Claire would forget to bring her EpiPen with her. She would work at our house and not have it with her. It made us so nervous that we bought one and kept it handy whenever she was around."

"Did you ever need it?" I ask.

"No," Mitchell and Zoe reply in stereo. "Thank goodness," Zoe adds.

Thinking back, when Claire attended the needle-felting exhibit at the store, she used a napkin to pick up the bookish cookie when I asked her if I could take a picture of her holding it. She didn't partake in any refreshments, avoiding the refreshment table altogether, and hanging out at the front of the store instead. To avoid touching anything, she kept her hands clasped behind her back. Actions that I interpreted as stand-offish might have been part of her safety protocol because of her nut allergy. Things aren't always as they seem.

We're still sitting at the harvest table at noon, albeit in a much more sombre mood, when our phones ding, chime, buzz, and vibrate.

"The statement about Claire's death," Adam advises us, standing up. "I should go. The mayor's office is issuing a statement about Claire's passing, since she died here and was attending our book fair."

Zoe thanks him for coming and gives him a big hug.

"I'll see you out," I say, standing up.

"Thank you for coming," I say at the back door. "I know Mitchell isn't your favourite person. I appreciate you putting aside your feelings."

Adam shrugs. "You and I are still family, Meg, therefore Mitchell is still my family, whether he likes it or not." He smirks and puts on his top hat. "I'll see you tomorrow at dinner."

I lock the door behind him and turn around. "Jeez!" I say, clutching my chest. "You scared the life out of me." Eric is standing partway up the stairs that lead to his apartment. How is this tall, muscular man so light on his feet?

"Sorry, babe," Eric says, chuckling. "I'll be upstairs talking to the coroner." He holds up the phone in his hand, then disappears upstairs.

I hope it's good news, if there is such a thing when someone dies young and unexpectedly. Good news would be if the coroner determines natural causes or a freak accident caused Claire's death. The anxious knot in my stomach isn't expecting good news.

CHAPTER 9

Only in Harmony Lake can the Paperbag Princess and Nancy Drew walk The Very Hungry Caterpillar on a leash, through the park, with no sideways glances or second looks.

"Do you think I should have taken off Sophie's costume?" I ask.

"She's fine," April says. "She doesn't even notice it."

"You're right." I nod in agreement. "Now reassure me that Claire didn't eat a nut product at Knitorious on Wednesday afternoon, then die from it twenty-four hours later."

"It's not possible, Megabean," April reassures me, mashing up her nickname for me with my father's nickname for me. "Besides, nothing had nuts in it. T made sure the bookish cookies were nut free. I helped you put the food out, you served nothing with nuts. Anyway, nut allergies kill in like thirty minutes or something." She stops walking and looks at me. "Did Eric tell you Claire died because of her nut allergy?"

I shake my head. "No," I reply. "He doesn't know her cause of death. He's talking to the coroner right now, though, so he'll know soon."

When we get to Artsy Tartsy, April and I hug goodbye, and I watch her cross the street and go inside the bakery. Then Sophie and I turn around and meander toward Knitorious. It's a beautiful spring day. The sun is shining, and the birds are singing. The temperature is a mild ten degrees—maybe a tad cooler this close to the lake.

Connie accompanied Mitchell and Zoe to chez Martel to help them settle in. I offered to go with them, but they said they have a lot to catch up on, and I didn't want to be in the way.

I closed Knitorious for the rest of the day since nobody is shopping today with the opening ceremony for the book fair and the news of Claire's death.

"Come here, Soph. Let's take off your costume." I crouch down to her level and undo the clasps that keep Sophie's costume in place, then pull it off. She gives herself a good shake. "Is that better?" I ask, scratching her neck and chest. "Who's a good girl?"

I give her a few dog treats, then take off my paper leaf bag and lay it over the back of one of the kitchenette chairs. I'm about to make lunch, and cooking in a paper dress isn't how I want to die. I take the glass container of stuffed peppers out of the fridge and climb the stairs to Eric's apartment.

"Shhh," I remind Sophie. "He might be on the phone." I open the door and Sophie rushes in ahead of me.

She jumps onto the leather sofa and parks herself next to Eric, who's leaning forward, focused on the laptop on the coffee table in front of him. His Sherlock Holmes costume lays over the back of the leather club chair. His phone is on the table next to his laptop, and there are no AirPods in his ears.

"Hey, Handsome," I say.

"Hey, babe!" He looks up at me and smiles. He's not on the phone. "No more Paperbag Princess?" he asks.

"Not until after lunch," I reply. "Hungry?" I ask, holding up the glass container.

"Starving," he responds. "What are we having?"

He's always starving. I've never seen Eric turn down a meal.

"Stuffed peppers," I reply. "The ones you like with the sausage, rice, and cheesy mushroom stuffing. How hungry are you?"

Still absorbed in whatever is on the computer screen, he holds up two fingers; he's two peppers hungry. I put the peppers in the oven and join him on the sofa. "Anything interesting?" I ask.

He sighs and turns the laptop so I can see the screen. "Crime scene photos," he explains. "From Claire and Dina's cottage."

Crime scene. He said crime scene, not death scene.

"The coroner concluded Claire was murdered?" I ask, flexing my deductive muscle.

"Fatal anaphylaxis," he replies, nodding. "I need to find the source of the peanut oil and retrace Claire's final steps to explain how she came into contact with it.

It could be accidental, but it's too suspicious. Too many things don't add up."

I take a deep breath and let it out. "So, it was her peanut allergy that killed her, not the felting needle?"

He nods again. "The coroner believes she fell on the felting needle when she collapsed. The puncture wound from the needle was not fatal."

"Why was she hanging out near the door with her felting needle?" I wonder aloud. "I mean, she probably realized she was in trouble. Why didn't she use the key? Or use her cell phone to call for help?"

The rental cottage—like the rest of Harmony Lake—is remote, but we have decent cell phone coverage. Unlike some remote towns, we lucked out with cell phone towers.

"The coroner says the allergic reaction could have made Claire confused, panicky, or both. Maybe she couldn't immediately find the key or her phone, but she found the felting needle. Or maybe she was already holding it when the reaction started."

I nod toward the laptop screen. "Are you searching the crime scene photos for the nut product she had contact with?" I ask.

He nods and sighs. "Officers are searching the cottage for anything that might contain nuts. So far, nothing, but they've collected a bunch of stuff for the lab to test."

"Is that the letter Jules asked me to give to Claire?" I ask, pointing at the handwritten note on the screen.

Eric nods. "I assume it is. It's signed by Jules." He

reaches for the laptop and zooms in on the photo. "Is that the envelope she gave you?"

"Yes," I confirm. "I remember her pretty, cursive handwriting."

The oven beeps, and I plate the stuffed peppers. Eric closes his laptop and joins me at the breakfast bar.

"Did your dad say anything after I left?" he asks.

I blow on a forkful of steaming hot stuffing before I reply. "He said lots of things," I tease. "Are you asking if he said anything about you?"

"I can't get a read on him. I don't think he likes me, but I can't tell for sure."

I shrug. "That's how he is," I explain. "You can't spend your life worrying about whether my dad likes you." I smile. "I already know how I feel about you, and his opinion won't change my mind."

"He posted a nice statement about Claire," Eric says, then takes a sip of water.

"Zoe or his publisher posted a nice statement," I correct him.

When Zoe and my dad met, she was an editor with the publishing company that handles his books. She still edits for him, but since Claire quit as his assistant ten years ago, Zoe stepped into that role too.

"Your dad lets other people post to his social media accounts?"

"*Only* other people post to my dad's social media accounts," I clarify. "I don't think Mitchell Monroe has ever made a social media post. I bet he doesn't even know how to access his accounts." We laugh. "I didn't know you follow my dad on social media."

"I don't," Eric explains, "but I'm monitoring the responses to Claire's death, and the responses to yesterday's post about retiring the Familia series."

I gasp. "You think an angry fan killed her because she was ending the series?"

"It's possible," he acknowledges. "Babe, there were some disturbing, threatening social media posts after her announcement."

"Ugh!" I roll my eyes. "Social media can be so negative and toxic."

"Interpol contacted me about one post in particular," he discloses.

"Interpol? The international police organization?" I ask.

After eating half of my pepper, I'm full. I use my fork to push the other half to the edge of the plate. Eric scoops up my abandoned pepper with his fork and transfers it to his plate. Where does he put all the food he eats? It's one of the great mysteries of the world; he eats enough for three people, yet there isn't an ounce of fat on him. I'm jealous.

He nods. "Claire has an overzealous fan from Britain who made some particularly vitriolic comments and vague threats yesterday when Claire announced the end of *Familia*. Authorities in Britain tried to question her, but she's abroad."

"Well, if she's not in Harmony Lake, she can't be a suspect in Claire's murder," I surmise.

"That's the thing," he says. "We think she's in Harmony Lake. She landed in Toronto a few days ago and rented a car at the airport. Her cell phone has been dinging off local cell phone towers. I'm waiting for the car rental company to call me back. I'm hoping the rental car she's using has GPS, and they can tell me where it is. I'd like to talk to her."

"Did you check the local hotels?" I ask.

He nods as he finishes his second pepper and digs into my abandoned half-pepper. "She hasn't checked in anywhere."

I bite the inside of my cheek. "Maybe she's renting one of the rental properties. I can ask around. What's her name?"

"Piper Peters," Eric replies, standing up and retrieving his phone from the coffee table. "I'll send you her picture. If you see her, let me know."

"Of course," I say, looking at my phone when it dings. Piper Peters is about my age. In this photo, her long, straight brown hair is in a low ponytail that hangs over her shoulder. She has deep-set brown eyes and fair skin. Her nose and mouth are small, and her lips are pursed in a tight line. "Is this a mugshot?" I ask.

"I think so," Eric responds. "She has a history of harassment and threatening. Brooks Wiley mentioned Piper yesterday when I asked him who might want to harm Claire. He said Claire got a restraining order against her last year when Piper showed up on her doorstep and demanded that she change the end of one of the *Familia* books."

"That doesn't sound like the behaviour of a mentally well person," I observe.

"It isn't," Eric agrees. "So, if you see her, please, please, don't approach her. Call me."

I nod.

"Promise?" he asks.

"Promise."

CHAPTER 10

"Hi, Dad." We kiss cheeks.

He's sitting in one of the living room chairs. His reading glasses are on the tip of his nose, and he's reading on his iPad.

"How are you, Bean?" he asks, looking at me over his glasses and smiling.

"Fine," I reply. "Where are Zoe and Connie?"

Mitchell closes his iPad and places it on the table next to him. He pats his lap, and Sophie jumps onto it.

"They went to the town square to revel in the book fair festivities," he replies, scratching Sophie between the ears.

"Maybe I'll join them," I suggest.

"They shouldn't be hard to find." He sounds amused. "Just look for Madame Defarge and Charlotte." He chuckles.

"Charlotte?" I ask.

"Yes, Charlotte," he reiterates. "Zoe dressed as Charlotte, the spider from Charlotte's Web."

"You didn't put on a costume and join them?" I smirk at the mental image of Mitchell Monroe dressed up as anything.

"It's not my scene," says the author about the book fair.

"Right," I say. "There's a strawberry dream cake in the fridge. Tamara made it just for you."

"I found it," he says, as if it's a secret. "And if Zoe asks, *you* had an enormous slice." He raises his index finger to his lips in a *shhh* motion. "I'm supposed to be watching my sugar intake."

"Got it," I say with a dramatic wink. "So how are you feeling?"

"Do you mean after the enormous slice of cake, or about Claire's untimely death?" he answers my question with a question.

"I know you weren't on good terms and hadn't spoken in ten years, but it must be a shock."

Mitchell sighs. "It is," he admits. "Regardless of our feelings toward one another, Claire was too young to die. She had her entire life to look forward to. I'm debating reaching out to her family. Zoe said we should send flowers and a note."

"That's a lovely idea," I concur. "Phillip can make you a floral arrangement."

I remind him that my neighbour at home and at work, Phillip, owns a florist shop. I'm about to tell my dad about the coroner determining Claire's death was murder, but my phone rings. It's Dina Langley.

"Excuse me, Dad."

He waves me away and puts his head back, closing

his eyes. He's still rubbing Sophie, who has fallen asleep in his lap.

"Hello?" I answer the call on the way to my bedroom.

"Hi, Megan! It's Dina."

"Hi, Dina. I've been thinking about you. I meant to text you, but I haven't had a spare moment."

"That's OK. I understand. Thank you again for stopping your life to come to the cottage yesterday. I appreciate it."

"No problem," I say.

Claire's death being declared a murder hangs between us like a dense fog.

"I have to collect the rest of my things from the cottage," Dina says. "There was a cancellation and the hotel manager said I can stay here. Since the cottage is a crime scene, I can't stay there, anyway." I hear her gasp. "Not that I'd want to stay there," she corrects herself. "I feel safer at the hotel. They have cameras here, and it's booked solid, so if something happens, someone will hear me scream." Another gasp. "That sounds awful. I'm not very articulate today. I didn't sleep well and…"

"It's OK, Dina," I interrupt her. "You don't have to explain. I get it. I can come with you if it would help. I closed the store for the rest of the day anyway…"

"Thank you, Megan! It would be easier if I'm not alone. I mean, I could ask Brooks to go with me, but he's not very warm and comforting, you know? He's all business, all the time. And I think Claire's… death created more work for him."

He didn't look all business, all the time when I saw

him kissing Jules Janssen and touching her butt. Just saying.

"Should I pick you up?" I offer.

"No, thank you," Dina replies. "I arranged a rental car, and Brooks drove me to pick it up this morning. I'm more emotionally stable than I was yesterday… well, somewhat… I'll drive myself."

We agree on a time to meet at the cottage and end our call.

"Dad, I have to go out. Do you need anything?" I call as I enter the living room. "Dad?" Where did he go?

"No, Bean. I'm fine." He's at the front door, putting on his shoes. "I think I'll take a walk and burn off the cake I ate, so I can eat more later." He winks.

"You mean you'll burn off the cake *I* ate." I wink back.

"That's my girl." He chuckles. "I'll take my granddog with me, and we can explore the neighbourhood." He refers to Sophie as his granddog.

"Take your cell phone, in case you need it," I remind him.

"Yes, Bean. Stop worrying. You get that from your mother."

We kiss cheeks. He attaches Sophie's leash, and they leave.

THERE ARE as many vehicles along the narrow, winding driveway as there were yesterday. Also like yesterday, I find a spot between two cars about halfway up, parallel park, and walk the rest of the way. I don't know if Dina is here yet because I don't know what kind of rental car she's driving.

I hear Lucas's voice before I see him. Lucas Butler is the rookie officer who was standing guard at the top of the driveway yesterday, the one who has a crush on my daughter.

"I'm sorry, sir, but you're not on the list. If you're not on the list, you can't pass."

"Of course, I'm on the list!" I recognize that dulcet accent. Brooks Wiley is here, and it sounds like Lucas won't let him access the crime scene. "I insist you let me pass, or I will call Chief Sloane, and he will have your badge!"

"Hi, Lucas," I say, approaching the two men.

"Hi, Megan!" Lucas smiles. "No water or cookies today?" he teases.

"Not today," I reply. "Is Dina Langley here?" Lucas purses his lips and shrugs. "Long blonde hair. Young"—well, young to me. I forgot I'm talking about a twenty-three-year-old—"she left with April and me yesterday."

Recognition flashes across his face. "Right!" he declares. "I remember her." He shakes his head. "I haven't seen her."

"I'm supposed to meet her here. Is it OK if I wait in the Muskoka chairs by the fire pit?" I ask, pointing toward the cottage.

"Of course," Lucas replies. "I'll tell her where you are when she shows up."

I thank him, smile at both men, and continue walking.

"So, you're telling me she's on the list and I'm not?" Brooks says, seething with frustration. "I need to get in that house. You don't understand. There's money at stake."

This gets my attention, and I stop walking.

"If you aren't on the list, you don't get in."

Lucas and Brooks continue arguing back and forth, Brooks holding up his phone, threatening to call Eric, and Lucas telling him to call whoever he wants. They're at an impasse. I'm about to continue on my way to the firepit when I hear Dina's high-pitched, excited voice.

"Call the police!" she yells. "Call the police!"

She's yelling this at a police officer. There are literally half a dozen cops here.

I jog down the driveway until she's in view. She's flailing her arms and running up the steep driveway like she's being chased.

"Brooks! It's her! She's here! Call the police," Dina yells when she spots Brooks. "She's crazy! She says Claire isn't dead!"

Who says Claire isn't dead?

Lucas puts his hand on his sidearm and positions himself in front of Brooks. With his other hand, he beckons Dina, encouraging her to keep running toward him.

"Who is Dina talking about?" I ask, running toward Lucas and Brooks.

"I don't have a clue." Brooks looks confused.

He mumbles something I can't hear as he jogs

toward her. Then he turns and, wide-eyed, runs back toward Lucas and cowers behind him. "That woman is crazy! Arrest her before she hurts someone!"

What woman is crazy? Is he talking about Dina?

Then I hear her shrieking British accent.

"I demand to know what's happening! Where is Claire Rivera! Who is in charge?"

Piper Peters. I recognize her from the photo Eric showed me earlier.

I move to the edge of the driveway and crouch between two parked cars. I've already dialed Eric's number.

"Hello?" He's in the car. I can tell from the echo.

"Piper Peters is here," I hiss.

"Where are you?"

"Rental cottage," I whisper, trying to talk to him and listen to Piper's ravings.

"Why are you at the cottage? Never mind. Are you sure it's her?"

"Positive."

"Don't approach her," he reminds me.

CHAPTER 11

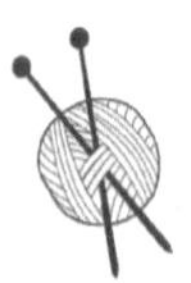

WE END our call and three officers run down the driveway from the cottage. They apprehend Piper without incident. I emerge from my hiding spot and join Brooks and Dina.

"The chief says to take her to the station for questioning. He'll meet you there," Lucas tells the officer who's placing Piper in his patrol car.

Piper looks at the three of us—me, Dina, and Brooks—from the backseat. Her face is taut, and her lips pressed into a taut line. She and I lock eyes until the patrol car drives away and forces us to break eye contact. There are so many questions I want to ask her.

Lucas clears up the confusion about Brooks being on the list and gives all three of us–me, Dina, and Brooks–permission to pass. The officer who accompanies us searches our bags and pockets to ensure we don't have anything that might contaminate the crime scene, then we proceed to the cottage.

It's large and modern. The entire back wall is floor-to-ceiling windows and French doors with a beautiful view of the lake. The space is open and airy, with simple, contemporary furnishings. With four bedrooms, it's large for only two people, but I understand why Claire and Dina chose this specific cottage in this precise location. It's tidy, clean, and private with a beautiful view.

The officer follows Dina into her bedroom, where she lobs an open suitcase onto the queen-sized bed. She tosses clothes and personal effects into the suitcase, packing as if her goal is to get out of here as soon as possible and organize her belongings later. I don't blame her. If my employer-slash-friend met a violent end here, I'd be in a hurry to leave too.

"How can I help?" I ask.

Dina stops tossing items into the suitcase and looks at me. "I left my swimsuit and towel on the clothesline by the dock. And my rubber shoes too."

I nod. "I'll get them," I tell her.

Brooks follows me down to the dock.

"Hi," he says, extending his hand. "I'm Brooks Wiley. I'm–I was–Claire Rivera's agent."

I shake his warm hand. His grip is firm and confident. "Hi, Brooks. I'm Megan Martel. I'm sorry for your loss."

"Oh!" A glint of realization shines in his eyes. "You're Mitchell Monroe's daughter."

"That's right," I affirm.

Did Jules tell him who my father is?

Brooks reaches into the pocket of his light grey, custom-tailored suit and pulls out a business card. "Do you know if your dad is happy with his current literary agent?"

I shrug. "I assume so, he hasn't said otherwise."

He pulls out another business card and hands it to me. "Just in case he's looking to make a change, please give him my card."

Dina wasn't joking when she said Brooks is all business, all the time. I understand Claire's death creates a gap in Brooks's client list, but it seems insensitive to replace her the day after her murder, at the scene of the crime.

"I'll pass it on." I drop the cards in my bag, then remove the towel from the line and fold it. "It's nice of you to help Dina pack her things. Claire's death really shook her up." I hand him the folded towel and pull the swimsuit off the line.

"If Dina is shaken up about anything, she's shaken up about losing her job," Brooks remarks with a contemptuous sneer. "That's what she and Claire were arguing about yesterday before Claire died. Dina was angry because their contract ends the day they release the last *Familia* book."

"Claire and Dina were arguing yesterday before Claire died?" I confirm. "How do you know?" I hand him the folded swimsuit, and he places it on top of the folded towel I gave him a minute ago.

"I rushed over here as soon as I saw Claire's post about retiring the Familia series," Brooks explains. "I heard them yelling from the driveway. Also, Claire told me once that the contract between them specifies that Dina's role as Claire's assistant ends when the Familia book series ends."

"It sounds like a unique arrangement," I say, gathering magazines and books from a nearby lounge chair. "Claire didn't tell you ahead of time that she was planning to stop writing *Familia*?" I ask.

He shakes his head. "I found out when I saw her social media post, just like everyone else. Dina seemed just as surprised as I was, so I don't think Claire warned her either."

If this is true, was Dina angry enough about losing her job to kill her employer? If Claire's death delays the release of the final *Familia* book, would it also delay Dina's last day on the job? Could Claire's untimely death delay Dina's unemployment status? I wonder if Dina told the police about her argument with Claire?

Claire is one of the world's most successful authors; she's likely Brooks's most successful client and his biggest source of income. Was he so shocked and angry by Claire's announcement that he killed her?

"I was kind of hoping her announcement was a publicity stunt or something."

"It wasn't," Brooks insists. "She was dead serious."

He doesn't seem to realize his unfortunate choice of words.

I add the pile of magazines and books to the towel and swimsuit in Brooks's arms.

"Their entire relationship was unique," he agrees. "They were very secretive, and Claire relied on Dina for almost everything. It was like she couldn't write without her. It doesn't matter what I asked her, Claire always had to check with Dina before she could answer me."

"She sounds like an excellent assistant," I point out. "My dad says an author assistant's job is to make sure the author has nothing to do except write. He says a good assistant takes care of all the menial tasks that writers use to distract themselves from writing." I pick up the rubber shoes, and we head back toward the cottage.

"Using your father's criteria, Dina is a fabulous assistant." Brooks chuckles.

"How did Claire and Dina meet?" I ask.

"I don't know," Brooks admits. "Dina was already her assistant when Claire and I met."

As we approach the back door, I realize this is my last chance to talk to Brooks without being overheard by either Dina or the officer chaperoning us. I stop walking. Brooks stops walking too and looks at me.

"What did you mean when you told the officer money is at stake?" I ask.

"The signed books," Brooks explains. "The ones in the cottage. They were to be sold at Claire's book signing this weekend. They're worth a lot more money today than they were yesterday. Now that Claire has died and can't sign any more books, those signed books will be a hot commodity among her fans and collectors."

"OK," I acknowledge. "Why are they at stake?"

"They can't stay here, Megan," he says, like I'm missing the point. "This cottage has no security. It's secluded and in the middle of nowhere. Do you know how easy it would be to sneak in and steal them?"

"The police are guarding the cottage and its contents," I remind him.

"Not good enough," Brooks counters. "Someone could drive up to the dock in a boat. Or they could sneak through the trees from another cottage." He shakes his head.

It sounds like Brooks Wiley has thought about how to get in and out of the cottage unnoticed.

"I'm supposed to remove them from the cottage and take them somewhere secure. The publishing company asked me to keep them safe until a courier picks them up on Monday," he adds.

We enter the cottage and find Dina in the washroom, stuffing toiletries into an overnight bag. I hold up the rubber shoes, and she puts them in the tote bag. As she takes them, I notice another bandage on one of her fingers.

"Another paper cut?" I ask, nodding to the bandage.

"This?" Dina asks, appraising her injured middle finger. "No. I bite my nails when I'm stressed." She fans out her hand and examines her short nails. "The last twenty-four hours have been extra stressful. I bit this one too low, and it bled."

Brooks extends his arms, showing Dina the towel, swimsuit, and reading material we collected from the dock.

"The magazines aren't ours," Dina explains, pointing to the magazines in Brooks's arms. "They were here when we arrived at the cottage. I took them down to the dock yesterday and forgot to bring them back."

Instead of moving them herself, Dina points to the edge of the tub while looking at the magazines, wordlessly instructing Brooks to place them there. Brooks complies and places the magazines on the tub, then Dina takes the remaining pile of stuff from him and drops it into her overnight bag.

"Good thing it didn't rain," I comment to break up the weird atmosphere between them.

"There," she declares, looking around the washroom. "I think that's everything."

"Dina, where are the books?" Brooks asks her.

"I figured that's why you're here," Dina replies with a slight huff. "Where will you take them?"

We follow her to the living room, where she points to the boxes of books stacked against a wall. Brooks and Dina discuss possible new locations for the boxes of books. They agree their hotel rooms would be too obvious to anyone hoping to get their hands on them.

Brooks excuses himself to call the hotel to ask if they have a safe or locked room that can accommodate the books.

"I'll ask Eric if there's anything the police can do to help store the books," I suggest, trying to help.

"Eric?" Dina asks.

"Chief Sloane," I clarify as I text him.

"You two are a couple?" she asks.

"Uh-huh,"

"I knew it," she gushes. "I could tell when you were

here yesterday. He kept touching you and walked you to your car."

"The books can't stay in the evidence lock-up because they aren't evidence," I say, changing the subject.

"The hotel doesn't have anywhere large enough to store them," Brooks announces upon his return.

"I might have space at Knitorious," I suggest. "I could lock them in the storeroom. They'd blend in with my father's books. The police chief lives in the upstairs apartment, so it's pretty safe."

"That would be perfect!" Brooks says.

"They'd be safe there," Dina adds.

"It will only be until Monday when the courier picks them up," Brooks reminds me.

With that settled, Brooks, Dina, me, and a few officers lug the boxes of books to my and Dina's cars. An officer checks our bags and pockets to ensure we don't leave with anything not on the list of items approved for removal. As much as Brooks insists he'd love to follow us to the store and help us unload the boxes, he has an important meeting and has to rush back to his hotel. How convenient for him.

CHAPTER 12

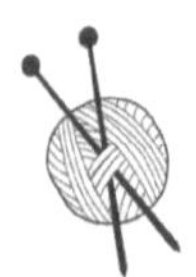

I PARK AS close as possible to the back door at Knitorious and prop open the door with a brick. One by one, Dina and I unload the boxes of books.

"What are you doing, my dear?" Connie asks.

I explain about transferring Claire's signed books from the cottage to the store for safekeeping.

"What are you doing here?" I ask.

"We parked here and walked to the book fair," Connie explains, gesturing to Zoe who is wearing a black spider costume. "It's a lovely day for a walk. Besides, parking at the venue is a hassle."

I nod.

"Megan, wouldn't it make more sense to take the books to chez Martel?" Zoe asks, all four of her right-side spider legs moving in unison when she gestures with her right hand. "You have that newfangled security system there."

She's right. I nod, then look at Dina and realize she hasn't met my stepmother.

"Dina Langley, this is my stepmum, Zoe Monroe." I gesture to my spider-costumed stepmum. "Zoe, this is Dina Langley, she was Claire Rivera's assistant." I gesture to Dina.

Zoe extends four arms, and after a moment of confusion while she determines which arm is real, Dina shakes Zoe's hand.

Connie and Zoe offer Dina their condolences. Then, after a brief conversation about how much we all love Charlotte's Web, I explain to Dina that my house has a state-of-the-art security system complete with cameras, motion sensors, and police monitoring.

I don't bore her with the details about why I have such an elaborate security system, but the short story is someone broke into the house, lay in wait for me, then tried to kill me. As a result, Adam had the house outfitted with a fancy security system to keep Hannah and me safe.

"I think the boxes would fit in the laundry room," I say.

"That sounds like a better idea," Dina agrees. "I'll call Brooks and make sure he's OK with it." Dina calls Brooks while I return the few boxes we've unloaded to my car. "He's not answering," she says, sliding her phone in her pocket.

"Moving the books without telling him feels sneaky," I say.

"It'll be fine," Dina reassures me. "I'll text him later and explain where we moved them and why."

Dina, Connie, and Zoe all insist it will be fine, and

storing the books at chez Martel is a better idea, so I agree and Dina follows me home in her car.

"HEY, BABE." Eric kisses me hello. "Where are Mitchell and Zoe?"

"They went into town to send flowers to Claire's family," I reply.

"Did Sophie go with them?" he asks, looking around his feet where the corgi always rushes to greet him.

I nod. "This is her fifth walk today." I exaggerate with a chuckle. "She loves it when her grandparents visit. We didn't expect you for dinner with the case and all."

"I don't want to miss dinner with your dad and Zoe," he explains. "I can go back to work later." He jerks his thumb toward the laundry room. "What's with the boxes?"

I explain how offering to store Claire's signed books at Knitorious morphed into storing them here. "I wish you'd shown up an hour ago," I tease. "We could have used your muscle to help carry them into the house."

"Brooks Wiley didn't help you?" Eric asks. "He's the person appointed by the publisher to look after them."

"Brooks rushed off to a meeting," I explain, drizzling olive oil onto the baking sheet of baguette pieces.

"What's for dinner?" Eric asks, rubbing his flat stomach. "I'm starving." He's always starving.

"Pesto chicken with roasted zucchini and red pepper panzanella salad," I reply.

"Can I help?"

I decline his offer, then add, "There are pita chips in the cupboard and hummus in the fridge to tide you over until it's ready. How's the case?" I ask.

"I questioned Piper Peters and released her," he replies as he sits at the table and digs into the hummus and pita chips.

"You released her?" I ask, sliding the baking sheet of seasoned bread into the oven. "She's not a suspect?"

"She has an alibi," Eric explains. "It's weak, but it's an alibi. I didn't have enough to keep her. It took a while to make Piper believe Claire is dead. She'd convinced herself it was some kind of elaborate media hoax."

"Denial can be strong," I say. "If Piper killed Claire, she wouldn't be in denial about her death, right?"

Eric shrugs and swallows a mouthful of hummus. "I've seen weirder things."

"Have you heard anything about Dina and Claire having a loud argument yesterday?" I ask, joining him at the table with a cutting board and knife to slice the red peppers and zucchini.

He shakes his head. "No, but it sounds like you have."

I tell Eric that Brooks claimed to hear Claire and Dina's argument from the driveway. Then I tell him about Brooks's revelation that Claire didn't warn anyone she intended to stop writing *Familia*, and Dina's job ends with the book series.

"I bet they were both angry with Claire," Eric theorizes, putting the lid on the hummus container.

"Angry enough to kill her?" I wonder out loud.

"We can't verify Brooks Wiley's alibi," he discloses as he seals the bag of pita chips. "We know he was at the cottage the morning before Claire died. He says he arrived at the hotel and was in his room working on his laptop until hours later when Dina called to tell him Claire died."

"No one saw him come in?" I ask.

"There is video footage of him entering the hotel, and one employee thinks he remembers Brooks entering the hotel, but isn't sure about the time," Eric explains. "Brooks didn't use his keycard. He didn't enter his room. He hasn't used his keycard since he left to go to the cottage yesterday morning. The main entrance is the only door with video surveillance. He could've come and gone through a different door."

"I see," I say, smirking.

"You know something," Eric accuses.

"I suspect something."

"I'm listening," he urges.

"Did anyone access Jules Janssen's room at the time Brooks claims he entered his room?" I ask.

I tell Eric about the intimate moment Brooks and Jules shared in the alley beside my store. "It definitely wasn't the first time they met," I say in conclusion.

Eric types a text to someone, instructing them to ask the hotel for the access history to Jules Janssen's suite of rooms. Then I remember the second time I saw Brooks Wiley.

"He was across the street when Claire and Dina were at Knitorious," I recount. "Dina told me who he was, so I assumed he was waiting for her and Claire." I put down the knife and look at Eric. "In hindsight, I wonder if Jules sent him," I theorize. "Maybe he was watching for Claire to leave with the gift bag from Jules. Maybe Jules dispatched him to report back to her."

"You think Brooks might be a double agent?" Eric asks, grinning with amusement at his pun. "You think he worked for both Claire Rivera and Jules Janssen?"

I shrug and carry the chopped veggies to the counter near the oven. "Maybe," I respond. "You always say motive comes down to either love, money, or ego," I say, removing the toasted bread from the oven and transferring the bread pieces to a bowl. "Think about it. Brooks would earn a lot of money if Jules convinced Claire to turn the *Familia* books into a movie. His fifteen-percent cut would be substantial. And from where I was standing, he looked smitten with Jules. Brooks has at least two motives to kill Claire, money and love." I add the chopped peppers and zucchini to the baking sheet the bread was on and slide it back into the oven.

"Claire can't agree to a *Familia* movie if she's dead," Eric counters.

"No, but her estate can," I remind him as I rub pesto into the chicken breasts. "Maybe Brooks thinks it'll be easier to convince her heirs than to convince Claire herself."

If Brooks killed Claire Rivera, did he act alone, or did he and Jules kill her together?

Sophie charges down the hall, followed by the thud of the front door closing.

"Hey, Soph." She stops long enough for Eric and me to greet her before continuing to her water bowl.

"Can you set the table, please?" I ask Eric while I brown the chicken.

AFTER DINNER, Zoe and my dad yawn and stretch, their eyes heavy with fatigue. It's only early evening, and so far today, they've had a long drive, learned about Claire's death, then learned her death was murder. Zoe walked around town, checking out the book fair dressed as a spider. My dad ate too much cake, and between them, they've put about fifteen miles on Sophie's odometer. They've had a long day, so I insist they relax and let Eric and me clean the kitchen. While Sophie and her grandparents sink into the sofa and watch the evening news with the volume turned up extra loud, we clear the table, load the dishwasher, and tend to the myriad of other tasks required to make the kitchen look like dinner never happened.

"I'll get this, and you can check in at work," I say, taking the broom from Eric and sweeping crumbs toward the hidden sweep inlet under the kitchen cabinet.

Eric turns on his phone and waits for it to come to life. He makes a point of turning it off every day for at least an hour—a gesture I appreciate—but I know when he's working a big case, it stresses him out to be unreachable.

He reads and replies to texts and emails while his phone dings, rings, buzzes, and vibrates.

"What's wrong?" I stop wiping the stovetop and look at him when he utters a curse word under his breath.

"I don't know how to tell you this, babe." He takes a deep breath. "Your dad is a suspect. I have to question him."

"What?!" I hiss, putting away the broom.

I peek in the family room. My dad is asleep with his head resting on the back of the sofa, and Zoe is asleep with her head on my dad's shoulder. Sophie is asleep, sprawled across their laps. I have to imagine their chorus of gentle snores because I can't hear anything other than the meteorologist on the twenty-four-hour news channel. Thank goodness, they watch the news with the volume so loud and can't overhear our conversation.

"Is this because he knew about Claire's nut allergy and made that stupid comment about how he thought her carelessness about it might kill her?" I struggle to contain myself to a whisper.

Eric shakes his head and opens his mouth to answer me, then closes it, and gestures for me to follow him. We tiptoe to the bedroom where I close the door while he turns on the TV and increases the volume.

"My dad couldn't have killed Claire. He and Zoe were two hours south of here when she died. They pulled off the highway for the night, remember?"

"After they checked in, your dad left the hotel alone.

For several hours," Eric explains. "The hotel has surveillance footage."

"OK." I shrug. "That doesn't mean he drove to Harmony Lake and murdered Claire," I claim.

"The problem is, I don't know where he went." Eric throws up his hands in frustration. "The man turns off his cell phone when he's in the car. Who does that?" He sounds flustered. "If I could track his cell phone location, this wouldn't be necessary."

"Why were you looking into him, anyway?" I ask, my voice full of agitation and my cheeks hot.

"I have to eliminate him as a suspect. He was close enough in proximity that it's within the realm of possibility. And because of Mitchell and Claire's troubled history, his name is being bantered around social media as a likely suspect." Eric places his hands on my shoulders. "You might want to avoid reading the social media comments. Some of them are pretty harsh."

I sigh and sit on the edge of the bed. "My dad isn't a murderer." I shake my head and blink away the tears that sting my eyes.

"I know, babe." Eric sits down next to me. "But you know how this works. I have to eliminate him so when we arrest the actual killer, they can't suggest Mitchell as an alternate suspect to create reasonable doubt." He turns his body toward me. "Look at it this way, when I eliminate Mitchell as a suspect, no one can accuse him of killing Claire. I'll make sure his name and reputation are clear."

"Do you have to question Zoe too?" I sigh again.

Eric nods. "I won't take them to the station," he

offers. "I can question them myself, so no one else has to know, and it won't leak to the media. I can question them here if they agree."

"My dad might lawyer up," I warn him. "He won't make it easy for you."

Eric shrugs one shoulder. "That's his choice. If it happens, we'll deal with it."

"Not tonight, please?" I implore. "You saw how tired they are. They're sound asleep on the sofa. Can we talk to them about this in the morning?"

Eric nods. "It'll give me more time to work up the nerve." He looks at me. "Your dad barely tolerates me already. He'll hate me after this."

If it proves he didn't murder Claire, it will be worth it.

Where was my dad when Claire was killed? Why did he leave the hotel after they checked in? Why was he gone for several hours? Does Zoe know where my dad was, and what he was doing?

Speaking of Zoe, what was she doing while Mitchell was unaccounted for? If they weren't together, does she have an alibi? Don't be silly, Megan. Zoe doesn't have a vindictive bone in her body. There's no way she'd kill Claire Rivera out of revenge for stealing her husband's idea. Would she?

CHAPTER 13

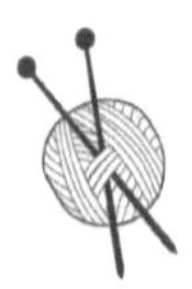

SATURDAY, April 17th

"Good morning, Bean!"

I almost jump out of my skin at the sound of the unexpected voice.

"Good morning, Dad," I say, clutching my chest.

I'm used to being the first person awake in my house. It freaks me out to have another morning person here. Eric is a morning person, but he doesn't hang around. He either goes for a run or goes to work, leaving me and Sophie to enjoy the early morning quietude on our own.

"You're an early riser. You get that from me," he informs me with pride. "Your young man is an early riser too. He's already gone for a morning run."

"How do you know?" I ask.

It's weird to be in your forties and have someone refer to someone else your age as young, but age is relative, I guess.

"I ran into him when I walked to the store to get a

paper." Mitchell holds up the newspaper as evidence and looks at me over his reading glasses. "He was heading to his apartment after his ten kilometre run. He said he'll come over after he has a shower."

Eric isn't staying overnight while my dad and Zoe are here. He's worried my dad will think it's inappropriate.

I open the sliding glass door, and Sophie launches herself into the backyard like a missile.

"You can read the news online, you know," I remind him in jest.

"It's not the same," he insists, turning the page and snapping the paper.

"You're right," I agree. "The newspaper is less up-to-date than the online sources."

"Are you sure you want to have this debate, Bean?" he teases, chuckling. "Because I'm more than happy to spend the entire day convincing you."

"I know better than to debate with you," I say, picking up Sophie's bowls so I can refresh her water and fix her breakfast. "How did you sleep?"

"Like this." He drops his head to his shoulder, closes his eyes, and snores.

I roll my eyes. "Hilarious. I'll assume that means you slept well."

He couldn't have slept worse than me. I tossed and turned all night, worrying about his alibi situation. I return Sophie's bowls to the floor and open the back door. She bolts past me and runs straight to her breakfast.

We're alone. Maybe I should ask my dad where he

was when Claire died. Maybe if I prepare him before Eric gets here, my dad will warm up to the idea of being questioned and cooperate.

"Dad." I swallow. He bends the top half of the newspaper toward him and looks at me.

"Yes, Bean?"

Sophie barks. I flinch. The front door opens and closes.

"Why are you so jumpy this morning?" my dad asks. "That's the second time you've startled in ten minutes."

"Good morning." Eric smiles. He's carrying a takeout tray with four coffees from Latte Da. He pulls one of the to-go cups out of the tray. "For you," he says, handing me the cup and kissing my forehead.

"Thank you." I crack the lid and inhale the comforting aroma.

I take a moment to savour the first sip of maple pecan latte and let the caffeine touch my soul while the warmth flows down my throat and emanates through my body. In the background, Eric explains to my dad he isn't sure what he and Zoe drink, so he got them each a medium roast and a bunch of coffee condiments on the side.

After a few minutes of awkward-for-me small talk, I announce I need to take Sophie for a walk, and my dad offers to join me. I thank him but decline his offer. Eric offers to join me in his place, and we tell my dad we'll leave him in peace to read his paper.

Coffees in hand, we step outside, and for the first time today, I feel like I can breathe. I inhale deeply and try to focus on the warm sun on my face and the birds singing their morning songs.

"You OK?" Eric asks. "It's like you're on pins and needles."

"I'm nervous," I explain, "and I didn't get much sleep."

"Are you worried about how your dad will react when I tell him I need to question him?"

I shake my head. "About his whereabouts when Claire was murdered." I take a moment to gather my thoughts. "What if his alibi isn't verifiable? What if you can't eliminate him as a suspect?"

"Heavy shoulders, long arms," Eric coaches me as we stop to wait while Sophie sniffs a fire hydrant.

Heavy shoulders, long arms is a mantra I learned in a yoga class in my twenties. I still use it today to remind myself to breathe and to release the tension in my neck and shoulders.

"I couldn't sleep last night, either," Eric admits. "Questioning them is just a formality. I'm sure I'll be able to eliminate him." The tension in his jaw and eye muscles when he forces a smile betrays the confident tone of his voice. He's trying to ease my stress about this situation.

"Thank you." I take his hand. "You're the best cop I've ever met. If anyone can prove my dad is innocent, it's you." I stand on my tippy toes and kiss him. "I know you're in a horrible position. You have my full support."

"The best way to eliminate Mitchell Monroe as a

suspect is to find Claire's killer." He smiles and hugs me. "So that's what I'll do."

Agreed. That's what I intend to do too.

To procrastinate the unpleasantness of telling my father he's a suspect as long as possible, we walk twice as long as normal. Sophie must wonder what is going on. Her walks are extra long and extra frequent this week. She's loving the extra attention.

I'm not in a rush. The store will be slow today because the book fair is in full swing. I texted Connie and Marla last night to arrange for them to open the store, and cover for me, in case I'm late today. They assume I want to spend time with Mitchell and Zoe, and I didn't correct them. It's kind of true.

"Ready?" Eric asks, before he opens the door to the house.

"Ready." I nod.

"You're back!" Zoe gives us each a hug. "We weren't sure whether to wait, so we ate without you. Can I get either of you some toast and half a grapefruit?"

"I already ate," Eric assures her, "but thank you."

"I'm not hungry," I add, my stomach in knots. I take a deep breath and pull up my proverbial big-girl pants. "Dad, we need to talk to you."

"Sounds serious, Bean." He takes his usual seat in the overstuffed chair in the living room. He pats his knee, and Sophie joins him, snuggling on his lap.

"It is," I confirm, sitting on the sofa cushion closest

to his chair. Eric sits next to me, and Zoe sits across from us on the loveseat. "Why did you get a hotel room on Thursday instead of driving straight to Harmony Lake?"

He looks back and forth between Eric and me. "For days I ruminated over a plot hole in my manuscript, and the solution came to me while I was driving. Just like it always does," Mitchell explains. "I needed to capture my thoughts before I lost them, so I pulled over." He shrugs.

"This is how your father works, Megan. It's part of his process," Zoe elaborates. "I was the one who suggested the hotel. I knew your father would spend hours working. By the time he finished, it would've been late, and neither of us likes to drive at night if we can avoid it."

"We went to the hotel and checked in," Mitchell adds, picking up where his wife leaves off. "The Wi-Fi was as stable as a two-legged stool, and the room was uninspiring. Zoe stayed at the hotel, and I went somewhere with better Wi-Fi and more ambience."

Eric reaches into his pocket and pulls out his small notebook and a pen. He flips to the next open page of the notebook and clicks the top of the pen, then writes. This incites my dad.

"Wait," my dad says with his index finger in the air. He looks at me. "Are you questioning me, Bean?" He looks at Eric. "Is this an interrogation, Chief Sloane?"

"I need to ask you a few questions, sir," Eric says.

With my father rendered momentarily speechless from shock, Eric explains he needs to ask my dad about his absence from the hotel. He tells them he can question them here, instead of the station, and offers to question them himself to ensure the utmost discretion and avoid the media finding out Mitchell Monroe is a person of interest.

"I want my lawyer," my dad proclaims.

Eric closes his notebook and clicks his pen closed. "Call them."

"He's at least a day away from here," my dad insists.

The doorbell rings. Sophie barks and jumps off my dad's lap. Zoe and I both startle. I excuse myself to answer the door.

"Hello, Mitchell," Adam says. "I understand you need a lawyer."

Is he psychic? How could he know my dad just demanded to talk to his lawyer?

"Who called you?" Mitchell demands, sounding just as dumbfounded as I am.

"I did," Zoe replies.

"Why?" My dad and I ask in stereo.

"How did you know Dad would need a lawyer?" I ask her.

"I didn't." Zoe shrugs. "I asked Adam for advice about the internet lies," she explains. She looks at my dad. "I saw some online comments and conjecture yesterday. I didn't tell you because I didn't want to upset you. I asked Adam what we can do to minimize the damage to your reputation. He offered to come by this morning and talk to me. I assumed you'd be writing, so I didn't bother to tell you he was coming over.

But with the brouhaha this morning, I forgot he was coming." She raises her eyebrows and leans toward her husband. "Wasn't it nice of Adam to offer to help us, Mitchell?"

"Why do I sense something bigger is going on?" Adam asks, lowering himself onto the loveseat next to Zoe. He surveys our blank stares. "Care to fill me in, Meg?" he asks, glaring at me.

"Your replacement, here, thinks I killed Claire Rivera!" Mitchell blurts out before I can answer.

"Mitchell!"

"Dad!"

Zoe and I admonish him in unison for his rude comment.

I gasp and use my scowl to reprimand him further for referring to Eric as Adam's replacement.

I look at Adam. "Eric needs to ask Dad a few questions, but he wants to wait for his lawyer who is far, far away," I summarize curtly.

"I see," Adam nods and sits back. He laces his fingers together and rests his hands on his lap. "Mitchell, would you like me to represent you while Eric questions you?"

"No, thank you!" my dad snaps. "I have a lawyer. He's just not here." He huffs. "Yet," he adds.

"I'd like you to represent me while I'm questioned, Adam," Zoe interjects.

"Zoe!" Mitchell exclaims. He draws his brows so close together they almost touch.

"What, Mitchell?" Zoe asks in a calm voice. "I have no desire to draw out this fiasco any longer than necessary. If answering Eric's questions will help him find Claire's killer sooner rather than later, he has my full cooperation."

"Coffee, Adam?" I ask, standing up. Sensing an opportunity, Sophie jumps onto the sofa and takes my spot.

Adam nods, so I excuse myself to the kitchen to take my time making the slowest coffee ever and give Zoe, my dad, and Adam an opportunity to talk alone.

"Well, this couldn't have gone worse," Eric says, following me into the kitchen.

"I'm sorry about what my dad said," I say to Eric as I pull the crock pot out from under the sink and hoist it onto the counter. "It was inexcusable. And not true."

"I know, babe. He was angry. People get defensive and offensive when they feel cornered by the police," Eric justifies.

"It doesn't matter," I respond. "Don't make excuses for him. What he said was unacceptable." I plug in the crock pot and turn it on, then I drop a pod in the coffeemaker and turn it on too.

I place a mug under the spout, then get the meatballs out of the freezer.

"What are you making?" Eric asks.

"Sweet and sour meatballs," I reply. "For the family dinner tonight. It's potluck."

"This might be the most awkward family dinner ever," he mutters.

I sweeten Adam's coffee with cream and sugar, then pour a jar of sweet and sour sauce over the meatballs, and close the lid on the crock pot.

"Good news," Adam announces as he enters the kitchen. "They both agree to answer questions. I'll represent them. They'd like Meg to be present." He smiles, accentuating the lines around his blue eyes, and scratches the back of his head, mussing his hair.

"Thank you, Adam," I say, handing him his coffee. "I'm sorry we dragged you into this."

He winks. "Life is more exciting than fiction when Mitchell comes to town." He sips his coffee and looks at Eric. "Dude, you will be so dead this time next year." He puts down his coffee and rubs his hands together. "How do you think Mitchell will kill you?" He chuckles, then adds, "In the literary sense, I mean. In a book. He'll kill you in a book."

I wish Claire's murder was a plot in a Mitchell Monroe book. Unlike real life, his books always end with the good guy figuring out whodunit and the culprit suffering the consequences of their evil deeds.

CHAPTER 14

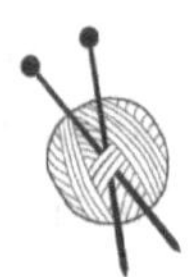

We regroup in the living room, and Eric starts by asking Zoe what she did while my dad was out. She claims she stayed in the room and watched a movie. The movie rental should appear on their hotel bill, and her cardkey should verify that she didn't leave the room.

"Also, my cell phone was on the entire time, so you'll be able to trace its location, right?" she asks Eric.

That was easy. I doubt questioning my dad will be as straightforward.

"Where did you go when you left the hotel, Mr. Monroe?" Eric asks.

My dad looks at Adam. Adam nods, and my dad looks at Eric.

"Some coffee shop not too far from the hotel."

"What was it called?"

Mitchell shrugs. "I can't remember."

"Did you keep a receipt?"

"I paid cash."

This is going nowhere.

"Describe the coffee shop, Dad. What was the first thing you noticed when you walked in?" I ask.

"It was one of those trendy places," he recalls. "It smelled like gourmet coffee and all the customers were on their laptops, cell phones, tablets, or all three. Most of the drinks had pretentious, hard-to-pronounce names."

"What did you order?" I ask, opening the internet browser on my phone and searching for coffee shops within a two-hour radius.

"I had two London Fogs and two cranberry biscotti. They had two menus, one vegan and one regular. I ordered from the regular menu. The manager recognized me from my book jacket and gave me the second London Fog and biscotti on the house." He sounds pleased with the amount of detail he's able to recollect.

"Tell us about the manager," I encourage, adding *vegan menu options* to my online search criteria.

"I wouldn't have known he was the manager if he didn't tell me. He wore the same black apron as his employees, and everyone was the same age. You know the type, well educated, overqualified, and full of existential angst." He gestures vaguely. "Typical young people."

I add *black apron* to my search criteria. The list is getting shorter. There are a surprising number of trendy coffee shops around.

"Did the manager have a nametag?" Eric asks.

"Yes!" Mitchell replies with enthusiasm and snaps his fingers. "And he introduced himself to me. We shook hands, and he asked if I would take a selfie with him." He bites his lip while he thinks. "What was the boy's name?" The boy is probably in his thirties.

"Did you take the selfie?" Eric asks.

"Yes," Mitchell replies. "I try to be approachable and friendly. It's important to me to accommodate my readers."

I close the internet browser on my phone and open a social media app. I type in #MitchellMonroe. Wow, my dad wasn't kidding. It looks like he takes a selfie with anyone who asks. There are pages of photos of him posing with random people. I filter the results by date and look at the most recent posts first.

"He had one of those man-buns that have become so popular." He holds his hand on top of his head to show us where the coffee shop manager's man-bun was. "And those earrings you can see through. You know where they train their earlobes to have holes in them?" Mitchell snaps his fingers again. "He had two last names. *Ooof!* What was his name? It's on the tip of my tongue."

"He had a hyphenated last name?" Zoe probes.

"No," Mitchell clarifies. "His first and last names were both common surnames."

"Does Smith Wilson sound familiar?" I ask, turning my phone toward my dad.

He raises his reading glasses to his face and looks at my phone. "That's him!" he shouts like he just won a game of bingo. "Well done, Bean!" We high five. "She gets her resourcefulness from me," he announces to no one in particular.

I tilt the phone screen so Eric can see it. "Smith Wilson is the manager at The Daily Grind." I flash a smug smile, pleased with my aptitude for online stalking.

I take a screenshot of Smith Wilson's post, just in case he deletes it or makes his account private or something.

"The Daily Grind! That was it!" Mitchell confirms. He looks at Zoe. "It's one of those hipster places with clusters of sitting areas. There are sofas, chairs, coffee tables. They look like leather, but they aren't leather. All the sitting areas have signs explaining the furniture is vegan leather. Vegan leather!" He huffs. "Vegan leather is an oxymoron. Just call it plastic, for goodness' sake...."

While my dad expounds the absurdity of referring to anything not sourced from an animal as leather, I clear away the takeout cups and Adam's mug. Eric follows me into the kitchen, typing on his cell phone.

"This should be easy to verify," he assures me. "If all goes well, I'll text you in a couple of hours to tell you we eliminated Mitchell Monroe as a suspect in Claire's death."

"Thank you," I say, hugging him.

"I have to get going." He kisses the top of my head. "I'll pick you up at closing time?"

"Perfect." I kiss him goodbye.

He says goodbye to my dad, Zoe, and Adam as I check the crock pot before I leave.

"Meg, I'm leaving," Adam says, looking at his watch as he enters the kitchen. "I'm on mayor duty today. I have to attend a luncheon at the town hall with the book club, have my photo taken with Jules Janssen at her book signing, then go to the library and read *If You Give a Mouse a Cookie* to The LitWits."

The LitWits is a reading group for local children at the Harmony Lake library.

"Busy day," I comment. "I hope you have time to come for dinner." Adam says he'll be here for dinner but won't have time to make anything for the potluck, so he'll bring wine. "The most important part of any meal," I quip. "I'll walk you to the door."

My dad and Zoe are already at the door.

"Thank you for your help, Adam." Zoe kisses Adam's cheek, then discreetly nudges my father's ribs.

"Thank you, Adam. We appreciate your time and expertise." My dad extends his hand.

"Don't thank me yet. You haven't seen my bill." Adam winks.

Zoe and I laugh, but Mitchell isn't amused.

"He's kidding, Dad," I assure him.

"Of course, he is," Mitchell chuckles. "I know that."

They shake hands, which is the closest thing to affection I've ever seen them share, then Adam and I exchange a double-cheek kiss, and he leaves.

I look at the time and realize it's almost lunchtime. Connie and Marla are working a half day today, and I have to relieve them. Zoe suggests we go together since she's going to Knitorious to meet Connie. They plan to wander around the book fair together, then go back to Connie's place and cook for the pot luck tonight.

Mitchell asks if Sophie can stay with him. He says

she's the perfect writing companion, good company without being demanding or distracting.

"You should write her into one of your books," Zoe suggests. "What book wouldn't be improved by a loyal animal companion?"

"You're right," I agree.

April: Dina Langley has been here all morning.

Me: At the bakery?

April: Yup. Working on her laptop. She really likes lemon meringue tarts.

Me: Who doesn't? T's lemon meringue tarts are the best! Has Dina said anything?

April: She says lots of things. She's chatty and outgoing. Nothing about Claire's murder, though.

The *Familia*-inspired needle-felt display was popular this morning. We sold at least half of the figures. I'm rearranging the leftover items so the display looks less sparse when my phone dings again.

April: Dina just left. She's meeting Brooks Wiley for lunch. Can you talk?

I scan the store, even though I know I'm the only person here.

Me: Yes! The store is empty.

Moments later, my phone rings. I put April on speaker while I dig out my AirPods from the bottom of my purse.

"Hello?"

"Hi, Megapop! Not that it's a surprise, but T and I are bringing dessert to the potluck tonight."

"I figured," I say, popping my AirPods into my ears. "What are you bringing?"

"Nanaimo bars and toffee pecan shortbread."

"Mmm..." Just hearing the words make my tummy rumble.

"Dina just left," April informs me. "She got here just after we opened. She said she gets lonely in her hotel room by herself, and Eric asked her not to leave town, so she's trying to make the best of it."

"You and I are the only people she knows in Harmony Lake," I remind April. "It must be hard for her being stuck in a strange town by herself."

"He's not local, but she also knows Brooks Wiley. When she packed up to leave, she said she was meeting him for lunch."

"Interesting," I think out loud.

"What's interesting?"

"I got the sense they don't like each other."

"I guess things change when you're both stuck in the same small town," April suggests.

"You're right," I agree, wondering if Brooks and Dina could be closer than they let on. I've caught him sneaking around with Jules, maybe sneaky relationships are his thing.

"She typed frantically for twenty-five minutes, then rewarded herself with a lemon meringue tart," April reports. "Then she typed frantically for twenty-five minutes again, then ate another tart. All morning."

"My dad does that when he's writing," I respond.

"He says it's part of his process."

"Eats a lot of lemon meringue tarts?"

"No, the frantic typing-thing," I clarify. "He writes uninterrupted for twenty minutes, then takes a five-minute break and does something he likes. He calls the frantic typing sessions, sprints."

"I guess non-writers do sprints too," April surmises.

"What was she doing?" I ask.

"She said she was replying to social media posts and condolence emails from fans who reached out about Claire's death," April mumbles with her mouth full.

"What are you eating?" I regret skipping breakfast.

"Chocolate croissant," she replies, swallowing. Then takes another bite. "Why? You want some?" she garbles.

"Yes. I'm starving. This morning was a fiasco, and I missed breakfast."

"I'll be there in two minutes. I want to know everything."

Before I can respond, April ends the call.

True to her word, two minutes later, the bell over the door jingles, and April swoops in carrying my favourite box: a white confectionery box with the Artsy Tartsy logo on the lid.

"Thank you," I say, taking the box from her. "You're saving me from an afternoon of hunger." I bite into a croissant and let my eyes roll back in my head. "I can't leave because I'm alone until closing time," I mumble with my mouth full of flaky pastry goodness.

"Business is dead," she informs me. "Everyone is at the book fair today. The only customers we've had want the bookish cookies and nothing else."

"It's the same here," I agree, using the half-eaten croissant in my hand to point to the needle-felt display. "The felted *Familia* figures are the only thing we've sold today." I shrug and take another bite of croissant.

"So..." April makes herself comfortable in the cozy sitting area. "Who do you think killed Claire Rivera? I know you've been sleuthing."

Swallowing a mouthful of croissant, I join her on the sofa. "I don't know," I admit. "A few people have motives. Eric is verifying alibis to determine who also had opportunity."

"Who do you think did it?" I ask.

"Dina Langley," April replies without hesitation.

"Why?" I ask.

"First, she was there when it happened. Second, she had access to Claire to give her whatever nut product was the murder weapon," April alleges.

"Makes sense," I agree, taking another croissant from the box and closing the lid. "But the employment contract Dina had with Claire stipulated that Dina's job as Claire's assistant ends the day they release the last *Familia* book. Why would she make herself unemployed sooner?"

"Hmm," April ponders, "that strengthens my case. Dina would be unemployed either way." She shrugs. "She had nothing to lose."

Ding!

A knot of panic swells in my belly when my phone dings. What if it's Eric telling me he couldn't verify my dad's alibi?

CHAPTER 15

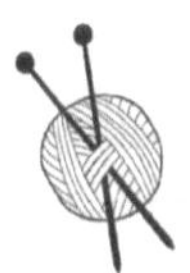

"PLEASE LET IT BE GOOD NEWS," I wish out loud as I pick up my phone from the counter.

Eric: He's eliminated! Do you want to tell him or shall I?

I let out a long, audible sigh of relief.

Me: Good job, honey! I'll let you deliver the good news.

"Good news?" April asks. "You look like a two-tonne weight just lifted off your shoulders."

I smile and nod, then return to the sofa and tell her about Mitchell going AWOL from his hotel room on Thursday, ending up on Eric's suspect list. I try to convey how awkward it is to watch your boyfriend question your father about a murder while you and your ex-husband try to support both of them.

"That explains why you missed breakfast," April sympathizes. "We all knew Mitchell didn't kill Claire," she reassures me. "Now everyone else knows too."

"I know," I agree, nodding. "But I want to eliminate

any possibility of doubt. The only way to do that is to find the killer."

"Just be careful." April's tone is serious, and her smile is tight and forced. "I don't want to embrace my inner sleuth to solve your murder."

She puts her hand on top of mine. I smile.

"Getting back to your theory that Dina is the killer," I say, guiding us back to our original conversation. "If Dina is the murderer, why was she afraid to be at the cottage after Claire died?"

"She was probably scared of Piper," April reasons. "From what you told me about this Piper person, she's not a good example of mental stability. With Claire dead, Dina likely worried Piper might shift her crazed obsession from Claire to her."

"Dina was terrified of Piper at the cottage yesterday," I reminisce. "You can't fake that kind of fear. It was real. I felt it."

"You think Piper killed Claire, don't you?" she asks.

"I did," I admit. "But now I'm not sure."

"What changed your mind?"

"A few things," I reply. "Piper is a huge *Familia* fan. If she killed Claire, there could never be a *Familia* revival, prequel, sequel, crossover series, or anything. Also, with Claire dead, Piper could never change her mind about retiring the series. You can't convince a dead person," I assert. "And Eric said when he questioned Piper, he had a hard time convincing her Claire was dead. He said Piper insisted Claire's death was a media hoax, or a publicity stunt, or something. If she was there when Claire died, how could she delude herself about it?"

"Maybe Piper was pretending she didn't believe Claire was dead, so she could claim mental incompetence if they caught her," April theorizes. My best friend has a knack for coming up with conspiracy theories; it's kind of her super power.

The bell over the door jingles, bringing our conversation to a premature end.

At first, it's difficult to make out her face through the black veil, but when we make eye contact, I recognize her.

"Speak of the devil," I mutter under my breath.

As I motion to get up, April touches my knee, and I look at her.

"Is that Piper?" she mouths.

I nod and get up.

"Hi there," I say, mustering my most cheerful voice and smile.

"Hello, there! You must be Megan Martel. I'm Piper Peters." She extends her gloved hand and smiles.

The bubbly voice is a stark contrast to her traditional Victorian-era mourning dress. Yes, mourning dress. Piper is wearing a floor length, black dress with long sleeves and a full skirt. The bodice buttons up to just underneath her chin where it's fastened with a cameo brooch. A black veil is draped over her black bonnet–yes, bonnet–obscuring her face.

All she needs is a black parasol and a case of the vapours, and I'd swear she just time-travelled here from 1850 England.

"Hi, Piper." I shake her gloved hand. "It's nice to meet you." Her black gloves feel like cotton. "Have we met before?" I ask, narrowing my eyes and tilting my head to one side. "You look familiar."

I don't know if she remembers me from the cottage yesterday, but I want to give her the opportunity to mention it without confronting her. I get the feeling it's a bad idea to confront Piper or back her into a corner.

"Yes," Piper responds. "I believe you were at Claire Rivera's cottage yesterday. We weren't formally introduced, but I never forget a face." She giggles.

Neither do I. Especially when we make eye contact through the window of a police car.

"I'm April." April extends her hand, and Piper shakes it.

I'm distracted by Piper's presence and didn't know April was behind me. I don't blame her for coming over for a closer look. Piper's attire is a lot to take in for the observer. Heck, I'm tempted to take a picture.

She must've brought the outfit with her. I can't think of anywhere local that sells this style of clothing. Is it a costume for the book fair? Some book fair attendees are cosplaying today, so maybe Piper is one of them. Cosplay is a word fans use to describe wearing costumes and accessories to represent a certain character. I learned it from Hannah.

"It's lovely to make your acquaintance, April. I'm Piper Peters."

"Your dress is beautiful. The attention to detail is incredible," April compliments. "Who are you supposed to be?"

"Excuse me?" Piper asks, tilting her veiled head to one side.

The sudden corrugation on her forehead and the hint of offense in her voice makes me think Piper isn't cosplaying; this is a legitimate mourning outfit.

I'm about to give April a discreet prod under the counter before she says anything else that Piper might find insulting, but I'm too slow. My finger pokes her hip just as she says, "You're dressed as a literary character, right?"

"I most certainly am not!" Piper barks. "I am in mourning!"

From the shocked expression on her face, I can tell April gets it now. "I'm sorry for your loss," April sputters. "Mourning attire isn't very common in Harmony Lake."

Or in the twenty-first century, but I digress.

"Mourning attire signals to the world that a woman has suffered a significant loss." Piper reaches under her veil and dabs her eyes with a handkerchief.

"Would you like to sit down?" I offer. Piper nods, and I gesture toward the cozy sitting area. "Would you like some water?"

"No, thank you," Piper replies, tucking her handkerchief into the cuff of her sleeve. When she sits, the spread of her skirt takes up the entire loveseat. "I've learned the hard way that when one is in mourning, it's best to avoid drinking anything unless absolutely necessary." She sighs. "You wouldn't believe how difficult it is to pee whilst wearing this dress," she overshares. "Very few public washrooms nowadays are spacious enough to accommodate a bustle."

I can't help myself; I have to know. It's driving me crazy. "Did you buy your mourning dress somewhere local?"

"Heavens, no," Piper replies. "When travelling, I always pack mourning attire. Just like the royal family, one must prepare oneself for any contingency." She giggles.

I make a mental note to ask Eric if packing a nineteenth-century mourning outfit constitutes premeditation.

I want to ask her what other contingencies she's prepared for, but I stop myself.

"Are you a knitter, Piper?" April asks.

"No," Piper retorts, vexed. "Why would you ask me that?"

I guess she hasn't forgiven April for thinking her dress is a costume.

"This is a knitting store," I explain. "Most people come here for yarn and knitting supplies."

"Right," Piper says, looking around and taking in the store from behind her veil. "I didn't realize."

"What brings you here today?" I ask, smiling and being as non-threatening as possible.

"Well, I was wandering through the exhibits at the book fair, and I noticed several people with small, felted figurines from the *Familia* books. I stopped one person, and she graciously told me you were selling them here. She even gave me your name."

"Yes, we sell them here." I gesture to the display. "A

local artisan handcrafted each character and location," I explain. "One hundred percent of the proceeds will benefit a non-profit organization that supports community-based literacy programs..."

"I'll take whatever you have left," she interrupts my sales spiel.

"Oh," I say, shocked. "Would you like a closer look? Or the price of each item before you decide?" I ask.

"No, thank you." Piper smiles. "I'll take them." She giggles. "Please pack them such that they will endure a cross-Atlantic voyage."

She makes it sound like she'll be sailing back to England on the Titanic.

"I'll help you wrap them up, Megnolia," April offers, already pulling out tissue paper from under the counter.

"Oh, is your full name Magnolia?" Piper asks. "Magnolia is a lovely name."

"No," I correct her. "My name is Megan. April just likes to change it up, sometimes." She looks disappointed my name isn't Magnolia. "Were you and Claire close?" I ask.

April shoots me a look that silently screams, *What are you doing? Don't poke the bear!* I remove a price tag from the bottom of a needle-felted church and hand the church to April for packaging.

"Yes," Piper replies. "Our connection was deep. So deep it transcended the necessity for written words and verbal communication."

I'd bet my yarn stash that the restraining order

Claire had against her is the real reason they didn't share written words or verbal communication.

"It sounds like a very special relationship," I sympathize, handing April a felt Mama and sticking the price tag to the counter.

"Yes," Piper agrees, "our souls were old friends."

A lovely sentiment that sounds ominous when she says it.

She wanders toward the back of the store.

"Were you shocked when Claire announced she was retiring *Familia*?" I shout so Piper can hear me. She's hovering near the back room.

"I didn't kill her, you know," she snaps as if one of us accused her. "What's in here?" She gestures to the back room. "Are there more felt figurines in here?" Her voice is now sweet and calm.

"Just a kitchenette, a back door, and some stairs," I assure her.

"She scares me," April whispers.

I nod.

"Do you want this one too?" I ask, holding up a tiny figure she won't be able to see from the back of the store through her veil.

"I want all of them," Piper reiterates.

She's distracted from the back room; mission accomplished. She walks toward the front of the store, craning her neck to look at the figure.

"Well done," April commends me.

"Thank you," I whisper.

"I know everyone thinks I killed Claire, but I didn't," Piper says matter-of-factly.

"We don't think you killed Claire," I say, trying to comfort her, though this interaction has moved her way up on my suspect list. "You're one of Claire's biggest fans, why would you harm her?"

"I'm not one of her biggest fans," Piper corrects me. "I am Claire Rivera's biggest fan! Why would I kill her? It would eliminate any chance of reading a new *Familia* book ever again!"

Her voice hitches on the last few words, and she pulls her handkerchief from her sleeve and dabs her eyes.

April finishes packing the felted items, and I ring up the sale. After Piper pays, I thank her for her business and put her receipt in the bag.

"May I ask you one more question?" I ask, handing her the bag across the counter.

"Of course," Piper replies.

"How did you know where Claire and Dina were staying? Their location wasn't public knowledge."

"A kind lady told me," Piper says. "I was in line at the library to get my free Between the Covers Book Fair swag bag, and she was behind me. She asked if I planned to attend Claire's book signing. I told her that of course I would. Claire's book signing is the reason I came to the book fair. Then she told me she knows where Claire is staying. She even gave me directions."

"Do you remember her name?"

"We didn't exchange names," Piper replies, her veil swaying when she shakes her head.

"What did she look like?" I ask.

"It's hard to tell from the way she dressed," Piper

explains with a one-shoulder shrug. "Not very tall, about your height. Baseball cap. Black backpack. Ginger-ish hair, I think. It was under her cap, so I can't say for sure."

"Lots of teeth?" I ask.

"Yes, now that you mention it. And her teeth were very white and very straight."

While April tells her about the *Familia*-inspired bookish cookies at Artsy Tartsy, I rush around the counter and hold the door for Piper. She thanks us for our time and help, and we wish her a good day. After her bustle has cleared the threshold, I close the door behind her.

"Lock it!" April hisses.

"I'm glad you were here," I lock the door and turn the sign to CLOSED for a few minutes so April and I can regroup. "I don't think I could do that scenario justice if I described it to you."

"I'm glad I was here too," April responds. "If she'd snapped, she could only kill one of us at a time. The other one could run for help."

"Why did you send her to the bakery?" I ask.

"T needs to share this experience with us. Otherwise, she'll think we made it up or accuse us of exaggerating."

"Fair point," I say.

"Can I change my answer?" April asks.

"Answer to what?"

"To who killed Claire Rivera," April clarifies. "I'd like to change my answer to Piper Peters."

I'm leaning toward that answer too.

CHAPTER 16

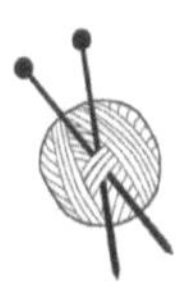

TIME PASSES SLOWLY WITHOUT CUSTOMERS. I'm out of things to do. I've dusted, swept, mopped, tidied, and packed the online orders to drop off at the post office. With three hours left until it's time to close the store, I sit down with my needle-felting project. I just need to finish Sophie's ears and face.

I'm about to open the camera roll on my phone and look at a photo of Sophie to make sure I get her markings correct, when the bell jingles. Next thing I know, the real Sophie is in front of me with her front paws on my lap.

"Hey, Soph! This is a pleasant surprise." I detach her leash, and she trots toward the back of the store, no doubt en route to her water dish in the kitchenette.

"Hello, Bean!"

"Hey, Dad! What are you doing here?"

"It was time for a break. I'm craving another coffee from Latte Da, so Sophie and I discussed it, and we decided to walk into town."

"How's your book coming along?" I ask.

"Slower than I'd like," he admits. "The manuscript is due at the end of the month, and I'm making some major last-minute changes."

"What kinds of changes?" I ask.

"It's time for Rock Granite to retire," my dad replies, then sighs like he's relieved to say it out loud.

"You're ending the series?" I stop stabbing and put down my felting needle so I don't stab myself by accident from the shock. "You're writing the last *Shark Attack* book? Ever?"

"That was the plan," he replies. "But our road trips to Toronto to visit Hannah, then to Harmony Lake to visit you have inspired me to go in a different direction." He winks. "I think I can keep the series fresh and still let Rock Granite enjoy his retirement."

"Wanna tell me about it?" I ask, knowing he won't give me any spoilers.

"You can wait and read it after it's published," he teases.

"Did Eric call you?" I ask, wondering if my dad knows Eric eliminated him as a suspect.

"He did better than that," he responds. "He stopped by the house to give me the good news in person. To say I'm relieved is an understatement."

"Listen, Bean," he says, sitting next to me on the sofa. "I owe you an apology. I'm sorry I was uncooperative and maybe rude earlier when you and Eric tried to question me." He shrugs one shoulder. "This is the first time I've been part of a real murder investigation. I panicked and got defensive. I shouldn't have said Eric was Adam's replacement. It was wrong."

"Thank you, Dad." I accept his apology. "I wasn't the only person hurt by your comment…"

"Yes, I know," he interjects. "I apologized to Eric when he came to the house."

"And?" I urge.

"And what?" he says, looking confused.

"Your comment was hurtful to Adam too. Don't you think you owe him an apology?"

He sighs. "I suppose."

"Maybe you could be nicer to Adam," I suggest. "We've been in each other's lives for over twenty years. He's Hannah's dad, and he's not going anywhere. It would mean a lot to me, and to Hannah, if you show him a little respect."

"It's not that I don't like Adam," my dad confesses. "It's just that I think marrying him held you back. If you didn't marry young, have a baby, and move here, you could've done great things."

"I did great things!" I throw up my hands in frustration. "Hannah is the greatest thing I've ever done. I have great friends. I have a great business. And I live in a great community. I have a great life. Adam didn't force this life on me," I enlighten him. "I wanted to live in a small town. I wanted to stay home with my daughter when she was young. Adam went along with my vision for our life, not the other way around." He appears shocked by this revelation. "And while we're on the subject," I add, "please be nicer to Eric than you were to Adam."

"I am nice to Eric," my dad says in his own defence, pulling himself up to his full-seated height.

"I don't mean tolerant and cordial," I clarify. "I mean, you need to give him a chance. He's a good person. I love him, and he's not going anywhere either."

Adam and Eric have different approaches for dealing with my dad. Adam gave up trying to impress my dad years ago. He accepted Mitchell would never feel warm and fuzzy toward him. Eric isn't like that. He won't give up. He'll drive himself—and me—crazy trying to impress my dad and win his approval.

"I understand, Bean," my dad concedes. "I'll do my best."

"Thank you," I say.

My dad and I should have had this conversation years ago. I should have stood up for Adam when we were married instead of two years after we split up. I won't make the same mistake with Eric.

"Now," my dad says, standing up and rubbing his hands together. "Can I leave Sophie here while I go to Latte Da and get another caffeine fix?"

"Of course," I say, glancing at Sophie who is sound asleep on her bed.

"Can I get you anything?"

"I'd love a maple pecan latte," I tell him. "Let me give you my loyalty card. I think my next coffee is free."

I pull out my purse from under the counter and rummage through it, looking for my wallet. Because my purse is a black hole of lost and forgotten items, I empty it item by item onto the counter. Keys... lip balm...

sunglasses... knitting... tissues… business card. I stop and look at the business card. It's the one Brooks Wiley gave me when he asked me to pass his card along to my dad.

"Here." I slide Brooks's card across the counter toward my dad. "It's from Claire's agent, Brooks Wiley. He asked me to give it to you in case you're in the market for a new literary agent."

"I've already got one," my dad says, patting his breast pocket. "You can keep it." He slides the card back toward me.

"Where did you get Brooks Wiley's business card?" I ask.

"He gave it to me," my dad explains. "A few minutes before we got here. Sophie and I were walking through the park across the street, and Brooks walked up to us and introduced himself. I'm happy with my agent, but I took the card to be polite."

"Was Brooks alone?" I ask, wondering if he and Jules Janssen were having a secret rendezvous in the park.

"He was with a woman," my dad replies, confirming my suspicion. "You should have seen her, Bean. She was wearing authentic 1800s mourning attire and eating one of the bookish cookies Tamara made." He shakes his head and gestures to his chest. "There were cookie crumbs all over her bodice."

Brooks Wiley hanging out with Piper Peters? If it weren't for my dad's accurate description of Piper's attire, I wouldn't believe it. There can't be two British women walking around Harmony Lake in mourning attire, can there? Yesterday, I watched Brooks run away from Piper and hide behind a police officer at the rental cottage. Why would he hang out with her in the park?

"Are you sure?" I ask, dumbfounded.

"About which part?" he asks back. "I'm certain about her outfit. I did a double take. It's not everyday you see a British woman in full period attire, Bean."

"How do you know she's British?" I ask.

"They were talking and laughing as Sophie and I walked past them," he explains. "Her accent was clear as a bell."

If they were laughing, it doesn't sound like Piper ambushed Brooks or was harassing him.

"Dad, did Brooks seem scared to you?"

"Scared?" he asks, astonished. "Scared of what? Of me?"

"No," I clarify. "Did he seem nervous about the woman he was with?"

"Not at all," my dad replies. "Like I said, they were laughing and smiling." He shrugs one shoulder. "They seemed to have a pleasant conversation. When I walked by, he excused himself from her and told her he'd be right back."

"Did you hear what they were talking about?"

He shakes his head. "No, but I wasn't eavesdropping, Bean. From what I hear about your sleuthing hobby, eavesdropping is more your thing than mine," he teases.

This is so strange, it's hard to believe. Maybe it wasn't Brooks?

"What did Brooks look like?" I ask, starting to sound like I'm interrogating my father.

"Handsome," he responds. "Expensive Italian suit, clean-shaven head… he has a unique accent. At first, I thought he was British, too, like his friend, but he has a distinct, Caribbean inflection."

Sounds like Brooks to a tee.

He kisses Jules Janssen in secret, has lunch with Dina even though he insinuates he doesn't like her, and now he's going for a walk in the park with Piper Peters, a woman he claimed to be frightened of yesterday. I need to talk to Brooks.

AFTER A LOVELY POTLUCK DINNER, everyone leaves with full bellies and containers of leftovers.

Adam was the last to leave and, to my and Zoe's surprise, Mitchell offers to walk him to his car. Under the guise of finishing an already complete crossword puzzle, Zoe makes herself comfortable in the living room chair with the best view of the driveway. I think she's just as curious as me about Mitchell walking Adam to his car.

"Have you seen my laptop cord?" Eric asks. I shake my head and sink into the family room sofa. "I could've sworn it was here," he mumbles, checking all the outlets, in case the cord is plugged into one of them. "Maybe I left it at the office."

"You can use my laptop," I offer.

"Thanks, but I can't access work stuff on your

laptop," he replies, sitting next to me. "I'll use my phone until I get to the office tomorrow." He unlocks his phone and opens his email. "The forensics team didn't find any traces of nuts on the items we confiscated from the cottage. How did the peanut oil get onto Claire's fingertips?" He blows out an exasperated breath.

"Maybe the killer took the murder weapon with them," I propose.

"That's what I assume," he responds. "I wish I had an inkling of what it might be. We've checked the woods around the cottage for clues, but we've found nothing. I was hoping the killer tossed the murder weapon into the trees when they left."

"I guess the killer didn't leave behind anything obvious like a hair or some fingerprints?"

"The forensics people only found two sets of fingerprints," he says. "Claire's and Dina's."

"Does that mean the killer wore gloves?" I ask.

Eric shrugs. "Either they wore gloves, or they didn't touch anything," he speculates.

He's looking at crime scene photos on his phone, and I'm looking at them, too, over his shoulder.

"How did the killer leave if the door was locked from the inside, and Claire had the only key?" I ask.

"The landlord says there's another key," Eric discloses. "It's missing. We contacted the people who rented the cottage before Claire and Dina, in case they accidentally took the second key with them when they left. They say they don't have it." He looks at me. "I think the killer took the key with them when they left, probably because it had their fingerprints on it."

"I assumed they left through the window," I say. "It's a large window, and it's on the main floor." I point to the photo on his phone. "The drapes are billowing in this photo. The window was open when you found Claire's body," I deduce.

"That's the other theory," Eric admits. "The window makes sense because the killer could avoid walking through the cottage, and Dina wouldn't see them because the window in the den faces the opposite direction from the dock where she was sitting. Or the killer waited inside the den until Dina came back to the cottage, then snuck out the window. This way they wouldn't risk bumping into her outside."

The thought of being that close to a murder-in-progress makes me shudder.

"I guess it's a good thing the second key was missing. If Dina found the spare key, she would've found Claire, and she would see that image in her mind's eye forever." Sadly, I speak from experience; finding a dead friend is something you can never unsee.

"Dina didn't look for the spare key," Eric explains. "She didn't know about the spare key. She said there was only one key when they arrived at the cottage over a week ago."

Did the killer plan Claire's murder far enough in advance to sneak into the cottage and steal the spare key before Claire and Dina even arrived?

"Why did Claire lock the door?" I wonder aloud. "Dina was the only other person there, and she was sitting by the dock. Claire didn't have to lock the door to be alone."

"Dina says Claire always locks herself away to work." He shrugs. "Apparently it's part of her creative process."

I guess it's not weirder than driving without a cell phone being part of my dad's creative process. But part of me wonders if Claire locking herself in the office is less related to her creative process and more related to Brooks's claim that Claire and Dina were having a loud argument that day.

"Did you ask the landlord about the spare key?" I ask.

Eric nods. "He says he was unaware the key was missing until I told him. But he also said he doesn't check for both keys when he inspects the cottage between renters. We asked the cleaner when she last saw the key, and she has no recollection." He lets out a frustrated sigh. "For all we know, that second key has been missing for months."

"Or the killer has it," I remind him.

"The other weird thing is we found more of Dina's fingerprints in the den than Claire's." He looks at me. "Does that seem odd to you? Dina said Claire used the den as her office, and she said Claire likes to work alone, in silence. Wouldn't you expect to find more of Claire's fingerprints than Dina's?"

I shrug, and I'm about to tell him I don't know when Zoe appears in the doorway.

"That doesn't sound odd to me," Zoe chimes in. "If

the police investigated Mitchell's home office, I'm sure they'd find more of my fingerprints than his."

"Why?" Eric asks.

"Because even though I don't spend as much time in Mitchell's office as he does, when I'm in there I touch more stuff," she explains. "Mitchell sits at his desk and types. He touches a few things on and around his desk, but I'm the one who tidies up after him, restocks his supplies, and organizes the things he moved around."

I guess that makes sense. I wonder if the police investigated Knitorious, if they'd find just as many of Connie and Marla's fingerprints as mine?

CHAPTER 17

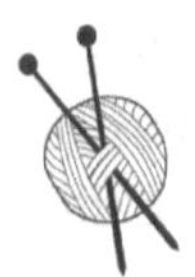

SUNDAY, April 18th

"Good morning, Bean!" my dad says without looking up from his laptop.

"Good morning, Dad. Do you always start work this early?" The sun just rose, and it looks like he's been hard at work for a while.

"Only when I'm up against a deadline," he replies with a chuckle. "I was just taking a break and reading some of Claire's online obituaries."

"Yes, there are some lovely articles about her life and career," I observe. "I read a few yesterday." I open the back door and let Sophie out, then freshen her water and fix her breakfast.

"Until today, I'd never read articles about her or interviews she gave," my dad explains. "It's strange... she said she always wanted to be an author. She said writing was her dream from the time she was a child."

"Why is that strange?" I ask.

"Because it's the complete opposite to what she told

me when I hired her as my assistant," he replies. "The Claire Rivera I knew had no interest in writing. She wasn't even a keen reader. As I recall, she preferred gossip magazines and tabloid newspapers to books. She didn't study writing, she studied graphic design in college."

"Why would she lie to you?" I wonder out loud. "Maybe she thought you wouldn't hire an aspiring author?" I suggest.

He shakes his head. "Poppycock. I've mentored plenty of young authors," my dad insists. "I don't think Claire lied to me, I think she lied in all these interviews." He gestures to his laptop.

"Why?" I ask.

He shrugs. "Maybe her publisher's PR people thought it was a good idea," he offers.

"She also talked a lot about her needle-felting hobby in those interviews," I comment. "She said needle felting was such an important part of her life that she included it in her book series as the main character's hobby. Did you know Claire was a needle felter?"

My dad shakes his head and closes his laptop. "I never saw her do it, and she never mentioned it to me," he says, opening the back door so Sophie can come inside.

It's possible Claire discovered her love of needle felting after she quit as my dad's assistant.

"Dad, why are you certain Claire took your idea and turned it into the Familia series?"

"It's a bit of a coincidence that when Claire worked for me, I was in the planning stages of a books series about an organized crime family headed up by a matriarch who knits, then less than a year after she quit, she released the first *Familia* book," he alleges.

"Do you think she copied your computer files?" I ask. "Or did you talk to her about your idea?"

My dad shakes his head. "I never give my assistants access to my computer or my files," he insists. "And the only person I bounce ideas off is Zoe. I think Claire pieced it together by going through my notebooks and the notes I collect."

"Ah," I respond with a nod.

My dad likes to capture ideas as soon as they come into his head. He keeps notebooks around his house, in his car, and even in his pocket for this purpose. In the event he has an idea when there isn't a notebook within arm's reach, he'll jot it down on whatever is handy. A napkin, the back of an envelope, a sticky note. When I was ten years old, he stopped the car and jotted down a note on a ten-dollar bill.

"I'm convinced Claire lied to me, Bean." His face is clouded with sadness. "She must've planned to use me all along. It makes little sense, but that's the only explanation."

"Claire came to see me the day before she died," I tell him. "She asked me to set up a meeting with you and her. She wanted to bury the hatchet."

We sit in silence while Mitchell takes a moment to contemplate what I said.

"I'm sad Claire died without resolving the issues between us, but I'm not sure I would have agreed to meet her, Bean," he admits.

There are too many inconsistencies between Claire Rivera, who worked as my father's author assistant, and Claire Rivera, the best-selling author. I can't help but think that hidden somewhere in all the inconsistencies is the reason someone wanted Claire dead.

"You got a waffle maker?" I ask, more excited than the sight of a countertop appliance should warrant. "I love waffles!" I approach the waffle maker on Adam's sleek and modern kitchen counter and open the lid.

"I know," he says. "You're the perfect guinea pig for me to try it out."

Every Sunday, Adam and I have brunch with our daughter, Hannah. Adam and I meet in person, and Hannah joins us by video chat. We alternate between his place and mine, but Adam always cooks. Since we split, Adam has become a culinary hobbyist, and I'm more than happy to let him cook brunch every week. Especially since I did all the cooking during our twenty-year marriage.

While Adam makes waffle batter, I cut up strawberries and prepare other waffle toppings.

"Thank you again for helping my dad and Zoe yesterday," I say, putting the strawberry pieces in a bowl. "I know Mitchell didn't seem appreciative, but he was."

"He thanked me last night," Adam says.

"When he walked you to your car after dinner?" I ask.

Adam nods. "Yup. He thanked me for helping him and Zoe yesterday, and he apologized for not liking me."

"That's how he said it?" I ask, shocked. "He said, I'm sorry for not liking you?"

"No, Meg. He was more sincere than that."

"Wow." I can't believe my dad apologized to Adam.

"He hugged me too."

"He hugged you?" I wipe my hands and sit down.

Adam nods. "I don't know what you said to him, Meg, but it worked. He's trying to make amends for over two decades of resentment and contempt."

"What makes you think I had anything to do with it?"

"Either you said something to Mitchell, or he's in the early stages of dementia," Adam replies.

"I asked him to be nice to you. I reminded him you're Hannah's dad," I confess. "And I might have cleared up a few misconceptions he had about our relationship." I open the fridge and find the whipped cream, then I look at Adam. "I regret not standing up for you sooner. I should've set Mitchell straight years ago, and I'm sorry I didn't."

"I don't think he would have been ready to hear it years ago," Adam says. "Mitchell needed someone to blame when you didn't choose the life he wanted for you, and I was the most logical choice."

"I get that now," I acknowledge, "and I cleared up his misconceptions."

"I bet he'll still kill me in his next book," Adam teases with a chuckle.

"Speaking of books," I say, changing the subject. "How was your photo op at Jules Janssen's book signing yesterday? I saw a photo of you and her on The Front Page. Are you starstruck?"

"I'm not starstruck, Meg," he replies, rolling his eyes at the suggestion that he could be awestruck by a gorgeous, charismatic, A-list celebrity. "Our meet and greet was short and sweet." We carry the waffles and toppings to the table. "She seemed friendly, but her handlers whisked her off as soon as the photographer got the shot. She mentioned she thinks Harmony Lake is a beautiful town, and she thinks it would be an ideal location for part of the *Familia* movie."

"I don't think there will be a *Familia* movie," I comment, picking up Adam's iPad and FaceTiming our daughter.

"That's what I said!" Adam agrees. "But Jules said she's optimistic. She said she just eliminated a major obstacle. She said she believes she's close to acquiring the movie rights."

Is it me, or does Jules' claim about eliminating a major obstacle sound like a confession?

While we eat waffles and drink fresh-squeezed orange juice, Adam and I have an enjoyable virtual visit with Hannah. She'll be home for the summer in less than two weeks. It's incredible how much I still miss her. I assumed I'd get used to her living away from home, since this is the end of her second year of university, but it's still hard to be so far away from her.

"I have to get to the store for Mitchell's book signing," I say after I help Adam clean the kitchen. "Thanks for breakfast."

"I'll see you there," he says. "I'm having my photo taken with him for The Front Page."

"I'll save you a copy of his latest *Shark Attack* book," I tease.

We exchange a cheek kiss, and I leave.

MITCHELL'S APPEARANCE is in thirty minutes, but there's already a line outside Knitorious when I arrive.

Knitorious is closed on Sundays and Mondays, but we're open today to host my dad's reading and book signing. He requested his appearance be at the store instead of the book fair venues.

"You're here early," I say when I walk through the backdoor to find Mitchell, Zoe, and Connie sitting at the harvest table at the back of the store, drinking coffee and eating coffee cake.

Sophie rushes over to greet me, and I bend down to rub her.

"Your neighbour dropped off this beautiful arrangement," Zoe says.

"They're gorgeous." I inhale deeply to take in as much of the floral scent as possible.

"It's your April bouquet," Connie explains. "Phillip thought it would brighten up the store for the book signing."

Early in our relationship, Eric and I went to a fundraiser with a silent auction. One prize was a year of monthly floral arrangements courtesy of Wilde Flowers, the florist shop next door to Knitorious. Eric had the winning bid and every month for a year, I received a beautiful floral arrangement. When my year of floral arrangements expired, Eric renewed it as an anniversary gift, so now I'm enjoying another year of floral arrangements.

When it's time to start, there are more people in line than will fit in the store.

"Hi, Megan!"

"Hi, Lucas," I greet the rookie cop who's leaning against the wall on the sidewalk just outside the door. "What are you doing here?"

"Crowd control," he replies. "Chief Sloane sent me."

I'm not sure how to manage a crowd this size. We've never had so many people in Knitorious at once.

"I'm glad you're here." The relief is clear in my voice.

"Leave it to me," Lucas assures me. "This is nothing compared to the crowd yesterday at Jules Janssen's book signing. This is manageable."

Reassured by the young officer's confidence, I turn the sign from CLOSED to OPEN and step aside.

The store is full, and Lucas leans against the door, keeping it open, so the people who can't fit inside can hear as Mitchell reads an excerpt from his book, from the comfort of one of the overstuffed chairs in the cozy seating area.

After the reading, my dad moves to the harvest table. Lucas organizes everyone in an orderly line extending from the harvest table, out to the sidewalk, and down Water Street.

After Mitchell signs a book, I direct the person toward the back door and hand them off to Connie. She wishes them a good day and sends them on their way. Zoe is busy selling books and taking photos for people who want a picture with my dad.

We take a quick break when Adam, in his role as Mayor Martel, and the photographer from The Front Page show up. While Adam and my dad pose for a couple of photos, I see Brooks Wiley next in line to meet my dad and get his book signed.

"Hi, Brooks," I say.

"Nice to see you again, Megan." Brooks nods and smiles. "I'm here to meet Mitchell Monroe and ask him to sign my book." He holds up a copy of the latest *Shark Attack* book.

"I hear you met him yesterday in the park," I say.

"In passing," Brooks acknowledges with a grin. "I gave him my card."

"Did you have a pleasant walk through the park with Piper Peters?" I ask.

Guiding me by the arm, Brooks leads me away from the people waiting in line. Lucas asks me if everything is OK, and I assure him it is.

"It wasn't how it looked," Brooks hisses when we're in front of the display window.

"It looked like you were laughing and having fun with someone you insisted was scary and dangerous the day before."

"I was humouring her," he explains. "She's... fragile."

"Fragile?" I ask, confused. "Like a flower?" Fragile isn't the first word I'd use to describe Piper Peters.

"Fragile like a bomb," Brooks clarifies. "I was being careful. I didn't want to set her off."

It's a fair observation. I sensed Piper had a short fuse when she was at Knitorious yesterday with April and me.

"What did you and Piper talk about?" I ask, knowing it's none of my business and expecting Brooks to tell me so.

"We didn't." He shrugs one shoulder. "She'd just approached me when your dad walked past us. I used him as an excuse to get away from her."

"I thought maybe you and Piper were having a secret rendezvous in the park," I tease.

"Why would you think that?" he asks, chuckling.

"You meet Jules in secret." I quirk an eyebrow. "Maybe secret meetings are your thing."

"Who?" he asks, trying to convince me he doesn't know what I'm talking about.

"Jules Janssen," I specify.

"I know who she is. I don't know her personally," Brooks lies.

"It looked pretty personal when you were kissing her and groping her butt in the alley beside my store." I escalate my voice toward the end of my sentence.

"Shhh," he says, his brows furrowed together. "Keep your voice down, woman!" he hisses. "Fine, Jules and I are friends."

I stifle a giggle and raise my eyebrows.

"Good friends. We're quite close."

"Did Claire know about your close relationship with Jules?" I ask.

"She did not," Brooks confirms. "My personal relationships were none of Claire's business."

"Even when your personal relationship is with someone who's trying to buy the film rights to her books?"

"I don't like what you're insinuating," Brooks challenges. "I always worked in Claire's best interest. Selling the film rights to *Familia* was in her best interest."

Claire believed otherwise. But I don't argue with him.

Zoe comes over and tells Brooks it's his turn to meet Mitchell.

"I don't want to lose my place in line," he says, looking at me. "Excuse me, Megan."

After he gets his book signed and takes a selfie with my dad, I escort Brooks to the back door. I'm about to hand him off to Connie when he tilts his phone toward me.

"Look at this," he says. "These are some emails and letters Piper sent to Claire," he explains. "I want you to see how disturbed she is, so you'll know I'm telling the truth when I say I wouldn't meet her alone in a park."

I scroll through the emails on his phone. I can't spend much time looking at each one, but Brooks is right, they are disturbing. It seems Piper believed that her and Claire's lives were intertwined and that Claire used her books to share secret messages with Piper. Piper also thinks things Claire said in interviews, and even certain outfits or colours Claire wore, were secret messages to Piper. It's creepy, and it's enough to convince me to avoid being alone with Piper.

CHAPTER 18

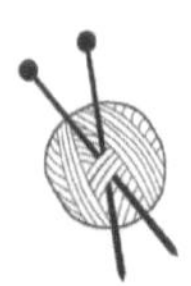

Today, I'm thankful I sell yarn and not books; boxes of the former are much lighter than boxes of the latter. I'm lugging the last box of *Shark Attack* books from the storage room into the store when Dina flags me down from her place in line.

"Hi, Dina," I say, wiping box-dirt from my hands onto my jeans. "How are you?"

"I'm OK," she replies, hugging me. "Excited to meet Mitchell Monroe. He's one of my mentors! I wrote a paper on his creative process when I got my Master of Fine arts." She spins around and shows me the black backpack she's carrying. "I brought my *Shark Attack* books." She smiles. "I understand if he doesn't have enough time to sign all of them."

"That looks heavy." If every book in the series is in there, it weighs about twenty pounds. "Would you like me to put it by the table for you?"

Dina dismisses my offer with a wave of her hand.

"It's fine. I'm a bookworm, I'm used to toting books everywhere." We laugh.

"If you were here earlier, you would've run into Brooks," I tell her.

"I've seen enough of Brooks this weekend," she says, shaking her head. "I don't need to see any more of him."

"Yes, I hear you had lunch together yesterday," I say.

"Yeah," she nods. "We went to the local pub. It was nice. They have excellent food. The Irish nachos are the bomb!"

"They are," I agree, suddenly craving a platter of Irish nachos. "Can I ask you something, Dina?" She nods, so I proceed. "I get the feeling you don't like Brooks. Why did you have lunch with him?"

"He said he needed to talk to me about Claire. He said it was important," she replies, not denying my allegation that she doesn't like him.

"Oh?" I urge.

Dina looks at the line of people behind her, then uses her chin to gesture to a quiet corner of the store. "If we step over there to talk, will I lose my place in line?"

I shake my head. "I'll make sure you don't."

Dina follows me toward the cozy sitting area.

"He wanted me to approach Claire's family and convince them to sell the *Familia* film rights to him and Jules Janssen," she whispers near my ear.

"Brooks wanted you to do that?" I clarify.

Her eyes are wide, and she gives me a deep nod. "He doesn't know Claire's family, but I do. They like me and I like them. He thought my relationship with them would give me an advantage."

"Did you agree to do it?" I ask.

"No! Of course not!" Dina sounds almost insulted. "I wouldn't take advantage of them in their time of grief. Even if they weren't grieving, I wouldn't do it. Claire was clear. She did not want *Familia* made into a movie or TV series."

"Good for you for doing what you felt was right," I commend her.

"He said they're going to approach Claire's family with or without me. If I helped them, they would've cut me in, but I don't care. I don't need the money bad enough to go against Claire's wishes or take advantage of her family's grief."

"They, who?" I ask. She looks at me confused. "You said they're going to approach Claire's family with or without you. Who are they?"

"Brooks and Jules," she replies. "They're partners."

Before I can ask her anything else, Zoe summons Dina to meet Mitchell and get her books signed.

While Mitchell and Dina talk, my back is to them as I empty the last box of books.

"Don't stab yourself," my dad teases with a jovial tone in his voice. "I guess that's one way to keep pick-pockets out of your stuff." He and Dina laugh.

I turn around to see what they're laughing about, but come face-to-face with a fan looking for Mitchell Monroe's previous books to purchase. By the time I refer him to Zoe, Dina and Mitchell finish their meet-and-greet, and I'm ushering Dina toward the back door.

"It was nice seeing you, Dina," I say as I gesture toward the back door. "Oops! You have a little something." I point to her shoulder. "May I?"

She nods, and I pick a piece of lime-green fibre fuzz from her shoulder. "A bit of fibre attached itself to you. It must be your magnetic personality," I tease, holding up the offending fluff.

Dina shrugs. "Well, I am in a yarn store." She giggles and waves goodbye on her way out.

Soon after Dina leaves, we run out of *Shark Attack* books. The empty boxes are strewn about the back room and kitchenette area because I've just been haphazardly tossing the boxes in there as I empty them. There hasn't been a spare second to tidy up.

Zoe announces to the fans waiting in line that we are out of books. A chorus of disappointed groans follows her announcement. She assures everyone that if they already have a book, they're welcome to wait and Mitchell will gladly sign it. The line reduces by half after the mass exodus of hopeful book buyers.

Only a few people remain when Piper Peters joins the end of the line. She's still grieving, as evidenced by the mourning attire she's wearing again today. I must be growing accustomed to her outfit, because I find it less shocking. Judging by the astonished expression on her face, this is Zoe's first time encountering Piper.

"Good afternoon, Piper," I greet her with a smile.

"Megan! How lovely to see you again." She extends her gloved hand toward me with her wrist limp and her fingertips facing the floor.

Unsure what to do with her extended, flaccid hand, I attempt a handshake and end up tugging her fingers.

"We're out of books, I'm afraid," I say, hoping this information will render her visit fruitless, and she'll leave.

"No worries," she assures me. "I brought my own." Her other hand produces a *Shark Attack* book from the multitude of folds in her full skirt.

"Awesome," I say as Zoe uses hand motions to beckon Piper to the harvest table.

I accompany Piper and stand nearby, keeping a close watch on their interaction, looking for signs that Piper's unhealthy obsession with Claire might transfer to my father.

Mitchell signs her book, poses for a selfie with Piper, and shakes her droopy, gloved hand. Zoe summons the next person in line while I usher Piper to the back room.

"Thank you for coming, Piper," I say when we reach Connie at the back door.

"It was a pleasure," Piper responds while Connie takes in her elaborate outfit. "Oooh, it's lovely back here," Piper comments, looking around the unremarkable, utilitarian back room. "What's in here?" She jiggles the handle of the storage room door.

"Yarn," I reply, guiding her gently by the arm toward Connie. "I had to remove most of the yarn from the store to make room for the books."

"Right. Of course," she responds. "Well, hello, there." Piper extends her limp hand toward Connie. "It's lovely to make your acquaintance. I'm Piper Peters." She grins beneath her veil.

Connie introduces herself, then shakes Piper's wilted hand, and uses it to lead her through the back door. "Have a wonderful day, Piper. Thank you for coming." Connie closes and locks the back door behind her.

Back in the store, my father is walking around, stretching his legs, and shaking out his right hand, which is probably cramping after signing several hundred books this afternoon.

I'm itching to lock the door, but one person is loitering near the front of the store, leafing through a knitting magazine.

I turn the sign from OPEN to CLOSED and thank Lucas for helping with crowd management.

"No problem, Megan," the rookie officer responds. "Enjoy the rest of your afternoon," he says before leaving.

From a distance, I watch the lone patron thumb through the latest issue of Vogue Knitting magazine and stare at the back of their head, using my non-existent powers of telepathy to will them to leave.

"Gross habit," my dad whispers in my ear.

I look at him, baffled. "What's a gross habit?" I whisper.

"Licking your fingers before turning the page," he specifies, glaring at the finger-licker. "And it's unacceptable when it's a magazine you don't own."

I nod. "It's a gross habit," I agree.

"Claire used to do that," he whispers, watching the finger-licker. "She couldn't turn a page without licking her thumb and forefinger first. I would look away when she did it because it grossed me out." He gestures vaguely in the general direction of nostalgia. "I remember warning her she'd catch a cold or worse, either from licking her dirty fingers, or from picking up whatever germs are lurking on the corners of the pages. But she never listened."

"You're right," I say, struck with an epiphany. "A person could catch a cold or flu because of that habit."

I bet they could pick up other things too. I think I just found the murder weapon that killed Claire, or at least narrowed down the options.

At last, the lone remaining customer closes Vogue Knitting, and as they motion to pick up another magazine, Zoe opens the front door, distracting them with the jingle of the bell, and wishes them a good day. Taking the polite hint, the customer leaves.

"Where is everyone?" Eric asks, looking deflated.

"Who?" I ask.

"Your dad, Zoe, all the people who want to get their books signed?" He crouches down and greets Sophie, who's wagging her entire back end because she's so happy to see him.

"Gone," I update him. "We ran out of books, so the signing ended early."

"I came to help, but I guess I'm too late. I thought we could take your dad and Zoe out for dinner." He looks around, surveying the empty boxes laying haphazardly around the back room.

When Eric kisses me hello, I sense his tension. His facial muscles are taut, and his body is more rigid than usual when he hugs me.

"Dad and Zoe are having dinner with Connie and Archie," I explain. "Then they're going to Connie and Archie's place to play euchre. If I'd known you were coming…"

"It's not your fault." He lets out an exasperated sigh. "I messed up this visit. I wanted to get to know your dad and Zoe. I booked the weekend off work to help with the book fair. Then this murder happened, and instead of making a good impression with your family, I'm interrogating your father, chasing witnesses all over town, and trying to get straight answers about anything."

"Honey, it's fine," I assure him. "You made a great impression. Everyone understands. A murder investigation takes priority over a book fair."

"I can't keep these witnesses in town forever, babe. I need to solve this case before they scatter and go back to where they came from." He watches me toss another flattened box onto the pile. "Let me help you put the store back together," he offers, picking up a box. "It's the least I can do, and it might be the only thing I accomplish today."

I take the box from him and toss it aside. "Maybe I can improve your day," I tease.

"I'm listening," he says.

The tone of his voice is serious, but the glint in his eye when he cocks his eyebrow and smirks tells me we have different ideas about how to improve his day.

Focus, Megan!

"What would you say if I told you I have a theory about how Claire ingested the peanut oil?"

"I'd apologize in advance for hugging you so hard you might break in half," he jokes. "Wait. Are you serious?" he asks, straightening his spine. "You figured out how Claire was poisoned?"

"I think so," I reply. "Maybe," I add to manage his expectations in case I'm wrong. "When Claire was here, she was flipping through a pattern book..."

I continue, telling him about Claire's habit of licking her thumb and finger with each page turn, and how my dad mentioned it was a habit she had back when she was his assistant. I tell him Mitchell's theory that such a habit is an effective way to catch a cold.

"If you can pick up a cold, you can pick up other things too. Like peanut oil," Eric surmises, coming to the same conclusion I did.

"Exactly," I concur.

"Babe, that's brilliant!" He wasn't kidding about hugging me tight. He lets go when I gasp for air. "But we checked every book in the den for traces of nut products."

"My dad says Claire preferred magazines to books," I tell him.

Eric unlocks his phone, and his thumbs move across the keyboard so fast they're practically a blur. "I'll send a team to confiscate every book, magazine, and piece of paper in the cottage, not just the den. We'll check all of them for traces of peanut oil."

It's ironic that a book, something Claire claimed to

love and is her legacy, might be the instrument of her demise.

While he types and sends instructions to his team, I attach Sophie's leash and put on my jacket.

"I'm going to walk Sophie." I kiss him goodbye.

"Wait, I'll come with you." He finishes typing, sends a message, and shoves his phone in his pocket. "Let's order dinner, and we can walk Sophie together before it gets here," he suggests.

"Aren't you going back to work?" I ask.

"We haven't seen each other all day," he reminds me. "What do you feel like for dinner?" he asks, holding the door for Sophie and me.

"I've been craving Irish nachos since Dina mentioned them earlier," I confess, stepping into the parking lot.

"You saw Dina Langley today?" Eric asks.

I nod. "I also saw Brooks Wiley and Piper Peters."

While we walk, Eric phones in our dinner order to the pub. Then I tell him about my discussion with Dina and her revelation that Brooks and Jules offered her money to convince Claire's family to sell the *Familia* film rights.

"Even if Brooks and Jules convince Claire's family to sell the rights, it won't matter," Eric says.

"Why not?" I ask.

"Because Claire bequeathed *Familia* rights to Dina," he discloses. "Claire's family has no say whether they will make the books into movies."

We arrive back at Knitorious, and I stop at the back door while Eric unlocks it. "Why would Claire leave something that valuable to her assistant?" I ask, flabbergasted.

Eric shrugs and holds the door for Sophie and me. "I don't know," he replies. "But I don't think Dina knows yet that she's the beneficiary."

"Being the beneficiary might make her the next target," I say.

However, if she did know, it also gives her a motive to kill Claire.

CHAPTER 19

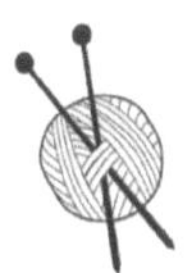

WHILE WE WAIT for dinner to arrive, we turn Eric's apartment upside down, looking for his laptop cord. He hoped it would be in his office at the station, but it's not.

"It's not here," I state the obvious, reassembling the sofa cushions.

"It's not anywhere," he grumbles.

"Did you check your car?"

He nods.

"My car?"

He nods.

"The store?

He holds up his index finger. "Not yet. But only because I never work in the store," he reasons, opening the door and thudding down the stairs.

"Bring my purse when you come back. I'll check it just in case," I call after him.

I doubt his cord is in my purse, but goodness knows

I've found stranger things in there, so there's no harm in looking.

While Eric searches the store for his laptop cord, I put his apartment back together and feed Sophie her dinner.

Our food arrives while he's searching the store, so he comes back upstairs with dinner and my purse, but no laptop cord. I search my purse while he unboxes the food and sets the table.

"No cord," I say, shoving everything back inside.

"It's like it disappeared," he says. "I swear I left it at the house the other day when I was working from home doing budget stuff," he insists.

"I'll look again when I go home."

"No point," he says, "I searched the house so thoroughly you'd swear I had a warrant."

While I satisfy my craving for Irish nachos, and Eric digs into his steak and fries, I tell him about my discussion with Brooks Wiley and his reluctant admission that he and Jules are close.

"We'll have to take Brooks's word for it," Eric huffs. "I haven't questioned Jules. I can't get near her."

"Why?" I ask. "Just because she's famous doesn't mean she's above the law."

"No, but it means she can afford to surround herself with multiple layers of handlers and lawyers who won't let me access her." He cuts a piece of steak. "I can't even get her on the phone, which means I can't verify whether Brooks was with her when Claire was killed. Until I talk to her, Brooks's alibi is unverified." He shoves a piece of meat in his mouth.

I think about the business card Jules gave me, and her request for me to contact her after I passed along her gift to Claire.

"What if I talk to her," I suggest. "Jules will meet with me. Alone." I sound more confident than I am.

Eric looks dubious. "Without her entourage?"

I nod. "She was alone when she visited me the first time," I reason. "And if someone is with her, I'll refuse to talk to her unless we're alone."

"The situation has changed since Jules visited you on Wednesday," Eric reminds me. "With Claire dead and Jules knowing I want to talk to her, she might not come."

"Her goal hasn't changed," I counter. "She and Brooks are still trying to secure the film rights to *Familia*." Full, I slide the rest of my nachos toward him. "I can try, and if she doesn't come, we're no further behind. Nothing ventured, nothing gained, and all that."

"Even if she shows up, I can't question her." He pushes his empty plate aside and pulls my leftover nachos into its place. "In fact, don't even tell me. Plausible deniability. It's better if I don't know what you're up to. Jules Janssen lawyered up. Anything she says to me wouldn't be admissible because I'm a cop."

"Lucky for you, I'm not."

AFTER DINNER we watch an episode of our favourite home renovation reality show. By the time I get home,

I'm physically spent from moving boxes of books, and mentally exhausted from trying to make sense of what we know so far about Claire's death. It's like trying to put together a puzzle that only has outside pieces—it doesn't make sense.

My dad and Zoe are already asleep, so I tread quietly through the house while I get ready for bed and put Sophie outside one last time before we turn in.

While Sophie is in the backyard doing her final perimeter check for the night, I walk through the house, gathering the dog toys she left scattered around the floor. I swear this corgi has enough toys for ten dogs. I'm about to drop the armload of squeaky, stuffy, bouncy toys into Sophie's toy box when I see it. Plain as day. Eric's laptop cord. Sitting in the bottom of the empty toy box. I must've gathered it up with Sophie's toys and dropped in there by accident. I unload the toys I'm carrying into the box and pull out the laptop cord. I snap a picture of the cord with my cell phone and text it to Eric.

Me: Look what I found!

Eric: OMG! Where was it?

Me: Sophie's toy box.

Eric: The one place I didn't look.

Me: Want me to drop it off?

Eric: Stay there. I'll pick it up. I'll be there in 10 minutes.

Me: Text me from the driveway so Sophie doesn't bark and wake up Dad and Zoe.

Eric: K.

Sure enough, ten minutes later, Eric texts to let me

know he's outside. I slip on the fuzzy slides I wear for excursions into the garage, grab the laptop cord, and silently close the front door behind me.

"Sorry," I say, hopping into the passenger seat of his car and lunging the cord at him.

"Sorry for what, babe? You found it!"

"I suspect I might also be the one who lost it," I explain, telling him how I probably scooped up the cord with Sophie's toys and deposited it in her toy box.

"Actually, I think it was me. On Thursday morning, when we expected your dad and Zoe to arrive before dinner..."

While Eric and I argue over who was the last person to clean up Sophie's toys and lose the stupid laptop cord, his phone dings.

"Phillip," Eric says.

Phillip is my next-door neighbour at home and at work. I glance over Eric's shoulder, and it doesn't look like Phillip is home; his house is dark, and his floral-wrapped delivery van isn't in the driveway.

"Is everything OK?" I ask.

It's late for Phillip to be texting without a reason. He gets up horribly early most mornings to receive deliveries at his florist shop.

"There's someone in the store," Eric replies, typing a response.

"Wilde Flowers?" I ask, assuming he's referring to Phillip's store.

Eric shakes his head. "Knitorious."

"What?!"

"You should wait here," he suggests, tossing the laptop cord in the backseat and starting the car.

I close the car door and buckle my seatbelt. "No way."

"Babe, you're wearing dragonfly jammies and fuzzy slides."

"Drive," I insist, unwilling to argue. "Or I can drive myself and meet you there."

On the short drive to Knitorious, Eric summons backup and reminds me three times to wait in the car.

He parks in the farthest parking spot and turns off the ignition.

"Wait. In. The. Car." He tries to look stern, but it doesn't suit him.

"Be careful," I say. "Maybe you should wait for backup."

"They're already here," Eric informs me. I look around. Nothing but bushes, darkness, and Phillip's floral-wrapped delivery van. "It's probably a false alarm anyway," he says, trying to ease my worry. "Phillip said he saw someone using a flashlight, but it could've been a head light reflecting off the display window," he reasons. "I'll be right back. I love you." He kisses me then exits the car, closing the door silently behind him.

A tap on the rear passenger-side window makes me almost jump out of my skin. Phillip is squatting next to the car and tapping the window with a key. I push the button on the armrest and unlock the door.

"Geez, Phillip, you scared the life out of me!" I say when he crawls into the backseat.

"Sorry, Megan!" he hisses. "I was hiding in my van," he explains in hushed tones. "There's someone in your store. I heard them through the wall. I didn't see your or Eric's car in the parking lot, and I worried it might be a critter. I looked through the front window and saw a silhouette. They were carrying a flashlight."

"Were they near the cash register?" I ask.

If I were going to rob a store, I wouldn't choose a yarn store. We have hardly any cash. We do a lot of sales online, and most of our in-store sales are debit or credit.

"No," he replies. "They were near the back room."

Maybe they're stealing yarn? What other reason could someone have for breaking into a yarn store?

"Did you get your April bouquet?" Phillips whispers. "I left it with Connie and Zoe yesterday."

"Yes," I reply. "Thank you. It's gorgeous, Phillip."

"Well, I got the most beautiful delivery of cherry blossoms. I know they're one of your favourites, and I thought they might add to the ambience at your dad's book signing..."

While Phillip and I discuss April flowers, I contemplate how absurd this is; we're out here talking about seasonal blooms while the love of my life is potentially taking down a dangerous intruder less than a hundred metres away. My phone dings, making Phillip and I gasp and jump.

Eric: Suspect apprehended! You can come inside.

Between the car and the store, Phillip and I ponder whether the intruder is someone we know, and why they broke into Knitorious. We can't remember the last time a local business was robbed. We're locked arm-in-arm and cling to each other for dear life.

I open the back door, and a uniformed officer stands aside so Philip and I can enter the store together, like conjoined twins, because I'm not letting go of him, and he's not letting go of me.

Three uniformed officers crowd the back room, plus Eric. One of the uniformed officers stands aside to reveal the intruder, cuffed and sitting on the stairs that lead to the apartment.

CHAPTER 20

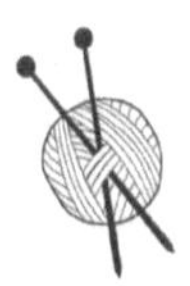

"PIPER PETERS!" I gasp and bring my hand to my mouth.

Phillip inhales sharply. "Piper!" he wheezes, sounding dramatic and horrified. Then he whispers in my ear, "Do we know her?"

"Yes." I nod. "We know her."

An officer approaches us and asks Phillip to go with him to provide a statement.

"Will you be OK without me?" Phillip asks.

"I think so." I nod, unable to take my eyes off Piper. "How about you?" I ask. "Will you be OK?"

"You'll know if I'm not," he says, prying our arms apart. "I'll scream your name so loud they'll hear me on the other side of the lake."

"I'll be right here, Phillip." I throw my arms around him. "Thank you!"

Piper isn't wearing her authentic Victorian-era mourning attire. She's wearing black leggings, black running shoes with black soles, and a black hoodie. A black backpack rests nearby. She looks like a cat burglar. She wasn't kidding when she said she packs an outfit for every contingency.

"Nice PJs," Piper says, smiling. "I love dragonflies." She greets me like we've bumped into each other under normal circumstances.

"Piper, what are you doing here?" I demand.

"Stealing Claire's books," she explains as though it were a foregone conclusion.

"What books?" I screw up my face in confusion and look back and forth between her and Eric.

"The signed books you helped Dina remove from the rental cottage," Piper explains calmly. "I was told they would be here. But it appears I was misinformed."

This explains Piper's preoccupation with the back room at the book signing today, and yesterday when she was here to purchase the felted items. She was casing the joint.

"Who told you that?" I ask, already knowing the answer.

"I'm afraid I'm not at liberty to say," she coos in her posh British accent.

"We asked her," Eric interjects. "She won't tell us either."

"I already know who told her," I inform him. "I just want to hear her say it." Piper extends her bottom lip out and blows a stray lock of hair from her face and rolls her eyes like a sulky teenager. "Why did Brooks Wiley tell you where to find Claire's signed books?" I inquire.

"I'm sorry, I don't know to whom you're referring," Piper insists, looking at her feet and feigning ignorance.

"How do you know it was Brooks?" Eric asks.

"Because when Brooks and Dina discussed where to move the books, I offered to store them here"—I gesture to the nearby storeroom—"but when Dina and I came here to drop them off, Zoe convinced us they'd be safer at chez Martel, so we took them there instead. Dina couldn't reach Brooks to clear it with him, but assured me she'd contact him and let him know about the last-minute location change. I guess she forgot."

"How were you planning to move the books?" Eric asks Piper. "There aren't any vehicles in the parking lot."

Good observation, Eric!

"Upon locating the books, I would contact my partner in crime, at which time he would arrive with a vehicle to transport them to an undisclosed location."

"Where's the undisclosed location?" I ask.

"I don't know," Piper admits. "He didn't disclose it to me."

I sigh. "How did she get in?" I ask Eric.

"She busted the lock," he replies, fanning the door to show me the damaged hardware.

"Where is Brooks now?" I ask, glaring at Piper.

Piper shrugs. "I've no idea," she replies.

"I think she's telling the truth," Eric says. "Piper, what were you and Brooks planning to do with the books?"

"I planned to preserve my half," she explains, "for posterity."

"You and Brooks planned to split the books?" I clarify. "He would keep half of them and you would keep half of them?"

"That's right," Piper confirms. "They've increased in value, you see. Because they are the last books Claire will ever sign. Brooks said he planned to capitalize on their value. Strike while the iron is hot, is how he said it, if I recall. He lined up buyers on an online forum for collectors. I have no interest in profiting from Claire's death, I just want to preserve the books for future generations."

Have the books increased so much that Brooks decided it would be worthwhile to kill Claire so he could sell them? Did Brooks and Piper conspire to kill Claire together? Or did they join forces just to steal the books? Why would Brooks want a partner to steal the books, anyway? If he stole them alone, he could've sold all of them instead of half. But this way Piper gets caught in the act instead of him. I think Brooks Wiley doesn't like to get his hands dirty. Or maybe Brooks had no intention of giving Piper half the books; that would explain why he didn't tell her where the undisclosed location is. Maybe after Piper stole the books and served her purpose, Brooks was planning to kill her too.

A uniformed officer stands guard over Piper while Eric and I walk through the store, making sure nothing is missing. Everything seems to be where I left it.

"We checked her backpack and there's nothing from the store in there. Just a burner phone, a small amount of cash, and the tools she used to break the lock on the back door," Eric says.

A burner phone is a phone purchased with cash. It doesn't have a monthly plan and can't be traced to an owner.

"Do we need to check the apartment?" I ask Eric when we re-enter the back room.

"Oh, I hardly touched anything in the upstairs flat," Piper interjects, giggling. "I'm not one for nosing through people's belongings," says the woman who broke into my store and touched everything.

"What do you mean you *hardly* touched anything?" Eric asks.

Piper shrugs. "I looked around. There were no books, so I left. There was no point in rifling through your drawers and cupboards." She giggles. "It's not like you could hide boxes of books in your underwear drawer." Then she becomes serious again. "Mind you, I relocated your Spathiphyllum wallisii."

"You relocated his *what*?" I ask, wondering what the heck she's talking about.

"His peace lily," she clarifies. "It was on the windowsill. They prefer indirect sunlight, so I moved it to the coffee table. And I watered it." She looks at Eric with a serious expression on her face. "The soil was dry to the touch. You must keep the soil moist," she scolds.

She's crazy. There's no other explanation. If she's not crazy, she deserves an Academy Award.

While Eric goes upstairs to make sure nothing is missing or damaged in the apartment, Phillip informs me he's finished giving his statement, and he's going home. I thank him again for having my back. We're hugging when Piper's backpack rings.

"Brooks!" I say to the uniformed officer who's guarding Piper. "It must be him."

I bet he's calling to find out why Piper hasn't contacted him yet.

"Chief!" the officer yells.

Eric's feet thump down the stairs as the uniformed officer unzips the backpack and holds it open toward him. Eric pulls the phone out of the laptop with his gloved hand and raises the index finger of his other hand to his lips in a *shhh* motion. We all nod in acknowledgement.

Eric accepts the call and holds the phone to Piper's ear, but she says nothing. He raises his eyebrows and nods at her, as if willing her to speak. Piper purses her lips and turns away from the phone, refusing to answer the call. He puts the phone near his ear.

"Brooks Wiley. I know it's you. This is Eric Sloane from the Harmony Lake Police Department. We know everything." He pauses, but I don't think Brooks speaks. "Let's do this the easy way. Tell me where you are." Eric pulls the phone away from his ear. "He hung up."

The collective sigh in the back room sounds like a deflating balloon.

Eric instructs the first uniformed officer to accompany Phillip to his van, then check on Dina Langley, and stand guard outside her hotel room. They leave.

He instructs the second officer to take Piper to the police station and lists various charges to file against her. The officer leads Piper away by the arm.

The third officer's instructions are to go to chez

Martel and stand guard over the books and the occupants of the house. The officer leaves.

"The occupants of the house?" I ask with a lump in my throat and my heart pounding in my ears. "Do you think Dad and Zoe are in danger?"

"No, I'm sure they're fine. I'm being extra cautious. The books are there, and Brooks wants them. I don't think he'd be dumb enough to show up there, though," Eric assures me. "But if it's all right with you, I'll stay over tonight." Despite his reassuring words, Eric is worried enough to break his self-imposed rule about not having sleepovers while my dad is in town.

He makes a phone call and dispatches officers to King of the Hill to check if Brooks is in his hotel room. He also orders a BOLO for Brooks and his car.

BOLO is cop speak for Be On The Lookout. Officers will keep an eye out for Brooks and take him into custody if he surfaces.

"I want to go home," I say.

Eric nods. "We'll leave through the front door," he says, sliding the barrel bolt—the only remaining functional lock—into the locked position on the inside of the back door.

His phone dings, rings, and vibrates non-stop on the short drive home, but he doesn't check it because he's driving.

As soon as he turns off the engine, Eric checks his phone.

"Brooks isn't in his hotel room," he advises me. "His things are still there, including his passport, so he hasn't gone far."

"What about Dina?" I ask.

"Dina's fine," Eric replies. "The last time she spoke to Brooks was yesterday. She told the officer she'll notify us right away if Brooks contacts her."

Brooks's unknown whereabouts is like finding a spider on the ceiling. The situation is tenable as long as you know where the spider is, but if you look up and the spider isn't there, you panic, wondering where it went and if it's closer to you than you'd like.

CHAPTER 21

MONDAY, April 19th

"Good morning, Dad!" I summon a chipper voice and a smile, hoping to hide my exhaustion after tossing and turning all night.

"Good morning, Bean!" He smiles at me over his newspaper and reading glasses.

"Did you walk to the store this morning to get a paper?" I ask, wondering if the officer parked at the bottom of the driveway stopped him.

"I tried," my dad replies, closing the paper and laying it on his lap. "But Eric asked me to stay here. He dispatched the officer who's guarding the house to get a newspaper for me."

"Where is Eric?" I ask, dropping a coffee pod into the coffeemaker.

"Running," my dad replies. "He said we'd talk about it when you wake up."

I nod and open the back door for Sophie. "Do you want to wait until Zoe wakes up?"

He shakes his head. "I'll catch her up later."

While Sophie eats breakfast, and I sip my coffee, I tell my dad everything that went down last night and explain why Eric deemed it necessary to post a patrol car outside the house.

"He's being extra cautious until Brooks is in police custody," I say in conclusion.

"Hang on," my dad says, then reaches for the notebook and pen on the table next to his armchair. "I want to take notes. I can use some of this in my book."

"Well, I'm glad we can help with your research," I half-joke as I get up to put my empty mug in the dishwasher.

I pick up my phone for the first time today, and scroll through the myriad of unread messages. Most from friends and neighbours wanting to know what happened last night, and why there's a patrol car outside the house.

First, I respond to Connie and April so our nearest and dearest will know we're OK.

Next, I text Ryan, Harmony Lake's resident handyperson, and ask him to stop by Knitorious to fix the broken lock. He replies, saying he'll meet me at the store later this morning.

Last but not least, I text Jules Janssen and ask her if she wants to know what Claire said about her gift on Wednesday. Jules Janssen isn't quick to respond.

While I'm busy reading and responding to texts, Eric comes home from his run.

"Was there a Brooks Wiley sighting overnight?" I

ask, hoping Brooks is in custody, and we'll finally get some answers about Claire's murder.

Eric shakes his head. "Nothing." He kisses me good morning, and I scrunch my nose at his post-run muskiness. "Wait for me. I want to drive you to work." It's a statement, not a suggestion or a question. He's in bodyguard mode.

"OK." I nod.

I feel safe going to the store on my own, but I'm too tired to argue.

He gets in the shower, and Zoe wakes up, so my dad and I update her on everything that happened while she slept.

Knitorious isn't open on Mondays, but I need to finish flattening and recycling the empty boxes from the book signing, and re-shelve the yarn we removed from the store to accommodate my dad's books. Also, I need to be there when Ryan fixes the back door.

When we arrive at Knitorious, there is a courier truck in the parking lot. A man wearing a courier company uniform waits by the back door. He's leaning against a hand truck.

"The books!" I exclaim, smacking my palm against my forehead. "Claire's publisher sent him to pick up the signed books. With all the kerfuffle over the past couple of days, I forgot."

"I'll take care of it," Eric offers. "I'll meet you inside."

As I walk around the corner to the front door, Eric squints into the morning sun and tells the driver there's a misunderstanding about the location of the books.

As soon as I'm inside the store, I call my dad and Zoe to give them a heads up about the courier's imminent arrival at chez Martel.

"Don't worry, Bean!" my dad assures me. "Eric sent a text, and the officer stationed outside is here with us. We'll be sure the courier picks them up."

I can't wait for those books to leave Harmony Lake. It will be a relief not to worry about anyone breaking into my house to steal them.

As soon as we end the call, my phone rings.

"Is everything OK in there?" Eric asks.

"It's all good," I reply. "Don't worry."

"OK. I'll see you in a few minutes."

He sounds distracted; he must've run into someone or got caught up talking to the courier.

I drop my cell phone in my purse and toss it onto the counter. Hands on hips, I exhale loudly and survey the store, deciding where to start.

"Megan, don't scream."

A scream escapes me, but I cover my mouth with both hands and stifle it.

"How did you get in?" I ask, wide-eyed and mortified.

"I picked the lock," he replies in his melodious creole accent.

He points at the front door. If he can pick this lock, he could've picked the lock to the den at Claire's rental cottage.

"What are you doing here, Brooks?"

He's standing in the doorway between the back room and the store.

"I want to explain myself," he says, his hands in front of him as if he's not a threat.

"Explain why you killed Claire Rivera?" I ask.

Brooks shakes his head. "I did not kill Claire."

He sounds adamant, but I remind myself he's a skilled liar.

"Why should I believe you?" I ask. "You lied about your relationship with Jules. You lied about being in your hotel room when Claire was murdered, and you lied about your relationship with Piper Peters."

Where's Eric? He can't still be talking to the courier.

"First," he raises his index finger. "The only thing I lied about is my relationship with Jules," he insists. "I lied to protect her privacy. Do you know how hard it is for her to avoid the tabloids?"

"Do I care?" My voice is thick with sarcasm.

"I didn't lie about my alibi," he continues. "I told your boyfriend I was at the hotel when Claire was murdered. I didn't say I was in my room."

A lie by omission is a lie, nonetheless.

"You were in Jules's room?" I presume.

He nods. "That's right. Ask her entourage, lots of them saw me."

"Jules and her people aren't cooperating with the police," I advise him. "Didn't she tell you? They lawyered up. As far as the police are concerned, you don't have an alibi." Brooks curses under his breath, and the muscles in his jaw clench and unclench.

"I didn't lie about Piper, either," he tells me. "She is crazy. Like a fox. I think she killed Claire because it upset her when Claire announced she was ending the Familia series. Those aren't just books to Piper, they're real. That's why she broke into your shop to help me get them. She's built her life around them."

"So have you. Claire was your biggest client and your biggest source of income," I point out. "Trying to recruit Mitchell Monroe to fill the empty spot on your client list the day after Claire's murder doesn't look good for you."

Now would be a great time to show up, Eric!

"I would have pitched my services to Mitchell whether Claire was dead or alive," he says, shaking his head and sitting at the harvest table. "It's all about the money. That's why I wanted the books. With Claire gone, my income from her will dry up. I panicked and thought I could sell the signed books for a good price to fill in the gap." He looks at me with pleading eyes. "Think about it, Megan," he taps his bald head with his finger. "Why would I kill Claire? She was my meal ticket."

I shift my weight from one foot to the other, but stay put, planted within arm's reach of the front door.

"Because she refused to sell the film rights," I speculate. "The film rights would earn you millions of dollars. That's why you approached her family to sell them less than two days after Claire's murder."

I wish Eric would hurry.

"The only reason I approached Claire's family is because Dina convinced me it was a good idea," he says, sounding desperate. "She told me Claire's family wanted to sell the rights. She told me they were huge Jules Janssen fans, and she even suggested that if Jules was part of the sales pitch, it would help to convince them."

That doesn't sound like Dina. It doesn't vibe with what Dina told me, and her story has been way more consistent than Brooks's story.

"Why should I believe you?" I ask.

"Because it's the truth." He smacks the tabletop with his open palm, and I take a step backward, toward the door. Brooks takes a deep breath and blows it out. "I might be shady, but I'm not a killer."

"Why did you tell Jules where Claire and Dina were staying in Harmony Lake? You know they wanted their location to remain private."

He shrugs. "Because she asked me. And I love Jules. I'd do anything for her."

Would he commit murder for her?

"Brooks," I say, trying to sound as composed as possible, "you need to tell your story to the police..."

"No way." He stands up, shaking his head. "They won't believe me. They're looking for evidence to charge me, not clear me." He backs away from the harvest table, toward the back room. "I've been here too long." He glances behind him, then looks back at me. "I have to go." He turns, and moments later, the back door slams shut.

I lunge toward the counter and grab my phone from my purse. I run toward the back door. Maybe I can tell which direction Brooks went. I throw open the door and run into the parking lot.

He's gone. There's no sign of him. The parking lot is empty except for Phillip's delivery van and Eric's car.

Where's Eric? Did he run after Brooks? Should I call 9-1-1? I turn my head in every direction, searching for a sign of either man.

"Megan?" His voice is distant. It's coming from inside the store. "Babe?" I turn toward the back door. Eric appears in the doorway. "What are you doing? Are you OK?" He's next to me now, turning his head. Scanning the parking lot. Searching with me, but he doesn't know what we're searching for.

"Brooks was here. I don't know where he went." I look up at him. "He's gone. I tried to keep him here as long as I could. I'm sorry."

"Are you OK?" He grips my shoulders and looks me up and down. "Did he touch you?"

I shake my head. "I'm fine. He stayed away from me."

Eric turns me around and guides me inside. I sink into the sofa in the cozy sitting area, and he hands me a coffee. Maple pecan latte. He went to get me a coffee.

"Thank you." I force a small smile.

"This is my fault, babe. I'm so sorry." He looks like he might cry.

"It's not your fault. Brooks's actions are Brooks's fault and no one else." I shake my head. "You did nothing wrong. Anyway, no one was hurt."

"I should've come inside ahead of you and cleared the store... rookie mistake," he says, shaking his head.

"The courier could've waited." He sounds angry. His thumbs move at lightning speed across the keyboard on his phone. "Everyone is looking for Brooks. When I get hold of him…" His voice trails off at the end of his sentence.

"He had no intention of hurting me," I assure him. "Why would he? I haven't done anything to him."

Eric sits next to me and pulls me into him. I rest my head on his chest and take a deep breath. He smells like a forest after it rains and the sun comes out. It's my favourite smell. He kisses the top of my head. He tells me he loves me and apologizes again. His guilt is palpable. His chin rests on the top of my head.

"We're getting a security system for the store," he says, like it's a done deal.

"We are?" I ask.

I don't think we need a security system at Knitorious, but now isn't the time to argue, so I swallow the urge to disagree with him.

I feel him nod. "We'll get the same system as the house." He squeezes me. "Two intruders are too many." He shakes his head. "This won't happen again. When I think about what could've happened…" He swallows hard. His hand clenches into a fist, then relaxes. "You're here fending off a dangerous fugitive while I was standing in line buying coffee..." His voice hitches on the last word of his incomplete sentence, and he squeezes me again.

"I didn't fend off anyone. Nothing happened," I remind him. "Everyone is fine."

"Do you need to look for him?" I ask, sitting up to sip my coffee.

"Every cop on the force is looking for Brooks Wiley," Eric reminds me, tucking a stray curl behind my ear. "How did he get in here?"

"He says he picked the lock." I point to the front door.

"If he could pick this lock, he could've picked the lock on the den at Claire's rental cottage," Eric points out, coming to my previous conclusion. "What did he want? Was he looking for the books?"

"I don't know if he was looking for the books," I reply. "He said he wanted to explain himself."

"Did he?"

I nod, then tell Eric about my conversation with Brooks.

"Do you believe him?" Eric asks at the end of my account.

"Which part?" I ask. "I feel like lying comes easy to Brooks, you know?"

Eric nods. "I'm familiar with the type."

"He makes a good point, though, about how killing Claire would kill most of his income. It wouldn't be a smart move, and while Brooks might be an accomplished liar, he strikes me as a smart person. Too smart to kill his biggest source of income."

"But she wouldn't be his biggest source of income if she stopped writing," Eric points out. "And Jules has a lot more money than Claire. Maybe now that he's with Jules, he decided Claire was expendable."

I startle at the sound of three sharp raps on the door.

Heavy shoulders, long arms, I remind myself, letting out a deep breath.

"It's probably Ryan," I say to Eric as he stands up to answer the door. My phone dings, and I glance at it. "Eric! Stop!"

He stops, and I tilt my phone so he can see it.

Jules: Are you there? The door is locked.

Eric blurts out a curse word. "I can't be here when you talk to her."

"Just a sec," I tell him as I type a response to Jules's text.

Me: I'll be right there. Give me two minutes.

"Leave through the back door." I jerk my head toward the back of the store.

"I'm not leaving!" He sounds offended. "What if Brooks comes back?"

"He won't," I insist, despite having no idea what Brooks Wiley's intentions are. "I'll text you as soon as Jules leaves. I'll be fine. Ryan will be here soon, and if I scream, Phillip will hear me through the wall." I nudge him toward the back of the store. "Just go. If you don't go, I can't talk to her."

With a frustrated groan, Eric disappears into the back room. I plaster a cheerful smile on my face and open the door.

CHAPTER 22

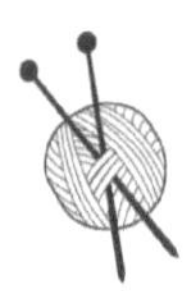

"HI, JULES!"

"Thanks for reaching out," she says, leaning in for an awkward side-hug where we touch each other's shoulders and kind of lean into one another. "You have good timing. I'm leaving town tonight."

She steps inside and watches me lock the door.

"We're closed on Mondays," I explain. "I came in today to clean up. The store is in shambles after the book signing. Can I get you a coffee, or tea, or anything?"

"No, thank you." Her smile displays a tremendous number of teeth. "I'm fine."

"Speaking of book signings, I hear yours went very well on Saturday."

"Yes, it was a huge success," Jules responds, taking off her sunglasses and laying her backpack on the floor at her feet.

While Jules gives me the highlights of her book signing, I join her in the cozy sitting area with my maple pecan latte. Just like the first time we met, Jules is incognito today. She's wearing a pair of leggings—the athletic kind you'd wear for running—a pink tank top with a pink running jacket zipped up halfway, and black running shoes. Her auburn hair is tucked into her black baseball cap with the bill pulled down to shield her face. She looks like any other yummy mummy running errands after dropping off the kids at school.

"Did Brooks Wiley come to your signing and get you to sign a book for him?" I ask.

A panicked micro-expression flashes across Jules's face.

"Who?"

I can see why she earned an academy award.

"Tall guy… handsome... expensive Italian suits... face that looks like it was sculpted by a Greek god… bald… sultry accent?"

She shakes her head. "Doesn't ring a bell," she says, "but if he looks anything like you describe him, I *wish* I knew him." We laugh.

"Weird," I comment. "I'm sure I saw you making out with him in the alley beside the store on Wednesday." I reach for my phone on the coffee table. "In fact, I think I have a photo of you kissing with his hand on your backside."

"Let's cut the crap, Megan," Jules says, her tone business-like. "Fine. I know Brooks." She points to my phone. "Delete the photo."

"There is no photo," I admit. "I wanted to see how far you'd take the lie."

She's not amused. Even her exhale sounds annoyed.

"I go to great lengths to protect my privacy," she explains.

"It's too bad you don't go to the same lengths to protect other people's privacy," I counter.

She narrows her eyes. "What is that supposed to mean?" she asks, defensive.

"It means you gave Piper Peters the address and directions to Claire Rivera's rental cottage." Jules's face softens, and her shoulders slump. "Why would you do that? Brooks told you Piper was unstable and had a history of threatening Claire."

"Look, it wasn't my finest moment," Jules admits. "I knew about Claire's trouble with Piper. Brooks told me about the disturbing letters and emails Piper sent. I empathize. I've dealt with more than my fair share of obsessed fans. A few months ago, when Brooks told me Piper showed up on Claire's doorstep, I reached out to offer Claire support."

"Moral support?" I ask.

Jules shrugs one shoulder. "Yes, and other support. I have a first-rate security team and legal advisers. They deal with fans like Piper Peters on the regular. I offered Claire their services. Free. No strings attached."

"Did Claire accept your generous offer?"

She shakes her head. "She didn't even respond to my offer. Brooks said Claire thought that if she accepted my offer, I'd use it as leverage to pressure her into selling me the *Familia* movie rights."

"That doesn't explain why you disclosed Claire's location to Piper."

"It made sense at the time. It was a spur-of-the-moment decision," she justifies. "I saw Piper waiting in line, and the idea jumped into my head. I acted without thinking it through," Jules explains, sitting up a little straighter. "Claire wouldn't talk to me at all. She wouldn't reply to emails, accept phone calls, or even meet with my representatives. I thought if Piper showed up on her doorstep in Harmony Lake, it would frighten Claire enough to contact me and take me up on my offer to help her."

"And the line of communication between you and Claire would be open," I conclude.

"That was my plan."

"That was a dangerous plan, Jules," I say, shaking my head. "What if Piper used the information you gave her to kill Claire?"

"I know." Jules raises her hand in a stop motion. "I realized it was a horrible idea as soon as I did it. I regretted it immediately."

"But you didn't regret it enough to warn Claire that Piper knew her location?"

"It never occurred to me that anyone would die!"

"Where were you when Claire was murdered?" I ask without warning so I can gauge her response.

"I was busy," Jules replies, shrugging one shoulder. "I'm always busy."

"Can you be more specific?" I urge. "If the police can account for your whereabouts, they'll eliminate you as a suspect and leave you alone."

"Let's see." Her gaze shifts to the right, like she's trying to remember something. "Thursday morning, I had a call with New York about an upcoming project."

She drums her meticulously manicured fingers on her lap. "Then I went swimming in the hotel pool." She looks at me. "The hotel manager closed the pool just for me."

"Did anyone swim with you?"

"No," Jules replies.

"What time did you finish swimming?" I ask.

"Lunchtime," she replies. "I went back to my room, showered, and got dressed. I ordered soup and salad from room service. My manager sat with me while I ate, and we went over my schedule for the New York project. After lunch, I had a massage and a facial." She smiles.

"At a local salon?"

Jules laughs. "No. I have my own people. They do everything for me. I received the spa treatments in my hotel room."

"You didn't mention Brooks. Was he with you on Thursday?"

She presses her lips into a thin line and shakes her head. "I didn't see Brooks until Thursday evening."

"Brooks says he was in your room all day on Thursday, starting from late morning."

"Which room?" she asks.

"How many rooms do you have?"

"The entire top floor of the hotel," she replies as if it should be obvious. "I need a lot of rooms, Megan." She counts on her fingers. "A room for me, a room for my manager, rooms for my security team, rooms for my glam squad, a room for my publicist, a room for my agent…."

I raise my hand in a stop motion. "I get it. You have an entourage."

"He could've been there, and I just didn't see him," she surmises. "But if he was there, someone saw him. My team is pretty busy. Lots of comings and goings."

"Jules, you need to let your team talk to the police. Unless someone says they saw Brooks at the time of Claire's murder, he'll stay on the suspect list. He needs your help."

"It's not up to me," she explains. "It's up to the lawyers."

"The lawyers work for you," I remind her. "If you tell them you want to cooperate with the police, they'll listen to you. Don't you want to help Brooks? He's on the run. He's practically a fugitive, and he's making poor decisions."

"Is that why he's not returning my texts?" she asks.

I get the sense Jules Janssen isn't very concerned about her boyfriend's legal problems. At all. It's like he's just another member of her entourage.

"Jules, he lied about his alibi to protect your privacy. He loves you."

"Lots of people love me." She shrugs.

"But I think Brooks believes you feel the same about him."

"He's so sweet." She tilts her ear toward her shoulder and smiles. "Brooks knows our situationship is casual."

"Situationship?" I ask.

"An undefined relationship situation," she explains. "Hanging out with Brooks is fun. And lord knows, he's hot." She fans her hand in front of her face. "We bonded over the common goal of making *Familia* into a movie, but I'm not looking for anything permanent. I made it crystal clear to him. If Brooks caught feelings for me, that's his problem. I warned him."

Sounds cold. I almost pity Brooks. Maybe he killed Claire to make Jules love him. Maybe, he thought with Claire out of the way, he'd be able to secure the film rights, and Jules would fall head over heels for him. Was Claire's murder Brooks's attempt to be Jules's knight in shining armour?

"Do you think Brooks loves you enough to kill for you?" I ask quietly.

Jules shrugs. "How would I know? I didn't ask him to kill anyone for me." Jules pulls her phone out of her jacket pocket and checks the time. "I have to get going." She stands up and grabs her backpack. "You didn't reach out to me to tell me what Claire said about the gift, did you?"

"It was my secondary reason," I admit. "She accepted the gift, but said she'd only give up the film rights over her dead body."

"Creepy," Jules remarks with a shudder.

Before she leaves, Jules agrees to give me the names and phone numbers of the people from New York who she spoke with on Thursday morning. I open my planner to a blank note page and hand her a pen. Using her phone for reference, she jots down five names and phone numbers.

"And I'll talk to my lawyers and ask them to be more cooperative with your local police," she says.

"Thanks," I reply. "One more thing," I say before I unlock the door. "At your book signing on Saturday, you told the mayor you were confident you'd acquire the film rights to *Familia* because you just eliminated a major obstacle. What did you mean? Were you referring to Claire?"

"No," she replies, laughing. "Of course not. On Saturday morning, I secured one of the best directors in the industry. I won't tell you his name, but I guarantee you've seen lots of his movies. He'll impress whoever ends up owning the *Familia* rights." I unlock the door. "That's all I meant." She waves. "Bye, Megan."

"Bye, Jules. Safe travels."

I take a picture of the names and numbers Jules wrote in my planner and text them to Eric. He asks me how our visit went and whether I learned anything that might help solve Claire's murder.

To be honest, I don't know.

Was Jules honest with me about everything she said, or was she acting? If she can sneak around town incognito to visit me, make out with Brooks, and talk to Piper without being recognized, she could easily go to Claire's rental cottage with no one noticing. And I'm sure Jules's team will verify her alibi; their livelihoods depend on it.

Other than Jules agreeing to let her entourage cooperate with the police, our conversation didn't rule out or further incriminate any of the suspects. Who killed Claire, and why, is still as clear as mud.

CHAPTER 23

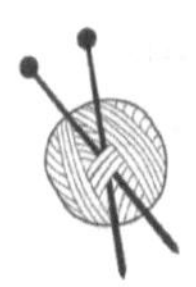

APRIL: The bakery is DEAD today. I'm sooo bored!

Me: As soon as I finish here, I'll come visit you!

April: Yay! I want to hear about everything that happened last night.

Me: Want me to call you? We can talk while I re-shelve the yarn.

April: I can't talk right now. Guess who is here again?

Me: Give me a hint.

April: She's blonde, bubbly, and loves lemon meringue tarts.

Me: Dina Langley?

April: Yup! She's been here all morning. Just her and me. All alone.

Me: Where's T?

April: She drove to Harmony Hills to load up on baking supplies. She'll be back later.

Me: I hope Dina hangs around until I get there. I want to ask her about some things Brooks said.

I just flattened the last box, and now I'm tying all the flattened boxes together with twine so they'll be easier to drag to the curb on recycling day.

Two sharp raps on the back door startle me, and I almost cut myself with the utility knife. I'll be less jumpy when Claire's murderer is off the streets.

"Who is it?" I shout through the locked door.

"It's just me, Megan."

"Hi, Ryan," I say with a smile when I open the door. "Thanks for fitting me in. I know it's last minute."

"*Pshaw*." He flicks away my comment with his hand. "That's what family is for."

Ryan and I aren't family in the biological sense of the word. Or in the related-by-marriage sense of the word. Ryan's dad is Archie. Archie is Connie's partner. Connie is my surrogate mum. According to Ryan, this makes us stepsiblings. Ryan is part of my modern, non-traditional family.

"*Phwoooooh*," Ryan whistles. "She sure did a number on this lock."

"Can you fix it?" I ask.

"Let me take a closer look," he replies, squatting and putting his face up to the broken mechanism. "If I have to replace it, I have locks in my truck. Either way, you'll have a functional lock when I leave."

"Thank you," I say. "It's a weight off my mind."

While Ryan works his magic on the back door, I walk to and from the back room, carrying skeins of yarn from the storage closet to the store. When he's finished fixing the lock and announces he's leaving, I've already re-shelved all the bulky, Aran, and worsted weight yarns.

I'M CHALLENGING myself to carry the last of the lace weight yarn in one armload when someone taps three times on the front door. It's busier here than at Grand Central Station. The knocking is followed by intense scratching; whoever it is has Sophie with them.

"Just a sec!" I holler from near the lace weight yarn shelves.

I dump the lace weight yarn into the shelves, creating yarn chaos, and jog to the front door.

"Hi, Dad!" We kiss cheeks. "Hi, Soph!" She puts her front paws on my knees, and I rub her. I stand aside so they can come in. "Where's Zoe?"

"Grocery shopping. She said to tell you not to worry about dinner tonight, she wants to cook."

"That's nice of her," I say. "Sometimes I wish you guys lived closer."

"So we can cook for you?" he asks, laughing.

"It would be a nice perk," I reply. "But it would be nice to see you more often."

"Even if we lived up the street, you wouldn't see much more of us," he reminds me. "We travel most of the year."

"I know." I sigh. "What brings you and Sophie into town?"

"It was time for Sophie's midday walk, and I

thought she could stay here while I take one of my favourite daughters out for lunch."

"I'd love that," I say, smiling.

"Can we go in a few minutes?" I ask. "I want to finish shelving this yarn."

I return to the yarn I shoved into the lace weight shelves and sort it by colour and brand as fast as I can.

"Ouch!"

"Dad, are you OK?" I ask from the back of the store where I'm finding shelf space for a few rogue skeins of yarn.

"Mmm-hmm," he replies with the tip of his index finger in his mouth.

I grab the first-aid kit and rush to his side.

"What happened?" I open the first aid box.

"I pricked my finger with that thing." He points to my felting needle. It's on the end table in the cozy sitting area, next to my almost-finished Sophie figurine.

"How?" I ask, using a piece of gauze to apply direct pressure to his wound.

"I just picked it up to look at it," he explains. "I was curious. It doesn't look as sharp as it feels!"

Tearing open an alcohol wipe, I explain the tool has small barbs near the end that make it sharper than it looks. He winces when the alcohol touches his finger.

"It hurts more when you pull it out than it does when it goes in," I explain.

"That Dina lady who came to the book signing yesterday had one floating around in her backpack, so I assumed it must not be very sharp," he says.

"Dina?" I ask. "The young woman who brought all the *Shark Attack* books with her?"

Dad nods. "That's right. Claire Rivera's assistant."

This must be what they laughed about when he signed Dina's books and made the comment about keeping pickpockets out of her backpack. But Dina told me she isn't a needle felter, so why would she carry a needle? And if she is a felter, why would she lie about it? It's hardly a controversial hobby; there's no reason to be a closet felter and keep her needle felting habit a secret.

"What else did you see in Dina's backpack?" I ask.

"I only had a quick peek when she pulled out the books," Dad replies. "The needle, a big sponge, and some balls of wool. White, orange, lime green, and brown, I think."

Everything a needle felter would need to work on a project.

I flashback to when I walked Dina to the back door and picked green fibre off of her sweater.

The knot in my stomach grows bigger as I apply a bandage to my dad's injured finger. Something isn't right; something way bigger than Dina lying to me about her crafting habit. I feel like I'm missing something right in front of me.

"You were very brave," I tease. "Would you like a sticker, lollipop, or small toy?" I produce a basket from under the counter. We give them to the children of customers to keep them occupied while their parents shop.

"I'd like sushi and a glass of wine with my daughter," he says, chuckling. "But I'll take a grape lollipop to sustain me until we get there." He reaches into the basket and takes a purple lollipop.

Putting away the first aid kit, my phone dings.

*April: I wasn't snooping, but when Dina went to the washroom, I *might* have nudged her table and woken up her laptop, then looked at the screen. Accidentally, of course.*

Me: It sounds very unintentional.

April: I knew you'd understand.

Me: What did you see?

April: The unreleased Familia book.

Me: Are you sure?

April: I've read every book in the series. This is new. Wanna know which one of Mama's kids dies in the next book?

Me: NO SPOILERS!

April: It's weird that Dina has the unfinished book open on her laptop, right?

Me: It seems weird, but I don't know.

April: I keep wiping nearby tables so I can spy on her. Dina is definitely typing words into the book.

Me: I'm going out for lunch with my dad, then I'm coming to the bakery.

April: OK. I'll keep wiping and snooping. Artsy Tartsy will have the cleanest tables in town!

"Ready, Dad?" I ask, walking toward him.

His bandaged finger reminds me of the bandages on Dina's fingers. She said one of them was a paper cut, and the other was her nail-biting habit, but now I wonder if they were needle-felting injuries.

"Ready, Bean!" he replies, standing up.

"Dad, can I ask you a work question?" I ask, retrieving my purse from under the counter.

"Of course," he replies.

"Does your assistant ever work on your unfinished manuscripts?"

He shakes his head. "No," he replies with conviction. "No one reads my first draft except me. Zoe is my wife and one of my editors, and I don't even share my first drafts with her. My assistant never has writing-related tasks." He points to his chest. "I'm the author. I'm the only one who does writing-related tasks."

Claire claimed to be an avid needle felter, but showed no interest in the felting display at the store or in the felting supplies we sell. Dina claims she is not a needle felter, but showed enthusiastic interest in all things needle felting when she was here, and carries felting supplies in her backpack.

My dad says Claire wasn't an avid reader and preferred magazines to books. Dina is a self-described bookworm who totes 20 paperbacks in her backpack without breaking a sweat.

Dina is more Claire-like than Claire.

My dad and I say goodbye to Sophie and are about to leave the store when my phone rings.

"It's Eric," I tell my dad. "Just one more minute." I accept the call and put him on speaker.

"Hey, babe! How's your day?"

"Good. I'm just about to have lunch with my dad. He's right here. You're on speaker."

"Hello, Eric," my father shouts from right beside me.

"Hi, Mitchell," Eric responds. "I thought I'd call and give you the good news."

"You found Brooks?" I ask.

"Not yet." he replies. "Other good news. Forensics found peanut oil on some items we took from the cottage yesterday. I have a theory."

"We're dying to hear it," I say.

"Yes, Eric, you can't leave us with a cliffhanger," Mitchell shouts.

"We found peanut oil on the pages of several magazines," Eric divulges.

I remember picking up magazines at the cottage when Dina sent me to the doc to collect her things. Could he be talking about the same magazines?

"Were the magazines inside the den with Claire?" I ask.

"No," Eric replies. "They were in the washroom. I suspect Claire went from the office to the washroom where she came into contact with the magazines, then returned to the office. Her allergic reaction started after she locked the door."

"Are you saying Claire's death wasn't murder after all? It was an accident?" Dad yells.

"That's what I'm saying. And the coroner concurs. He's going to change Claire's death from murder to accidental."

"Eric, were the magazines on the edge of the bathtub?" I ask.

"They were."

"Are there fingerprints on the magazines?" I ask.

"From three people," he says with hesitation. "Why are you asking? You have that tone in your voice, like you've figured something out."

"Were the fingerprints Claire's, Brooks's, and mine?" I ask.

"That's right," Eric says. "But you aren't a suspect, babe. You were at the scene when you helped Dina pack. We expected to find your fingerprints there."

"I'm not worried about that." I shake my head even though Eric can't see me. "The only way Claire touched those magazines is if she went down to the dock." I explain to Eric how Brooks and I went to the dock on Friday to fetch Dina's stuff when we were helping her pack. "I assumed the magazines were part of her stuff and brought them back to the cottage. Dina told us the magazines were already at the cottage when she and Claire arrived. Brooks put them on the edge of the tub. Dina seemed to avoid touching them. I remember our conversation clear as day. Dina mentioned she took the magazines down to the dock on Thursday. I commented it was a good thing it didn't rain since they were down there overnight."

"Why aren't Dina's fingerprints on the magazines?" Eric sighs on the other end of the phone. "If she took them to the dock, her fingerprints should be there."

"Because she doesn't want them to be?" I suggest.

"I have to locate Dina Langley."

I gasp. "I know where she is."

Panic radiates from the knot in my stomach to the rest of my body when I realize Dina is at Artsy Tartsy.

With April. Alone. My best friend is alone with a murderer. My best friend is in danger.

"Stay here with Sophie," I instruct my dad as soon as Eric and I end our call.

"You aren't going there?" my dad asks, incredulous.

"And text April," I add, ignoring his question. "Tell her to unlock the back door without Dina noticing." I'd do it myself, but I'm not coordinated enough to run and text at the same time.

"This isn't a good idea, Bean. She's dangerous!"

"I'll be back soon." I shove my phone in my back pocket, throw open the door, and run toward Artsy Tartsy.

I'm coming, April. If Dina plans to put up a fight, she'll have to go through both of us.

"Bean! Megan!" My dad's voice grows fainter the farther I run.

CHAPTER 24

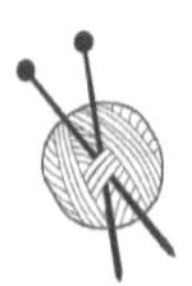

I SLOW down to a walk a few doors from the bakery and catch my breath. I don't want to rush in there all flustered and tip off Dina.

"Hey, Megastar!" April flashes me a wide smile when I enter the bakery.

"Hey!" I say, smiling.

Her phone buzzes, and she looks down. The cheerful expression disappears from her face. Her brows furrow toward each other, and she swallows hard. She must have read the text my dad sent. April looks up at me with a blank expression on her face. I give her an exaggerated smile, reminding her to act natural. Picking up on my hint, April smiles, then snaps her fingers.

"I saved you a slice of pistachio cake with strawberry meringue," she says. "I'll just nip to the kitchen and get it."

"Sounds yummy," I say. "You and T spoil me." April disappears into the kitchen.

I'm sure the cake is an excuse to unlock the back door.

I cough to cover the clicking sound when I lock the front door. Then, keeping my eye on Dina the entire time to make sure she doesn't look up from her laptop screen, I flip the sign from OPEN to CLOSED.

Dina is laser-focused on her laptop. She hasn't looked up once since I walked in the door.

"Here you go, Megadoodle." April slides the plate and a glass of water across the counter to me.

"Thanks," I say, taking them, and sitting at the table behind Dina. "I can watch the bakery if you have paperwork to do in the office," I suggest. "I'm finished at Knitorious for the day."

Will April take the hint and leave through the back door she just unlocked? There's no point in both of us locking ourselves in here with a potential killer.

"Don't be silly," April responds. "I wouldn't ask you to do that." She shrugs. "Besides, the paperwork is all caught up."

She won't leave. I don't blame her. I wouldn't leave her alone, either. I give her a trace of a smile, and she winks in return.

"Hi, Dina," I exclaim.

Dina raises her index finger. "Just give me one minute." Her index finger returns to her laptop keyboard. I have a few mouthfuls of cake while April repeatedly wipes the same area of countertop. "And… done!" Dina slams her laptop shut, looks up at April with a satisfied grin, and says, "One lemon meringue tart, please!"

"Coming right up!" April says.

Dina spins around in her chair. "Hi, Megan!" She smiles at me. "April told me what happened at Knitorious last night. I couldn't believe it! Piper Peters broke in and tried to steal the *Familia* books?! It's a good thing we let your stepmum convince us to move them, huh?"

April places a plate in front of Dina, who says thank you and takes a big bite of tart.

"Yes," I agree. "And it's a good thing my neighbour noticed someone in the store."

"I can't believe Brooks told her where to find the books." Dina shakes her head. "With all the activity and confusion this weekend, I forgot to tell him we moved them. Thank goodness. Otherwise she might have tried to break into your house."

"Have you heard from Brooks?" I ask.

Dina shakes her head. "No. Not since we had lunch on Saturday. But I told the police I'll tell them if Brooks tries to contact me."

"Do you know if the police have found him yet?" she asks me.

"As far as I know, they're still looking," I reply. "But they almost caught up with him this morning. He was at Knitorious when I arrived."

"Inside?" Dina asks wide-eyed before putting the rest of the tart in her mouth.

I nod. "Inside. Brooks is a decent lock picker."

"Wow," she garbles with her mouth full of tart. "Maybe he picked the lock in the den at the rental cottage," she mumbles, her words difficult to understand. Then she swallows. "Did he try to hurt you? Are you OK?"

"I'm fine," I assure her. "He didn't harm me. He didn't even threaten to harm me. He wanted to talk."

"About what?" Dina asks.

"He wanted to clear his name. Brooks insists he did not kill Claire."

She rolls her eyes. "Of course, he does. He'll say anything to avoid jail."

"Dina," I say, about to change the subject. "My dad mentioned you had a felting needle and some fibre in your backpack yesterday. Why do you have them if you're not a felter?"

Dina looks down, avoiding eye contact with me. "They're Claire's," she confesses. "I took them from the rental cottage when we were there on Friday." She shrugs. "I wanted something of hers. Something important to her, but not expensive, you know?"

She's lying. The police checked our bags before and after we left the cottage. Dina did not have any needle felting supplies.

"Silly me. I thought the needle felting stuff belonged to you," I laugh. "And your bandaged fingers resulted from needle-felting accidents." I laugh, and April laughs with me.

"Why would someone lie about a hobby like needle felting?" April asks with a shrug.

"Exactly," Dina agrees. "That wouldn't make any sense."

"You're right," I concur. "But something else doesn't add up," I suggest.

"What?" Dina asks, the smile disappearing from her face.

"According to Brooks, you suggested he approach Claire's family and offer to purchase the *Familia* rights from them. He says you even suggested it might help if Jules approached them because Claire's family are Jules Janssen fans."

"What?" she asks, overdramatizing her skepticism. "That's not true." Dina shakes her head. "Either he lied, or he misunderstood me," she insists. "Yes, I told him that Claire's family are huge Jules Janssen fans because it's true. But I didn't tell them to ask her family to sell the rights. I suggested it might mean a lot to them if Jules reached out personally and offered condolences for Claire's death. That's all I said, I swear." She's talking fast now. Too fast. She's rattled. "Remember, I told you I think it's tacky to talk to Claire's family about business while they're grieving. He's just angry because I refused to be part of their scheme."

"You're right," I reply. "Your version makes more sense." Relief washes across Dina's face. "Especially since Claire's family won't inherit the rights to *Familia,* you will."

"Me?" Dina pokes herself in the chest. "How do you know that?" She narrows her eyes and looks at me sideways.

I shrug. "I heard it somewhere. The rumour mill around here is incredibly accurate and efficient." I take a sip of water. "You don't seem shocked, Dina. Did you know Claire was bequeathing you the rights to her books?"

"To be honest, I'm not as shocked as I should be," Dina admits. "Claire must've left the rights to me because she knew I would respect her wishes and not sell them."

"Did the contract between you and Claire stipulate you would inherit the rights if she died?"

"Who told you about our contract?" She sounds defensive now.

"Brooks," I reply. "He mentioned it at the cottage. He didn't have many details, only knew a contract existed and said it made for a strange working relationship between you and Claire."

"We've already established that Brooks is a liar," Dina reminds me.

"Was he lying when he said the contract stipulates that when the Familia series ends, the working relationship between you and Claire also ends?" I ask. "When Claire announced the next *Familia* book would be the last, she essentially fired you over social media. It would be understandable if that made you angry."

"You don't understand what you're talking about," Dina says snidely. "Claire couldn't fire me, even if she wanted to." She glares at me through squinty eyes. "And the rights were never Claire's to bequeath."

"What does that mean?" I ask.

"Never mind." She dismisses my question with a flick of her wrist. "I don't want to talk about this anymore. You're making me feel like a suspect."

If the shoe fits...

"I'm sorry," I say. "I didn't mean to upset you. If it makes you feel better, I have it on very good authority that, as of fifteen minutes ago, there were no suspects in Claire Rivera's death."

This piques Dina's interest, and she inches her chair closer to my table.

"Did your boyfriend tell you that?" she asks. "Chief Sloane? What did he say?"

"If I tell you, it can't leave this bakery," I say.

Dina nods with enthusiasm. "Of course not." She makes an X over her chest with her index finger. "Cross my heart and hope to die."

"He said they found traces of peanut oil on some magazines at the cottage. Eric theorizes that Claire left the office, touched the magazines, then returned to the office, and died after she locked the door."

"So, he thinks Claire's death was accidental," she summarizes, smiling. Dina inhales a deep breath, then blows it out. "That's fantastic news! There's no murderer."

"That was as of fifteen minutes ago," I remind her. "As of ten minutes ago, we think there is a murderer."

"Who?"

"What did you and Claire argue about before she died?" I ask, ignoring her question.

"Claire didn't give me any warning before she sent out the social media post saying *Familia* was over," Dina reveals. "It took me by surprise, and I was angry." She sighs. "Just because we argued doesn't mean I killed her."

"Did Claire lock herself in the den to escape the argument?" I ask.

"No," Dina replies, looking me in the eye.

"So, you didn't expose Claire to peanut oil then lock her in the den, forcing her to use a felting needle to pick the lock and save herself?"

Dina sits back and crosses her arms in front of her chest. "How could I, when the only key was inside the den with her?"

"You're the only witness who claims there was only one key," I challenge. "No one else can remember. The cleaner didn't notice how many keys were there. The landlord didn't notice how many keys were there when he inspected the cottage between renters. The previous tenants aren't sure whether there was one key or two because they claim they didn't lock the den during their stay."

"There you go." Dina shrugs. "You can't prove there was a second key."

"You're right," I accede. "But people don't notice things unless they change. If there are always two keys and one key is missing, it would stand out, and the cleaner or the landlord would notice. If both keys were there, neither would notice because nothing was out of place."

Dina shakes her head and laughs. "I don't think your theory will be admissible in court." She lurches forward and puts her forearms on my table, causing me to flinch. From the corner of my eye, April startles behind the counter. "What motive would I have to kill Claire? Why destroy a job I love sooner than I have to?"

"Maybe you were so angry that you weren't

thinking straight," I suggest, hoping to give her an opening to confess. "Or maybe this super-secret contract you and Claire had would be void if she died." I slide my chair back a little in case my next statement tips Dina over the edge. "Or maybe with the rights to *Familia,* you wouldn't have to worry about finding another job."

"I already told you the rights weren't Claire's," she snarls. "Claire and I were friends. We'd worked together since before the first book came out. I wouldn't kill my friend."

"Claire told me you weren't friends," I counter. "If I recall, her exact words were, *we're barely friends*."

"I would *never* put *Familia* at risk." Dina bangs the table with her fist, her face flushed with angry heat. "I love the Familia series just as much as Claire did."

"I think you're lying," I accuse.

"What?" she says through clenched teeth.

"I think you love the Familia series *more* than Claire did." Confusion clouds Dina's face. "Because you're the author and Claire was your assistant."

"You sound ridiculous," she hisses, rolling her eyes and shaking her head. "Utter nonsense."

"Let's look at the facts," I suggest, counting on my fingers. "The author of *Familia* is a needle felter. There is zero evidence Claire was a needle felter, whereas you have needle felting supplies in your backpack." I lower one finger. "Claire studied graphic design, and you have a Master of Fine Arts degree in creative writing." I lower another finger. "Claire never talked about her dream of being a writer until after she released the first

Familia book. You are a lifelong booklover who studied writing." I lower my third finger. "Claire wasn't much of a reader except for gossip magazines. You are a bookworm and always have multiple books and ebooks with you." I lower my fourth finger.

Dina holds up her hands in surrender. "OK, Nancy Drew, you win." She laughs. "I'll admit it. I'm the ghost writer behind the *Familia* books. All of them."

A ghost writer is someone who is paid to write for the named author. Ghost writing is surprisingly common. It's almost always a secret because ghost writers aren't credited for their work, and they sign contracts swearing them to secrecy about what they write and for whom. Fun fact: all the Nancy Drew books were ghost written by different, uncredited authors. The credited author, Carolyn Keene, is a pen name for the many authors who contributed to the series.

"Why?" I ask. "Why didn't you take credit for your own work? You're such a talented writer."

After a deep sigh and contemplative look that makes me think she's not sure how much to tell me, Dina runs her hands through her blonde hair and speaks.

"I was very young when I thought up the idea for the Familia series," she explains. "I wrote the first three books when I was still a teenager. Literary agents wouldn't take me seriously. Most of them didn't believe I was the author because of my age. When I approached Brooks, I lied and told him I worked for the author, so he wouldn't write me off because of my age like everyone else. He liked my books, and I didn't want to ruin it by meeting him in person and having him realize how young I was. So, I hired a lawyer who helped me find and hire Claire. She had the skills to act as my author assistant, and she had the perfect personality to represent the books. We hired her away from your father." Dina touches my hand, and I suppress a wince and fight the urge to yank it away. "I always felt guilty about that. Especially after your father accused us of stealing his idea."

"Did you steal his idea?" I ask.

"No," Dina insists, "and I can prove it. By the time I hired Claire, I had already written the first three books in the series. My series predates your father's idea." She shrugs. "It was an unfortunate coincidence." I slide my hand out from under hers. "Anyway," she says. "The lawyer was the only person who knew about our arrangement. Everything happened so fast after Claire was onboard. Brooks met her and took her on as a client. We got a publishing deal. Then the first book was released, and it was an enormous success. We were stuck. The world believed Claire was the author, and I was her assistant. It terrified us that if we told the truth, the fans might not trust us anymore, and it would ruin *Familia*."

"Claire must have wanted to end your arrangement badly if she announced the end of the Familia series without checking with you first."

"She wanted out for the past couple of years," Dina admits, "but I kept convincing her to stay. Claire started to believe our lie. She wanted to write her own books and publish them under her own name. The woman had written nothing longer than an email, but she knew that because she was Claire Rivera, best-selling author in over twenty countries, whatever she wrote would earn money. She would have published poorly written books and earned money because of the success she had with my writing. She was planning to profit from my hard work. I couldn't let that happen." Dina stops talking, like she realizes she might say something she couldn't take back.

"How did you stop her?" April asks, leaning on the counter, engrossed in Dina's version of events.

She crosses her arms in front of her chest. "You can't prove I killed Claire! Anyway, how could I have killed Claire? I was sitting on the dock when she died. There were eyewitnesses, the neighbours saw me. And I was on the phone with my parents."

"I think you went down to the dock after Claire's anaphylaxis started, or maybe even after she died," I hypothesize. "I think you already laced the magazine pages with peanut oil and left them in the den where Claire would find them. You knew Claire would read them because she loved gossip magazines. When Claire ran into the den and locked the door to escape your argument, she flipped through the pages of at least one magazine and ingested the peanut oil when she licked her fingers to turn the pages. I think you held the door closed from the outside so Claire couldn't escape and save herself. She probably thought the key wasn't working and tried to pick the lock with the felting needle *you* left in the den."

"Oooooh, you're so close," Dina says, her words

laced with a bizarre sense of smug satisfaction. "I sensed Claire was planning to do something drastic to end our arrangement. I bought a bunch of mind-numbing gossip magazines and laced them with peanut oil, just like you said. I scattered them around the cottage when we arrived. I wore gloves when I touched them so they could never be traced back to me. Claire didn't go near the magazines. She kept playing games on her stupid phone and texting her lame friends."

Dina rolls her eyes. "She'd do anything to avoid reading. Anyway, when she posted the social media message that destroyed my career, we had a huge argument. It was nasty, and we both said horrible things. Claire ran into the den to escape and locked the door. After we had time to calm down, I knocked on the door. She didn't answer. I used the second key to let myself in. Claire was in the throes of anaphylaxis. She couldn't speak. She was writhing on the floor, looking at me with desperate, pleading eyes. I told her I would get her EpiPen. I promised I would be right back. I put on latex gloves, took her phone and both keys, and left. I locked the door behind me. I walked around the cottage and gathered up the magazines I'd laced with peanut oil. Then I got the peanut oil from my room. I put my ear up to the den door, and it was silent. I knocked and called her name. Nothing. I unlocked the door.

"I promised myself if Claire was still alive, I would save her. She wasn't. I had to squeeze past the door because she died right behind it. I left her phone and one key on the desk, then removed the peanut-oil-laced magazine she touched. I locked the door behind me with the second key. At the dock, I took off the rubber gloves, placed the key and the small jar of peanut oil inside them, and tied them shut. I skipped rocks while I figured out what to do next. The neighbours came out. We said hi. They went back to their cottage, and while I was throwing rocks, I threw the glove into the lake, then phoned my parents. I wasn't sure how to dispose of the magazines. I decided not to. My fingerprints aren't on them. I made sure I never touched them. The police will never link them to me."

"Yes, we will," Eric says from the doorway between the bakery and kitchen.

He tells Dina that she's under arrest and reads out her rights. Two other officers cuff and search her.

The police escort Dina to a waiting patrol car, and April and I fall into each other's arms. We scold each other for taking risks; her for refusing to leave when I gave her the chance, and me for goading a disturbed killer instead of waiting for the police to arrive.

"Bean! Never scare me like that again!" My dad chastises as he puts his arms around April and me. "I can only handle this much excitement in a book, not my daughter's life!"

"Why are you here? You were supposed to stay with Sophie," I say.

"Would you stay with the corgi if Hannah ran down the street chasing a murderer?" he asks.

He makes a good point.

Eric asks April and me if we're OK, then tells us we need to give statements.

"Well done, Eric!" My dad hugs him, which takes Eric, and the rest of us, by surprise. "Good job, son!"

April, Eric, and I exchange a look in silent agreement never to tell Adam about Mitchell calling Eric, *son*.

"Thank you, sir, but I can't take all the credit. I have a brilliant partner." He winks at me.

CHAPTER 25

MONDAY, April 26th

I trap a crab sashimi with my chopsticks and dip it into the soya sauce before popping it into my mouth.

"I'm glad we finally got to have our sushi lunch," my dad says between salmon-avocado rolls.

"I'm glad you extended your trip for a few days so we could make it happen," I reply.

"I was on a roll," he says, laughing. He holds up a salmon-avocado roll between his chopsticks. "Pardon the pun." I groan at his attempt to be punny. "I didn't want to interrupt my flow by packing up and driving away," he says. "Can you believe I finished the first draft of the next book and submitted it early for a change? They're probably still in shock at my publisher's office." We laugh.

"Whatever the reason, it was nice to have you and Zoe around for a few extra days," I say.

"We might be back sooner than you think. Eric said

if Dina goes to trial, I might have to testify." He sounds excited at the prospect.

"It was just a warning," I tell him. "I've been a witness in more than one murder case since Eric and I met, and I haven't stepped inside a courtroom yet." I shrug one shoulder. My dad lets out a disappointed sigh. "He thinks Dina will take a deal," I say. "The evidence against her is solid."

After Dina confessed, the police searched the lake at the rental cottage and found the latex gloves with the key to the den and the bottle of peanut oil inside. Both the key and the bottle had Dina's fingerprints on them.

When he searched her credit card transactions, Eric discovered where and when Dina purchased the magazines. The store where she bought them provided surveillance video of her purchase to the police.

The cleaner and landlord at the rental cottage confirmed there were no magazines at the cottage prior to Claire's and Dina's arrival. The landlord has a strict rule about removing personal items and food left by previous renters before the new renters arrive. The cleaner confirmed she strictly enforces this rule and removed any trace of the previous renters.

When the cyber crimes unit searched Dina's computer, they found manuscripts for three unpublished *Familia* books. Dina admitted she planned to claim she found the manuscripts after Claire's death. She hoped to convince the publisher to publish them posthumously, extending the life of the Familia book series. Sadly, it's unlikely they'll ever get published now.

The lawyer who helped Dina find and hire Claire to be the credited author of the Familia series provided a copy of their contract to the police. Dina was telling the truth; she was the author, and Claire was her assistant, whose duties included being the credited author of the books and the public face of the series. Claire was well paid for her part in the scheme, and she and Dina shared the rights to the Familia series, with a clause that, in the event of Claire's death, Claire's half of the film rights would revert to Dina. Selling the film rights would have been a complication that neither woman wanted. It would have risked exposing their arrangement.

"If there is a trial, will the British woman fly back to testify?" my dad asks.

"You mean Piper Peters?" I confirm.

He nods. "Yes, the lady with the mourning attire. Such an intriguing persona." He winks. "She might inspire a character in a future book."

"I don't know," I admit. "I'll have to ask Eric. Maybe she could testify over video chat or something."

Piper avoided charges in relation to the break-and-enter at Knitorious in exchange for her immediate departure to England and a signed oath that she won't come back. If she does, she'll face charges for the crimes she committed. Eric was so eager for her to leave that he confirmed with the airline she had boarded her flight.

"What about Claire's agent?" my dad asks, dipping a California roll into some soya sauce. "I hope he faces the consequences of breaking into your store."

"He won't," I tell my dad. "I don't want him to. He didn't hurt anyone or damage anything. I just want to put this entire book fair behind us and move on."

Piper's partner-in-crime, Brooks Wiley, turned himself into police as soon as he heard about Dina's arrest.

True to her word, Jules Janssen and her entourage cooperated with the investigation and provided statements that eliminated Brooks as having any involvement in Claire's death. He wasn't charged with breaking into Knitorious because I asked Eric to let it go; Brooks wasn't a threat to me, and the last thing I want to do is give another statement. He also avoided charges for his role in conspiring with Piper to steal the books because that would require Piper's testimony, and Eric isn't keen to engage her ever again. Last I heard, Brooks was working and travelling with Jules; he's become part of her entourage.

"Are Brooks and the movie star still an item?" my dad asks.

"I have no idea," I admit. "But Adam said she called him to discuss making a movie in Harmony Lake."

I tell my dad how Jules Janssen gave up her pursuit of the *Familia* film rights and, instead, is working on a film inspired by Claire's murder. She contacted Adam to talk to him about filming part of it in Harmony Lake. The film is a fictionalized version of events. They'll change names and places to avoid lawsuits and such. Adam says Jules plans to play the role of Dina. I wonder who will play me?

"I wonder who will play me?" my dad asks; great minds think alike.

"Why would you be in it?" I ask.

He shrugs. "Why wouldn't I?" he answers my question with a question.

I check the time on my phone. "We better get a wiggle on, Dad. Zoe is waiting for you, and if you don't hit the road soon, you'll find yourself driving at night."

"I don't enjoy driving at night," he says, shoving the last piece of sushi in his mouth.

WE WALK BACK to Knitorious because that's where I parked the car, but when we get there, everyone is waiting outside in the parking lot.

"I thought we were leaving from chez Martel?" my dad asks Zoe.

"We were, but I grew tired of waiting for you," she says. "The car is packed, and we have to get on the road. We don't want to stop for the night at a hotel."

"I'm not doing that again." He chuckles. "Last time we ended up in the middle of a murder investigation."

Dad and Zoe take turns saying goodbye to everyone, starting with Sophie, who is excited that her favourite people are all here. Next, they hug and kiss Connie and Archie, then April and Tamara, who give them a box of baked goodies for the road. Next, they move on to Adam. Zoe gives Adam a warm hug and kisses him on the cheek. My dad shakes Adam's hand and pats his shoulder—which is practically a hug—and thanks him again for his help. Zoe gives me a tight squeeze and promises they'll come back before fall. I tell her I'll hold her to it. I thank her for all the cooking and mothering she always squeezes into our visits. She moves onto Eric and gives him a hug and cheek kiss. When my dad hugs me goodbye, he slips a small USB drive into my hand.

"What's this?" I ask, holding up the drive.

"It's the first draft of my next book," he replies.

"But no one gets to read your first draft," I remind him of his own words. "Never."

"I'm making an exception," he says. "You and Eric may read it." He winks. "I can't wait to hear what you think of it."

We wave them off, and after Mitchell and Zoe drive away, we scatter, exhausted from the week's events. Adam goes back to the town hall, April and Tamara return to their bakery, and Connie and Archie go home. Eric and I head upstairs to his apartment.

"Piper was right about one thing," I say, sinking into the leather sofa. "Your peace lily is much happier in its new location." I nod toward the plant that has sprouted blooms since Piper moved it.

"Maybe it would have bloomed on the windowsill," he responds, sitting next to me. "We'll never know."

I hold up the USB drive between us. "Who gets to read it first?" I ask.

He takes the drive from me and looks at it up close. "Let's read it together," he suggests. "Then we'll discover at the same time how your father kills me in his new book." He gets up and retrieves his laptop from the breakfast bar.

"He might not kill you," I say in defence of my dad.

"I interrogated him and told him he was a suspect," Eric reminds me. "I think my literary death is a done deal."

"You also eliminated him as a suspect, caught the real culprit, and love his daughter."

"I planned to ask your dad for permission to propose to you," Eric admits. "But I decided against it."

"Against asking Mitchell's permission, or against proposing?" I tease, knowing it's the former, not the latter.

"Against asking Mitchell," he clarifies. "I know it's traditional to ask the bride's father, but nothing about our relationship or family is traditional. I was asking the wrong person."

"You were," I agree. I'm about to launch into a lecture and tell him I'm a forty-one-year-old woman who makes her own decisions, and he doesn't need anyone's permission to propose to me other than mine.

Before I open my mouth he says, "I need to ask Hannah and Connie."

Sigh. Eric is traditional at heart. He wants to do things right. He's eager for us to get married, but he's waiting for me to be ready, which I'm not. Yet. Soon, though.

"I hope our life goes back to boring now that the book fair is over, and you solved Claire's murder," I say, eager to change the subject.

"You mean, *we* solved Claire's murder," he corrects

me and inserts the USB drive into his computer. "It'll be nice and boring until the next murder." He chuckles.

I swat his arm. "That's not funny," I say. "You'll tempt fate saying stuff like that."

"I'm sure fate would agree that we've solved our share of murders," he reassures me. "I have a feeling life will be wonderfully boring from now on."

I wish I had the same feeling.

EPILOGUE

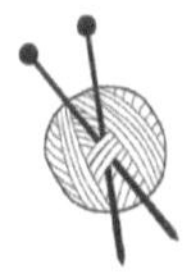

Eric and I finished reading the first draft of my dad's book, *Shark Attack: Fresh Blood*.

Good news: He didn't kill Eric. Bad news: He killed Adam. Again.

The protagonist, Rock Granite, is ready to retire but not ready to give up on capturing Alan Mandell, AKA The Shark. Rock takes on two proteges, Aaron Stone and Michelle Moldavite. Aaron's physique and strength are imposing, and he has experience in personal combat, while Michelle is clever and saves them from dangerous situations by outwitting their opponents. The chemistry between Aaron and Michelle is intense, but they try to ignore it. They have a Springer Spaniel sidekick named Stella.

Aaron and Michelle take up the mantle of hunting The Shark while the retired Rock Granite acts as their mentor and guide. Just like Rock Granite, Aaron and Michelle track down The Shark, and their final confrontation results in The Shark's apparent demise, though his body is not found.

Not only did Mitchell not kill Eric, but he made Eric a hero.

A Knitorious Murder Mystery Book 8

Rest in Fleece

REAGAN DAVIS

COPYRIGHT

Sign up for Reagan Davis' email list to be notified of new releases: www.ReaganDavis.com

ISBN: 978-1-990228-00-1 (ebook)

ISBN: 978-1-7772359-9-4 (print)

FOREWORD

Dear Reader,

Despite several layers of editing and proofreading, occasionally a typo or grammar mistake is so stubborn that it manages to thwart my editing efforts and camouflage itself amongst the words in the book.

If you encounter one of these obstinate typos or errors in this book, please let me know by contacting me at Hello@ReaganDavis.com.

Hopefully, together we can exterminate the annoying pests.

Thank you!

Reagan Davis

CHAPTER 1

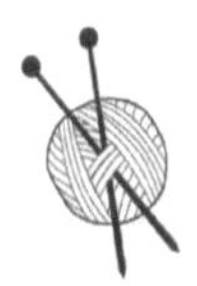

Saturday, June 12th

Shanice Bickerson rules her domain with awe-inspiring efficiency and a blind, three-legged Jack Russell Terrier named Kilian. She has an important job. As head librarian at the Harmony Lake Public Library, Mrs. Bickerson is a pillar of our community and one strand of the fibre that weaves our tight-knit community together.

The Harmony Lake Public Library is a hub of our small town When residents visit the library, they get more than books. Mrs. Bickerson fosters a haven of community, companionship, and offers programs for residents of all ages.

"I'll be right with you, Megan," Mrs. Bickerson says, smiling and holding up her index finger.

"No worries," I reply.

But she doesn't hear me. Mrs. Bickerson's attention is focussed on her husband, Boris Bickerson. They're standing at the periodical shelves. Mr. Bickerson crosses his arms in front of his broad chest and furrows his brow. His bushy mustache twitches when he speaks. Mrs. Bickerson's hands are on her hips, and she's shaking her head at whatever Mr. Bickerson is saying. The Bickersons are bickering.

Leaning against the counter, I pretend to browse the display of community flyers while discreetly monitoring the Bickersons in my peripheral vision.

Mr. Bickerson uncrosses his arms and gesticulates animatedly. Mrs. Bickerson throws up her hands in frustration and walks away while he's mid-sentence. Mr. Bickerson stomps his foot, scoffs, and marches out of the building.

"Sorry about that, Megan," Mrs. Bickerson says with a warm smile. Despite their domestic drama, Mrs. Bickerson remains poised. "How can I help you?" She pats her short, black, curly hair, then corrects her posture and squares her shoulders.

"I have a couple of blankets for you," I respond, smiling and placing a bag on the counter. "I have three today and should have more next week."

Mrs. Bickerson peeks inside the bag. "Wonderful!" she exclaims. "Thank you so much for doing this. The more isolated residents in our community love getting these lap blankets."

"Don't thank me," I insist. "All I do is crochet the squares together. It's The Charity Knitting Guild members who knit the squares and organize everything. I'm just their delivery service."

The Charity Knitting Guild teamed up with the Harmony Lake Public Library for their current project: lap blankets for the Outreach Reading Program. Every week, Mrs. Bickerson gathers books and magazines from the library and visits residents who can't get to the library as often as they'd like. This month, she's giving them a lap blanket with their book of choice.

The charity knitters knit the squares and drop them off at my yarn store, Knitorious. I use some yarn and a crochet hook to crochet the squares together into lap blankets, then drop them off at the library.

"It's wonderful having Hannah here, by the way," Mrs. Bickerson informs me as she stashes the bag of blankets somewhere under the counter. "I'm so happy she's working at the library this summer."

"She's happy to be here," I respond. "Thank you for letting me borrow her until the end of the month." It feels and sounds odd to thank someone for lending me my daughter.

Hannah is almost twenty. She just finished her second year of university in Toronto and is home for the summer. She has a summer job at the library, but Mrs. Bickerson let me borrow her until the end of the month while my two part-time employees sip their way through the vineyards of Italy and France on a wine crawl.

Mrs. Bickerson giggles. "It's the least I can do." She gestures somewhere below the counter. "These blankets mean more than you know to the people who receive them."

Mr. Bickerson stomps back into the library, glances at Mrs. Bickerson, then sneers at Kilian who is resting on a dog bed near the door. Mr. Bickerson huffs, turns, and stomps out again.

I lean over the counter and lower my voice. "Is Mr. Bickerson OK?"

Mrs. Bickerson rolls her eyes and flicks her wrist dismissively. "He's angry about the money I spent on Mysti," she explains. "But she's worth every penny. I get more value from the time I spend with Mysti than Boris gets from the time he spends fishing and listening to stock market podcasts."

"Mysti?" I ask.

"You know," she replies, "the fortune teller who set up a booth at the lakefront?"

"I've seen her around, but I haven't met her," I say.

The town is abuzz about the mysterious fortune teller who arrived here last week. Some people say she's blessed with a gift, and some say she's a con artist whose only gift is separating the residents of Harmony Lake from their money.

"Oh, Megan, you must pay her a visit!"

"Fortune telling isn't my thing…" I start.

"Mysti's gift goes way beyond telling fortunes," Mrs. Bickerson interrupts, her eyes wide with enthusiasm and her voice hopeful. She leans into me. "Mysti can contact the dead," she adds in a whisper.

"Really?" I ask, skeptical and concerned at the same time.

"My parents send messages through her," she whispers, then gives me an exaggerated nod.

Mrs. Bickerson's parents passed away last year, a few months apart, after living long, happy lives. The

Bickersons were their caregivers, and the double loss was hard for Mrs. Bickerson. Their deaths left Mrs. Bickerson with an empty nest. The Bickerson children are adults and out in the world, living their lives. Following her parents' deaths, Mrs. Bickerson transferred her maternal fussing to the library. The town benefits, but I'm not sure Mrs. Bickerson does.

"I'm glad you find comfort in your visits to Mysti." I smile, sympathetic to her situation.

My mother died when I was twenty-one. She died shortly after Hannah was born, when I needed a mother more than ever. Almost twenty years later, I still have moments when I would give anything to see her, hear her voice, or ask her for advice.

I hope Mysti isn't exploiting Mrs. Bickerson's grief for money. But if Mrs. Bickerson finds comfort from the "messages" Mysti gives her, maybe it isn't a waste of money.

"Well," I say, pushing myself off the counter and pulling myself up to my full height, "I should get back. Hannah is alone at the store. I hope you and Mr. Bickerson work things out."

"There's nothing to work out," Mrs. Bickerson says, resolute. "Mysti's gift is priceless. You cannot put a price on the peace of mind she provides."

On my way out, I stop to visit Kilian. When I put my hand in front of his nose, he wags his tail and looks in my direction with his closed eyes, sniffing the air. I tell him he's a good boy, give him a few head rubs and a scratch between the ears.

Today is one of the first summer-like days of the

year. The sun is bright, the air is hot, and a warm breeze blows off the lake. I lower my sunglasses from my head to my face and stroll down Water Street toward Knitorious. The sidewalk is busy with smiling people soaking up the sun and window shopping. On the other side of the street, walkers, joggers, dogs, kids, and strollers dot the lakefront park.

I'm wearing my first sundress of the season. Sundresses are one of my many guilty pleasures. Despite living where it's winter up to six months of the year, I have an extensive sundress collection. Today's selection is an-off-the-shoulder maxi dress with purple and blue flowers.

I'm a few stores away from Knitorious when its door opens.

"Megastar! There you are!" April calls, her impossibly long legs skipping toward me. "Hannah said you went to the library." She hooks her arm through mine.

April likes to come up with nicknames that sound like puns of my actual name.

"I did," I confirm. "And now I'm going back to work."

"Not yet." April grins, veering us off the sidewalk and onto the curb. She looks both ways then drags me, running, across Water street.

"Where are we going?" I ask.

"To find out the future," April replies. "There's a fortune teller reading tarot cards in the park. I thought it would be a laugh!"

I love April. She was my first friend in Harmony Lake. We've been best friends since our daughters were in diapers. We met at a mummy-and-me playgroup when I moved here. Our daughters are best friends too. They attend the same university.

"I have to get back to the store," I protest. "Hannah's been alone for a while…"

"The store is empty," April argues. "Hannah said it's been dead all day. She gave me her blessing to kidnap you for as long as I want."

April takes long strides, and I trot to keep up with her. April is tall, and I am short. We're kindred spirits, but physical opposites. She's blonde, I'm brunette. Her hair is straight, mine is curly. Her eyes are blue, mine are hazel. April has a perpetual tan, and I look anemic. I'm not anemic, I just look that way. April's tall, lean body looks like it just stepped off a runway at a Milan fashion show, while I'm shorter and curvy with round hips, big boobs, and a small waist.

"I'm not wearing any SPF," I declare, worried about my exposed shoulders.

"You'll be fine," April assures me. "She's reading tarot cards under a tree. We'll be in the shade."

"I don't believe in fortune tellers and psychics," I protest.

April shrugs. "It's for fun. It's just entertainment. We won't make major life decisions based on what she tells us."

"Do you believe in supernatural stuff?" I ask.

She shrugs again. "I don't know. I mean, I'm open minded. If that makes sense. On one hand, I like to think there's a plan, and all this"—she gestures around us—"isn't just random chaos. But I also like to think we control our own destinies."

This conversation is too deep for a Saturday morning.

The fortune teller is under a huge sugar maple tree. She has a large blanket laid out with a crystal ball, tarot cards, and crystals placed around the perimeter in a circle. A handwritten sign leans against the tree.

MYSTI CALLY ~ SPIRITUAL HEALER ~ GUIDE ~ SOOTHSAYER

"Is that Mr. Bickerson?" April asks, lifting her sunglasses and squinting to confirm her sighting.

"Looks like it," I reply. "I saw him at the library earlier, and he was wearing the same outfit. And his moustache is twitching like when he was bickering with Mrs. Bickerson."

"I'd never guess he's into predicting the future and having his tarot cards read," April observes.

"He's not," I confirm.

I tell her about the heated exchange between Mr. and Mrs. Bickerson, and Mrs. Bickerson's confession that they argued about how much money Mrs. Bickerson spends on Mysti.

We keep a respectable distance and watch their interaction from the shade of a nearby oak tree. They seem oblivious to us, and their discussion appears to escalate into a disagreement. The longer they talk, the more exaggerated their facial expressions become, and their body language grows increasingly defensive. Both parties have their arms crossed in front of them and only uncross them to point or gesture at the other person.

Mr. Bickerson takes an aggressive step toward Mysti and enters her personal space. She seems intimidated and backs up. He steps forward again.

"Is everything OK here?" April shouts, taking long strides to bridge the gap between the shade of our oak tree and the shade of their sugar maple.

I hustle to catch up to her, like a toddler chasing their mother.

"I was just telling this charlatan that the residents of this town don't appreciate her and her con-artist trickery setting up shop here," Mr. Bickerson booms.

"I think she got the message," I say, smiling.

"I doubt it," Mr. Bickerson says, then looks at April and me. "I'd advise you ladies to keep an eye on your wallets." He takes a deep breath and lets it out. "Have a pleasant afternoon."

April and I say goodbye to Mr. Bickerson's back as he storms away.

"Are you OK?" April asks Mysti.

"I'm fine." Mysti's trembling hands say otherwise. "Some people don't like the messages they receive." She shrugs. "But I can't control what the spirits tell me. I'm just the messenger."

We sit on Mysti's blanket, inside the crystal circle, and decide April will go first. While Mysti shuffles her deck of tarot cards and recites some kind of incantation under her breath, I take in our surroundings. A woman on a nearby bench is reading a book. Her gorgeous sundress catches my attention. It's flowy and a beautiful vivid yellow. The wide brim of her straw sunhat hides her face. She's also wearing sunglasses. I can't distinguish her features. Her nails are the same shade of yellow as her dress. Admiring her dress, I realize the sundress isn't the only thing catching my interest. She's wearing a wide-brimmed sunhat and sunglasses *in the shade*. And she hasn't turned the page of her book the entire time I've been watching. It's odd. It's almost like she's trying to go unnoticed, but she's trying so hard, it's backfiring and making her stand out.

"Earth to Megatron," April says, bringing me back to the here and now. "It's your turn. Mysti wants you to shuffle the deck."

"Right," I say, picking up the oversized cards. "Sorry, my mind wandered."

The cards are too large for my hands, but I attempt to shuffle them before handing them back to Mysti.

"It's not really about the shuffling," Mysti explains, taking the cards and giving them a proper shuffle. "It's more about you having contact with the cards so they can absorb your energy." She smiles.

Mysti is pretty. She has long, light brown, wavy hair and small freckles spray the bridge of her nose. Her brown eyes and smile are warm. Unlike Mr. Bickerson, I don't pick up a dishonest or predatory vibe. She seems timid and vulnerable to me. The word *lonely* comes to mind. I'd guess she's in her late twenties, but her high-pitched, child-like voice makes her sound younger and adds to her air of vulnerability.

Mysti lays out three cards: The Page of Cups, The Tower, and Death.

At first glance, my future doesn't look very optimistic.

"The page is a young man," Mysti interprets, pointing to the first card. "Pages are messengers. This young man will bring you a message."

"A good message or a bad message?" April asks, fully immersed in the experience.

Mysti points to the tower card next to the page of cups and makes eye contact with me. "A message that will turn your world upside down and shake you to your foundation."

"Sounds ominous," I respond.

"Not necessarily," Mysti says. "Sometimes good news rocks our world too. And sometimes something that seems negative at first turns out to be a blessing in disguise."

So much wisdom from one so young.

"What about the death card?" I ask, nodding toward it.

"The death card rarely signifies a literal death," she explains with a chortle. "The death card usually portends a transition from one state to another. Something ends so something new can begin."

"But it can signify an actual death, right?" April clarifies.

"It can," Mysti replies, then looks at me. "But you have to consider the cards around it. A young man will give you a message that will turn your world upside down, and things will never be the same. I can't say if the change will be good or bad."

"When can I expect this young man to bring me this message?" I ask.

Mysti shrugs. "Sooner than you think."

CHAPTER 2

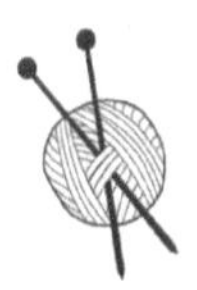

"IT WAS VAGUE. It could mean anything," I say to April in response to her enthusiasm about a mysterious young man showing up any second with a life-changing message. "This is how they operate. My fortune could apply to anyone. About anything. It's a setup, so the next time I talk to any young man, and he tells me anything, I'll believe Mysti's prediction came true and rush back to her with more money."

"She seemed sincere, Megnolia," April insists, opening the door to Knitorious and gesturing for me to go ahead of her. "I'm not saying it's true, I'm suggesting we keep our minds open to the possibility."

"Hey, Hannah Banana," I say to my daughter who's standing behind the counter. I scan the floor around my feet, expecting to find a dog clamouring for my attention. "Where's Sophie?"

Sophie is my corgi. She comes to work with me.

"Eric picked her up. They went to the dog park,"

Hannah replies. "He said to tell you they won't be long."

Eric Sloane is my boyfriend, dog walker, and the chief of our local police department.

"Was it busy?" I ask, stashing my purse under the counter.

"Other than Aunt April and Eric, only one person came in."

"Do you want to take your lunch?" I ask.

Hannah shakes her head and raises her eyebrows like she knows a secret.

When she shakes her head, her long curls bounce and sway around her shoulders. Hannah has my hair, except her curls are tighter. She also has my eye shape, but her green eyes are a blend of my hazel eyes and her dad's blue eyes. Lucky for her, Hannah inherited some height from her dad, so she's a couple of inches taller than me. We have the same fair skin, and similar hourglass figures. She can thank both of us for her sarcastic sense of humour. I like to take credit for her resourcefulness and intelligence.

"Someone is waiting to see Eric," Hannah says. "He got here a few minutes ago."

April pokes my rib. "A mysterious man," she whispers. "The Page of Cups."

I give the empty store a cursory glance. "Where is he?"

"He's in the back." Hannah jerks her head toward the backroom. "I thought the fewer people who see him the better."

"Why?" I ask.

"You'll see," she replies.

"Did you text Eric?" I ask.

"Not yet. I wanted to wait for you."

April sighs. "I should get back to the bakery."

April and her wife, Tamara, own Artsy Tartsy, the local bakery. Tamara is a talented pastry chef, and her creations are locally famous. They spoil me with treats.

"I should talk to the mystery man." April and I hug. "Thanks for the glimpse into our futures."

"Aunt April," Hannah blurts out. "You should go with Mum."

Now I'm equal parts concerned and curious. What the heck is going on?

"Do you have time?" I ask April.

"I do now," April replies, her curiosity piqued.

"Maybe Mysti's prediction is coming true," April whispers when we're almost at the door that separates the store from the backroom and kitchenette.

"Doubtful," I whisper in response.

A young man wearing a baseball cap sits at the table in the kitchenette. His head is lowered, and he's focussed on his cell phone. Because of his brimmed cap, I can't make out his face.

"Hi there," I say.

The young man's head jolts up from his phone. Our eyes meet. I hitch my breath to stop a gasp from escaping me and reach out, clutching April's forearm to steady myself. Blinking, I do a double take, stunned by the young man sitting in front of me.

"Holy smokes," April mutters under her breath, "they're identical."

I acknowledge her remark with a barely discernible nod.

"Hi. I'm Jaxon Squires." The young man stands up and takes off his green baseball cap. "You can call me Jax."

Even their voices sound hauntingly similar.

Speechless, I reach out by instinct and shake his extended hand. When he smiles, my knees feel like they might give out. Jaxon Squires is the spitting image of Eric. The resemblance is undeniable. He has Eric's brown hair and eyes, complete with honey-coloured flecks, and Eric's smile. This is what Eric would have looked like twenty years ago. They're even the same height and have the same muscular build. *What's going on? Who is this boy?*

"Megan," I mumble, pulling my hand back. April touches my back reassuringly. I clear my throat. "I'm Megan Martel." I introduce myself in a clearer voice, and plaster a smile on my face. "What can I do for you, Jax?"

"The lady at the library said I might find Eric Sloane here," Jax replies with a nervous chuckle. He rubs the back of his neck the same way Eric does when he's nervous or embarrassed. "I went to the police station, but they said he's not working today. I didn't want to leave a message, so I tried the library." He shrugs. "I thought they might have a town directory or something with Eric's address. The librarian said I should try here."

I pull out a chair and sit at the small table, gesturing for Jax to join me. April joins us, too, sitting in the chair beside me. At a loss for words, I can't stop staring at this Eric-identical young man.

"Is Eric expecting you?" April asks, taking the conversational reins while I compose myself and recover from the shock.

"I doubt it," Jax replies. "We've never met." He wipes his palms on his denim-covered thighs and does his nervous chuckle again. "In fact, I'm pretty sure he doesn't know I exist."

"Why are you looking for him?" I ask, afraid I already know the answer.

"Eric Sloane is my father."

I inhale deeply and hold it. Jax's phone dings, and he looks at it. His facial muscles tense as he reads the screen.

"Is everything OK, Jax?" April asks.

Thank goodness she's here to be my voice when I can't speak.

"Yeah. Kind of," he replies. "A friend of mine is having an issue." He scans the room and nods toward the back door. "Can I use that door? I just want to call my friend to make sure everything's OK." He stands up.

"Of course," I say. "I'll text Eric while you're gone."

"So, I came to the right place?" Jax's eyes brighten with enthusiasm. "Awesome. Thank you. I'll be right back." He smiles.

"Eric has a son?" April hisses when the back door shuts with a thud.

"He's never mentioned it," I respond. "April, if Eric has a son, I don't think he knows."

"The resemblance is incredible. They could be..."

"Father and son?" I ask, finishing her sentence.

"I was going to say twins," she says. "But there's your page of cups and your tower."

She's right. This mysterious young man brought me a life-changing message.

I unlock my phone and text Eric.

Me: There's someone at Knitorious to see you.

Eric: Who?

Me: Jaxon Squires.

Eric: I don't know him. Work or personal?

Me: He says he's your son.

Eric: On my way.

The dog park is a ten-minute walk from here. If they run, they'll be here in five.

I place my phone on the table and take a deep, cleansing breath. *Heavy shoulders, long arms,* I remind myself, then take another deep breath. Heavy shoulders, long arms is a mantra I learned at a yoga class in my twenties. It helps release the tension in my neck and shoulders when I'm stressed.

"Are you OK, Megnificent?" April cups my cold, trembling hand in her warm, steady hand.

"A bit shaky and nauseous," I reply. "And curious. I have so many questions."

"Not as many as Eric, I bet."

April gets me a glass of water while I peek my head into the store to make sure it's not busy and Hannah can cope on her own. She's talking to a couple of knitters who are knitting in the cozy sitting area. I close the door to the store and make sure it clicks. It's difficult enough to keep anything private in this town, without having our family dramas unfold at the store during business hours.

We sit in silence, and I sip my water.

"It's been a few minutes since Jax left," April observes. "Should I check on him?"

I nod, unsure if I hope he's there or hope he had second thoughts and left.

"He's there," April confirms, closing the back door quietly. "It sounds like he's finishing his call."

I nod, both relieved and disappointed.

"Maybe we should take Jax upstairs." She gestures to the stairs that lead to the upstairs apartment. "They'll have more privacy up there."

I open my mouth to agree with April when the back-door and store door open simultaneously.

Both men enter the room at the same time. They lock eyes and freeze, stunned by the future and past versions of themselves. An eerie Twilight Zone tension fills the room.

Silence.

Oblivious to the thick fog of tension blanketing the room, Sophie trots in and breaks the silence by lapping water from her bowl, the metal tag on her collar clanging against the metal rim of the bowl. Water drips from her chin when, tail wagging, she prances over to greet me.

"Hey, Soph," I whisper, stooping down to pet her.

"You must be Jaxon." Eric speaks first.

Jax nods. "Eric?"

Eric nods and steps forward. Jax steps forward too, and they shake hands.

"Maybe you and Jax should talk upstairs," I suggest quietly to Eric.

"Good idea," April adds. "I'll take Sophie and help Hannah in the store."

"Don't you have to get back to the bakery?" I ask.

"Nope," April assures me as she walks past me to the door. "No way. Not until after." She opens the door and whistles for Sophie. They disappear into the store, closing the door behind them.

She means after I give her an update. I don't blame her. If our roles were reversed, I wouldn't leave, either.

I touch Eric's arm. He looks at me, and I take the leash and dog toy he's holding.

"If you need me, I'll be in the store." I place the leash and toy on the counter.

"Do you mind if Megan comes with us?" Eric asks, looking at Jax. "She's my partner, and I'd like her to be there."

"Sure." Jax shrugs. A micro-expression of comprehension flashes across his face, and his eyes brighten. "Wait!" He points to me and smiles. "You're my stepmum? I've never had a stepmum before."

"I've never been a stepmum before," I respond, trying but failing to match his enthusiasm.

"Does that mean the girl in the store is my sister?" he asks.

"No," I reply, shaking my head. "Hannah's father and I are divorced."

"Oh, right," Jax responds.

Eric gestures for me to go ahead of him. The three of us climb the stairs in silence except for the fourth step, which creaks when each of us steps on it.

CHAPTER 3

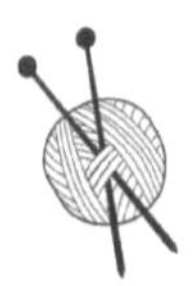

While Eric invites Jax to have a seat, I open the fridge and offer him a drink. There aren't many options because we don't eat or drink here anymore. Before he moved in with me, this was Eric's apartment. The apartment is still furnished, but his personal belongings are gone. The space feels soulless now, like a collection of furniture instead of a home. We should find a new tenant. Now isn't the time to think about that. Focus, Megan.

Jax says yes to a diet soda. I take two cans from the fridge, one for him and one for me.

"Thank you," Jax says when I hand him the can.

The leather chair creaks when he leans forward to place the can on the coffee table. The leather sofa wheezes as I sink into it beside Eric. He shifts closer to me until our arms and thighs touch. His body is tense and rigid, like he's ready for something to happen. He reaches into a nearby drawer and pulls out a small notebook and pen. One of his cop notebooks. He finds a blank page, clicks the top of the pen with his thumb and positions the pen, poised to write.

"Who's your mother, Jax?" Eric asks, using his cop voice. "First name, maiden name, and date of birth."

"Jax isn't a witness you're interrogating," I remind him just above a whisper. "He's a young man looking for his biological family."

"Right." Eric clicks the pen again, and closes his notebook, leaving them on the arm of the sofa.

"It's cool that you're a cop," Jax says. "I want to be a firefighter. I took a firefighting and fire systems program. I just graduated, and I have a few interviews lined up with fire departments in nearby towns."

"Near Harmony Lake, or nearby where you live?" I ask.

"Near Harmony Lake," Jax replies, "so we can get to know each other."

I nod. "You just graduated from college?" Jax nods. "Congratulations. So, that would make you… twenty-one, twenty-two?" I probe.

"I turned twenty-two last month," he replies.

Eric's gaze shifts to the distance, and I can tell he's doing mental math. If Jax is twenty-two, and Eric is thirty-nine, Jax was conceived when Eric was…. SIXTEEN!? Oh my. I sip my diet soda and swallow hard. Beside me, Eric's body and posture relax. He lets out a sigh of either relief or disappointment. I hand him my can of diet soda, and he takes a sip, then hands it back to me.

I sit in silence, sipping my soda while Eric and Jax talk. Jax is from Nova Scotia, a province on Canada's east coast. His maternal grandparents, however, are from a small town on Prince Edward Island, another province on the east coast. His maternal grandparents live in the same small town Eric is from. Jax tells Eric his mother's name and a bit about his childhood.

His parents live in Nova Scotia. His mum and stepdad raised him. He grew up believing his stepfather was his biological father. He has two younger sisters.

"When did your parents tell you about your biological father?" Eric asks.

"They didn't," Jax replies. "We visited my grandparents when I was eighteen, and someone in their town called me Eric. They said I was the spitting image of you and asked me if I was a Sloane," he explains. "Everything made sense. We never visited my grandparents, they always visited us. I'm sure my parents didn't want anyone to see me and figure it out. The only reason we went when I was eighteen was because my grandpa had a heart attack. Also, I look nothing like my dad or my sisters. And there are no photos of my parents together before I was a few months old. I found you on the internet, and now that I see you in the flesh, I know you're my father."

"Your parents know you're here, right?" Eric asks.

Jax shakes his head. "They think I found a summer job planting trees in Quebec." He must see the worried expressions on our faces because he quickly adds, "I didn't tell them because I don't want them to feel bad. I had a great childhood. I love my dad, and I don't want him to think I looked for you because I was unhappy, or he was a terrible father."

"I need to speak to your mother," Eric says.

Jax nods. "Should I phone her?"

"If you don't mind," Eric points down the hall. "You can go into the bedroom and speak to her in private."

Jax stands up and takes a deep breath. He taps his phone screen, puts the phone to his ear, and walks down the hall. We listen for the bedroom door to close.

"Babe, he's not mine!" Eric blurts out as soon as the door shuts. "I've been dying to tell you since Jax told us his age and his mum's name, but I think it's best if she explains it to him." He lets out a sigh, rubbing his temples with his thumb and forefinger. His shoulders slump.

Is he disappointed? Is Eric sad Jax isn't his son? Eric always insisted he never wanted kids. But maybe, faced with the possibility of being a father, he's having second thoughts.

"Umm... you looked at him, right?" I ask, worried Eric is in denial. "He looks like you went for a swim in the fountain of youth."

"That means nothing." Eric waves away my statement. "We all look the same."

"We, who?" I ask.

"Me and my brothers," he replies. "We're practically identical. People confuse us all the time."

It never occurred to me that Jax could be Eric's nephew and not his son. Eric is the middle of three brothers. And he's right, they all look very similar.

"Do you know Jax's mum?" I ask.

Eric nods, swallowing the last of my diet soda. "Her parents live down the street from my parents." He puts the empty can on the coffee table. "Jason and Jax's mum were in the same year at school. They had a fling the summer after they graduated."

My turn to do some mental math. Eric's older brother, Jason, is a year older than Eric. If Jax turned twenty-two last month—and assuming he was born after a full-term pregnancy—he would have been conceived in August of the year Jason finished high school. The timing works.

"I swear, babe, I was never intimate with Jax's mother," Eric says as if he can read my mind. "I was a gawky sixteen-year-old, I wasn't intimate with anyone. Jax is Jason's son. To be honest, his existence isn't a huge surprise. Him showing up here, thinking I'm his father, is the surprise."

"Really?" I ask, recalling Eric's surprised expression when he saw Jax for the first time.

Eric nods. "Jax's mum went away to university. Soon after she left, there were rumours she was pregnant. Jason contacted her and asked her if she was pregnant and if it was his. She denied it. The rumours died down. Then we heard rumours she had a baby. Jason told our parents about their fling, and our parents knocked on her parents' door. They insisted the baby wasn't Jason's. They said she met someone at university, and it was his. But we always wondered."

"Wow," I respond, rubbing his slumped shoulder.

I'm about to ask him how he feels about Jax not being his son, when the bedroom door opens.

"Eric." Jax appears in the doorway, holding out his cell phone. "My mum wants to talk to you."

Eric squeezes my knee and stands up with a sigh. He takes Jax's phone and disappears into the bedroom, closing the door.

The leather chair moans when Jax drops himself into it. He picks up his can of soda and takes a swig.

"I guess you're not my stepmum, after all," Jax says after swallowing the soda.

"No, but I'm excited to have a new nephew," I say, trying to reassure him.

"I feel like such an idiot." He shakes his head. "I was so sure Eric was my father."

"You were close," I console him. "Did your mum tell you who your father is?"

Jax nods. "Jason."

"How are your parents?" I ask. "They must be shocked."

"My dad's not home. He's driving my sister somewhere," Jax explains. "My mum is shocked. The three of us are going to talk tonight. She's not mad though."

"I'm sure all of you will get through this," I assure him. "Jax, where are you staying in Harmony Lake?"

He finishes his soda and crushes the can with one hand. "A place near the highway called the Hav-a-Nap motel. Have you heard of it?"

I nod. "I have. Nice place. But we have a spare room..."

Jax smiles and shakes his head. "That's nice of you, Megan, but I'm staying with a friend as a kind of favour. I don't want to go back on my word."

"I get it," I respond. "I'll give you my number. If you want a hot meal or anything, call me." I hold out my hand and wait for Jax to hand me his phone so I can put in my information.

"Eric has my phone," he reminds me, pointing toward the bedroom.

I reach for the notebook and pen Eric left on the arm of the sofa and write my number on a blank page. I tear out the page and hand it to Jax.

"Your mum wants a quick word before she hangs up," Eric says, entering the living room and thrusting the phone toward Jax.

"How did it go?" I ask Eric when Jax closes the bedroom door.

"I have to call Jason and tell him about Jax," Eric replies. "I'm not looking forward to it."

"I'm sorry," I say, unsure if I'm sorry Eric has to be the bearer of shocking news, or if I'm sorry he doesn't have a son.

He puts his hands on my waist and pulls me toward him, kissing my forehead. "Thank you for your support. I love you."

When Jax returns, I excuse myself to check on the store and leave them alone to talk.

"ARE YOU A STEPPARENT?" April asks when I walk into the store.

"I'm an aunt," I reply.

I tell her about the revelation that all Sloanes look alike, and Jax is Eric's nephew, not his son.

"Eric must be relieved," April comments.

"I think so?" I say, uncertain.

"You *think* so? What does that mean?"

"I don't know," I admit. "Eric was either relieved or disappointed. I couldn't tell. He kind of... deflated when he realized Jax was his nephew."

"I'm sure it was a relief," April says. "Eric is happily child-free. He's been adamant about not having kids. He wants to focus on his career."

"I know," I agree, "but I sense regret." I shake my head and pull myself out of my thoughts. "Where's Hannah?"

"I sent her home," April replies. "I hope that's OK. It was dead in here, and she missed her lunch. Also, she's excited about her date with Lucas tonight, so I told her to go home and get ready."

Lucas Butler is Hannah's boyfriend. He's a rookie cop with the Harmony Lake Police Department.

"It's fine," I say. "I would've done the same thing."

April pulls out a bag from under the counter.

"One of the charity knitters dropped this off." She places the bag on the counter. "She said you'll know what to do with it."

I open the bag. More knitted squares for lap blankets. Without counting, I'd say there's enough here for two blankets.

"Thank you for watching the store, and for taking care of me when I was in shock. You're a good friend."

She hugs me tight. "You'd do the same for me, Megawatt."

"Tell T I'm sorry I commandeered you for the afternoon."

T is what we call April's wife, Tamara.

"It's fine. Both kids are working at the bakery today anyway, so it's not like she was short-staffed."

April and Tamara have two kids, Rachel, who is Hannah's best friend, and Zach, a sixteen-year-old hockey player with a mammoth-sized appetite.

April leaves, and a little while later, Jax leaves too. He pops into the store to say goodbye on his way out.

The store isn't busy, but it's steady. Two customers ask me about the rumour that a young version of Eric is roaming around town, looking for Eric. I'm not surprised. This is a small-town hazard. Everyone knows everyone else's business, and secrets are almost impossible to keep.

I don't confirm or deny anything. Instead, I feign ignorance and say, "Hmmm. That's interesting. Let me know if you find out anything."

CHAPTER 4

SUNDAY, June 13th

"Wow," Adam says, whisking the hollandaise sauce. "I can't imagine not knowing Hannah existed until she was twenty-two years old. This must be hard for Jason."

"I know, right?" I agree, sautéing the fiddleheads.

Fiddleheads are a local spring vegetable. They're a cross between asparagus, okra, and green beans. They often grow in the wild and are only available for a few short weeks each year.

Adam is my ex-husband and Hannah's dad. When we split up, we started a tradition of having Sunday breakfast together. It was a way for us to spend family time with Hannah while she was at university, but we continue the tradition when she's home for summers and holidays too. When she's at school, Hannah joins us by video call, and when she's home, she joins us in person. We alternate between my house and Adam's condo, but he always cooks. Adam learned to cook when he moved out, and I'm thrilled to let him do it after I did all the cooking during our twenty-year marriage.

"Morning, Dad," Hannah says, kissing Adam's cheek.

"Good morning, Princess," Adam says. "You didn't have to dress up for us," he teases.

She's not dressed up, just less casual than her usual Sunday morning attire of jammies and a messy bun.

"I'm not dressed up, and it's not for you," Hannah justifies. "Lucas is picking me up later. I'm going with him to look at apartments." She smiles.

Adam does not smile. He pinches his thick, dark brows together and narrows his blue eyes. He's beating the hollandaise sauce so hard you'd think it insulted his mother.

This is Hannah's first adult relationship. Adam is struggling with not being the only man in her life.

To distract from her father's reaction, I ask Hannah to set the table. When she leaves the kitchen, I take the fiddleheads off the stove and whisper to Adam, "Your disapproval is showing. Maybe you can tuck it in."

He grunts in acknowledgement.

I ignore Adam's reaction, intent on not arguing with him.

"Ready?" I ask cheerily in my normal tone of voice.

"Ready," Hannah and Adam say in unison.

As we settle in for a yummy breakfast of eggs benedict and sauteed fiddleheads, Hannah asks me where Sophie is.

"Eric took her to the dog park," I reply. "Again. It

seems to be their new favourite place."

Hannah smirks and pushes her fiddleheads around her plate.

"How does Eric feel about his new nephew?" Adam asks.

I shrug. "I think he's still processing it. He hasn't said much since he talked to his brother yesterday."

Adam and I are still close. When our marriage ended, we were determined to keep our family intact and be friends. We still love each other, but not the romantic way spouses should. We forged a new friendship based on our shared past and mutual love for our daughter. Despite this, I don't share with him my suspicion that Eric is disappointed Jax isn't his son.

"I'll call Eric later. See if he wants to go golfing to take his mind off it," Adam suggests between mouthfuls.

"Good idea," I agree.

Yes, my ex-husband and boyfriend are friends. And yes, it's weird sometimes. Eric was new in town and didn't know anyone. Adam didn't have any friends here because he was a workaholic who spent most of his time at his office in the city. He was a senior partner at a large law firm, but since we split up, he left the firm and opened a practice in Harmony Lake. We spend more time together divorced than we did married. Adam is our town's only lawyer, and as of earlier this year, he's also the mayor. He and Eric bonded over a mutual love of golf, and the rest is history. Their friendship is another non-traditional piece of our modern family.

"Lucas and I are going to a bonfire tonight," Hannah adds. Adam rolls his eyes at the mention of Lucas's name, but Hannah doesn't notice because she's focused on cutting her egg. "We can invite Jax to come with us. He can meet some people." She shrugs.

"That's thoughtful, sweetie. Thank you." I smile.

"Did you tell Connie about Jax?" Hannah asks.

Connie is my surrogate mother and Hannah's surrogate grandmother. She took us under her wing when we moved to Harmony Lake. She's the original owner of Knitorious, and now that I own the store, she works for me part-time. Connie is getting wine-drunk in Italy and France with her friends until the end of the month. She sends us daily texts with photos from her European adventures.

I shake my head. "I'm waiting until the DNA results are back," I explain. "You know how Connie is, she'll worry. I don't want to interfere with her trip. She's looked forward to this tour for months."

"Do you think Jax will stay in Harmony Lake now that Eric isn't his father?" Hannah asks.

"I'm not sure," I answer honestly. "He has interviews lined up with local fire departments, but I don't know if this will change his plans."

"Is Jason planning to meet Jax soon?" Adam asks.

"Jason and his wife are flying in sometime this week," I tell them. "They have to make childcare arrangements and book time away from their jobs. Eric said Jason will let us know when they confirm their travel plans."

"Will they stay at chez Martel?" Hannah asks.

Chez Martel is the nickname for our house. Adam is French, so at the time it seemed fitting.

"We think they'll be more comfortable in the apartment above the store," I explain. "They'll have more privacy, and it'll give them somewhere to spend time with Jax."

"Makes sense," Adam comments.

I tell them Eric and I are going to the apartment later today to give it a thorough cleaning and stock the kitchen and washroom with some essentials before Jason and his wife arrive.

"I hope Jax is a real Sloane and doesn't just look like one after all the trouble you're going to," Hannah comments.

"Jason ordered a DNA test," I disclose. "They'll ship one swab to chez Martel and the other to Jason PEI. He ordered it with overnight shipping. Jax's swab should arrive today."

PEI is short for Prince Edward Island, Canada's eastern-most and smallest province.

We finish eating, and Adam and I pour ourselves a second cup of coffee when Hannah's phone chimes.

"Something came up and Lucas is running late," she announces with a slight pout. She puts her phone on the table and takes a deep breath. "Can I ask you something?"

We nod.

"You know how the apartment above Knitorious is just sitting there? Empty?"

"Yes," I reply with a nod.

Under his breath, Adam mutters, "No way," like he knows what she's about to say.

Hannah either doesn't hear him or ignores his comment.

"Would you consider renting it to Lucas?" she pleads. "He's been searching for a decent apartment for months. There's, like, no rental housing in Harmony Lake aside from vacation rentals, and everything else is too far from work. He commutes for, like, an hour. One way." She lays out her argument like a lawyer. She is her father's daughter.

I look at Adam. He looks at me. His jaw is tense, and he's flaring his nostrils. He doesn't like this conversation.

"We'll think about it," I tell her.

"Think about what?" Hannah asks. "You have an empty apartment, and Lucas is a rent-paying tenant. He's a cop, so the store would be safer with him there," she argues. "You and Dad own the apartment, so it's not like you have to ask anyone."

Actually, I own the store and the apartment. I also own the house—now with Eric—and Adam owns his condo and the law practice. I own both cars, and our investments are still joint. It's complicated. Sometimes I find it confusing, so I can see why Hannah is confused. It's difficult to divide assets after a long marriage, so we left most of them commingled for the sake of simplicity.

"Eric's stuff is still in the apartment, Princess," Adam says. "Let us think about it, and we'll talk to you and Lucas about it soon."

"Thank you," Hannah says, standing up. "I'm going to finish getting ready."

"Leave it, sweetie. We'll take care of it," I say when she motions to pick up her plate.

After a quick peck on the cheek for each of us, Hannah disappears, and moments later, her bedroom door closes with a dull bang.

"We're losing her, Meg," Adam says with a heavy sigh.

"We aren't losing her, Adam. She's growing up. She still needs us, she just needs us differently," I say, not sure if I'm trying to convince myself or him.

"Lucas monopolizes her time. And he's too old for her. She's too young to be this serious about a *boy*."

He spits out the word *boy* like it leaves an unpleasant taste in his mouth.

"My dad said the same things about you," I remind him.

"She shouldn't be helping him find an apartment. At her age, she should have fun with her friends and hang out at the lake."

"Hannah and Lucas are the same age you and I were when we got married," I point out.

Hannah will be twenty in August, and Lucas just turned twenty-three; the same ages Adam and I were on our wedding day.

Adam freezes and looks up for a second. I'm sure he's doing the math, intent on proving me wrong.

"It's not the same thing, Meg, and you know it." He sips his coffee.

"I know you aren't happy about Hannah and

Lucas's relationship, but she's an adult, and we can't choose her partner," I say. "It would help if you could be supportive."

"I don't like him," Adam insists.

"You don't know him," I counter. "The four of us should have dinner together."

Adam's eyes narrow, and he taps his fingers on the table. "Clever, Meg," he says. "Maybe if you, me, and Eric have dinner with Hannah, we can convince her that Lucas isn't right for her..."

"No," I interject, waving my hands. "That's not what I mean, and you know it. I mean you, me, Hannah, and Lucas should have dinner together. We'll take them to a restaurant. Somewhere neutral. We can get to know him, and he can get to know us."

"Can Eric come?" Adam asks.

"No." I shake my head.

"Why not?"

"You know why not," I reply. "Eric is Lucas's boss and the chief of police."

"Exactly," Adam says.

"You're the mayor, which is intimidating enough. We want Lucas to feel comfortable, not threatened."

"*You* don't want him to feel threatened," Adam mumbles, rolling his eyes.

"Pardon?" I say, pretending I didn't hear him.

"Nothing," he mumbles.

"Try to treat Lucas the way you wish my dad treated you."

"Fine," Adam cedes with a sigh. "We'll have dinner, and I'll keep an open mind."

CHAPTER 5

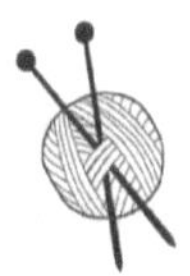

WE ZIP along the highway between Harmony Lake and Harmony Hills. The day is bright and clear. Eric and I are on our way home to Harmony Lake to drop off some essentials we picked up for the apartment.

Harmony Lake is a tiny town and doesn't have the same amenities as larger towns. We don't have big-box stores, chain restaurants, or a movie theatre, for example.

"How's Jax today?" I ask. "Have you spoken to him?"

"We exchanged a couple of texts. He seems fine," Eric replies. "We're going to meet after dinner to do the DNA swab."

"Why don't you invite him for dinner?" I suggest, looking through the window and admiring the cloudless blue sky against the mountains.

I don't mind making trips back and forth to Harmony Hills. I'd rather live in my picturesque, cozy town than in the suburbs any day. Harmony Lake is on the south side of the Harmony Hills mountain range. We're sandwiched between the mountains and the lake. There's no room for expansion, but nature gave us the perfect setting for a tourism-based economy. Tourists flock to Harmony Lake in the summer to be near the lake, and they flock to us in the winter to ski, snowboard, and skate.

Right now, we're on the cusp of tourist season; the tourists are just trickling into town. After the July long weekend, throngs of city-escapees will descend on Harmony Lake until Labour day.

"I don't think that's a good idea, babe," Eric replies.

"Why not?"

"Because we don't know him. He's a stranger who literally showed up out of nowhere twenty-four hours ago."

"He's your nephew," I remind him.

"That doesn't mean he's a good person," Eric explains. He places a hand on my knee. "I know you want everyone to feel welcome and included, and I love that about you, but we don't know Jax. I'm uncomfortable with him having that kind of access to you and Hannah. We should get to know him better before we welcome him into our home."

Now would be a bad time to tell him I already offered Jax our guest bedroom and told him to call me if he wants a home-cooked meal.

"OK," I agree, smiling.

"I'll run his name when I get to the office tomorrow, and we'll take it from there."

Eric's phone rings. His car has Bluetooth, so he

answers it hands free, and the caller's voice echoes through the car's speaker system.

It's dispatch. There's a dead body at the Hav-a-nap motel.

"That's where Jax is staying," I say. "Oh my god, Eric! What if it's him?"

Eric presses his foot on the gas pedal and asks the dispatcher for more details. The deceased is a woman. There are no obvious signs of foul play.

I blow out a relieved breath.

"Want me to take you home?" Eric asks without taking his eyes off the road.

"No way."

As we approach the motel, uniformed officers detour traffic to prevent rubberneckers from seeing the crime scene. We slow down as they wave Eric through, moving pylons and tape to accommodate his car.

"You know the drill," he reminds me. "Touch nothing. Stay in the car." He gives me a side glance. "Well, do your best to stay in the car."

"Got it." I nod and jerk my thumb toward the backseat where my bag is. "I brought lap-blanket squares. I'll crochet them together while I wait."

Eric complains that I never stay in the car at a crime scene when he asks me to. Is he right? Maybe. In my defense, I only exit the car with good reason. As a compromise, I text him to let him know where I went.

The police cordoned off the parking lot at the Hav-a-nap motel with police tape. Most of the action is at a north-facing room. Officers in white bunny suits enter and leave the room. Bunny suits are not rabbit costumes, they're what the police call the white HAZMAT-type suits that the forensics people wear to minimize contamination when they are at a crime scene.

Eric pulls into an empty spot near the motel office, turns off the engine, but leaves the fob key in the cupholder between us.

"Text me if you need me." He smiles and winks, making the butterflies in my tummy flutter.

I nod.

I turn on the stereo and use my phone to set my playlist to shuffle. As the opening bars of Wonderwall by Oasis fill the car, I twist my upper body and retrieve my bag from the backseat. Through the back window, I glimpse Carlo Viscardis, the manager of the motel. He's sitting alone on the curb smoking a cigarette. For an instant, I debate getting out of the car to check on him. I decide against it because, for once, I'd like to surprise Eric by actually staying in the car.

I open the window to let in some fresh air, then pull the knitted squares from my bag. I lay them across my lap and begin moving them around, arranging them until I'm satisfied with how they look. With my phone, I snap a picture of the final arrangement, in case they get mixed up later, then I stack them in the order I'll crochet them together.

"Hey, Megan."

I'm rummaging through my bag, searching for my

crochet hook, and almost jump out of my skin when I hear my name so close to my ear.

"Hi, Carlo," I say, hand on my chest. He's leaning in the open window with his forearms resting on the door. "You startled me. I didn't hear you coming."

"How could you with the music so loud?" he teases with a grin.

It's not *that* loud.

"You want to get in?" I jerk my head toward the driver's seat next to me. He nods.

Carlo walks around the front of the car and climbs in. I turn off the music and rest my hands on the bag in my lap.

"Lots of excitement today," I say, stating the obvious. "How are you doing?"

Carlo's chest expands when he inhales deeply. "Anxious," he replies. "A housekeeper found her. She was pretty shaken up. The police are talking to her now."

"Did you see the scene?" I ask.

He shakes his head. "I stood guard until the police arrived but didn't go in. The housekeeper said the dead woman was on the bed, fully clothed. She was face down and her upper body was lying on the bed and her feet were on the floor. Like she fell forward onto the bed, or something." Fidgety, Carlo picks at the fabric of his cotton trousers. When I glance at his hairy knuckles, I notice his hands are trembling.

I sympathize. I tremble around death too.

"It sounds like it wasn't violent," I say, looking for a

bright side to this tragic event. "Maybe she had a heart attack or something."

"I'm not a doctor or anything," Carlos disclaims, "but I think she was too young for a heart attack. Unless she had an underlying condition or something," he speculates.

"How old was she?" I ask.

He shrugs. "I dunno, late twenties or early thirties." Beads of perspiration dot his brow. He seems nervous. It's not hot in here. I press the button on the armrest and lower the driver's side window. The cross breeze is refreshing.

"Is she staying in the room alone?" I ask, wondering if her family knows what happened.

"She checked in alone, but a friend joined her a couple of days ago. He wasn't there when the housekeeper found her."

"Well, you have her name and address from when she checked in, right? The police might ask for it to notify her family."

"She paid cash, Megan. I don't know her name or address," he admits, sounding nervous about the transaction. The cross breeze isn't stopping the beads of perspiration from forming on his brow. Now they're forming in the thick stubble on his upper lip too. Carlo is the type of man who has a five o'clock shadow by noon. "She paid for a week in advance. She signed the registration form as M. Cally." He shrugs. "We called her Ms. Cally."

Carlo's twitchy demeanour is making sense. A guest

who wanted to remain anonymous died under mysterious circumstances in her room.

I flashback to the handwritten sign leaning against the tree the fortune teller sat under yesterday.

MYSTI CALLY ~ SPIRITUAL HEALER ~ GUIDE ~ SOOTHSAYER

"Wait." I reach out and touch Carlos's arm while I connect the mental dots. "Is the dead woman the fortune teller everyone is talking about?"

Carlo nods. "That's her."

Mysti is dead.

CHAPTER 6

A POLICE OFFICER comes to the car and asks Carlo to go with him.

"My turn to give my statement," Carlo says with a weak smile as he opens the door and gets out.

"Good luck," I say, unsure of the appropriate send-off in this circumstance. "I hope you feel better," I add to cover my bases.

I turn on my music again and find my crochet hook at the bottom of my bag. I sing along to Mysterious Ways by U2, making progress on the lap blanket when the driver's side door opens.

"Wow. I didn't think you'd still be here," Eric jokes with a chuckle.

"Ha-ha," I respond, pleased to have shocked him with my compliance.

"Was it natural causes?" I ask. "Do you know how Mysti died?"

Confusion clouds Eric's face. "How do you know who died?"

"I don't have to leave the car to find stuff out," I tease, not using Carlo's name so he won't get in trouble for talking to me.

"Did you know her?" he inquires. "The fortune teller, I mean."

"I met her," I reply, nodding. "She read tarot cards for me and April yesterday."

"I didn't think you believed in that kind of thing," he comments with a smirk.

"I don't," I confirm. "It was for fun. It was April's idea, and I promised her I would keep an open mind."

"Do you believe in fortune tellers and psychics?" I ask, knowing Eric is a show-me-the-evidence kind of guy.

"No." He chuckles, rubbing the back of his neck with his hand. "But I didn't believe in women's intuition before I met you, and now I trust your intuition more than actual evidence sometimes."

"You say the sweetest things." I lean over and give him a quick kiss.

"Did you have any other interaction with her?" he probes.

I shake my head. "No. She read our cards, then April and I went to Knitorious where Jax was waiting to meet you. Are you questioning me?" I ask. "Is Mysti's death a murder investigation?"

"I'm not sure yet," Eric replies. "I'm waiting for the coroner to look at her and give his opinion. We'll treat it as a suspicious death until we know otherwise." He produces a small, clear, plastic evidence bag and smoothes it on his lap. "We found this in her room."

I look at the contents. A torn piece of paper with my first name and phone number in my handwriting. The piece of paper I gave to Jax when I told him to call me if he needs anything.

"I gave that to Jax yesterday." I gasp and bring my hand to my mouth. "Is Mysti the friend Jax was staying with?" I ask out loud.

"We found men's belongings in the room," Eric admits. "And both beds look slept in. Jax is staying with a friend?" Eric asks. "I knew he was staying at the motel, but he didn't mention a friend."

I tell Eric what Jax said about staying with a friend.

"He sounded concerned about his friend," I say. "It might be the same friend he talked to on the phone before you showed up."

"Did you overhear the conversation?" Eric asks.

I shake my head. "He stepped outside to make the call. He said his friend had a bad day or something. He wanted to check on them."

"Did he mention a name? Or any identifying information."

I wrack my brain trying to recall the details.

"I don't think so." In front of us, a luxury sedan parks and a middle-aged man gets out of the car. He's wearing golf pants, a golf shirt, and a golf hat with the Harmony Hills Golf & Country Club logo embroidered on the front. "Coroner," I say, nodding toward him.

Eric looks up and waves. The man comes over and leans in the driver's side window.

"Eric! Great day on the links. Too bad you couldn't join us."

"Well, someone has to work in this town," Eric responds. The two men laugh.

"Hello, Megan." He tips his hat. "Long time no see."

"Hi, Raj," I say, smiling. "Shame your round was cut short."

"What room?" Raj asks.

"107," Eric replies. "I'll meet you there in a minute."

Raj nods, tips his hat at me again, and returns to his car where he retrieves what I assume is coroner stuff from his trunk.

"I have to go," Eric says, then leans over and gives me a kiss. "Do you want a patrol car to take you home, or are you taking the car?"

"I'll take the car," I offer. "I need to drop off the stuff we bought at the apartment."

He kisses me again, tells me to drive safely, and gets out of the car.

I pack up my crochet supplies and toss them onto the backseat. Walking around to the driver's side, I see Jax Squires talking to a uniformed officer at the parking lot entrance. Jax is pointing toward room 107, and the officer shakes his head. My uneducated guess is that Jax wants to get to his room, but the officer won't let him.

I pause and bite the inside of my cheek, debating what to do. I know what I want to do. But it could interfere with the investigation if the coroner and police determine Mysti was murdered. The distressed expression on Jax's face helps me decide.

"Hi, Jax!" I say, approaching him and the officer he's talking to.

"Hi, Megan," Jax replies, shocked to see me. "What are you doing here?"

"Wrong place, wrong time," I reply. "Eric is here. I was just leaving." I look at the officer. "Can Jax join me in the car?" I ask, pointing to Eric's black Dodge Charger parked about fifty feet away.

"You can't go near the room," the officer warns Jax.

Jax nods.

"We won't get any closer than the car," I assure the officer. He smiles. "Thank you." I smile.

"What room are you staying in?" I ask Jax on the short walk to the car.

"107," he replies, holding up his room key.

The Hav-a-nap motel is an older establishment, and it predates keycards and other high-tech conveniences most modern hotels have. The Hav-a-nap has real keys. Upon registering, they issue guests an actual key on an oval metal key chain with their room number etched in white. It's quite charming in a retro way.

We get in the car and close our doors slightly out of sync.

"What's going on? Why can't I go to my room?" Jax asks, watching the commotion surrounding room 107.

"Your room is part of a police investigation," I explain. I pull out my phone and unlock the screen. "I'll just let Eric know you're here."

Me: I'm still here. Jax is in the car with me. He was staying in room 107.

Eric: He can't leave with you. We need to talk to him.

Me: OK.

Eric: Text me when you leave.

Me: OK.

"Is Mysti OK?" Jax asks. "What happened?"

"I don't know the details," I reply truthfully.

Two officers position themselves in front of and behind the car, staring at us inside. Courtesy of Eric, no doubt.

"Why are they here?" Jax asks when he notices the officers.

I shrug one shoulder. "It's their job," I say nonchalantly, as if it would be weird if two police officers *weren't* surrounding the car and watching us.

"Is Mysti OK?" Jax asks again.

"I don't think so," I reply.

Panic seizes Jax's face, and his breathing hastens. "He came back for her, didn't he?"

"Who came back for her?" I ask.

"If something happened to her, it's my fault," Jax blurts out, ignoring my question. He's on the verge of hyperventilating. "She was scared, and I told her I would protect her."

In response to Jax's change of demeanour, the officer in front of us takes a protective step forward. I look at him and shake my head. He acknowledges me with an almost indiscernible upward nod.

"Deep breath, Jax." I place a gentle hand on his arm and inhale an exaggerated breath, hoping he'll follow my lead.

Jax and I make eye contact, and he takes a few deep breaths, redirecting his anxious energy to his leg, which bounces with a chaotic rhythm.

"Start at the beginning," I suggest, trying to guide him. "How long did you know Mysti?"

"We met on Friday," he replies. "When I arrived in Harmony Lake."

"How did you become roommates if you just met?" I probe.

"I came to the motel looking for a room," Jax explains. "They didn't have any. They were booked. I was walking back to my car to leave when I saw Mysti in the parking lot arguing with some guy. It looked intense. I assumed she was fighting with her boyfriend or something. I got in my car and monitored the situation for a few minutes. I didn't want to leave if she was in trouble."

"That was very valiant of you," I tell him. "A very Sloane-like reaction."

Jax grins, and I detect a hint of pride at the comparison.

"The dude's body language got more and more aggressive. Mysti cowered, and I could tell he scared her. That's when I went over. The guy backed off as soon as I approached them."

I'm sure he did. Jax is over six-feet-tall and well-muscled. When motivated, I'm sure he could intimidate most people.

"I swear, Megan, I didn't touch the guy." Jax puts his hands in front of his chest, palms forward. "I stood between him and Mysti and asked him if there was a problem. He said there was no problem. I suggested he was just leaving, and he agreed. He turned and high-tailed it away from us."

"Did you hear any of their argument?" I probe.

Jax shakes his head. "When I approached them, he was jabbing his finger toward Mysti,"—Jax jabs his index finger into the air in front of him—"and he said, *it'll be the last thing you ever do!"*

Sounds like a threat to me.

"Did Mysti tell you his name?" I ask.

"No," Jax replies. "But she made it clear he wasn't her boyfriend. She said she didn't know him. She didn't tell me much. I got the feeling she was afraid."

I got the same feeling yesterday when April interrupted Mysti and Mr. Bickerson's interaction.

I unlock my phone and open a social media app.

"Is this the man who was with Mysti?" I show him a picture of Boris Bickerson.

Jax shakes his head. "No. The dude she was arguing with was younger than him."

"Have you seen him since?"

Jax shakes his head. "No. But I hung around after he left. You know, in case he came back. Mysti asked what room I was in. I told her they were booked, and I couldn't get a room. She offered me the spare bed in her room."

"Just like that?" I ask, bewildered. "She offered her spare bed to a huge guy she just met?" This sounds unbelievable to me.

Jax nods. "I think she was scared," he surmises. "She relaxed a lot when I accepted her offer. I got the feeling she felt safer with a roommate. And that was fine with me. I like to help people."

Another Sloane-like trait.

If what Jax says is true, Mysti must have been beyond scared. I would have to be downright terrified for my life before I'd ask a big, scary stranger I just met to share my motel room.

"You need to tell this to Eric," I tell him.

"Mysti's dead, isn't she?" Jax asks. "Was she murdered?"

"Yes, she's dead," I reply. "But they don't know yet if it was murder. They're gathering evidence, and the coroner is examining her. They'll know more about how she died soon. In the meantime, they have to treat it like a crime scene."

"In that case, there's more I should tell you," Jax says.

"Like what?"

"Mysti was on the run."

"From the police?" I ask.

"From her family."

"Was she escaping an abusive relationship?"

"I don't think so," Jax responds. "It had something to do with a family business. Mysti said her family wanted to kill her because of the family business. She thought they had hired a hit man to take her out. That's why she moved from town to town. She was trying to stay ahead of the hit man. She planned to leave town tonight. Someone owed her money, and they were supposed to pay her today. She said as soon as she got the money, she was outta here."

"Did Mysti think the man you saved her from was the hit man?"

Why would a hit man risk being seen by arguing in public with his target?

Jax shakes his head. "She said he was a dissatisfied customer."

"Why didn't Mysti go to the police if she feared for her life?"

"She thought the police would arrest her because of her scam."

"What scam?" I ask.

"She moved from town to town offering her services as a fortune teller," he explains. "She chose small towns because they have a lot of gossip. When she arrived in a new town, Mysti would change her look and blend in with the locals. She'd hang out at the local gathering places like pubs, parks, libraries, and stuff. She kept her eyes and ears open for gossip and personal stories, learning intimate details about the town's residents and their lives."

"Mysti confessed to you that her gift was fake," I say. It's a statement of fact, not a question.

Jax nods. "After she learned about them, she would set up her fortune-teller booth," he continues. "When the locals came to her for spiritual guidance, she would amaze them with details about their lives and problems. Believing her gift was real, they'd give her more money for more guidance."

Jax says Mysti was skilled at reading people and asking questions. When answering her questions, Mysti's clients unknowingly disclosed private information about their friends and family—also town residents

—that Mysti would use in her readings with those people.

I'm processing what Jax is telling me and watching room 107. Eric just exited the room and is heading toward the car, no doubt to talk to Jax.

"Where were you this morning?" I ask.

"I went to a restaurant for breakfast, then hung around the waterfront. I waited for Mysti to come and set up her booth, but she didn't show up. I texted her and phoned her, but she didn't answer. I thought maybe she left town without saying goodbye. I came back to the motel to check on her. Instead, I found you and a crime scene."

After Jax's explanation about Mysti's scam, I feel vindicated that my instincts about her gift being an elaborate swindle were right.

Her gift might have been fake, but it sounds like Mysti Cally the fortune teller may have predicted her own murder.

CHAPTER 7

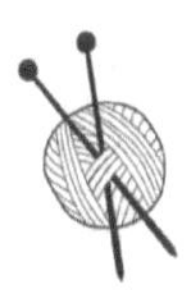

Me: I'm in the lobby.

Eric: I'll be right there.

The secure door opens, and Eric appears. He holds the door, and I stride through it into the inner workings of the Harmony Lake Police Department.

"This is a nice surprise," he says as we stroll down the corridor. "You hardly ever visit me at work."

"Because I don't want to distract you," I tease with a wink as we enter his office.

"You distract me whether you're here or not," he says quietly, then taps my bottom.

Shocked, I spin around to make sure no one saw, relieved to see he'd closed the office door behind us.

With a glint in his eye, Eric smirks and cocks an eyebrow. "How do you plan to distract me?" he asks as he leans against his desk.

A familiar tingle of temptation tugs at me down low, but I remind myself why I'm here and banish all inappropriate thoughts from my mind. *Focus, Megan.*

"A courier delivered this to the house about an hour ago." I reach into my bag and hand him the box from Let Me Take A Cellfie; the box that contains Jax's half of the DNA test. "Also, I thought you might want your car back." I hand him his keys.

"I'll get a patrol car to take you home," he says, putting the keys and DNA kit in his desk drawer, then sitting on the sofa adjacent to his desk.

"No need," I tell him. "Hannah's coming to pick me up. She came home to get ready for the bonfire tonight, and I asked her to pick me up in my car."

"Thank you for dropping that stuff off." He pats the sofa cushion next to him, coaxing me to join him.

"There's more," I inform him, ignoring his invitation. "I thought you might be hungry." Eric is always hungry, so this assumption isn't much of a stretch on my part. I sit next to him, put my bag on the floor, and pull out a glass food-storage container. "Chicken wraps and pasta salad for you." I hand him the container and pull out a second, identical container. "And for Jax." I hand him the other container. "I assume Jax is still here?"

"He's still here," Eric confirms, putting the containers on the end table next to the sofa. "His statement was long. He's waiting to sign it before he can leave."

"He had a lot of information considering he only knew Mysti for two days," I concur.

"Do you believe him?" Eric asks, narrowing his eyes and rubbing his thumb and forefinger along his chiseled chin.

"That he only knew Mysti since Friday?" I clarify.

He nods.

I sink back into the sofa and sigh.

"I'm not sure," I admit. "He seems sincere, but I don't know him well enough to know if he's lying. Also, I find it hard to believe that Mysti, a woman travelling alone, would invite a guy she just met to share her motel room. Especially a guy like Jax. He's physically intimidating."

Eric nods in agreement. "I had the same thought."

"Do you suspect Jax and Mysti knew each other before Friday?" I ask.

He shakes his head. "There's no evidence to support that," he says. "Using receipts and social media posts, we traced Jax's trip from Nova Scotia to Ontario. He didn't cross paths with Mysti, and he wasn't in any towns she visited."

"You traced Mysti's whereabouts before she came here?" I ask, amazed.

"It wasn't difficult," he replies. "She left a path of angry people in her wake." He stands up and picks up a file folder from his desk, then sits back down. "She lived as a transient fortune teller for a few months. Mysti Cally wasn't her only alias. She also called herself Lady Karma, Luna Soleil, and Claire Voyant. She scammed people in small towns, and several of her victims filed police reports."

"People can file a police report because the fortune teller they paid was a fraud?" I ask.

He opens the folder and shows me several grainy and low-quality photos of what *might* be Mysti, but I can't say for sure. Most of them look like still shots taken from surveillance camera footage.

"The scam she told Jax about wasn't Mysti's only scheme," Eric explains. "According to the complaints, Mysti used the more scandalous information she learned about people to blackmail them."

Chances are, not everyone who Mysti blackmailed went to the police. If they filed a complaint, they'd have to tell the police what information Mysti used to blackmail them, a conversation some victims might prefer to avoid. The reports that Eric uncovered likely represent only a fraction of her victims.

"This explains why she told Jax the police would arrest her if she went to them for help," I deduce.

"She's wanted in at least three jurisdictions," Eric confirms.

Anyone Mysti blackmailed or swindled in these towns could have hunted her down, seeking revenge.

"So, if Mysti was murdered, the suspect pool would be huge," I speculate.

"There's no *if*," Eric corrects me. "Mysti Cally was murdered." He opens the folder again and flips through the pages. "The coroner found these." He removes two sheets of paper from the folder and hands them to me. "The killer stuffed them down her throat after she died."

The first sheet is a photo of the death card from Mysti's tarot deck. It has lines and crease marks like someone crumpled it up. The killer must've scrunched it to make it fit in her throat.

"The death card came up when Mysti read my cards," I say.

"How prophetic," he responds dryly.

The next sheet of paper is a photograph of a handwritten note. Like the death card, the note has lines and creases as if someone crumpled it up. The note says: *$10,000 and your secret is safe with me.* It's written in blue ink, on notepaper with the Hav-a-nap motel logo.

Are the death card and the note a message? Or does the killer have a sick and twisted sense of humour?

"I hate to stereotype," I say, "but this looks like a woman's handwriting."

The penmanship is neat and curvy, with rounded letters that are uniform in width and height. The printed letters look like they were written without lifting the pen from the paper. I don't know many men whose penmanship has these characteristics.

"The note was most likely written by a woman," Eric agrees. "I'm waiting to hear from the handwriting expert, but at first glance, she also speculated a woman wrote it."

"Do you think Mysti wrote it?" I ask.

He shrugs. "Possibly. We found samples of Mysti's handwriting with her belongings. The expert will compare them and get back to me. We're testing the pens from the room too. To see if any match the ink on the note."

"Jax said Mysti planned to leave town today. He said someone who owed her money was supposed to pay her today, then she was leaving. Maybe this note refers to the money she was waiting to collect."

"Maybe she blackmailed someone local, and they killed her," Eric theorizes.

"April and I saw Mysti and Mr. Bickerson arguing on Saturday," I say. "We couldn't hear what they were arguing about, but it was intense enough for April to intervene."

I also tell Eric about my conversation with Mrs. Bickerson at the library on Saturday morning, and the Bickerson's domestic dispute near the periodical shelves.

"Did the tarot card and note cause Mysti's death?" I ask. "Did she choke on them?"

Eric shakes his head. "The coroner thinks the killer smothered her with a pillow from the motel room," he confides. "He found a few fibres inside her nose. They're being tested against fibres from the room. He said he'll know more after her autopsy. If she was smothered, he expects to find more fibre samples in her lungs."

The mental images of the autopsy and the smothering make me shudder. Eric puts his arm around my shoulder and pulls me into him.

"Since Mysti Cally was an alias, how will you notify her family without her actual name?" I ask.

"We found her ID in the motel room," Eric explains. "Her driver's license, bank card, and credit cards."

"What's her real name?" I ask.

Eric sits up and rifles through the papers in the file, and hands me a photocopy of Mysti's driver's license. She was twenty-nine years old and had an upscale

Toronto address. Her name was Everley Leighton Moregard-Davenhill.

"Wow! Impressive moniker," I comment under my breath.

"She probably got writer's cramp signing her name," Eric jokes. "No wonder she shortened it to Mysti."

"That's not what I mean," I clarify. "The Moregard-Davenhills are one of the wealthiest families in the world."

Eric sits up at attention, pulling himself up to his full seated height.

"You've heard of them?" he asks, incredulous.

"You haven't?" I reply, equally incredulous. "The Moregard-Davenhill family owns MD Biocorp, one of the largest biotech companies in the world. You use their products every day. They make the vitamins and supplements you take and the cold medication we keep in the medicine cabinet." I stand up and open his desk drawer, removing the Let Me Take A Cellfie box. "See?" I hold it in front of him, pointing to the small print that says: Let Me Take A Cellfie: a division of MD Biocorp.

"Wow," Eric declares, shaking his head. "I had no idea."

"Is MD Biocorp the family business Mysti told Jax about?" I wonder out loud.

It feels wrong to call her Everley. She introduced herself as Mysti, and that's the name she called herself, so it's what I'll call her too.

"This changes things," Eric says, sitting at his desk and making notes on a piece of paper in Mysti's file. "I assumed she was talking about a regular family business, not a multi-billion-dollar, multinational corporation."

"Maybe Mysti was right about her family being out to get her," I suggest. "Considering who her family is and the amount of money that could be at stake, maybe she wasn't exaggerating. Maybe when she told Jax she feared for her life, she had a legitimate reason to be scared."

"I need to find out more about her relationship with her family and her role in the business," Eric says. "It's possible she's a distant relative and has nothing to do with the business."

"True," I say. "Have you contacted them yet?"

"I'm waiting for someone to call me back," he replies. "This isn't the kind of news you leave in a voicemail message."

Fair point.

Deep in thought, our eyes meet, and we're struck by the same idea simultaneously. We both look at the laptop on Eric's desk. He taps on the keyboard, and I rush around to his side of the desk where I can read the screen over his shoulder.

According to the internet, Everley Leighton Moregard-Davenhill was a major shareholder of MD Biocorp, along with her parents and two siblings. All family members own an equal number of shares. It would take three family members to control the company, which sounds like a recipe for a family feud.

"And the list of potential suspects gets bigger," Eric mutters under his breath.

While he prints some of the information we found online, I settle on the sofa and unlock my phone to snoop Everley Leighton Moregard-Davenhill's social media accounts.

She was active on social media, posting almost every day, and sometimes multiple times a day. Her most recent post was... an hour ago?! Impossible! She died over six hours ago. I scroll below the post to read the comments. She responded to a comment less than fifteen minutes ago. This must be a fake account. But it looks so real.

"What's wrong, babe?" Concern seeps onto Eric's face as he stands up. "You look like you've seen a ghost."

"Sort of," I acknowledge as he joins me on the sofa.

I tilt my phone and show him my post.

"What the?" he mumbles, taking my phone and scrolling down to the comments like I did moments before. "It has to be fake," he insists.

Speechless and confused, we stare at the post in silence. It's a photo of a takeout coffee cup from a national coffee chain with the name Beverley handwritten on the side of the cup in black marker. The caption reads, "When you place the same order at the same coffee shop every day, and they still get your name wrong." Followed by a facepalm emoji.

"We don't even have one of those coffee shops in Harmony Lake," I point out.

"Someone else must have access to Mysti's social media accounts," Eric concludes. "It's the only explanation. Otherwise, this is a very convincing fake account."

He opens his phone and types something. "I'll look into it," he says.

Someone knocks on the door.

"Come in," Eric bellows.

"Hi, Jax," I say.

"Hi, Megan," he replies.

"Eric, I signed my statement."

"Good," Eric replies. "Megan brought your DNA swab. Want to do it now?"

"Sure." Jax nods with enthusiasm.

I sit on the sofa and watch while Eric and Jax open the box and read the instructions. Seconds later, Jax swabs the inside of his cheek and drops the swab in a vial. I offer to take the swab with me and drop it off at the post office tomorrow. With any luck, we'll have the results in a couple of days and at least one mystery will be solved.

"Are you hungry?" I ask Jax.

He nods, rubbing his stomach. "I haven't eaten since breakfast."

I shoot Eric a dirty look, and Jax adds, "Eric offered me lunch, but I wasn't hungry. Not after what happened to Mysti."

I give him a sympathetic smile. "How are you feeling now?"

"Hungry."

I hand him one of the glass containers.

"Go find the lunchroom," Eric instructs. "I'll meet you there in a few minutes, and we'll have dinner together."

Jax thanks me for the food and closes the office door behind him when he leaves.

"I can't tell you how many people have commented on the resemblance," Eric says, shaking his head.

He's referring to the resemblance between himself and Jax.

"How do you explain it?" I ask.

Eric shrugs. "I ignore it."

"How's Jax doing?" I ask. "A murder investigation on top of finding your biological family is a lot to process."

"I think he's over the shock, and he's cooperative with the investigation," Eric replies. "There are no available rooms at the Hav-a-nap. He can't go back to room 107 because it's a crime scene. Is it OK with you if he stays in the apartment above Knitorious tonight?"

"Of course, it's OK with me," I say.

"I'll stay with him," Eric adds. "I don't know him enough to know if he's really OK. And he's a person of interest. I need to make sure he doesn't leave town."

"Has Jax told his parents what's going on?" I ask.

"I suggested he call them, but he refused. He said they'll panic and book plane tickets. He doesn't want to worry them."

"Jax seems like a considerate, caring person," I say. "Very Sloane-like," I add with a smile. "Does Jason know Jax is involved in a murder investigation?"

Eric nods. "I told him. He told me to keep him updated," he says, his voice full of disappointment. "I don't get it, babe. Jason's so casual about Jax. Jason and his wife haven't even firmed up their travel arrangements yet. And he only spoke to Jax on the phone once, for two minutes, and hasn't reached out to him since." Eric shakes his head and leans against his desk, crossing his arms in front of his chest. "I don't understand how he can be so uninterested." He shrugs and shakes his head. "If I had a kid somewhere, I'd drop everything and go there."

"I know you would," I say, running my hands up and down his biceps. "Your brother might need more time. His situation is complicated. Jason has a wife and three kids who are affected by this. Lucky for Jax, he has an attentive uncle in the meantime."

I knew it; I saw it in his eyes when he told me Jax was his nephew and not his son. For a few moments, Eric thought he might be a dad, and the disappointment when he found out he wasn't made him realize he wishes he was.

I've been a parent for twenty years. I love Hannah with all my heart. She's the best thing I've ever done. But I've been raising her since I was twenty-one, and I don't want to do it again. I don't want to go through late night feedings, toddler tantrums, potty training, PTA meetings… just thinking about it overwhelms me.

My phone dings.

"It's Hannah," I say. "She's outside. I should go."

Eric thanks me for dinner and everything else, and we kiss goodbye.

We leave his office together. At the end of the hall, he turns right toward Jax, and I turn left toward the exit.

CHAPTER 8

Monday, June 14th

Early bird that I am, I arrive at the post office five minutes before it opens. Even after taking my time assembling a lap blanket and taking Sophie for a longer walk than usual.

I don't mind waiting outside in the warm morning sun. Most businesses aren't open yet, so Water Street is still quiet. I lean against the wall outside the post office and raise my face toward the sun, listening to the birds in the park across the street.

The ding of my phone distracts me from my meditation.

April: What are you doing out there?

The post office is next door to Artsy Tartsy. April must see me through the window.

Me: Waiting for the post office to open.

April: Are you coming in when you're done?

Me: Of course!

April: I want to hear everything!

Harmony Lake is a small town, and Mysti Cally's death is public knowledge. I don't think her true identity is public knowledge—yet—but her death and the mystery surrounding it is.

Dropping my phone in my bag, I spy someone across the street. They're standing still and watching me, just standing there with their hands at their sides. A woman. Her wide-brimmed, straw sun hat is familiar, but the rest of her isn't. I contemplate crossing the street to talk to her, but the click of the lock on the post office door startles me. I turn and smile at the postal worker as she flips the sign from CLOSED to OPEN. She smiles back and holds the door open for me. I turn to check on the woman across the street. She's gone. Poof. Vanished. Weird.

A few minutes later, I drop off Jax's DNA swab, and I'm on my way next door to see April and indulge in one of Tamara's sweet treats. Leaving the post office, I hold the door for someone struggling to see over the massive box they're carrying.

I step onto the sidewalk and lower my sunglasses to my eyes from the top of my head.

"Excuse me!"

I turn toward the unfamiliar voice.

"Hi," I say to the woman in the wide-brimmed straw sun hat. "Are you talking to me?" I ask.

She nods. "My name is Renée Dukes." She extends her hand for me to shake, and I immediately recognize her long, manicured, vivid yellow nails.

"Megan Martel," I say, shaking her hand. "I've seen you around."

"I work for the Moregard-Davenhill family," Renée explains. "They hired my firm to locate their daughter."

This must be why Renée was sitting near Mysti's fortune-telling blanket at the park on Saturday, pretending to read the book she was holding.

"How can I help you?" I ask, wondering what Renée could want with me.

"I was hoping we could talk," she replies. "Maybe share some information about Everley's death and her movements before. My client asked me to cooperate with the investigation to the fullest extent possible."

"You should talk to the police," I advise. "I can give you a number for the lead investigator." I reach into my bag and rummage around for my wallet so I can give her one of Eric's business cards.

"Aren't you the police?" Renée asks, looking confused as she takes off her sunglasses.

"No, I'm not." So far, she's not wowing me with her investigative skills.

Renée shakes her head. "I'm sorry. I assumed you were with the police. You were at the crime scene, and yesterday you were at the police station. Also, Everley's roommate was in your car."

How did Renée have such a good view of the crime scene yesterday? How did she know I went to the police station? Is she watching the police, or Jax?

"You're right," I confirm, "but I'm not with the police." I decline to provide further details about my involvement with the case.

"Well, whatever your involvement, be careful," Renée warns. "I wouldn't invite that roommate into my car if I were you. I think he's the key to what happened to Everley."

It's weird to hear someone refer to Mysti as Everley.

"Why do you say that?" I ask.

"A hunch," she replies, shrugging a shoulder. "I've done this a long time. I have pretty good instincts about people. My instincts about this boy are that he's dangerous. Everley was on the run alone for months and nothing happened to her. Then as soon as this guy shows up, she's dead? That can't be a coincidence."

As much as I hate to admit it, Renée has a point.

From the corner of my eye, I spot April watching our exchange through the bakery window.

"There's a great little bakery right here," I gesture toward Artsy Tartsy. "I was just going to treat myself. Would you like to join me? We can compare notes, and I'll buy you a pastry."

Renée smiles. "Sure. I'd like that. I haven't eaten breakfast yet."

We stop at the counter and assess the yummy, fresh-made pastries under the display glass. We choose one of the secluded bistro tables at the back of the bakery. Without taking my order, April brings over a medium roast coffee with two sugars and one cream—just the way I like it.

I thank her and she recommends the scones with clotted cream. Renée and I agree it sounds wonderful, and April disappears behind the counter to prepare our order.

"Do you work for the Moregard-Davenhills too?" Renée asks.

"No," I reply. "In fact, I didn't know Mysti was a Moregard-Davenhill until yesterday. Her true identity isn't common knowledge."

"I see," Renée acknowledges. "I suspect we aren't the only firm they hired to find their daughter, but I don't know for sure."

"How long were you looking for Mysti?" I ask.

"Almost three months," Renée replies. "Until Harmony Lake, I've always been one town behind her. She was good at staying hidden. The only reason I caught up with her is because she re-used one of her aliases."

Renée tells me that Mysti hadn't used any credit cards or bank accounts since her disappearance. She left her cell phone at home and has contacted no one from her old life. Whatever Mysti ran away from, she did everything possible to make sure it wouldn't catch up with her.

April delivers Renée's tea and our scones and clotted cream. Then she pulls up a chair from a nearby table and joins us at the small bistro table. Renée looks at me, shocked.

"This is April," I explain. Then I look at April. "April, this is Renée Dukes. She works for Mysti's family."

"Ah," April says with an understanding nod. "It's nice to meet you, Renée."

The two women shake hands, and I explain to Renée that April knows everything I know. Renée seems fine with it.

"When I searched Mysti—erm, Everley's—name on

the internet, there was nothing about her being missing," I say, smothering a scone with clotted cream. "In fact, if her social media accounts are anything to go by, she's living her life as usual and joking with friends and family in the comments. "

Renée holds up her finger while she swallows a mouthful of scone. "That's by design," she explains. "Everley is worth *a lot* of money. Her family was concerned for her safety. If her disappearance was public knowledge, and the wrong people found her, Everley would be a target for kidnapping, or worse. The firm I work for hacked into her social media accounts and took them over to create the impression that Everley isn't missing."

This explains how Mysti has continued to post and comment after her death, and why her posts include photos that weren't taken anywhere near Harmony Lake.

"What did Mysti say when you found her?" I ask.

"I never spoke to her," Renée replies, then sips her tea. "I confirmed Mysti Cally and Everley were the same person on Saturday. I notified her family on Saturday evening. They asked me to continue surveillance until they got here. They were making travel plans and said they would be here Sunday night. They didn't want me to approach their daughter and risk her running again. This type of transient lifestyle isn't safe for someone like Everley," Renée continues. "If someone recognized her, she could be in danger. She died the next day, before her family got to Harmony Lake."

"But they knew where she was?" I clarify. "You told them she was staying at the Hav-a-nap and what her alias was?"

"Of course," Renée confirms. "They're my clients, they're paying me to find this information."

So, the night before Mysti's murder, the people she believed wanted to kill her discovered her location. The Moregard-Davenhills might not have come to Harmony Lake themselves, but maybe someone they hired—or even Renée herself—acted on their behalf.

"Mysti didn't know you were following her?" April asks, sounding skeptical.

I'm skeptical too. With her vibrant yellow dress, nails, and giant sunhat, Renée didn't blend in with the crowd. I noticed her on Saturday, and I wasn't even looking for her. Mysti was on the run and afraid; she must have noticed Renée hovering and lurking, pretending to read a book.

"I don't think so," Renée shrugs, smearing clotted cream onto another scone. "I think she would've taken off and tried to lose me if she knew."

"Mysti said she was on the run from her family because she believed they wanted to kill her," I say, watching Renée's face closely for a reaction. None. Her brown eyes and the rest of her face remain relaxed and unresponsive. "She said it was because of the family business but didn't elaborate."

"The Moregard-Davenhills love Everley," Renée insists. "They're concerned for her well-being. Everley overreacted to a family misunderstanding and ran away."

Renée explains that despite being married for over thirty years, in private, Mysti's parents live separate lives and are married in name only. They keep up the facade because their separation would spook investors and hurt the share price of MD Biocorp. In other words, their net worth would take a hit. According to Renée, Mr. and Mrs. Moregard-Davenhill can't be in the same room without arguing. She says they often drag their three kids into their disagreements. It was one of these disagreements that drove Mysti into hiding. Mr. and Mrs. Moregard-Davenhill disagreed on a major business decision regarding the European division of MD Biocorp. To out-vote the other, each parent solicited their children for support in a race to get the majority of votes. Each of Mysti's siblings supported one parent, leaving Mysti as the deciding factor. Whichever parent she sided with would win. Overwhelmed by the pressure, she ran. Renée speculates Mysti misunderstood her parents' and siblings' aggressive lobbying and felt threatened.

"Everley wasn't like the rest of the family," Renée discloses. "She was sensitive and creative. Her parents and siblings are business-minded and analytical. She didn't understand them, and they didn't understand her."

"Where were you when Mysti died?" I ask.

"If she died Sunday morning, I was at the park," Renée responds, "sitting on a park bench and waiting for Mysti to set up shop for the day."

If Renée is telling the truth, and Jax is telling the truth about his alibi, they must've seen each other.

"Did you see Mysti's roommate at the park?"

Renée shakes her head. "I don't think so. Should I? Was that his alibi?"

"I don't know his alibi," I fib. "I'm not the police."

Renée asks me about my involvement with Mysti and the investigation. I answer her questions and tell her April and I met Mysti for the first time when she read our tarot cards on Saturday.

"I saw you on the bench near Mysti's tree," I tell her. "Your yellow maxi dress is gorgeous. I couldn't keep my eyes off it. And the matching nails are a nice touch." I nod toward Renée's fingertips.

Flattered by the compliment, Renée tells me where she bought the dress and suggests it might still be on sale. She opens her phone and texts me a link to the dress at an online store. We now have each other's contact information and I have a dress to order.

Renée asks more questions, which seems fair since I just interrogated her. I explain that I was at the crime scene because I was in the car with Eric when dispatch called him to the motel. I tell her Jax is a relative we don't know very well, who arrived in town two days before Mysti's murder.

"Don't you think the timing is suspicious?" Renée asks. "He shows up and, just like that, they share a room? And now she's dead?"

I do find it suspicious but don't admit this to Renée because I find her suspicious, too, and I don't trust her.

Renée looks at her watch and tells us she has to go. We thank each other for taking the time to talk, and she thanks April for the scones and tea, then Renée leaves.

"What do you think?" I ask April when we're alone.

She shrugs. "I think the Moregard-Davenhills can afford a better private investigator. Instead of blending in, her wardrobe choices make her stick out like a sore thumb. There's no way Mysti didn't know Renée was tailing her."

I nod. "I thought the same thing," I agree. "But that yellow dress she wore on Saturday was so gorgeous."

"Also, I doubt her clients would be comfortable with her disclosing their personal business. Their family dysfunction and secret separation are secret for a reason."

She's right.

"Do you think Renée killed Mysti?" I ask.

April takes a deep breath and lets it out. "I think she's a good contender, unless Eric can confirm her alibi. Or maybe she looked the other way while someone else killed Mysti. Someone sent by Mysti's family."

"If Hannah were missing, I'd tell everyone who would listen," I speculate. "I'd want the entire world searching for her. I wouldn't cover it up like Mysti's parents."

"We're not super rich," April reminds me. "All that money seems to complicate things."

"You're right," I agree, knowing I can't relate to a mother with billions of dollars and a huge corporation to consider. "Is Mysti's family worried about her safety?" I ponder aloud. "Or are they worried the MD Biocorp share price and their net worth would plummet if the media found out someone who controls twenty percent of the company was missing? If the media looked into Mysti's disappearance, they'd uncover the family dynamics that lead to it. What do you think?"

"I think money is the root of all evil," April replies.

Me too.

CHAPTER 9

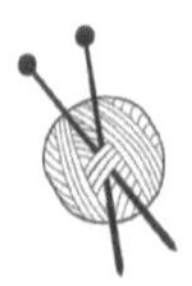

SOPHIE'S DOING A NEW THING; no matter which toy I throw, she brings back a different one. It's so random. She's never done this before. Until today, she always brought back the toy I threw.

I turn off the hose, throw Sophie's braided rope toy across the yard, then wind the hose around the hook on the wall.

"Hey, handsome," I say when Eric steps out of the house and onto the back deck. "Why are you home in the middle of a workday?"

I'm home because Knitorious is closed on Mondays. Today is the day I clean the house and run errands. Right now, I'm pulling weeds in the backyard, watering the hanging baskets, and playing fetch with Sophie.

"I miss you." He tips the brim of my sunhat and stoops down to kiss me. "And I need to pick up some clothes for tomorrow. I think I'll stay at the apartment with Jax again tonight."

I nod. "How is he today?"

"He seems OK," Eric replies with a sigh. "He's on his way to Harmony Hills for an interview with the HH fire department."

"So he's staying in Harmony Lake?" I ask. "Even though you aren't his father?"

"I don't think he's decided," Eric says. "But the interview was already scheduled. And if it distracts him from Jason and Mysti, it can't hurt."

"I'm sure you're right," I agree.

Sophie drops her green tennis ball at my feet.

"Watch this," I say, picking up her frisbee and throwing it.

Sophie scampers after it, skidding to a halt when she reaches the frisbee's landing place. But she ignores it. Instead, she sniffs around and finds an orange tennis ball nearby, picks it up and prances back to me proudly, dropping it at my feet.

"Good girl, Soph!" Eric crouches down and rubs the corgi.

"Don't you think it's strange?" I ask, wondering why he didn't comment that she switched toys. "I threw the frisbee, and she brought me the ball," I explain in case he missed her switcheroo. "She's never done this before, but she's been doing it all day."

"Hm." Eric shrugs. "Who knows?"

I guess it's not a big deal. It's just weird.

"Does she do it when you take her to the dog park?"

"Speaking of the dog park," he says, ignoring my question, "I was hoping to take her today, but I don't think I'll have time. Maybe I'll ask Hannah to take her after her shift at the library. What do you think?"

"She'll survive," I say. "I walk her three times a day," I remind him. "Skipping the dog park for one day won't traumatize her."

"I know," he says, "but she has friends there, and Sophie loves the dog park. Besides, it's part of her routine now."

Whatever.

"Lemonade?" I ask, taking off my hat and using the back of my hand to wipe beads of sweat from my brow.

"I brought you an iced vanilla latte," he responds. "It's in the kitchen."

"Just when I think you couldn't be more perfect." I stand on my tippy toes and give him a thank you kiss.

Eric pours himself a glass of lemonade while I wash my hands and freshen Sophie's water.

"How's the case?" I ask, joining him at the kitchen table and sipping my latte.

"More complicated than yesterday," he says with a sigh. "The fingerprint report landed in my inbox this morning." He unlocks his phone and opens the email. "They found four sets of prints that could be of interest."

"OK," I say with a sneaking suspicion he's about to drop a bombshell.

"Jax Squires."

Not the bombshell I was expecting.

"He was staying in the room," I remind him. "It would be more suspicious if Jax's fingerprints *weren't* there."

"Renée Dukes."

"How did you get a fingerprint sample from her?"

I ask.

"She's a licensed PI, her prints are on file," Eric explains.

"Renée didn't say anything about being inside Mysti's room," I say, recalling our conversation at Artsy Tartsy this morning. "In fact, Renée told me she never spoke to Mysti."

"You spoke to Renée Dukes?" he asks, wide eyed and incredulous. "She's coming to the station later. I haven't even spoken to her yet."

I nod. "She approached me this morning outside the post office." I shrug a shoulder. "We had scones and clotted cream at Artsy Tartsy with April."

I tell Eric about my conversation with Renée and her theory that Jax murdered Mysti.

"She lied to you," Eric says when I finish my recap. "She didn't contact the Moregard-Davenhills on Saturday night. I spoke with Mysti's parents myself. They haven't heard from Renée in almost a week."

"Maybe the Moregard-Davenhills are lying," I suggest. "Maybe they killed Mysti and don't want to admit they knew where she was."

"Renée is a private investigator. If she killed Mysti, she'd be smart enough not to leave fingerprints behind," Eric surmises.

"I don't know," I rebut. "She wasn't smart enough to figure out I'm not a cop. Or to turn the page on the book she pretended to read."

"Who did the third set of prints belong to?" I ask, redirecting our conversation back to the fingerprint report.

"Boris Bickerson."

This is a small bombshell.

"Oh my." I sigh. "I wonder why he was in Mysti's room."

"Possibly to murder her," Eric states.

I can't tell if he's being sarcastic.

"I mean, assuming Mr. Bickerson didn't kill Mysti," I clarify. "Why would he go to her room? Was he trying to get Mysti to give back the money Mrs. Bickerson paid for readings?"

"I'd ask, but the Bickersons lawyered up," Eric says. "It's not as easy for me to question them now."

I wonder if they'll talk to me? I add The Bickersons to my mental to-do list.

"It's possible the killer didn't leave fingerprints in Mysti's motel room," Eric reminds me. "In fact, if they're smart, they didn't."

Why is he managing my expectations? Is it because the next name is the bombshell I've been expecting?

"Who is it?" I ask, cutting straight to the point.

"The last set of prints belongs to Lucas Butler."

Yup. There's the bombshell. Kaboom!

"Hannah's Lucas?" I ask, wide-eyed and stunned.

Eric nods.

"What did you say about Lucas?" Hannah asks, walking into the kitchen.

"Aren't you working at the library today?" Eric asks, surprised.

"Her shift ended at noon," I tell him.

While Hannah pours herself a glass of lemonade,

Eric tells her that the police found Lucas's fingerprints in Mysti's motel room.

"Of course, his prints are there!" Hannah declares, like it's the most obvious thing ever. "It's a crime scene, and he's a cop." She shrugs.

"He didn't work yesterday," Eric reminds her. "Lucas wasn't at the crime scene."

Panic and confusion cloud my daughter's face.

"Don't worry. I'll get to the bottom of it," Eric assures her. "I'll talk to Lucas this afternoon."

"No need," I say with confidence. "I think Lucas is being summoned by a power greater than his boss." I nod toward Hannah who's tapping her phone like a fanatic.

"An angry girlfriend is scarier than I could ever be." Eric smirks and I playfully swat his shoulder.

Hannah either doesn't hear us or ignores us as her thumbs fly across the keyboard. Her phone rings while she's still typing.

"Tell him to stop whatever he's doing and come to the house," Eric says as she accepts the call.

Hannah puts the phone to her ear and disappears into the next room.

"Where were Lucas's prints?" I ask, hoping to come up with a reasonable explanation. "Were they in one specific location?"

Eric shakes his head. "They were all over the room, babe," he discloses. "Every doorknob, light switch, even the shower door."

I sigh. "Were the police ever called to room 107 before Mysti died?" I ask, grasping for reasons to explain why Lucas's fingerprints would be all over Mysti Cally's motel room.

"No," Eric confirms. "I checked."

"Do you think Lucas and Mysti had an affair?" I whisper.

Eric shakes his head. "There's no evidence to support that."

Except his fingerprints all over her room and on her shower door.

"Lucas cares about Hannah. He'd never mess around behind her back," I say, trying to convince myself.

My heart thumps double time. Just thinking about the possibility that Lucas two-timed my daughter makes me flush with anger. I take a long sip of my iced latte to cool off.

"I think Lucas Butler is a stand-up guy," Eric assures me. "I don't think he'd mess around." He rubs my shoulder. "Also, he knows Adam and I would kill him," he mutters under his breath.

"Don't say that!" I admonish. "This is a murder investigation. It's not funny. Even if you're joking."

"Who's joking?" he asks. "What if Lucas can't explain these fingerprints? Am I supposed to look the other way if he cheated on my stepdaughter?" Now Eric's flushing with angry heat.

Eric and I aren't married, so Hannah isn't his stepdaughter. But he's so riled up about Lucas's fingerprints in Mysti's motel room, that I let it go without correcting him.

We talk about marriage often. Because Eric brings it

up often. He's made his intentions clear; Eric wants us to get married. I want us to get married, too, but I'm not ready yet. I'm still getting used to living together.

Eric and I met just as my marriage to Adam was ending. I had a post-divorce plan that included being single and living alone—something I'd never done. Meeting a kind, thoughtful, gorgeous, funny man and falling in love was not part of the plan, but here we are. Eric's latest negotiation tactic is a long engagement, which is hard to argue with. So I agreed, provided we don't have to set a date yet. I know he's planning to propose any minute. I suspect this murder investigation has sidelined his proposal plan. For now.

"Let's see what Lucas says," I suggest, trying to calm both of us down.

"The coroner found fibres in Mysti's lungs," Eric says, changing the subject.

"She was definitely smothered, then," I conclude.

Eric nods. "But so far, nothing in the room matches the fibres in Mysti's nose and lungs. They're still processing samples, so hopefully the murder weapon is in the to-be-processed pile." He takes a sip of lemonade. "And I heard from the handwriting expert."

"What did she say?"

"Mysti wrote the note we found in her throat," he confirms. "And forensics confirmed she wrote it with the complimentary note paper and pen from room 107."

"If Mysti wrote the note while she was staying at the Hav-a-nap motel, it was likely intended for someone local," I surmise. "Her killer might be someone we know."

CHAPTER 10

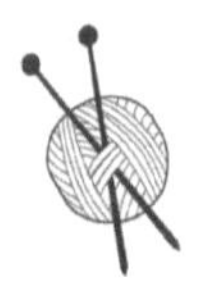

"HE'S PULLING INTO THE DRIVEWAY," Hannah announces, still holding her phone to her ear. "K. See you in a minute. Bye." She hangs up.

Hannah opens the door for Lucas while Eric and I get up from the kitchen table.

"Be nice," I whisper.

"I'll be nice as long as he's honest," Eric mutters in reply.

Lucas stands in the entryway and fidgets with his peaked cap, which is in his hand.

"Chief," he says, nodding at Eric with a tight-lipped smile. "Hi, Megan," he says, the dimple on his right cheek winking at me when he smiles.

Lucas calls Eric "chief" when he's on duty.

"Hi, Lucas." I muster my friendliest tone of voice, hoping to ease his palpable anxiety. "Come in and sit down." I gesture toward the living room. "Can I get you a drink? We have lemonade."

"No, thank you, ma'am." He and Hannah sit next to

each other on the sofa, and Sophie joins them, making herself comfortable on Hannah's lap.

Lucas's curly dark hair is damp with sweat either from wearing his dark uniform on a warm day, or because he's nervous, or both.

"Tell them what you told me," Hannah instructs, nudging her boyfriend.

Eric and I sink into the armchairs across from the sofa.

"We're listening," Eric says in his cop voice.

"I was in room 107 at the Hav-a-nap motel on Saturday," Lucas confesses.

"Why didn't you log it?" Eric asks, leaning forward and putting his elbows on his knees, his fingertips touching in front of him.

"I forgot," Lucas admits, sounding disappointed with himself. "I'm sorry. It was near the end of my shift. I guess I was in a hurry to leave, and it slipped my mind. I didn't know about the murder until I clocked in a couple of hours ago. I was going to talk to you later today." He reaches into a pocket and produces a small notebook. "But I have notes." He flips through the pages, then hands the notebook to Eric.

Eric reads the notes, then hands the notebook back to Lucas.

"Tell me everything," Eric instructs. "From the beginning."

Lucas tells us he was on patrol on Saturday afternoon and pulled into one of the metered parking spots on Water Street, so he could go into a local store to buy a drink. Walking from the car to the store, he heard someone yell, *police*. He says a woman was flagging him down and running toward him.

"What did she look like?" Hannah asks.

I smirk with smug pride at her instinct for focussing on the important details; I like to think she gets it from me.

Lucas describes Mysti to a tee. Right down to the spattering of freckles across her nose.

"She was scared," Lucas says. "I could tell. She was jumpy and kept looking behind her. She said a dissatisfied customer was harassing her, and she thought they were following her."

"Did you see anyone following her?" Eric asks.

"I don't think so," Lucas replies, sounding less than confident. "There was this one guy. I'm not sure if he was following her or just walking fast in the same direction. We made eye contact, and he turned and went the other way. Water Street was busy on Saturday, and I assumed he was trying to get through the crowd." He shrugs. "I pointed him out to Mysti and asked her if he was the guy who was bothering her, but she said it wasn't him."

"What did he look like?" Eric asks, with his own notebook open and his pen in his hand.

"He was younger than you, but older than me. He was taller than me but shorter than you."

This vague description applies to half the men in Harmony Lake.

"What about his hair?" I suggest.

Lucas shakes his head. "I didn't see his hair. He

wore a baseball cap. It was black and said, *Dad in charge,* in white letters.

"What else was he wearing?" Eric asks.

"A baby," Lucas replies.

"He was wearing a baby?" Hannah and I ask in stereo.

Lucas looks at Hannah. "Yeah, you know, those baby backpacks that parents wear in the front?" He gestures toward his upper torso to describe the man's baby carrier, then he looks at me. "It was a cute baby." He shrugs one shoulder. "It was facing me. It was smiling, and it's sunhat was too big for its little head."

"Any other identifying features?" Eric asks.

Lucas shakes his head. "No. That's it. I only saw him for a second.

The man Lucas describes sounds like an unlikely suspect. Do killers take their babies when they stalk their victims? I doubt it. First, only a sociopath would take a baby to a murder scene. Second, babies are unknown variables. What if the baby cried, or spat up, or left a clue behind? Or what if the baby was injured? No, this doesn't sound like a solid lead to me, but I'll leave it to the professionals to decide.

"What happened next," Eric probes. "After Mysti flagged you down and told you someone was following her."

"I asked for her name and address." He points to his notebook. "And wrote them down so I could log them later, but I forgot."

"Did you ask to see her ID?" Eric asks.

"Yes, but she didn't have any. I had to take her word

for it. I would've run her name when I logged our interaction, but I forgot to log it."

I have a mental flashback to Renée telling me she caught up to Mysti in Harmony Lake because Mysti reused one of her aliases. Oh my! If Lucas had logged his interaction with Mysti, he would've seen that she was wanted in other jurisdictions and taken her into custody. If she were in police custody, instead of her motel room, would Mysti still be alive?

"Tell them the part about the motel," Hannah urges.

"I could tell she was still scared, so I offered to drive her home—to the motel," Lucas reveals. "She accepted my offer. When we arrived, she was antsy and looked around like she expected someone to jump out at her. I offered to clear her room, so she would relax."

"Did you clear the room?" Eric asks.

"Yes," Lucas confirms. "And she was much calmer when I told her it was clear. I offered to help her file a report about the customer who was bothering her, but she didn't want to. She said disgruntled customers take out their frustration on her sometimes. She said it was an occupational hazard. I asked her for a description, and she blew me off, saying it didn't matter."

Eric, Hannah, and I sound like a leaky air mattress as we let out a collective sigh of relief. This explains why Lucas's fingerprints were all over Mysti's motel room; he turned on every light and opened every door to make sure no one was there.

"Then you left?" I ask.

"Yes, but first, I offered to wait while she called someone to come and stay with her," Lucas explains.

"She said her roommate would be back soon, and she would be fine." He looks at Eric. "I saw evidence of a male roommate when I cleared the room, so I assumed her husband or boyfriend would be back soon. She went inside, and I left."

"Let's talk about the importance of logging every interaction," Eric says, noticeably more relaxed than he was before Lucas got here.

Again, I offer Lucas a drink, and he accepts a glass of water. Thank goodness. I don't need to sit here while Eric lectures him about work stuff. Hannah follows me into the kitchen.

"I told you he would have a good explanation!" Hannah declares, relieved she was right.

"I didn't doubt it, sweetie," I fib.

"Are you going to tell Dad about this?" she asks. "I don't want him to know. He doesn't need to know. This will give him another reason to hate Lucas."

Until this moment, I wasn't sure if Hannah was aware of Adam's feelings about her boyfriend.

"I won't tell him," I assure her, "but you know what this town is like. Dad will probably hear about it from someone. Wouldn't it be better if one of us tells him?"

"I know, but Dad will use it as an excuse to hate Lucas. He'll say Lucas is a suspect until the police arrest someone else."

She's not wrong; she knows her dad well.

"I can be there when you tell him," I offer. "It's up to you."

Hannah nods with tears in her eyes. "Thanks," she mumbles.

"Come here, Hannah Banana." I envelop my daughter in a tight hug. We sway, and I smooth her long curls with my hand. "Dad doesn't hate Lucas," I explain while I hold her. "He hates the idea of Lucas. Dad is used to being the number one man in your life. He loves you so much that he thinks no one could ever love you as much as him. He'll come around," I assure her.

"But until the police charge someone else with Mysti's murder, Lucas is a suspect," Hannah says when we pull apart. "He slept in yesterday. Remember? He was late picking me up to go apartment hunting. Mum, he doesn't have an alibi for when Mysti was killed."

I brush a stubborn curl from her face and tuck it behind her ear.

"Then we'll have to find Mysti's killer and make sure they're held accountable."

CHAPTER 11

"BYE, LUCAS," I say, as he steps out of the house.

"I'll be right back," Hannah beams. "I'll just walk Lucas to the car."

Eric and I nod. Sophie leaps onto the back of the living room sofa, so she can watch Hannah and Lucas on the driveway.

"What do you think?" I ask when the door closes.

"The poor guy. He's wracked with guilt," Eric says.

"About what?" I ask, wondering if Lucas realized running Mysti's alias through the computer might've saved her life.

"He's convinced whoever was following Mysti came back for her after he left."

"He might be right," I suggest. "If Lucas ran Mysti's name through the computer, would she have been in police custody when her killer went to her room?"

"Unlikely," Eric says. "She didn't have a record. And they wanted to question her, not charge her." He shrugs. "We would've processed her, then released her. She would've been back at the motel by dinnertime."

"Renée Dukes was surveilling Mysti on Saturday," I say. "April and I saw her on a park bench near Mysti's fortune-telling blanket. If Mysti had an altercation, or ran away, Renée should've seen what happened. But she didn't mention it when April and I talked to her." Renée's story and role in Mysti's case aggravates the knot in my stomach. I don't trust her. "Maybe Renée was the person who was chasing Mysti."

"Didn't Lucas say Mysti was running from a man?" Eric asks, with his gaze focused down and to the left; his favourite gaze for thinking.

"Did Lucas say it was a man, or did we *assume* it was a man because he saw the dad with the baby walking fast behind Mysti?"

"I'll talk to Lucas and clarify," he says. "Do you believe Lucas's story?"

"I have to," I reply with a sigh. "Hannah believes him, and she needs me to trust her instincts about him. She already knows Adam doesn't like him. She needs one parent to support her."

"I get it, babe," Eric responds. "It's stressful for older, established couples to cope with one of them being a person of interest in a murder investigation, never mind a young couple in a new relationship."

"I need Adam to adopt that point of view," I say. "Is the baby-wearing dad a good lead?"

"I'd like to talk to him," Eric replies. "If he wasn't following Mysti, maybe he saw who was."

"Mysti must have been terrified, Eric," I say. "She

told Jax she didn't want to go to the police because she was afraid they would arrest her, but she flagged down Lucas for help. Mysti took a big risk when she approached him. She'd only do it if she was desperate."

"I know." He hugs me and rubs circles on my back. "I have to go to work. Can I show you something before I go?"

"Sure," I reply.

Eric opens his phone and shows me a photo. It's a selfie of Mysti and another woman. They're about the same age. Their arms are around each other's shoulders. Both women are mid-laugh and look like they might be intoxicated.

"Where did you get this?" I ask.

"We recovered it from Mysti's burner phone," he says. "She took them last week."

"Them?" I ask. "There's more?"

He nods.

"May I?" I ask before I swipe to the next photo.

"Of course," he replies. "They took the photos at the same time and place. Every photo has the same background, and their clothing doesn't change. I suspect they were drinking."

I swipe through the photos. Mysti and her friend make faces for the camera. They look like they're having fun, and I can't help but smile at their exaggerated facial expressions. The photos are a tad blurry, adding to my hunch that the ladies in the photos were inebriated. They remind me of April and I; we sometimes take silly selfies after a few glasses of wine. The background is familiar. I zoom in on one familiar head in particular.

"This is The Embassy," I say, handing the phone with the zoomed-in photo to Eric. "That's Sheamus."

The Irish Embassy—known to the locals as The Embassy—is our local Irish Pub. Sheamus is the owner. His full head of brilliant ginger hair makes him stand out in the background, even if he is blurry.

"You're right," he agrees, taking the phone and inspecting the background on the other photos. "Do you recognize the woman in the photos with Mysti?"

"No," I reply. "But if you send me the least blurry picture, I'll ask around and keep an eye out for her."

Unless this mystery woman is slightly blurry and makes duck lips in person, I'm not sure I'd recognize her, but I'll keep my eyes open.

"Thanks." Seconds later, my phone dings when he texts me the picture. "I'll send someone to The Embassy to ask around and look for her."

"Jax might know who she is," I suggest. "He was Mysti's roommate, after all."

"I'll ask him when he gets back from his interview."

Eric kisses me goodbye and passes Hannah at the door on his way out.

"How do you feel?" I ask, rubbing Hannah's arm.

"I'm OK," she replies with a sigh. "Lucas is upset. He feels like Mysti might not be dead if he pushed her harder to talk about who was following her, and if he ran her name through the computer."

"Eric said even if Lucas arrested her, it wouldn't have changed Mysti's outcome," I assure her.

Hannah nods. "I know. He said the same thing to Lucas. But he still wonders *what if,* you know?"

"How was your shift at the library this morning?" I ask.

"Fine," she says, shrugging. "Kind of slow. People do outdoor activities when the weather is good."

"How was Mrs. Bickerson?" I specify.

"Not her usual cheery self," Hannah admits. "She and Kilian stayed in her office with the door closed. Mrs. B never closes her office door. It goes against her open-door policy."

"Mrs. B was close with Mysti," I explain. "Mysti's death might be hard for her."

"I know," Hannah tells me. "The other summer interns said Mrs. B told everyone who came to the library last week how amazing Mysti was. She praised Mysti's gift and tried to convince everyone to see her." Hannah fidgets with her hands like she's trying to figure out what to say next. "Mum, I think Mrs. B might know something about what happened to Mysti."

"Did you tell Eric?" I ask.

She shakes her head. "I was going to, but the situation with Lucas's fingerprints made me forget. I didn't remember until now when you asked about Mrs. B."

"Why do you think Mrs. B knows something?"

"Because when she left her office to take Kilian outside, she was crying. I took some tissues and followed her outside. When I handed her the tissues, she thanked me and I asked her if she was OK. She said she was fine, but *poor Mysti was right about the woman coming to get her.*"

"Were those her exact words?"

Hannah nods. "Yes. I should tell Eric, right?"

"For sure," I reply. "Send him a text. Tell him what you told me."

That's the rest of my day sorted. If anyone needs me, my crochet hook and I will be binge-watching Netflix and finishing a few lap blankets, so I can drop them off at the library tomorrow and visit Mrs. Bickerson.

CHAPTER 12

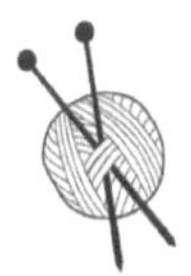

TUESDAY, June 15th

"Wow! That's a lot of mail, Soph," I say as Sophie innocently traipses across the scattered envelopes on her way into the store.

I stoop down and pick up yesterday's mail off the floor. There's more than usual. I sign up for electronic correspondence and opt out of snail mail whenever possible. We never get this much physical mail anymore.

Knitorious has a new postal carrier. On Mondays, she pushes the mail through the mail slot in the front door. I'm not complaining, it's her job. But I miss our old carrier, who held on to Monday's mail and delivered it the next day with Tuesday's mail.

Flipping through the envelopes, it becomes clear why there's so much; I have mail for three other Water Street stores. *Sigh.* I sort the non-Knitorious mail into piles and set them aside. I'll deliver them to their intended destinations when Hannah starts her shift at lunchtime.

Just after I flip the sign from CLOSED to OPEN and unlock the door, Hannah arrives.

"What are you doing here?" I ask. "You don't start until noon."

"I told Eric I'd take Sophie to the dog park," she replies, squatting down to rub Sophie, who's super excited to see her.

"I already walked Sophie," I say. "We had a nice leisurely stroll before I opened the store."

"I promised, so I feel like I should take her."

"Why does Sophie have to visit the dog park every day?" I demand. "She coped just fine when we only took her a few times a week. Why, all of a sudden, does she have to go every day?"

Hannah shrugs. "She likes it there. She has canine friends that she plays with, and it's part of her routine now."

Am I having déjà vu or is this what Eric said word-for-word yesterday when I asked him the same question?

"Did Eric tell you to say that?"

"Pretty much," Hannah admits, picking up two of Sophie's toys and getting her leash.

"Good morning!" Jax appears in the doorway between the store and the back room.

Hannah and I greet him and ask how he's doing. He tells us he's fine, and we exchange pleasantries about the wonderful weather we've been enjoying.

"How was your interview yesterday?" I ask.

"I think it went well," Jax replies. "I guess I'll find out for sure if they offer me the job. I have another interview this afternoon. With the Harmony Lake Fire Department."

"I didn't know you applied there," I comment.

"I didn't," Jax responds. "Adam introduced me to the fire chief last night at The Embassy." He shrugs. "Now I have an interview."

The Harmony Lake Fire Department has been one firefighter short of a full roster since January. I assumed they hired someone by now, but I guess not.

"Good luck," I say. "I'm sure they'll love you."

"How did you meet my dad?" Hannah asks.

"Eric had to work late last night on Mysti's case," Jax explains. "I was bored in the apartment by myself, and Eric suggested I go to the pub for dinner. He said it was steak and mushroom boxty night, and his friends would be there watching the game. When I got there, Adam recognized me and waved me over. I sat with him and a bunch of other guys. The fire chief was there, and Adam told him about my training."

I didn't give Adam details about Jax's training or job search. He and Eric devised this scheme on their own. I suspect Eric hopes Jax will settle in or near Harmony Lake.

"We'll ask everyone to put in a good word for you," Hannah says.

"Thanks," Jax replies, then looks at me. "Megan, can I ask you a favour?"

"Of course," I reply. "What do you need?"

"Eric said I can go to room 107 and collect my stuff. I don't want to go alone, and Eric has to work. He said you might come with me."

"Sur…"

"I'll go with you," Hannah offers, interrupting me before I finish my sentence. "We're practically step-cousins." She shrugs with a smile. "Can you wait until I get back from the dog park?" She points to Sophie, sitting at her feet, staring at the dog toys in Hannah's hand.

"Can I go to the dog park with you?" Jax asks. "It'll give me something to do other than obsess about my interview."

"Sure!"

"Before you go," I interject, just as Hannah bends down to attach Sophie's leash, "can you watch the store for a few minutes?" I pick up the piles of mis-delivered mail from the counter. "I need to drop off some mail."

"Sure."

"No problem."

"Thanks," I say, grabbing my phone and slipping it in my pocket. "I'll be back soon."

TWO DOWN, one to go. After I drop off Wilde Flowers' mail, I can go back to Knitorious.

Wilde Flowers is next door to Knitorious; we share a wall and a parking lot. The owner, Phillip Wilde, is my next-door neighbour at home too. We're work and home neighbours.

"Good morning, Phillip," I say loud enough for him to hear me over the jingle of his door.

"Why, Megan Martel!" He comes out from behind the counter. "To what do I owe this unexpected pleasure?" Phillip bows, his right hand spiralling in front of his chest with a dramatic flourish.

"I come bearing gifts," I say, playing along, "of the postal variety." I slap the envelopes on his counter.

"Again?!" He stands up. "I like the new postal carrier," he says. "She's friendly and chatty and all that good stuff, but she's not very detail oriented, is she?"

I shake my head. "Where's Kevin?" I ask, looking around for Phillip's beloved Chihuahua, expecting to find him perched atop his royal blue velvet pillow with gold piping and tassels. "He's not on his pillow."

Kevin and Phillip are always together. I can't remember the last time Wilde Flowers was open for business and Kevin wasn't here.

"He's at the vet," Phillip replies. "Getting his teeth cleaned. Plaque is a horrible thing, and it gives Kevin the worst halitosis."

"Thank goodness," I say. "I worried for a second." Glancing at the counter, it looks like Phillip was in the middle of ringing up a sale before I interrupted him. "Were you in the middle of something?"

Phillip flicks his wrist. "I'm waiting for a customer to come back. He left his wallet at the park or something. I have time for a quick chat." He smirks and gives me a sideways glance. "What's the latest on the fortune teller's murder?"

"How would I know?" I tease.

"Because you always know."

"I know the police have a lot of suspects and a lot of evidence to sift through," I tell him, hoping to satisfy his curiosity.

"You know more than that," he says. "I'll tell you something juicy if you tell me something juicy," Phillip suggests.

"Deal."

"OK." His eyes light up like a Christmas tree. "According to Trudy, Mrs. Willows said Artie saw Eric coming out of Charmed and Dangerous last week."

Charmed and Dangerous is our local jewellery store.

"You call that juicy?" I smirk. "It's fourth-hand gossip at best."

Phillip shrugs. "It's been a slow week for me."

"Eric could've been there for anything," I assert. "It could have been work related. He could've been getting a new battery for his watch..."

"Or an engagement ring," Phillip finishes my sentence. "I sense there's a wedding in our future, sweetie, and I'm already thinking about the flowers. What do you think your colour scheme will be? In which season will the nuptials take place?"

I feel my face blushing. "Artie is legally blind in four provinces. He probably saw someone who looked like Eric," I say, ignoring Phillip's questions.

"Speaking of people who look like Eric," Phillip

probes, "what's the story behind the mini-Eric staying at your apartment?"

"There's nothing mini about Jax," I correct him.

"You can say that again," Phillip agrees with a wink.

"I promise to tell you more about that later this week." I smile.

"You owe me something juicy."

I think hard about what I can tell Phillip that will satisfy his curiosity without compromising the investigation.

"OK," I say, leaning toward Phillip like I'm about to tell him something that will blow his mind. "The fortune teller's true identity is a closely guarded secret, but when it becomes public, her death will make headlines all over the world."

Wide-eyed, Phillip gasps and brings his hand to his mouth. "Tell me!" He swats my shoulder. "You can't leave me hanging! Who is she?"

Saved by the bell. A man sweeps in, rushing to the counter.

"Sorry about that!" the mystery man says, "but I'm here now." He turns to me. "I'm sorry, were you in the middle of a transaction?" He smiles.

Speechless, I shake my head, unable to stop staring at him or the baby he's wearing in his baby-carrier. A cute, smiling baby whose sun hat is too big for his little head.

The man turns back to Phillip. "I found it," he explains, holding up his wallet. "It was buried in the bottom of the diaper bag." He chuckles, and Phillip joins him.

While Phillip finishes ringing up the mystery man's transaction, I reposition myself to better view the man's hat. A black baseball cap with white letters that say *Dad in charge.*

No way! This is the baby-wearing dad! I need to take a picture and send it to Lucas. But how, without being obvious? Before I can think through my dilemma, Phillip hands him his receipt and wishes him a good day.

"Have a great day," the man says, turning to leave.

"Bye," I mumble.

When the door closes behind him, I rush to the window. He crosses the street and walks toward the park. He veers toward the playground, waving to someone I can't see.

"Who was that?" I demand.

"Some guy who bought flowers for his wife," Philip shrugs. "Pink peonies."

"What's his name?" I clarify.

"I have to protect my client's privacy, Megan."

"Phillip. There's no such thing as florist-customer confidentiality," I reason. "I *need* to know his name."

He narrows his eyes. "Does it have anything to do with the fortune teller's murder?"

I nod.

"In that case, his name is Cole Duffy with two f's. His wife's name is Kelsi with an i. They aren't local. They have a vacation rental until the middle of July. He paid with cash."

I pull out my phone and make a quick note of the names.

"Thank you, Phillip!" I say, shoving my phone in my pocket. "I have to go."

"If you wait ten minutes, I'll be finished with your June arrangement, and you can take it with you."

"I'll come back for it," I call on my way to the door.

"It's OK, I'll drop it off later." His voice grows fainter as the door closes behind me.

CHAPTER 13

"C'MON, SOPH!" I blurt out, spying her leash and rushing to snatch it off the counter.

"Mum, what's wrong?" Hannah jumps off the sofa in the cozy seating area.

"The baby-wearing dad is across the street!" I exclaim, attaching the leash to Sophie's collar.

"Are you sure?" she asks.

"Same hat, same baby," I say, leading Sophie toward the door.

"Why do you need Sophie?"

"So I can take his picture without being obvious," I explain. "I'm just a woman walking her dog."

Hannah nods, fast. "We can send it to Lucas to confirm it's him."

"Exactly."

Hannah turns to Jax. "Can you go with her?" she asks. "In case this guy is dangerous?"

"For sure!" Jax rushes to the door.

As we cross the street, I give Jax the short-version

explanation of who the baby-wearing dad is and how he might help Eric find Mysti's killer.

"Got it," he says, like I just gave him a life-or-death assignment. "Black hat, cute baby, big sunhat."

"Last I saw, he was headed toward the playground," I say, steering us in the right direction.

"We should slow down," Jax advises. "You look like you're on a mission. It'll draw attention to us."

I nod and take a deep breath.

"Good call," I say, slowing my pace, much to Sophie's relief as she stops to sniff a nearby tree.

This is the first time I've been alone with Jax since Saturday. I should use this opportunity to check in with him.

"How are you doing, Jax?" I ask. "You came to Harmony Lake expecting to find your biological father, and instead, you found an uncle, a murder investigation, and some pretty quirky people."

"Actually, I like it here. Especially the quirky people." His chuckle sounds so much like Eric's it makes me hold my breath for a moment. "Everyone is really nice and accepting of me. People make me feel welcome. Even if I don't develop a relationship with my father, I'm glad Eric is my uncle."

"I think he's glad he's your uncle too," I say. "He's eager to tell people who you are. But he's waiting for the DNA results."

"I know," Jax responds. "Jason isn't as eager. He won't book a plane ticket until the DNA results come back." He sighs. "We only spoke on the phone once, and he didn't ask for my number or email address or anything. But Eric shows me family photos and tells me about my other relatives. He asks me about my life and asks to see my family photos. For brothers who look almost identical, Eric and Jason couldn't be more different."

"I'm sorry Jason isn't as enthusiastic as you hoped," I commiserate. "He might need time to process everything. His wife and other kids might need time too. The rest of the Sloanes will be excited about you, regardless of Jason's reaction. And if Jason never gets used to the idea, it's his loss. You're a great person, and he should be proud you're his son."

He nods. "My dad said the same thing," Jax says, referring to the dad who raised him. "If I ask you something, Megan, will you be honest?"

"I'll do my best," I say, sensing he's about to ask me something serious.

Jax inhales and blows it out. "Do you think I killed Mysti?"

"No," I reply without hesitation, shaking my head.

"You sound sure."

"I am sure," I admit. "I was pretty sure until this morning, but now I'm one hundred percent sure."

"What happened that made you sure?"

"It was when Hannah offered to go to the motel with you," I explain. "I didn't feel any anxiety or hesitation. If *any* part of me believed there was even a slight chance you did anything to Mysti, my instincts would've kicked in, and I would've panicked about Hannah being alone with you." I shrug. "But my first instinct was that I'm happy you're getting to know each other."

"I didn't hurt Mysti," Jax insists. "I swear on my family's lives. I know her fortune-telling job was a con, and I know she was wrong to trick people, but she didn't deserve what happened to her."

"I agree with you," I say.

"And she wasn't all bad," he adds. "Mysti said most of her clients knew her gift wasn't real. They saw her for entertainment. Mysti's readings cost the same as going to a movie. She also said some sad and broken people went to see her. Mysti said they were grieving and in pain. She tried to tell those people what they needed to hear to bring them comfort and give them peace. So they could move on. A bad person wouldn't do that."

My thoughts instantly turn to Mrs. Bickerson and the sense of comfort she exuded when she told me how Mysti's readings helped her to find peace after her parents' deaths.

As we get closer to the playground, I spot the baby-wearing dad near the monkey bars with a little girl. She's about three, and he hovers nearby, ready to catch her if she falls. A woman, who I assume is his wife, follows a toddler around the perimeter of the whirl spinner. Three kids under four! Cole Duffy and his wife are busy parents!

Jax stops walking and faces the other way.

"What's wrong?" I ask.

"If he sees me, he'll bolt," Jax replies.

"Why?"

"He's the guy who argued with Mysti at the motel on Friday."

"The baby-wearing dad is the man you scared off when you met Mysti?"

"Yup," Jax confirms. "There's no doubt about it. That's him."

Interesting.

A woman is walking a chocolate lab about fifty feet behind us. Jax nods toward the lab.

"I'll hang back here," he suggests. "Close enough to reach you, but too far away for him to see me."

Before I can respond, he's walking toward the lab with his hand out and asking the owner the dog's name. I hear her respond, "Guinness," as Sophie and I walk farther away from Jax and closer to the playground.

I unlock my phone and open the camera. I turn the front-facing camera on and turn my back to the playground, positioning myself until Cole Duffy is on my screen and in focus. Pretending to take a selfie, I snap a few photos of him. With my back still toward the playground, I open the photo app to ensure the photos are usable and clear enough that Lucas will recognize the baby-wearing dad. They're perfect.

I open the text app, and I'm about to send the photos to Eric when I'm interrupted by a tiny voice behind me.

"Excuse me, may I please pet your dog please?"

Cole Duffy and his daughter are less than two feet away from me. The little girl is adorable, and when she says please twice, I almost melt from the cuteness.

"Absolutely," I say, smiling.

While I shorten Sophie's leash and tell her to sit down, Cole praises his daughter for using her good manners when she asked to pet Sophie.

"Her favourite spot is between her ears," I tell the little girl as I crouch down next to Sophie and grip her collar.

Sophie is a good girl. She loves people—kids are her favourite kind of people—and she's the gentlest dog you'll ever meet. But just in case, I always stay extra close and have extra control when new people approach her.

"What's her name?" the tiny voice asks.

"Sophie," I reply.

Cole Duffy shows his daughter how to close her hand and extend it for Sophie to sniff before petting her. By the time the tiny hand touches her, Sophie is practically vibrating with anticipation.

"Good girl, Soph," I whisper to the patient corgi.

And just like that, the little girl decides she's finished petting Sophie, turns around, and hightails it back toward the playground.

"What do you say, Pumpkin?" Cole calls after the tiny escapee.

"Thank you," the tiny voice calls, sounding even tinier because she's running away.

"Thank you for your patience," Cole says. "To you and Sophie." He rubs Sophie between the ears.

"Your kids are adorable," I say, smiling at the kicking baby who's grinning at me from the baby carrier on Cole's chest.

"Thanks!" He smiles. "There's one more,"—he points toward the playground—"over there with her mum."

"Is that your wife?" I ask, nodding toward the woman trying to follow a toddler and a preschooler in different directions.

"That's her," he confirms.

"You have a beautiful family."

"Yes, I do," he agrees. "But at their current ages, it's a handful."

"I can only imagine," I say, distracted by the adorable baby cooing at me and reaching for me with his chubby hands.

"I'm Cole, by the way." He smiles and extends his hand.

"Megan." I smile and shake his hand.

"Do you have kids?" he asks.

"One," I reply, holding up my index finger. "My daughter is an adult now. I'm about seventeen years ahead of you."

"Well, it's nice to meet someone who made it through this parenting gig and came out the other side. It gives me hope my wife and I will survive."

We laugh.

"You're not local, are you?" I ask. "If you were local, we would've crossed paths before."

"We're vacationing here for another month," Cole confirms. "We're renting a lakeside cottage. It's a beautiful town."

"Yes, it is," I agree. "I hope the murder on Sunday at the local motel didn't lower your opinion of us." I'm trying to introduce Mysti's murder without being confrontational.

"Not at all," Cole responds. "It's tragic, but these things can happen anywhere. I heard she was a transient with a shady fortune-telling gig. She probably pissed off lots of people."

Not very sympathetic, Cole.

"Are you one of those people?" I ask.

He scrunches up his face and shifts his gaze from side to side, like my question is preposterous.

"Why would you ask that?"

"Because one person saw you arguing with Mysti and another saw you chasing her on Water Street." So much for avoiding confrontation!

"I never met that woman." He shrugs and shifts his weight from one foot to the other while giving the baby a gentle bounce. The baby giggles with glee. Cole narrows his eyes. "Are you a cop or something?"

I shake my head. "No." I smile. "Just a concerned resident."

"Look." He takes a deep breath and turns his head, checking our surroundings. "I had words with the fortune teller, OK?"

"Words about what?" I inquire.

"We were at the beach last week, and the fortune teller offered my wife a reading," Cole explains. "My wife wasn't interested, but the fortune teller wouldn't leave her alone. She kept pressuring her to get a reading. Kept lowering her price, stuff like that. We were trying to spend quality time together as a family, but she wouldn't take no for an answer. I finally told her to back off."

"This happened at the beach?" I confirm.

"Yeah," he insists. "It was a weekday, and it wasn't very busy. I don't know if anyone witnessed it."

"Wow," I say. "Thanks for clearing that up, Cole. I hope the rest of your vacation is less eventful."

He turns to check on his wife and other children.

"I have to go. My wife is outnumbered over there."

"Bye, Cole. It was nice to meet you," I say as he rushes away. "Ready, Soph?" I ask, steering us toward Jax.

Jax and his new best friend, Guinness, are playing fetch while Guinness's owner sits on a nearby bench, chatting with a friend.

"How'd it go?" Jax asks as Sophie and I approach him.

"Interesting," I reply.

Sophie and Guinness greet each other the way dogs do. When Guinness's owner whistles, he picks up his tennis ball and obediently trots over to her.

"Bye, Guinness." Jax waves at the chocolate lab. "Bye, ma'am." He waves at the owner, who waves back.

"He mentioned nothing about being at the Hav-a-nap motel," I tell Jax.

"He was there," Jax insists. "And he was angry."

"He lied to me at least once."

"How do you know?" Jax asks.

"He contradicted himself," I reply. "First, he said he never met Mysti, then he admitted he had words with her on the beach."

"Did you get his picture?"

I snap my fingers. I forgot about the picture!

"Yes," I reply, stopping to open my phone and text the photos to Eric.

Me: Found the baby-wearing dad! Cole Duffy is at the playground on Water Street right now.

Eric: Thanks, babe! Followed by a red heart emoji.

While the photo app is open, I show Jax the selfie of Mysti and her friend.

"Did Eric show you this?" I ask, handing him my phone.

We resume walking toward Knitorious.

"Yeah," Jax says, nodding. "I don't know her, but I think it's Happy Hour."

"You think they took the photo during happy hour at The Embassy?" I clarify.

"No," Jax replies. "I think the mystery woman in the photo is Mysti's friend, Happy Hour."

"Her name is Happy Hour?" I ask, incredulous that a sane parent would name their child Happy Hour.

"I don't think it's her actual name," Jax explains. "I think Mysti couldn't remember her name, so she just called her Happy Hour." He shrugs like this is a reasonable explanation.

"Did she tell you about Happy Hour?"

"A little," he replies. "Mysti met her at the pub one night, and they got drunk together. She said Happy Hour was breaking up with her boyfriend. They drank to take her mind off it. Mysti said Happy Hour's boyfriend was a jerk, and Karma would give him what he deserved."

Was breaking up could have multiple meanings. Did Mysti mean Happy Hour just broke up with her boyfriend? Past tense. Or did she mean Happy Hour was about to break up with her boyfriend? Future tense. I wonder what Happy Hour's boyfriend did to warrant Mysti calling him a jerk and wishing karmic comeuppance on him.

"Did Mysti ever see Happy Hour again?" I ask. "Did they stay in touch?"

"She didn't say," Jax responds. "She said Happy Hour was in town visiting her boyfriend." He shrugs. "I assumed the boyfriend lives in Harmony Lake, but Happy Hour doesn't."

For the rest of the walk back to Knitorious, I wrack my brain trying to remember if I've heard any recent break-up rumours about anyone local. Nothing comes to mind.

CHAPTER 14

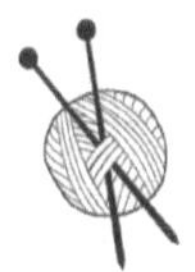

THIS FEELS like the millionth lap blanket I've crocheted together. Two charity knitters brought me enough squares for two more blankets. At this rate, every book lover in the world will have a lap blanket, not just Harmony Lake.

"Is this beautiful bouquet from Eric?" Mrs. Vogel asks.

"Yes," I reply, smiling. "It's my June floral arrangement. Phillip delivered it while Sophie and I were at the park earlier."

"How thoughtful and romantic of him," Mrs. Vogel says.

"Yes," I agree, assuming she means Eric, not Phillip.

On one of our first dates, Eric and I attended a fundraiser with a silent auction. One of the silent auction items was a year's worth of floral arrangements. Eric had the winning bid, and each month for twelve months, I received one of Phillip's gorgeous floral creations. Earlier this year, on our first anniversary, Eric renewed the floral deliveries, so now I'm midway through the second year of monthly flowers.

"I hope Hannah gets back soon," Mrs. Roblin says.

"She shouldn't be long," I say. "She's running an errand with Jax."

"We never get to see her anymore since she lives in Toronto most of the year," Mrs. Vogel comments.

"I know," I agree. "I miss her when she's not here."

The ladies knit in silence, making more squares for me to assemble into lap blankets, and I hook in silence, trying to assemble blankets as fast as the charity knitters produce new squares.

The jingle over the door interrupts the soothing, rhythmic clicking of their needles.

"Eric!" Mrs. Roblin declares, placing her knitting in her lap. "What an unexpected, pleasant surprise."

If I didn't know better, Mrs. Roblin's enthusiasm would lead me to believe a rock star just walked into Knitorious.

Eric smiles. "Good afternoon, ladies." He hands me an iced vanilla latte.

"Thank you," I mutter with a smile.

Eric doesn't look right. His hair is mussed, and he didn't shave today. He hates being unshaven.

"If I'd known you would be here, I would have brought you some cabbage rolls," Mrs. Vogel says with a hint of disappointment. "Eric loves my cabbage rolls," she says, smiling and looking at Mrs. Roblin.

"Yes, you keep saying," Mrs. Roblin responds with polite curtness.

The charity knitters *love* Eric. In private, I call them

his fan club. They love to feed him and, for reasons unknown, believe he requires a constant supply of food he cannot obtain for himself.

"That's very kind of you, Mrs. Vogel, but I just had a sandwich." He grins at her, tapping his finger on the counter and shifting his weight from one foot to the other.

"Next time," she responds.

"I can't wait," Eric says in a tone that I know is sarcastic but seems to encourage the charity knitters. He looks at me. "Can I talk to you for a minute, babe?"

We ignore the quiet, simultaneous *aww* sounds coming from Mrs. Roblin and Mrs. Vogel.

Waiting for my response, Eric rubs the back of his neck and rocks on his heels. He's not his usual composed self. He's twitchy and can't stay still. Something's going on.

"Well," I hem and haw. "I can't leave the store right now. Today is Stitch-Fix. I need to be here in case a knitter shows up."

On Tuesday afternoons, Knitorious hosts Stitch-Fix, a clinic for knitters to bring in their knitting problems and mistakes so Connie and I can help fix them. Some Tuesdays are so busy we get more knitting issues than we can fix in one afternoon, and other weeks only one or two knitters bring in their knitterly frustrations.

"We'll watch the store, Megan," Mrs. Roblin offers. "Mrs. Vogel and I have yet to encounter a knitting problem we can't solve."

"You can say that again," Mrs. Vogel says with a

giggle. "Between us, we have over a hundred years of knitting experience."

Wow. I've never thought of it like that.

"Are you sure?" I ask. "I don't want to impose or interrupt your own knitting."

"Go!" Mrs. Roblin shoos us away with her hand. "Take all the time you need."

Eric and I thank them and retreat to the upstairs apartment.

"What's up?" I ask my jittery boyfriend.

"Nothing," Eric replies, kissing me hello. "Why? Do I look like something's up? I just want to ask you about your encounter with Cole Duffy."

While Eric paces and nods, I tell him about my conversation with Cole Duffy.

After my statement, Jax returns to the apartment. He's wearing a hiking backpack, and he's lugging a huge rucksack.

"Hannah's downstairs with the knitting ladies," he says. "One of them asked me twice if I like cabbage rolls as much as Eric."

"Unless you like them a lot, tell her you have a cabbage allergy," Eric suggests, grinning.

Eric doesn't like cabbage rolls very much, but he eats one in front of Mrs. Vogel whenever she gives him some because he doesn't want to disappoint her. He does this with all the food his fan club gives him, even food he doesn't like. Wouldn't it be hilarious if Mrs. Vogel hates making cabbage rolls and only makes them because she thinks Eric loves them?

"I'm going to unpack and do my laundry," Jax says, then disappears into the spare bedroom.

"Did you find Cole Duffy at the park?" I ask, returning to our previous conversation.

"Uh-huh," Eric replies, pacing around the living room. "He was with his wife and kids. He's going to the station when their kids go down for a nap." The red veins in his eyes are more prominent than usual.

"Do you think he'll show up?" I ask, trying to determine if he's under-slept, over-caffeinated, or both.

The good news is this incarnation of Eric—jittery and exhausted—means we're about halfway through the investigation. This happens when he has lots of pieces of the investigative puzzle and is trying to figure out how they fit together.

"I know he will," Eric says with a confident chuckle. "He's terrified his wife will find out we want to talk to him. He'll show up so we won't go looking for him."

Wouldn't Cole *want* the police to talk to his wife? If he was honest with me about his altercation with Mysti, Cole's wife would have witnessed it and can verify his story.

Eric sits next to me and rubs his stubbled chin.

"How much coffee have you had?" I ask.

"Today?"

I nod.

He shrugs. "I don't know." He smiles. "It's not like I write it down, babe."

Eric has two cups of coffee. Every day. No more, no less. Always before noon. Dark roast, double-double.

"Did you sleep last night?"

"Of course, I slept," he scoffs.

"How long?"

"Almost two hours," he says, like it's an achievement.

Eric is brought to us today by not enough sleep and too much caffeine.

"Tell me what happened last night."

He groans. "It was that selfie from Mysti's phone." He leans back and laces his fingers behind his head. "Something about it bothered me, but I couldn't put my finger on it. Every time I closed my eyes, I saw that picture."

"The selfies you showed me of Mysti and Happy Hour?"

He nods. "I finally realized why it bothered me."

"What was it?" I'm enthralled.

"Mysti's shirt," he replies, unlocking his phone and handing it to me with the duck-lipped selfie of the two young women on the screen. "It was missing."

I look at the photo, paying particular attention to Mysti's shirt, a blush coloured, cap-sleeved boatneck. The selfies only show Mysti and her friend from the chest up, so I can't see the bottom half of their outfits, but judging from these photos, there's nothing extraordinary about Mysti's shirt.

"Mysti's shirt was missing?" I ask, making sure I understand.

"It wasn't with the rest of her stuff, and she wasn't wearing it when she died," Eric clarifies, sitting up. "Mysti was a light traveller. She had a small wardrobe. We collected and catalogued all her belongings. The shirt wasn't there. It was driving me nuts, so I went to room 107."

"What time?" I ask.

"Just after midnight?" he says with a facial expression that tells me he's not sure.

"Was her shirt in room 107?"

"No," Eric replies. "I looked everywhere. I even searched Jax's stuff in case her shirt got mixed up with his things. Nothing."

"But you found the shirt somewhere?"

He nods. "In a garbage can outside. Turns out, it's not a shirt. It's a dress. One of those long, flowy dresses like the ones you like to wear."

"You went through the garbage?" I ask, scrunching my nose. "Eww."

"It's not always a glamorous job, babe."

Confused, I shake my head. "I think I'm missing something. Why is the shir—dress significant?"

"Why would she throw it away?" he asks, answering my question with a question. "Mysti had a very limited wardrobe. And why use a garbage can outside when there were two garbage cans inside the room?"

"I don't know," I say, shaking my head. "Was the dress torn? Did it have a stain?"

"No, and no," he replies, smirking and leaning in closer. "I don't think Mysti put the dress in the garbage can. I think the killer did after they used it to kill her and exit the motel room without leaving fingerprints."

"You think the dress is the murder weapon?" This blows my mind.

He nods. "I think it's possible. At the very least, I suspect the killer used it to exit the room without leaving fingerprints behind. The coroner found fibres in Mysti's lungs. We know the killer smothered her. But we haven't found anything in the room that matches the fibres."

"So, part of your jitteriness is because you're on pins and needles waiting for the forensic report to confirm the dress is the murder weapon," I deduce.

Eric's eyes light up with relief. "You got it."

"Is it possible the killer left their DNA on the dress?" I ask.

"Maybe," he replies. "It's possible but not probable that they left touch DNA."

Touch DNA is the term for the microscopic skin cells we leave behind when we touch almost anything. Science has evolved to where they can extract these tiny samples and analyse them.

"Babe,"—Eric takes my hand and rubs his thumb in circles on the back of it—"the dress is a hold back."

"Got it," I say, nodding.

A holdback is evidence only the killer, or someone who was at the crime scene, would know about. Police use holdback evidence to eliminate false confessions—a false confessor wouldn't know about the holdback evidence—and to verify the killer. If the killer mentions the holdback evidence, it confirms they were at the crime scene.

"You need a good night's sleep," I say, "in your own bed."

"What about Jax?" Eric asks. "Babe, I want to come

home, but I don't want to leave him. What if his DNA results come back, and he's alone?"

"Jax is an adult," I remind him. "We'll invite him to either stay in our spare room or stay here. Either way, he'll be fine. You won't. You need sleep. What if you make a mistake because you're overtired, and it compromises the investigation?"

Eric looks at the ceiling and sighs. "You're right." He squeezes my hand. "I have to talk to Jax about your walk to the park and ask him where he wants to stay. Then I'll go to the station to interview Cole Duffy. After that, I'll come home."

"Good," I say, leaning into him. "I miss you."

"I miss you too," he says, then kisses the top of my head. "This apartment doesn't feel like home anymore. Home is where you are."

CHAPTER 15

"YOU'RE KNITTING?!" I clutch my chest dramatically as if I'm having a heart attack.

"Don't make a big deal out of it, Mum." Hannah rolls her eyes. "I know how to knit."

"I know you *can* knit. I just haven't seen you do it since you were twelve."

"Thirteen," she corrects me.

"And she's doing a marvellous job," Mrs. Vogel interjects. "Hannah is helping us make lap blanket squares." She smiles.

"Looks like I'll have more lap blankets to assemble." I grin.

"Can I relieve you, Mrs. Roblin?" I ask.

Mrs. Roblin is helping a stitch-fix knitter fix a mystery hole in a sock-in-progress.

"No, thank you, Megan," Mrs. Roblin replies with a giggle. "I'm quite enjoying this." The knitter she's helping looks at her like she just said she quite enjoys eating mud.

"And I got to help someone pick up stitches," Mrs. Vogel boasts. "It was lace so not as easy as you'd think."

"Thank you, ladies." I smile.

"We know we aren't Connie, but we're happy to help you until she gets back," Mrs. Roblin says. "In fact, we'll come back every Tuesday until Connie gets back from Europe."

"I appreciate it," I say, trying not to tear up from their kindness.

"Tell your handsome young man that next week I won't forget the cabbage rolls," Mrs. Vogel adds.

"I will," I promise.

"We might be helpful in other ways," Mrs. Roblin adds with a wink, leaving her knitter to resume knitting now that the mystery hole has been fixed.

"How do you mean?" I ask.

"Well, Connie holds down the fort while you pursue your… *hobby,*" Mrs. Roblin replies. "And we cleared our schedules to come to Knitorious any day you need us. So, you can pursue your *hobby* without worrying about the store."

"I'm sorry, I don't understand," I say, shaking my head. "My hobby is knitting."

We're talking about different things. What other hobby do I pursue and leave Connie to hold down the fort at Knitorious? *Hobby* is a euphemism for something. But I don't know what.

"Your *other* hobby." Mrs. Vogel touches my arm and gives me an exaggerated wink.

"They mean the sleuthing, Mum," Hannah interjects. "You know when you talk to people and help Eric solve crimes?"

I look at Mrs. Roblin and Mrs. Vogel. Both women nod and smile.

"Oh," I say. "I guess I've never considered it a hobby."

"Call it whatever you want," Mrs. Roblin says. "Harmony Lake needs a murderer off our streets, and you and Eric are good at doing that."

"The charity knitters have your back and will do whatever necessary to help you and Eric clean up the streets," Mrs. Vogel adds.

She makes it sound like we're trying to bring down a drug cartel.

"You can't be chained to the store when there's a murder to solve," Mrs. Roblin explains. "We need you pounding the pavement, doing whatever it is you do."

"We promised Connie we would keep our collective eye on you while she's away and accommodate your hobby if you need us," Mrs. Vogel adds.

"I think I understand," I respond, hoping this conversation is almost over because looking back and forth between the two women is making me dizzy. "Thank you for explaining it to me." I smile. "And I thought you only came in today to drop off squares and knit."

Mrs. Roblin and Mrs. Vogel giggle.

"There's always more to us than meets the eye, Megan," Mrs. Roblin teases in a way that sounds kind of ominous.

There's an undercurrent of truth to her joke. The

charity knitters are an organized network of matriarchs from established Harmony Lake families. They wield a lot of power and influence in the community and use their influence to protect our small town and ensure that Harmony Lake remains… harmonious. The charity knitters helped to convince Adam to run for mayor. They've taken on and defeated big-box corporations who tried to bully their way into our lakeside haven and have caused more than one real estate developer to run away with their tails tucked between their legs.

The Charity Knitting Guild has a complex organizational structure with the older, more mature women holding the highest positions while recruiting and training the next generation to take their place. I suspect Mrs. Roblin is their queenpin, but I'm not sure. They're secretive about who holds what role. Connie is a member of the Charity Knitting Guild, but I'm not. Connie tries to include me and convince me to get involved. The charity knitters meet at Knitorious every Wednesday afternoon to knit, plan future charity projects, and order supplies, so I'm often privy to their coded conversations, but have no idea what they mean. Kind of like the conversation I just had with Mrs. Roblin and Mrs. Vogel about my *hobby*.

"Aren't you handsome!" Mrs. Roblin declares, bringing her hands together in front of her chest.

"He looks just like Eric!" Mrs. Vogel proclaims. "He's the spitting image!"

Intimidated by their enthusiasm, Jax inches into the store from the backroom. He's interview-ready in a suit. His hair is parted and neat. The Sloane genes are so strong, if someone told me Eric's doppelganger time-travelled here from twenty years ago, I'd believe them.

"Ready for your interview?" I ask.

"I think so," he replies, nodding. "But I'm nervous."

"You'll be fine," Hannah assures him.

"I hope so," Jax says, taking a deep breath.

"Trust us, Jax," Mrs. Roblin says. "You'll be fine." She winks.

Is this interview a formality? Is the outcome already decided? Maybe I was wrong about Eric and Adam plotting to introduce Jax to the fire chief. Maybe the charity knitters were behind it.

WHEN JAX LEAVES for his interview, and the satisfied Stitch-Fix knitter leaves with her repaired, hole-less sock, I check the time on the cash register. Three more hours until closing time. I sigh, trying to figure out if today has been one of the longest or shortest days ever. Somehow, it's both. I was hoping to drop off some lap blankets to Mrs. Bickerson today and check in with her after what Hannah told me yesterday.

I join the charity knitters and Hannah in the cozy sitting area, picking up my crochet hook and the lap blanket I was working on before Eric interrupted us.

"Mum, weren't you going to drop off lap blankets to Mrs. Bickerson at the library today?" Hannah asks as if she can read my mind. "Mrs. Roblin and Mrs. Vogel are here if someone needs knitting help, and I'm here for everything else."

"You should go," Mrs. Vogel adds. "We're all worried about Shanice Bickerson. It's no secret she spent a lot of time with the fortune teller. We hear she's downright despondent because of the girl's murder."

"And from what we hear, Boris Bickerson isn't very sympathetic to his wife's sadness."

I'm glad they use their powers for good.

"You've convinced me," I say, placing my crochet hook and lap blanket on the coffee table and standing up. I collect the bag of completed lap blankets from under the counter and throw my bag over my shoulder. "Text me if you need me."

"Meg!"

My eyes search the courtyard for the source of my name.

"Mayor Martel!" Adam and I exchange a cheek kiss.

"Are you looking for me?" Adam asks, his blue eyes squinting into the afternoon sun.

Harmony Lake Town Hall and The Harmony Lake Public Library are in adjoining buildings. The locals call the area in front of the entrances The Courtyard.

"No," I reply. "I wouldn't just show up at your office without calling first. I know how busy you are."

"I'm never too busy for you, Meg." Adam smiles. "Hannah told me about Lucas," he says, taking my arm and leading me to a shady spot under a nearby tree.

"Good," I respond. "She was scared to talk to you about it."

"I could tell," Adam nods. "She called me last night. I could hear the hesitation in her voice."

"What did you say?" I ask, hoping he didn't mess this up.

"I was supportive," he says. "Thankfully it was over the phone, and she couldn't see me roll my eyes."

I sigh and roll my eyes, but Adam can't see them behind my sunglasses. "Hannah is more perceptive than we give her credit for," I say. "She's quite aware of how you feel about her boyfriend."

"She gets that from you," Adam muses. "Hannah's coming to my place for dinner tonight. We're going to eat pizza and download a new romantic comedy she wants to watch."

"You hate rom-coms," I point out.

"I love our daughter more than I hate sappy, romantic humour," he admits. "You like rom-coms. You should join us."

"I can't," I fib. "I have plans. And I don't want to interrupt your quality time with Hannah."

He scoffs. "You wouldn't be interfering..."

"But thank you for being supportive of her," I interrupt before he lays out a logical, lawyerly argument convincing me to go, "and tolerating a movie you won't like to take her mind off everything. And while I'm thanking you, thank you for introducing Jax to the fire chief."

"It was a straightforward decision, Meg," Adam replies. "He's a firefighter looking for a job, and our fire department is looking for a firefighter."

Was the introduction a fluke, a plot thought up by

Adam and Eric, or did the charity knitters mastermind the entire thing? I'm about to ask him, but he opens his mouth to speak.

"Are you on your way to the town hall?" Adam asks. "I'm leaving for the day, but I can come back..."

"I'm going to the library," I interrupt, pointing to the library entrance. "Lap blankets," I explain, holding up the bag.

"Ah," he says. "Hannah told me Mrs. B was upset about the fortune teller who died."

"She told me the same thing," I admit. "Have you seen Mrs. B lately?" I ask, realizing they work next door to each other, so it's plausible. "How does she seem to you?"

"I haven't seen her," Adam insists. "I keep my distance since her blind dog peed on me."

I snort, trying to muffle an outburst of laughter. "Kilian peed on you?" I explode into laughter at the thought.

"It's not funny, Meg," Adam retorts. "I think he mistook me for a tree. Or maybe a hydrant. It happened right there." He points to a nearby bench. "He just walked over to me and relieved himself. It's amazing how well that dog can balance on two legs."

"What did you do when you saw him peeing on you?" I ask, trying to picture the event in my mind's eye.

"Nothing," Adam replies with a shrug. "By the time I realized what was happening, he was almost finished, so..." He stops talking to force down a chuckle. "If I made a scene, I would've looked like a bully. Someone could've recorded it, and it could've gone viral. I don't want to be known throughout history as the mayor who was mean to a blind, three-legged dog, Meg."

I laugh so hard, my side aches. I grab my side, and Adam takes my elbow while I compose myself. I raise my sunglasses to the top of my head and dab the tears from my eyes.

"Poor Kilian," I mutter between outbursts of laughter.

"Poor Kilian?" Adam mimics me. "How about poor Adam? He peed on the leg of my light grey suit, Meg. That suit was custom-tailored. And he ruined my lucky shoes."

"They don't sound very lucky," I spit out, overcome by a renewed fit of giggles.

"They were my lucky court shoes." Adam rolls his eyes. "You know, the cognac-brown wingtips I wear when I have court."

I dab my eyes and swallow the urge to laugh. "It sucks that a blind, three-legged dog mistook you for a tree, and you lost your lucky shoes." I snort but manage not to succumb to another fit of laughter. "I'm sorry for laughing."

"It's OK," Adam replies. "Now that I say it out loud, it is kind of funny. And it's worth it to be the person who makes you laugh again."

"Mrs. Bickerson must have been mortified," I say, still dabbing at leftover tears of laughter.

"I don't think she knows," Adam replies. "She was bickering with Boris, and they didn't seem to notice. I wasn't about to interrupt their money argument to point out that their dog just ruined my custom-tailored suit and expensive leather shoes."

"How do you know they were arguing about money?" I ask, my interest piqued.

"I heard them. They were only six feet from me. They were so into it they forgot they were in the middle of The Courtyard."

"What did they say?"

"He told her she needed to rein in her spending,"—he puts air quotes around *rein in her spending*—"then, he said he'd *rather go to jail for killing the trickster than go to the poorhouse because you wasted our money on a scam.*" He mimics Mr. B's voice and uses air quotes again.

"Sounds serious," I agree. "When was this?"

"Last week," Adam replies. "Friday. I remember because I used to wear my light grey suit on Fridays, but now I'm considering something more casual. Golf pants and golf shirt."

"Good call," I concur. "You're more approachable when you don't wear a suit."

While Adam contemplates his Friday wardrobe options, I wonder if the trickster Mr. Bickerson was referring to was Mysti and if his threat was serious or if he was just blowing off steam.

CHAPTER 16

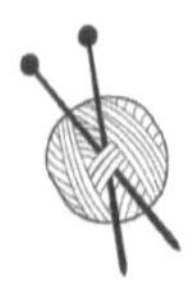

"Mrs. Bickerson will see you in her office." The summer intern points down a long hallway and smiles.

I thank the intern and take a deep breath, hoping one day Mrs. Bickerson will forgive me for what I'm about to do—ask if she thinks her husband could be a murderer. If I'm lucky, one day she'll even speak to me again.

I knock lightly and wait. No response. I crack open the door and peek in. Mrs. Bickerson is at her desk with her head in her hands. I open the door enough to poke my head inside.

"Come in, Megan." Mrs. Bickerson summons me with a wave.

Her closed-mouth smile is tight, and her eyes are puffy and red.

"Hi, Mrs. B," I say softly, sitting across from her and trying not to stare at the small mountain of wadded up tissues in front of her.

"Hi, Kilian." The dog rests his only front paw on

my knee while I rub the top of his head. Recalling Adam's recent experience with Kilian, I wrap my dress around my legs and tuck my feet under my chair, as far from Kilian's line of fire as possible. "Who's a good boy?"

"Kilian is the best boy," Mrs. Bickerson agrees, her voice thick from crying. "You're a nicer boy than your daddy, aren't you, Kilian?" She sniffles. "Yes, you are."

I get the impression Mysti's death isn't the only thing Mrs. Bickerson is crying about today.

Kilian wanders back to his dog bed in the corner, and I unclench my legs, letting them relax into a more natural position.

"I'm sorry about Mysti," I say, and watch tears well up in Mrs. Bickerson's eyes. She nods and pulls a fresh tissue from the box to dab her eyes. "Is there something else going on?" I ask. "Aside from Mysti?"

"Boris," she says with a frustrated groan. "As usual." Her voice hitches on the last word. "Oh, Megan, he was awful," Mrs. Bickerson warbles, her voice almost unintelligible because of the sobs. I place a gentle hand on top of her hand. "Do you want to talk about it?"

"Do you know what Boris said when Mysti was murdered?"

"I have no idea," I reply.

"He said, and I quote,"—Mrs. Bickerson pulls herself up to her full seated height, puts her hands on her hips, and tucks in her chin toward her neck—"*A real psychic would've seen it coming.*" She does a decent impersonation of her husband. "Then he laughed!"

"Oh my," I commiserate. "I'm sorry he wasn't more sensitive to your feelings."

"He was less than insensitive, Megan," Mrs. Bickerson confides, sounding exasperated. "Insensitive I can handle. But I can't handle happiness. He was happy someone murdered that girl. Since we found out, he's been all smug and self-satisfied. Gloating because *at least everyone's money is safe now that she's gone*." She once again impersonates Mr. Bickerson.

"Everyone reacts to death in their own unique way," I suggest, trying to comfort her.

"I don't think I can stay married to someone who celebrates the death of a fellow human being."

Oh, my. This is beyond the Bickersons usual bickering about day-to-day stuff.

"Have you told Mr. Bickerson how you feel?" I ask, venturing into couples' therapist territory, a place I'm neither comfortable nor qualified to venture into.

She shakes her head. "We haven't said a word to each other since Sunday night."

Sunday night? Mysti's death became public on Monday morning. Mysti's true identity, Everley Leighton Moregard-Davenhill, still isn't public. Eric says he's waiting for direction from her family. Sounds like the Harmony Lake rumour mill was busy on Sunday night.

I have a lot of questions for Mrs. B, but it's obvious she's not in a state to answer them. Mysti's murder and Mr. Bickerson's reaction are too much for her. I can't do anything to bring Mysti back, but I can support Mrs.

Bickerson while she works through her issues with her husband.

I take a deep breath.

"Why don't I go back to Knitorious and relieve Hannah," I suggest. "She can help at the library and you can visit Mr. Bickerson and work it out."

"No way." Mrs. Bickerson shakes her head. "If Boris wants to work this out, he knows where I am. He could talk to me instead of going fishing every day. At least I know where I am on his priority list. After fishing. Fishing, then Shanice!"

"Fishing?" I ask. "Off the pier?"

She nods. "Every morning, rain or shine. I thought under the circumstances he might skip a morning, but noooo."

One pier in particular is popular among the locals for fishing. We call it the fishing pier. You'll almost always find six to twelve people fishing there. Regular fishing in the warm months, and ice fishing in the winter months.

"How did you and Mr. Bickerson find out about Mysti?" I ask.

"I overheard two ladies in The Courtyard talking about it when I left the library on Sunday," she explains. "One of them said her sister was the maid who found Mysti's body."

"You were at the library on Sunday?" I ask. "Isn't the library closed on Sundays?"

"Yes, but I love to be here when it's quiet. And I get a lot done. The library is my happy place. And last Sunday the steam cleaners came to shampoo the carpets. I had to be here to let them in and keep an eye on things."

"Were you here all day?" I ask, wondering where the Bickersons were when Mysti was killed.

"Kilian and I came here after church. After the cleaners left, I met a friend for a late lunch, then came back."

"Mr. Bickerson was fishing?" I presume.

"He doesn't fish on Sundays," Mrs. Bickerson informs me. "After church, he goes home and listens to his podcasts." She wads up her tissue and tosses it on the mountain of tissues in front of her. "He listens to a bunch of stock market and investment podcasts on Sundays."

"Alone?"

As in, with no witnesses to confirm his alibi?

"Yes." She pulls another tissue from the box and comprehension flashes across her face. "I know what you're getting at, Megan. Boris did not kill Mysti."

I say nothing.

"Yes, he hated Mysti," Mrs. Bickerson continues. "And yes, he's not sad she's dead, but Boris is not a killer. He'd never raise his hand to someone. It's like my mother used to say." Mrs. Bickerson waggles her finger at me. "Shanice! Alligator lay egg, but him no fowl!" she says, manifesting her late mother's Jamaican accent.

"Things aren't always as they seem?" I ask, attempting to translate.

"Exactly." She smiles, seeming to find comfort from invoking her mother's words of wisdom.

"It's no secret that Mr. Bickerson didn't like Mysti," I

point out. "Multiple people saw them exchange hostile words." By multiple people, I mean April and I.

"That doesn't mean he harmed her," Mrs. Bickerson defends.

"And at least one person overheard Mr. Bickerson say he'd rather go to jail for murder than to the poorhouse, or something along those lines," I say, struggling to recall Adam's exact words.

"He didn't mean it," Mrs. Bickerson responds, not denying he said it. "He was venting." She blows her nose into her tissue. "If the police think Boris killed Mysti, they're barking up the wrong tree. They need to find the woman who was following her." A fresh supply of tears wells up in her eyes, and her chin quivers.

"What woman?" I ask.

"The woman her family hired, Ren—"

We startle when the office door swings open.

CHAPTER 17

Mrs. Bickerson and I recoil when the door slams into the wall with a heavy *bang*, shaking the office walls.

Confused, Kilian jumps off his dog bed and yowls—something between a bark and a howl—then sniffs the air and makes a hasty retreat to the safety of his owner, cowering under Mrs. Bickerson's desk.

"I'm sorry, Mrs. B," the intern sputters. "I told her you were busy."

Renée Dukes positions herself in the doorway, forcing the intern to stay in the hall.

"It's OK, Cecily," Mrs. Bickerson calls to the intern, then stands up behind her desk.

"Should I call security?" Cecily asks from the hallway.

"In fifteen minutes," Mrs. Bickerson responds. "If Ms. Dukes hasn't left the building in fifteen minutes, call the police. Do you hear me, Cecily?"

"Yes, Mrs. B," Cecily's concerned voice responds. "Fifteen minutes. I'll set my watch."

Mrs. Bickerson called Renée, Ms. Dukes. How do they know each other?

"How do you know my name?" Renée asks, looking Mrs. Bickerson up and down and closing the door behind her.

"Our mutual friend told me," Mrs. Bickerson replies, her gaze steady on Renée.

Renée scowls at me.

"Wasn't me," I clarify, pointing to my chest and shaking my head. "We haven't gotten to you yet."

"Someone at your store told me you were here," Renée says, still scowling at me.

I knit my brows together, confused. "You're looking for me?"

"Who else would I be looking for?" She answers my question with a question.

This conversation feels like a competition in confusion.

"You found me," I announce, correcting my posture. "What's so important that you had to burst into someone's office and terrify a young intern?" I glare at her with one brow arched.

"What did you say to the police about our conversation yesterday?" Renée demands.

I shrug. "Nothing that wasn't true. Why?"

"Because whatever you said convinced them to search my motel room and seize my car. Now I can't escape from this backwards little town, and it's your fault."

Backwards little town? You want to be nasty, Renée? Bring it.

"Your legal issues have nothing to do with me," I proclaim, crossing my arms in front of my chest and crossing my legs. "If the police are suspicious, maybe it's because you lie like a cheap watch."

"Lie about what?" Renée challenges.

She takes a step uncomfortably close to me, and her grip on the back of the chair next to me is so tight her knuckles are white. I refuse to let her intimidate me.

"Let's see," I say, getting ready to count her lies on my fingers. "You said you contacted Mysti's family on Saturday night. That was a lie." I push down one finger with my opposite hand. "You said you'd never spoken to Mysti. That was a lie." I push down another finger with my opposite hand. "You left out the part where a terrified Mysti fled the park and flagged down a police officer for help." I push down another finger with my opposite hand. "You probably left that out because you were the person chasing her."

"What are you talking about?" Renée narrows her eyes and turns her head, looking at me sideways.

"On Saturday?" I remind her. "When you were at the park, *surveilling* Mysti, as you put it."

Renée's face clouds with confusion, and she shakes her head.

"If you were watching Mysti, like you claim, you must've seen her pack up her stuff and take off."

Renée shakes her head again.

"Mysti ran along Water Street. She flagged down a cop because she thought someone was following her." I nod upward toward Renée. "You're the only person we know who was following Mysti."

"What time did this happen?" Renée asks.

"You tell me," I reply with an unintentional snort. "You're the detective."

"So, that's where she went," Renée mumbles under her breath, her gaze fixed on the wall.

"Excuse me?" Mrs. Bickerson asks, cocking her ear in Renée's direction. "You said something?"

"I left the park and went to the deli across the street," Renée explains. "I ordered a sandwich and used the washroom. When I got back fifteen minutes later, Ev—Mysti had disappeared. I thought she was trying to lose me."

"You're denying you chased her?" I confirm.

"I never chased Mysti," Renée insists.

"Why should we believe you?" Mrs. Bickerson asks. "You lie like a rug."

"How would you know?" She scoffs at Mrs. Bickerson. "Just because *she* says so?" Renée glances at me like you'd glance at a pile of dog poop when you warn someone to watch their step. "She doesn't know what she's talking about," Renée chortles, sneering at me. "She's a small-town busybody who thinks sleeping with the local police chief makes her a murder investigator."

Ouch! Her comment hurts more than I expect.

"At least I don't forget to TURN THE PAGE OF THE BOOK I'M PRETENDING TO READ!" I shout, standing up and sinking to her level.

Renée steps back and almost touches the office door.

"Or blend in with the crowd by WEARING THE BRIGHTEST COLOURS I CAN FIND." I gesture to her lime-green, short-sleeved, capris jumpsuit, which is actually super cute, but I'm angry and hurt and want her to feel the same. "Worst PI ever," I mutter under my breath, and sit down again with a huff.

"I knew who you were when I approached you outside the post office, you know!" Renée rolls her eyes.

Is she telling the truth, or trying to make it look like she confided in the small-town busy body and police chief's girlfriend on purpose? Who knows?

"Well, duh!" I roll my eyes. "I should hope so. It's your job to snoop."

"I have your number, Ms. Dukes," Mrs. Bickerson says. "I know all about you."

"You don't even know me!" Renée smacks her chest and looks at Mrs. Bickerson again. "I was trying to help Mysti. Her family was worried about her," she claims. "Are you judging me because of what *she* said?" she spits out the word *she* like it tastes bad and jerks her thumb toward me.

"*She* wants to know why you lied about being in Mysti's motel room," I interject, using the same tone of voice as Renée.

"I didn't lie to you about that," Renée insists.

"You told me you'd never spoken to Mysti," I clarify. "If that's true, why were you in her motel room?"

"How do you know I was in her motel room?" Renée narrows her eyes and scowls at me with more intensity.

Shoot! How do I talk my way out of this? I can't admit I know Renée's fingerprints were on the forensics report. Eric shows me evidence in confidence. He could get in trouble, and it could compromise the investigation. *Think, Megan, think!*

"I saw you."

Renée and I turn and look at Mrs. Bickerson.

"You saw her?" I clarify. "You saw Renée either enter or leave Mysti's motel room?"

"Both," Mrs. Bickerson replies. "Mysti saw her too. Friday morning. Mysti and I planned to meet at the park. I arrived first. When Mysti got there, she realized she forgot her cell phone. I drove her back to the Hav-a-nap motel to get it. When we got there, we saw Ms. Dukes picking the lock to room 107. I wanted to call the police or the motel office, but Mysti wouldn't let me." She points at Renée. "You were inside for less than five minutes. Then you left."

Mrs. Bickerson opens a desk drawer and pulls out her phone. "Mysti wouldn't let me call anyone, but I took your picture." She extends the phone toward Renée. "Want to see?" Mrs. Bickerson thrusts the phone toward Renée, but Renée doesn't take it. "You can take my phone, destroy it, and wipe the memory. I have copies in multiple locations online and offline. I'm a librarian, I know where to put stuff."

Busted!

"You and your friend here"—Renée flicks her wrist in my direction—"manipulated those photos with photo editing software."

"Maybe we should let the police decide. Hmm?" Mrs. Bickerson suggests, though it sounds more like a threat than a suggestion. "I gave physical copies of the photos to Mysti when she told me you blackmailed her.

I think you killed her when she confronted you with them."

"You blackmailed Mysti?" I look at Renée wide-eyed while I process this latest bombshell.

"Of course not!" Renée retorts. "Mysti approached me when she realized I was tailing her. I admitted her family hired me to locate her. She begged me not to tell them where she was and offered me ten thousand dollars to keep her secret."

"That's not how Mysti told it," Mrs. Bickerson says with a chuckle. "Mysti said you blackmailed her, and I believe her."

"Mysti isn't even her name," Renée hisses.

"I know," Mrs. Bickerson whispers with a wink, then raises her index finger to her lips in a *shhh* motion.

"That entitled brat tried to fleece *me!* Not the other way around!" Renée stomps her foot. "She counter blackmailed me. She told me she'd report me for breaking into her room if I didn't give her ten grand. I'd lose my PI license with charges for a crime like that!"

Sounds like a motive to me. No wonder Renée didn't look at the photos on Mrs. Bickerson's phone; she knows they exist because she saw them when Mysti showed them to her. Eric hasn't mentioned anything about the police finding photos of Renée breaking into Mysti's motel room.

"Your story keeps changing, Renée," I say in a calm voice. "It's getting hard for a small-town busybody like myself to keep up."

"Humph!" With her nose in the air, Renée swings the

door open, points her chin in the air, and marches out of the office and down the hall.

"She left within the fifteen-minute time limit." Mrs. Bickerson comes out from behind her desk and closes the office door.

"Was that true?" I ask. "Do you have pictures of Renée coming and going from Mysti's room?"

"Mmm-hmmm." Mrs. Bickerson nods, unlocking her phone. "I'll text them to you."

"Thanks," I say, still shocked by the exchange and disappointed that I allowed myself to sink to Renée's level. "I have to share them with the police."

"I know." Mrs. Bickerson nods. "It's time I talked to them anyway," she adds. "I know Mysti's story. I know who she was. And I know why she ran away from her old life. She told me about her scam and how it works, but despite that, Mysti didn't con me. Her gift was genuine, Megan. The messages she gave me were real. When I tell the police that, they'll dismiss me as a deluded, desperate woman who's wasting their time. They'll discount everything I say. Even the part about Renée Dukes."

"I don't think they'll discount you. I'm sure they'll believe you," I assure her. "Why did Mysti confide in you about her old identity?" I ask.

"She didn't," Mrs. Bickerson explains. "Boris did."

"How did Mr. Bickerson figure out Mysti's true identity?" I ask, interrupting her.

"He's a stock market hobbyist," she explains. "He recognized her from research he did on MD Biocorp stock. They include photos of the majority shareholders and board members in the annual report or something. He showed me her picture on the company website."

If Mr. Bickerson knew how wealthy Mysti was, no wonder he resented the money Mrs. Bickerson paid for readings.

"Mysti admitted it when you confronted her with her photo," I surmise.

"She told me everything." Mrs. Bickerson pulls a new tissue from the bottomless tissue box and dabs her swollen eyes. "It was like a dam had burst, Megan. That poor child was so relieved to have someone to talk to. She was the loneliest soul I've ever met."

Unable to hold it in any longer, my eyes also fill with tears for the tragic, lonely end of Mysti's life. Mrs. Bickerson slides the tissue box across the desk. Holding hands with Mrs. Bickerson, I use my free hand to take a tissue from the box and dab my eyes, hoping to contain the mascara before it runs down my face.

"Police!" Eric bellows, throwing the door open with one hand while his other hand holds his sidearm. His eyes dart around the room, assessing the situation. "What's going on?" he asks, perplexed by the sombre scene.

He shouts something over his shoulder to the officers in the hallway and holsters his weapon.

I'm crying, Mrs. Bickerson is crying, and we're holding hands over the mountain of tissue between us. Kilian emerges from under the desk to sniff around Eric's feet. I silently hope he doesn't decide to pee on Eric like he did on Adam.

"We're fine," I say with a sniffle. "Why are you here?"

"Hannah called me," he replies.

"Hannah?" I jump to my feet. "Is she OK?"

"She's fine." He puts a hand on my shoulder. "She thought you and Mrs. B were in trouble."

"Why would Hannah think that?" Mrs. Bickerson asks.

"Because her friend Cecily sent her a text saying a woman burst in and was holding you two hostage," Eric says with a chuckle.

I shrug. "We weren't hostages, per se."

"But it was a heated discussion," Mrs. Bickerson interjects.

"It's true?" Eric asks, stunned.

"No, but I can see why Cecily had that impression." Mrs. Bickerson stands up. "I'll be right back. I need to check that everything is OK in the library."

Eric closes the door behind Mrs. Bickerson when she leaves.

"Babe, why are you crying?" He sits in the chair next to me and takes my hand. "What happened?" He uses his thumb to wipe a tear from my eye.

I tell him everything, starting with Renée Dukes's confrontational entrance, and ending with Mrs. Bickerson's revelation that she knew all about Mysti and tried to help her when Renée allegedly blackmailed her.

"Looks like I'll be late tonight," he says with a sigh when I finish.

I nod.

CHAPTER 18

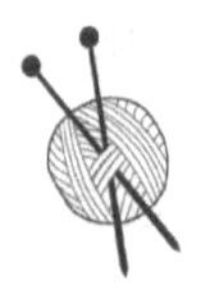

Wednesday, June 16th

April: Think we'll catch anything in the rain?

Me: Mrs. B said rain or shine, so I hope so.

April: See you soon!

When I got home last night, I called April and updated her on everything that happened yesterday. We found ourselves with a sudden, overwhelming urge to visit the fishing pier. We're angling for one fish in particular—a cantankerous, frugal species called Boris.

"Wanna go outside, Soph?" I wrap my fluffy robe around me and tie the belt at my waist.

Sophie leaps off the bed, and when I open the bedroom door, the corgi sprints down the hall. The door to Eric's home office is closed, so I assume either he's in there, or Jax accepted our invitation and is asleep on the pullout sofa.

According to the evidence, Eric slept here last night. His dirty clothes are in the laundry hamper, and judging by the damp towel on the towel rack, someone used the shower before me.

Yesterday was busy and exhausting. After I brought April up to speed, I had some leftover chicken salad, ran a hot bath, and went to bed early. I was sound asleep when Eric came home.

Sophie catapults into the backyard when I open the door. While she does her business and completes her first perimeter check of the day, I prepare her breakfast and put it on the floor.

Next, I rummage through our collection of coffee pods, searching for inspiration. Hazelnut vanilla sounds like it will hit the spot.

I wipe Sophie's wet paws with a towel we keep by the back door for this purpose. While she eats, I take my coffee upstairs to have a shower.

"Good morning, sleepyhead!" Eric says as I pass his office, the door now open.

That's one mystery solved.

I give him a facetious eye roll for calling me sleepy head. It's barely 6:30 a.m. for crying out loud.

"Hey, handsome," I say, leaning against his desk and putting my mug on his coaster. "I wasn't sure you were in here."

"J stayed at the apartment. He'd already unpacked, so it made sense," Eric explains. "I was on the phone. I didn't want to wake you and Hannah, so I closed the door."

"Who else is up this early?" I ask.

"The cops staking out Renée Dukes's motel room."

"You're watching her?" I ask, wondering what I

missed while I slept.

"More like waiting for her," Eric clarifies. "She disappeared after she left the library yesterday. We finally found her late last night when she sauntered into The Embassy. She was already drunk, so I told the officers not to approach her, just tail her. She stayed until last call, then took a cab to the motel. They're still keeping an eye on her. When she surfaces, they'll bring her in for questioning."

"Have you heard the saying, the only honest people are toddlers and drunk people?" I ask. He shakes his head. "Wouldn't it make sense to question Renée when she's drunk? She'd be less inhibited and might be more likely to tell the truth."

"It would be inadmissible," Eric says. "The court would consider her incapacitated."

"Renée and Jax have the same alibi," I say. "If she confirms that she saw him at the park when Mysti was killed, it will eliminate Jax as a suspect, right?"

"I'm not hopeful, babe," Eric confides. "Jax didn't recognize Renée when I showed him her photo. He didn't see her at the park on Sunday morning. We've canvassed like crazy, and we can't find any witnesses who can place Jax or Renée at the park when Mysti was murdered. If she doesn't verify his alibi, it's like neither of them were there."

"We'll just have to find another way to eliminate Jax," I say with more confidence than I feel. "Did you find the pictures of Renée breaking into room 107?" I ask. "The ones Mrs. Bickerson took on Friday morning. I assume Renée took them when she killed Mysti."

"They weren't with Mysti's belongings, and they weren't in Renée's motel room or car when we searched them," Eric replies. "Renée probably destroyed them. She wouldn't want anyone to find them."

"Why did Renée break into Mysti's room?" I ask. "Mrs. B said Renée was only inside for a few minutes. Whatever she was looking for, she found it fast."

"She wasn't looking for anything," Eric reveals. "She was leaving something. We found a GPS tracking device in the lining of Mysti's suitcase. I suspect Renée broke in to plant the device in case Mysti tried to skip town and give Renée the slip."

"That sounds less than legal," I comment, realizing the more I learn about Renée Dukes, the more I dislike her.

"It is," he confirms. "It's one of the many reasons she's avoiding us."

"You look better than yesterday." I run my fingertips along his clean shaven, chiseled jawline. "More like the Eric I'm used to." I comb my fingers through his well-groomed hair.

"I feel better," he says, pulling me onto his lap. "I slept for like six hours." He kisses me good morning.

He smells so good; I missed his woodsy scent. I wrap my arms around his neck and breathe him in for a moment while he spins us in slow semi-circles in his office chair. He spins us toward the door when we hear the *clickety-clack* of Sophie's nails trotting down the hall.

"Hey, Sophie." Eric rubs her head when she puts her front paws on his chair. "Did you miss me? Wanna go to the dog park?"

Sophie hops onto the sofa across from us and rests her chin on the armrest.

"Were you late because of Mrs. Bickerson's statement?" I ask.

"No," he replies. "Her statement didn't take as long as you'd think, considering how much information she shared," he says, still spinning us in lazy half-circles. "If only her husband was half as cooperative," he mumbles.

"Did Mrs. B know Happy Hour's true identity?" I ask. "I was going to show her the picture of Happy Hour and Mysti, but I didn't get a chance."

"She knew the same as Jax. Mysti met Happy Hour at The Embassy where they got drunk and commiserated about Happy Hour's boyfriend. According to Mrs. B, Mysti *had a feeling* Happy Hour's boyfriend *would get what was coming to him.*"

"Ominous," I comment.

"Anyway, after I questioned Mrs. B, I had to finish questioning Cole Duffy," Eric explains. "I was in the middle of interviewing him when I got Hannah's call that you were in trouble."

"You just left him there?" I ask. "At the station? The entire time?"

"It was unavoidable, babe." He shrugs. "He called a lawyer while I was gone, so the interview was over, anyway."

"I'm sorry you rushed to the library for no reason," I say. "Mrs. Bickerson and I were never in danger. Renée was loud and obnoxious, but she wasn't dangerous."

"I'm just glad I got the call," he says. "I turn my

ringer off when I'm in an interview. If anyone other than you or Hannah called, it wouldn't have come through."

"You have Hannah's number on bypass?" I ask, touched.

Bypass means even when Eric turns off his notifications, or mutes his phone, calls and texts from Hannah and me still get through.

"Of course." He winks. "My two most important people."

That comment earns him a kiss.

"Did you learn anything useful before Cole Duffy's lawyer showed up?"

"He denied arguing with Mysti at the Hav-a-nap on Friday. And he denied being on Water Street on Saturday afternoon, despite Lucas positively identifying him as the man he saw following Mysti."

"I'm not surprised," I admit. "He denied it to me too." I sip my coffee. "What else did I miss while I slept?"

"Let's see," he says, looking up at the ceiling. He brings the chair to a halt. "The dress I found in the garbage can is the murder weapon."

"Wow! Good job, honey!" I commend.

"Wanna see the report?" he asks proudly.

"Sure," I say, getting off his lap.

He leans forward and touches his mouse to wake up his laptop. When the screen comes to life, there's a full-screen photo of a baby looking back at us.

"Umm... who's baby?" I ask.

"Isn't he adorable?" Eric gushes. "The pregnant

officer at work had her baby last night," he replies. "Another reason I was late."

"How did someone else's baby make you late?"

"She wasn't due for another three weeks. When she went to the hospital, I had to find someone to replace her. She was on desk duty, assigned to the evidence room. She thought she had indigestion. Another officer convinced her to go to the hospital." He points to the screen. "This little guy was born a few hours ago. She emailed his photo to the department. He's cute, eh?" He leans forward and closes the email with the baby's picture.

Does Eric have baby rabies? I've never seen him swoon over a baby before.

I'm worried the brief moment he thought Jax might be his son triggered Eric's biological clock or something. Do men have biological clocks?

"I'll pick up a baby gift," I say.

"We already got them a gift," he reminds me. "Last month, remember? From their baby registry. One of those spinny, musical things that hangs over the crib."

"A mobile," I say. "I remember now."

Eric shows me the forensic report that explains how the fibres in Mysti's lungs and nose match the fibres on the dress he found in the garbage can.

"Oh my gosh!" I declare, noticing the time on his laptop. "I have to get dressed and leave." I grab my coffee from his desk and turn toward the door.

"Isn't it your morning off?" Eric asks, looking disappointed. "I thought Hannah was opening the store today?"

"She is," I confirm. "I'm meeting April," I explain, being purposefully vague.

"I was hoping to have breakfast with the woman I love." He grins, taking my hand and pulling me toward him.

"Well then, I'll leave you alone so you can call her," I tease.

"That's not funny," he says, laughing. "Seriously, babe, we haven't had a meal together since Saturday."

"My errand with April won't take long. Can we have breakfast after?"

"Breakfast at Tiffany's?" he suggests. "9 a.m.? That gives me enough time to take Sophie to the dog park."

"You're going to the dog park in the rain?" I ask.

"It's only misting," he justifies, shrugging.

"Why are you so obsessed with the dog park?"

Smirking like he has a secret, Eric leans back and laces his hands behind his head. "Come with us and find out." It sounds like a dare.

"Not today," I respond. One mystery at a time. First, I'll help Eric solve Mysti's murder, then I'll get to the bottom of his obsession with the dog park. "I'll meet you at Tiffany's."

"Do I want to know what you and April are up to?" Eric asks, narrowing his gaze and tapping his finger on the desk.

"No," I reply, "but I'll tell you if you want me to."

He shakes his head. "Be careful, please."

"Always." I smile.

CHAPTER 19

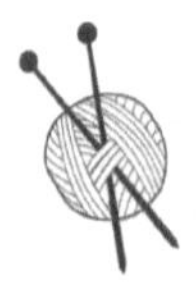

OCCASIONAL DROPS of rain hit the windshield. I run the wipers once to whisk away the rain that has accumulated since we've been here. While Mother nature alternates between drizzle and light rain without committing to either option, April and I strategize our next step.

"If we just walk along the pier until we find him, it'll be obvious we're looking for him," I say. "And it won't be private. Fishing is a quiet activity, the other anglers will hear everything we say."

"We can't wait for him to come to us. We could be here all day," April counters. "You should've brought Sophie. Walking the dog would've been a perfect excuse."

"She had to go to the dog park," I huff, rolling my eyes.

"Right," April responds with an understanding nod like she knew Sophie would be at the dog park but forgot.

"What's going on with the dog pa—?" I'm mid-question, when April interrupts me by pointing and nodding toward the far end of the small parking lot.

Mr. Bickerson opens the trunk of his car and his upper half disappears inside, like he's rummaging around for something.

"We should approach him before he finds whatever he's looking for and goes back to the pier," I say unbuckling my seat belt.

"Easiest fishing trip ever." April smiles. "We just have to reel him in, Megnifico." She makes a reeling motion with her hand.

"Ready?" I ask, distracted from my dog park question and eager to get this conversation over with.

She nods, and we exit the car, stepping onto the wet gravel.

Mr. Bickerson is whistling "Dock of The Bay" by Otis Redding. Loudly. He whistles the same handful of bars on repeat, like a scratched record stuck on the same few notes.

April and I close the car doors, looking at Mr. Bickerson for a reaction. Nothing.

"I bet he can't hear us over his whistling," I suggest, joining April on her side of the car.

"What he lacks in variety, he makes up for with volume," she whispers, making me laugh.

We approach his car, and Mr. Bickerson pops his head out of the trunk when the wet gravel crunching under our rain boots matches the volume of his whistling.

"Hi, Mr. Bickerson." I smile. "Fish biting today?" I

ask, hoping it's something you ask someone who's fishing. As a non-fisher, fishing etiquette eludes me.

"My dad swears fish are more likely to bite when it's raining," April adds.

"Nonsense," Mr. Bickerson responds, closing the trunk of his car with one hand and holding a plastic rain poncho with the other. "No doubt started by a fisherman trying to justify fishing in the rain to his carp of a wife."

I giggle at his pun.

"What's so funny?" he demands, his thick moustache twitching.

"Your fish pun," I reply. "It's clever."

"It was unintentional," Mr. Bickerson insists.

"The cleverness or the pun?" April mutters next to me, making me giggle again.

"You ladies here to fish?" he asks, unfurling the poncho. "Fishing for gossip is more like it." He laughs at his own joke as he slides the poncho over his head, then straightens his wide-brimmed boonie hat, adjusting the laces under his chin.

"We aren't here to gossip," I assure him.

I'm already frustrated by his insinuations that all wives are carping nags, and because April and I are women, our only pursuit is gossip. We have many interests aside from gossip. I remind myself that, somewhere deep inside, Mr. Bickerson must have a redeeming quality or two. Otherwise, why is Mrs. Bickerson so committed to him?

"If your boyfriend sent you to ask me about the fortune teller, don't bother," Mr. Bickerson warns. "My lawyer told me not to talk to the police without him present."

"Eric doesn't know I'm here." I hold up my hand like I'm swearing an oath. "And I'm not the police."

"But you'll tell Chief Sloane about our conversation, right?" he asks.

"That depends on what you tell me," I answer.

"Here's what you can tell your police-chief boyfriend," Mr. Bickerson says, wagging his finger at April and I. "That fraudster took advantage of my wife's kind nature to swindle her out of our money. It was only a matter of time." He shakes his head, and his laces sway under his chin. "She fleeced the wrong person and got what was coming to her."

"Were you the wrong person, Mr. B?" April asks, getting straight to the point. "I saw how angry you were with Mysti on Saturday. Remember? I intervened before you did something you'd regret." Mr. Bickerson opens his mouth to speak, but April speaks over him. "I can only imagine how hostile you were when you were alone with her."

Apparently, we're using a good-cop, bad-cop strategy, and April is the bad-cop. Except we aren't cops and we didn't discuss this before we left the car.

"I was never... I never touched that woman!" he retorts, appalled at the notion.

"But you don't deny being alone with her?" I clarify.

"I didn't say that either." He scowls at us. "Stop putting words in my mouth. You don't know what happened!"

"You're right," I agree. "We don't know what

happened because you won't tell anyone. We have to piece it together using the snippets of truth we know."

"If you think what we're saying is bad," April interjects, "you should hear the conclusions other people are jumping to." She rolls her eyes dramatically from one side to the other, while raising one corner of her mouth and making a *tsk* noise.

"Like what?" he asks, twitching a bushy eyebrow.

The idea of being fodder for the local rumour mill seems to bother Mr. Bickerson.

I look up at April, confused. Seriously? There are rumours? Why didn't April tell me? April widens her eyes and gives me a knowing nod. Ohhh, she's making it up. There are no rumours—aside from the ones I've already heard. I shake my head and refocus.

"Your poor wife is trying to defend you to the entire town, and you aren't making it easy for her," I add, hoping Mr. Bickerson has some capacity for guilt. "This situation is stressful enough for her without having to defend you too. Have you spoken to your wife since yesterday?"

Mr. Bickerson looks at his feet, digging the toe of his rain boot into the wet gravel.

"We're busy people," he says, without looking up. "Sometimes our schedules don't sync for a few days at a time." He shrugs. "Like all married people."

As someone who hasn't had a meal with the love of my life since Saturday, I can't judge him for that comment.

"Well, she spoke to the police last night," I inform him, "because she wants to put this behind her. Behind both of you. If you didn't kill Mysti, why not cooperate with the police? Tell them why you were in her motel room. Do it for Mrs. Bickerson, to ease her stress."

"How do you know I was in her motel room?" he asks, glaring at me. "Does Shanice know I was in Mysti's room?" Looking toward the dreary sky, he lets out a breath, then looks at me. "It was that maintenance guy, wasn't it?"

"Sorry?" I ask, confused.

This is the first I've heard about a maintenance man.

"The maintenance guy at the Hav-a-nap," Mr. Bickerson clarifies. "I should've known he'd finger me."

"You've lost us, Mr. B," April says. "What maintenance guy?"

"After you interrupted my conversation with the fortune teller on Saturday at the park, I met her at her motel room."

"What time?" I ask.

"I don't know," Mr. Bickerson replies. "After you came along, but before dinner."

After April chased off Mr. Bickerson, Mysti read our tarot cards. Soon after, Lucas said Mysti flagged him down on Water Street. He said he drove her to the motel, cleared the room, then left. Not long after that, Jax left Knitorious and said he went straight to the motel. Where does Mr. Bickerson fit in? Was he the person Mysti believed was following her when she flagged down Lucas?

"Mysti's whereabouts are pretty well documented on Saturday," I say. "She had a pretty tight schedule."

"After I left the park, I drove to the motel," he

explains. "I was going to the office to ask which room was Mysti's when I saw a maintenance guy fixing the ice machine. I told him I had a meeting with Mysti to find out my future but forgot her room number. He told me to try room 107."

"Was she there?" I ask.

"No," Mr. Bickerson confirms. "I knocked, but no one answered."

"But you said you were in her room," April reminds him.

"Not yet," he responds, holding up his index finger. Then he looks at me again. "I parked in sight of room 107 and waited."

"How long did you wait?" I ask.

"A while," he replies. "But I had podcasts to listen to, so I was fine," he explains, as if his ability to amuse himself while he waits is my biggest concern.

"When Mysti showed up, did you ambush her?" April asks.

"She came home in a police car," Mr. Bickerson says, wide-eyed. "I thought maybe she was under arrest, and he brought her to collect her things."

"Did you see the police officer she was with?" I ask, unlocking my phone and finding a picture of Lucas in uniform.

"That new officer. The young one who is always with Hannah," he replies.

"Him?" I show him Lucas's picture.

"That's him," Mr. Bickerson confirms. "He walked Mysti to her room. They talked outside for a few minutes, then she handed him her room key. The officer went inside, alone. She stood in the doorway, looking around, all nervous and jittery. When the officer came out, he handed her the key. She went inside and closed the door, then he left."

"How long was the officer inside Mysti's room?" I ask.

He throws up one shoulder. "Maybe two minutes. Three tops."

I let out a sigh of relief. I believe Lucas's story, but it's still nice to know someone can corroborate it.

"How did you get from your car to inside her room?" April asks.

"After the cop left, I knocked on her door," Mr. Bickerson replies. "She answered." He shrugs.

"And she just let you in?" I ask, dubious that Mysti would welcome the man who aggressively confronted her at the park, then showed up at her door unannounced.

"Not quite," he admits. "She took some persuading."

"How did you persuade her?" I probe.

"I threatened to yell her Christian name at the top of my lungs," he replies. "She opened the door but left the chain lock engaged. I whispered her name, so she knew I wasn't bluffing."

"And she let you in?" I ask.

He nods. "She begged me not to tell anyone who she was. She swore she'd leave town and not take another cent from Shanice."

"Result," I say. "You got what you wanted."

"Almost," Mr. Bickerson says. "I wanted our money

back. I told her she had twenty-four hours to give it to me, or I'd contact her family and anyone else who might be interested in her whereabouts and her current occupation. Also, I warned her never to contact my wife again."

"You blackmailed her," I clarify.

"Call it whatever you want," he concedes. "What I did was nothing compared to her lying about her gift to take advantage of innocent people. And I didn't demand a penny more than Shanice gave her. I wasn't looking for a profit. I just wanted our money back."

"Of course," April sighs beside me.

"What?" Mr. Bickerson challenges, crossing his arms and adopting a defensive stance. "If you knew who Mysti was, you wouldn't judge me for wanting my money back."

"I know who Mysti was," I tell him. "I know she was… affluent."

He scoffs. "She had so much money, she made affluent people look poor."

"Did she agree to refund the money Mrs. Bickerson paid her?" I ask, circling the conversation back to the topic at hand.

"She said she needed a day. She said she would give me cash on Sunday, then leave town on Sunday night."

"But Mysti died before she could give you the money," I speculate.

"That's right," he confirms. "One of her other scam victims must have got to her."

"You didn't go back to her room on Sunday to collect?" April asks.

"No, of course not," Mr. Bickerson baulks like he's offended by the suggestion. "I was at home. By myself. Shanice took the car to the library. We only have one car. Do you think I walked all the way from home to the Hav-a-nap motel? It's on the other side of town. I guess you think I killed the fraudster, then walked home again?" He throws his hands in the air and rolls his eyes. "Preposterous!"

Mrs. Bickerson told me she was at the library all day on Sunday, except for a quick outdoor lunch with her friend. In theory, Mr. Bickerson could've picked up the car from the library and returned it without Mrs. Bickerson's knowledge.

"Did Mysti say anything else?" I ask. "Or mention anyone? Did anything about her room or her stuff seem weird to you?"

He blinks at me like I'm asking in a foreign language.

"She said her roommate would be back any minute. She mentioned her roommate twice. And she was jumpy. I assumed it was because I was onto her and knew her true identity. She kept looking through the peephole and peeking through the curtains. And she asked if I saw anyone outside." He gestures vaguely. "Lurking, was how she said it. She asked if I noticed anyone lurking outside her room."

"Did you?" I ask.

He shakes his head. "No. I assumed she wanted me to think she was expecting someone, so I'd leave." He snorts. "Or maybe she wasn't all there, you know?" He twirls his index finger in a circular motion beside his temple, an offensive gesture indicating mental health issues. "She said someone was following her, and she hoped I didn't lead them to her."

"Did she say who?" I ask.

"No," he replies. "But she used feminine pronouns. Like it was a woman. She seemed scared. I believe she was scared, but I'm not sure I believe what she feared was real, if you get my drift." He twirls his finger near his temple again.

"Well, she died less than twenty-four hours later," April states accusingly. She digs her fists into her hips and steps toward Mr. Bickerson. I reach out and touch her elbow, prepared to pull her back if necessary. "Maybe her fears were genuine, after all. Maybe she was running for a reason. Did that *ever* occur to you? Just because she had money doesn't mean she didn't have problems. Maybe if you offered to help her, instead of blackmailing her, Mysti would still be alive."

"This isn't my fault!" Mr. Bickerson shouts, jabbing his chest with his stubby finger. "I never touched that woman. I have no responsibility for her death or the choices she made. My conscience is clear!" He leans toward me, narrowing his gaze and pointing. "Make sure you tell your boyfriend that!"

Sputtering unintelligible words under his breath, Mr. Bickerson turns on his heel and stomps toward the pier, his blue plastic poncho wafting like a cape in the lake breeze.

CHAPTER 20

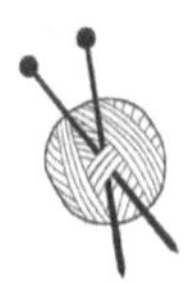

THE DRIVE to Water Street is quiet except for the intermittent scraping of the wipers across the windshield and an occasional huff from April, followed by words like, "insensitive" and "infuriating."

"I didn't realize you were this upset about Mysti's death," I say as we pull into a parking spot behind Knitorious.

"It's not so much about Mysti as Mr. B," April explains. "He's a bully who only cares about getting his money back."

"Mr. Bickerson is the opposite of his caring wife, that's for sure," I agree.

"He held back information that would be valuable to the case," April vents. "Information that cleared a suspect—Lucas—and he's indifferent to his wife's feelings about everything."

I nod. "On the surface, he's difficult to like," I acknowledge. "But he must have some redeeming qualities. Mrs. Bickerson is a practical, intelligent woman with strong opinions. If she puts up with him, there's a reason."

"Do you believe his story, Megpie?" April asks.

"Maybe?" I shrug, unsure. "The part about Lucas driving Mysti to the motel is consistent with Lucas's version of events."

"Because Mr. B knows Hannah and Lucas are a thing. He had to cover his butt in case Lucas saw him in the parking lot. He had to tell the truth about the part you could verify."

"Good point," I acknowledge. "I don't know if I believe his alibi. Maybe he took the car from the library, killed Mysti, then returned it without Mrs. Bickerson knowing."

"Maybe he was watching Mysti and caught her trying to skip town without giving him the money," April theorizes.

"Mysti told Jax she was leaving Harmony Lake on Sunday, after she collected money someone owed her," I think out loud. "I think whoever she blackmailed didn't want to pay her, but didn't want her to share their secret, either."

"According to Mr. B, he blackmailed Mysti, not the other way around," April reminds me. "Maybe he's not a murderer, just a cranky, miserly man."

I check the time on the console. "I'm meeting Eric for breakfast at Tiffany's. Do you want to join us?"

"No, thanks." April smiles. "T needs me at the bakery so she can pick up some supplies. But I'll walk with you."

"Sounds like a plan," I say, sending a quick text to

Hannah to make sure she's awake and on track to open the store. I also let her know that Mr. Bickerson verified Lucas's explanation for his fingerprints in Mysti's motel room.

MOTHER NATURE'S oscillating rain-and-mist routine takes a break for our walk along Water Street. The sidewalk is empty except for the odd bird splashing in a puddle.

Taking full advantage of our rain boots, we walk slowly, scanning the sidewalk for the next puddle, then race to stomp in it first.

"Two to one, Megastar!" April declares, jumping in a puddle with both feet.

"I can't compete with your ultra-long legs!" I tease, envious of her long, sinewy limbs.

We resume our slow amble, scanning the sidewalk for the next puddle.

The sky is dreary and grey, and the air is unseasonably cool yet somehow still humid. I'm preoccupied by my hair. I swear I feel it expanding at an alarming rate as it sucks the humidity from the air. Curly hair problems.

"Mrs. B might have a point about Mysti," April speculates.

"How so?" I ask, gathering my curls into a topknot and securing it with the hair tie I always keep on my wrist.

"Maybe Mysti's gift was genuine," April suggests.

April is the open-minded yin to my skeptical yang. She loves conspiracy theories, supernatural phenomena, and the idea that the paranormal is real.

"She told Jax and Mrs. Bickerson how her scam worked," I remind her.

"I know, but you said Mrs. B believed that despite the scam, Mysti told her things that were real." I open my mouth to object, but April points at me and keeps talking. "You said yourself that Mrs. B is an intelligent, practical woman. She would be hard to fool."

I hate having my own words used against me.

"But Mrs. Bickerson *wanted* to believe," I argue. "She's still grieving the deaths of her parents and had a vested interest in Mysti's comforting messages."

"Mysti's predictions about you were dead on," April counters.

"Pardon the pun," I say, bursting with giggles.

"Oh. Oops. Unfortunate choice of words." April laughs. "Admit it, Megadoodle, she nailed your tarot card reading. She predicted a mysterious young man would bring you a message that would change your life, and she was right!" She nudges my shoulder and races ahead of me to the next puddle. "Jax showed up that same day." She stomps her right foot and droplets splatter her jeans way above her knee. "And she predicted death."

"Three to two!" I shout, pouncing into the next puddle before April sees it. "When Mysti read my cards, Jax was her roommate, remember? He probably told her he came to Harmony Lake to find his biological father. Mysti was in town for almost a week when she met Jax. If she saw Eric around town, it would be easy to make the connection. Chances are, she saw Eric and me together, and based her reading on what Jax confided to her, and what she deduced from watching people. She said the death card wasn't literal death. She said it's a transformation from one state to another or something."

"You became an aunt," she responds, glancing over her shoulder. "That's a transformation." April grabs my hand, and dragging me along behind her, she speed walks past the next store. Then she slows us down and drops my hand, glancing over her shoulder again.

"I think someone is following us," she whispers. "Don't look!" she hisses when I turn my head to look behind us.

I hold up my index finger while I pull my phone out of my jacket pocket. Employing the same trick I used to take a discreet photo of Cole Duffy, I open the front-facing camera. April plays along, bending her knees and pressing her cheek against mine. We smile, and I pretend to take selfies of us but bring the person two stores behind us into focus and snap a photo.

"You think a mum with a baby is following us?" I whisper, looking at the photo. "She's familiar. Have you seen her before?" I hand April my phone.

"Either she's playing our puddle-jumping game by herself, or she's following us. She speeds up when we speed up, and she slows down when we slow down," April whispers, inspecting the photo. "I've never seen her before."

"Maybe she's keeping a safe distance because two

middle-aged women playing in puddles is weird," I suggest, not joking.

"Maybe," April says with hesitation.

"Excuse me!"

We turn toward the unfamiliar woman's voice.

"Woo-hoo!" She waves to us with one hand, the other hand steering the stroller toward us as fast as she can without breaking into a run.

Assuming she's a mum in a hurry, April and I separate, making a path for her and the stroller to charge through. But she doesn't charge through. Instead, she and the stroller come to an abrupt halt in front of us.

"You," she says, glowering at me.

Between Renée Dukes, Mr. Bickerson, and now this lady, I swear I've been scowled at, glared at, and huffed at more this week than the entire rest of my life combined.

"Me?" I ask, pointing at my chest and checking behind me in case she's referring to someone else.

"I know who you are," she says in an angry, threatening tone.

April and I step toward each other, closing the gap between us.

"I don't know who you are—wait!" I take a second to process the spark of recognition that ignites in my brain. A glance at the chubby baby and I know for sure. "Mrs. Duffy? Cole Duffy's wife?"

"He told you about me, then!" It's a declaration, not a question.

"No," I clarify. "He pointed you out at the playground yesterday." I extend my hand. "My name is Mega—"

"I don't care what your name is," she snaps, her eyes full of anger and fear. "I'll just call you home-wrecker since that's what you are!"

"Excuse me?" I demand.

I look around, making sure no neighbours or fellow shop owners are around to witness or hear this.

"You heard me, you… you... FLOOZY!"

Is floozy a popular word again? Does it mean something different now? Is it still a 1910 insult for a woman of questionable morals? It's so hard to keep up with the evolution of language. According to Hannah, *bad* means good, and *sick* means something is amazing.

"Floozy?" April repeats, confused.

Aghast and speechless, my jaw hangs open, and I stare at the woman and baby in front of me, processing her accusation. Mrs. Duffy's furious voice doesn't match her body language. Her grip on the stroller is shaky, and her knuckles are white. Her chin quivers, and she swallows hard, like she's fighting back tears. She has the heavy, exhausted eyes of a mother with young children, and her short, wavy hair is damp, either from the rainy weather or a recent shower. She's a woman in survival mode. I remember the overwhelm of having one baby. I can't imagine it three times over.

Mrs. Duffy adjusts the stroller's rain cover, peeking at her sleeping baby. I'm struck by the realization that she chose the word *floozy* to get her point across, without exposing her son's tiny ears to the much nastier insult she wanted to hurl at me.

"You heard me," Mrs. Duffy says, pointing her chin so it's parallel to the ground. "Don't deny it. I've known about you and Cole for months." Her eyes narrow, and she hisses the word *months*. "I'll kill you before I let you tear apart my family."

"Whoa!" I say. "Let's not say anything we'll regret." By *we*, I mean Mrs. Duffy.

"This woman?" April looks at Mrs. Duffy, but points to me. "This woman right here? You think she's having an affair with your husband?" April laughs, like Mrs. Duffy just told us a joke. "That's absurd."

"It is absurd," I agree. "But. It's. Not. Funny." I say to April through clenched teeth.

April stops laughing.

"Mrs. Duffy, I don't know why you think... what you think.... but you're wrong. I only spoke to your husband once. Yesterday at the playground. Your daughter wanted to pet my dog. Your husband and I made small talk. That's it. I swear."

"You're lying," Mrs. Duffy insists, but the tone of her voice doesn't match her confident words. "You're gaslighting me. Just like Cole does."

Gaslighting is when someone tries to convince you that your perceptions aren't real. The gaslighter says and does things to make their victim question reality and second guess what they know or believe to be true. They challenge their victim's recollection of events until the victim questions their own memories and experiences. Or they trivialize their victim's thoughts and feelings until the victim believes every thought and feeling they have is an unjustified overreaction. Gaslighting is a form of emotional abuse that's difficult to see because it's subtle to the observer and often happens within personal relationships.

"We aren't gaslighting you," April assures Mrs. Duffy, her defenses softened by the woman's obvious distress.

"I believe you, Mrs. Duffy," I say. "If you believe your husband is having an affair, I do too. But it's not with me."

It's obvious this conversation is too big for the side-walk in front of Tiffany's. I invite Mrs. Duffy and baby Duffy to join me for a coffee. Reluctant at first, the fraz-zled mum finally agrees, and I hold the door for her while she maneuvers the stroller inside.

CHAPTER 21

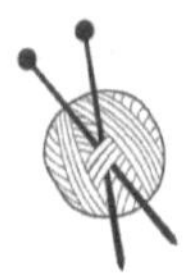

"YOU CAN GO. I'll be fine," I whisper to April after Mrs. Duffy is inside the diner. "Don't you have to work at Artsy Tartsy today?"

"No way!" April hisses. "She threatened to kill you. I'm not leaving you alone with her, and I'm not hearing about this second hand." She unlocks her phone. "I'll get one of the kids to cover for me." April walks past me into the restaurant.

Tiffany's is an homage to the iconic Audrey Hepburn movie, Breakfast at Tiffany's. The booths, chairs, and stools feature Tiffany-blue pleather upholstery and framed images from the movie adorn the walls. Because it's a breakfast restaurant, mornings are their busiest time. Like now. Scanning the sea of heads, I don't spot an empty table or booth.

"A booth just freed up," the cheerful hostess tells us. "I'll seat you in two minutes." She holds up two fingers. "We just have to clean it first."

"Great," April says. "Thanks."

While we wait for our table, the hostess offers to park Mrs. Duffy's stroller as it's a safety hazard to park it near the table and block the aisle. The baby, now awake, loves this idea and looks over his mother's shoulder with his smiley, drooly face, taking in the new scenery. I offer to take the diaper bag for her while the hostess parks the stroller. Checking the time on my phone, I remember I'm supposed to meet Eric here in ten minutes.

Me: I'm sorry to do this, but can we push back breakfast? Something came up.

Eric: Is everything OK? How long do you need?

Me: Yes. 30 minutes? Or we could do dinner instead?

Eric: I'll see you at 9:30 a.m.

Me: Thank you!

We order three coffees and diffuse the awkwardness by oohing and aahing over baby Duffy, who's bouncing on his mother's lap. He's learning to use his fine motor skills by picking up pieces of dry cereal with his thumb and index finger. He's six months old and not a very good sleeper, though he's a wonderful eater. Teething is hard, and Mrs. Duffy jokes that she has the bags under her eyes and a laundry pile of drool-soaked bibs to prove it.

The server delivers our coffees and disappears. By instinct, we move the mugs of hot liquid out of the baby's reach before adding our preferred condiments.

While we sip our coffees, and Mrs. Duffy bounces the baby on her knee, pulling various toys and snacks out of the diaper bag to keep him amused, she tells us how she found out about her husband's affair.

"Did you confront him with your proof?" I ask, engrossed by her story of months spent stealthily collecting texts, cell phone records, and credit card statements to prove his infidelity.

"Cole is very persuasive," Mrs. Duffy explains. "He has a way of convincing me it's me. Like I read too much into things or misinterpret everything he does. He has an excuse for everything, and by the time we finish discussing it, he has me convinced he's the victim, and I'm paranoid and suspicious. I end up apologizing to him."

"I'm sorry," I say, wondering if she recognizes Cole's actions as abuse.

"I came to my senses a couple of weeks ago," she says. "The night we arrived at our rental cottage in Harmony Lake. I forgot baby food, can you believe that?" She laughs. "I left it in a cooler bag on our kitchen counter in the city. After we put the kids down for the night, I got in the car to find some."

We pause briefly and discuss the various local options for procuring baby supplies. After two weeks in Harmony Lake, Mrs. Duffy has already discovered most of them.

"Anyway, when I returned to the cottage, Cole was inside on his cell phone. His phone connected to the Bluetooth in our car. He didn't know it happened. I heard their entire conversation."

"Was it the other woman?" April asks, enthralled.

Mrs. Duffy nods. "She's in Harmony Lake." Her chin quivers, and she blinks tears out of her eyes. "They were planning a rendezvous."

April and I gasp.

"Does she live in Harmony Lake, or is she visiting?" I ask.

"I'm not sure," Mrs. Duffy admits. "But this trip makes so much sense now." She shakes her head. "Under the guise of a family vacation, Cole could keep me busy looking after three kids while he had booty calls with his girlfriend," she sneers. "He thinks I don't notice he takes three hours to buy diapers? Or two hours to pick up takeout? Either he's dumber than he looks, or he thinks I am."

"It's him," April and I assure her in stereo.

A familiar, unpleasant stench fills the air, and Mrs. Duffy throws the diaper bag over her shoulder and excuses herself to change the baby.

"Her husband sounds like a total…"

The server comes by with the coffee pot, interrupting April's profane assessment of Cole Duffy, and offers to refill our coffees. We thank her and decline, then she moves to the next booth.

"The man his wife describes is the opposite of the devoted, proud family man I met at the park yesterday, or in Wilde Flowers," I say, remembering that Phillip told me Cole bought flowers for his wife.

"What if Cole Duffy's mistress was Mysti?" April hisses.

"I don't think so," I whisper. "The Duffys arrived in Harmony Lake on the first of the month. Mysti checked into the Hav-a-nap on the sixth. Mrs. Duffy said the mistress was in town when they got here."

"Maybe Mysti stayed somewhere else first," April suggests.

"You could be right," I agree. "I'll ask Eric where Mysti was on the first."

"If Mysti was Cole's mistress, maybe he killed her because she threatened to tell his wife," April theorizes. "Or maybe she blackmailed him, and he killed her."

"Or maybe Mrs. Duffy killed her," I theorize. "If she mistook me for Cole's mistress after one brief encounter at the park, maybe she also accused Mysti and killed her." It sounds far-fetched when I hear myself say it, but it's not impossible.

"You think Mrs. Duffy killed Mysti, then realized Mysti wasn't the other woman, and continued to hunt for her husband's mistress?" April paraphrases.

"I don't know," I whisper. "But she threatened to kill me on the sidewalk."

"When my kids were babies, I was too tired to kill anyone," April says. "And I only had two kids. She has three. Under age four. Ugh! Just thinking about it makes me want to take a nap."

As Mrs. Duffy weaves through the tables and booths on her way back from the restroom, I tell April I'll be fine if she leaves.

"I've monopolized enough of your day with my drama." I smile.

"Are you kidding?" April says. "I love your drama. It's the only drama I get in my boring life."

"Mrs. Duffy won't try anything in a packed restaurant. Besides, I think she knows I'm not the woman she's looking for."

"Only if you're sure," she says, finishing the last mouthful of coffee in her mug.

When Mrs. Duffy returns to the table, April excuses herself and says goodbye to Mrs. Duffy and the baby.

"Call me," April mouths over her shoulder on her way out, bringing her thumb and pinky finger to her face like a phone.

"I want to apologize for accosting you earlier," Mrs. Duffy says, handing baby Duffy a bottle of something milky. "When I saw you talking with my husband at the park yesterday, and you laughed together, I got the wrong idea." Her mouth smiles, but her eyes don't. It's a sad smile. "I added two plus two and got five. The sleep deprivation on top of everything else doesn't help."

"I understand," I say. "What will you do?"

"I don't know," Mrs. Duffy says with a hopeless sigh. "I can't continue looking for her, though. It's become an obsession. I suspect every woman I see." She exchanges the baby's damp bib with a fresh one from the bottomless diaper bag. "My parents want me to leave him," she discloses. "My mother is a psychologist, and she says Cole is a narcissist. My father spends his time devising escape plans for me and the kids." She sighs again. "Until today, I would have done anything to save my marriage. But why should I be the only one trying?" She shrugs. "I think I'll call them when I get back to the cottage."

"Listen, Mrs. D—"

"Call me Angela," she interrupts.

"Angela?" I confirm.

I'm sure Phillip said Cole's wife's name was Kelsi with an i. Phillip never forgets a name; details are his thing. If Cole was having an affair with Mysti, who's Kelsi?

"OK, Angela." I smile. "I'm Megan."

Angela Duffy extends her hand, and I shake it.

"Well, Megan, I should get going," Angela says, tossing stuff into the diaper bag. "This one still naps in the mornings, and the other two will be running their father ragged."

"Angela,"—I place a gentle hand on her wrist and lean toward her—"Cole bought flowers yesterday."

"How do you know?" Her eyes narrow into angry slits.

"I was at the florist when he paid for them," I explain. "The florist is my neighbour."

"Cole hasn't bought me flowers since Valentine's Day."

"Pink peonies," I add. "I'm sorry, I thought you should know. I'd want to know."

She nods and, without another word, slings the diaper bag over her shoulder and stands up.

"This isn't the most stroller-friendly establishment," I say, standing up. "I'll help you out."

As we pass the server, I explain that I'm not finished with the booth, and I'll be right back to order breakfast. The restaurant is wall-to-wall people, and Mrs. Duffy decides to settle the baby in the stroller outside.

"Can I ask you one last question?" I ask as we wait for the line of diners waiting to be seated to let us pass.

"Sure," she says, threading through the line with the baby smiling at me over her shoulder.

"Where were you and Cole on Sunday morning?"

"Let's see…" She stops in front of the first set of doors. "Cole was on a three-hour diaper run,"—she snorts—"and the kids and I waded in the lake for crayfish with the family next door."

Angela opens the first set of doors and steps aside while I push the stroller through. She's about to open the second door, but someone outside beats her to it.

"Hey, babe!" Eric beams at me, holding the door open with Angela's hand still on the handle. He looks from me to Angela. "Can I help?" He uses his foot to hold the door open to free up his hands.

Angela looks at me. "You know him?"

I nod. "Eric Sloane, Angela Duffy." I gesture between them. "Angela, this is Eric, our local police chief."

"Let me take that," Eric says, eyeing the stroller and extending his hands.

"Thank you," Angela grunts, thrusting the baby into his waiting arms.

I don't think either of us saw that coming.

Shocked because he expected the stroller, Eric embraces the baby who coos and smiles at him. Eric gushes at the squishy, squirmy bundle of warmth while the baby charms him with gurgly baby noises and drooly, gummy smiles. Baby Duffy giggles with glee when he reaches out to touch Eric's face, and Eric pretends to snap at his chubby, dimpled fingers.

I hand the stroller to Angela. She prepares it for the

baby and tucks the diaper bag in the basket underneath, while I watch Eric with the baby. The contrast between this handsome, muscular, strong man, and the tiny, vulnerable baby he holds gently with such tenderness almost makes my ovaries explode. Almost.

"Here you go," Eric says, passing the baby to Angela. "I think you have an appointment at the station this afternoon."

"That's right," Angela confirms, taking the baby and easing him into the stroller. "At naptime. I should be there around 1 p.m."

"We can come to your cottage if it's easier for you," Eric offers.

"No way," Angela chuckles. "I'm not giving up the chance to go somewhere alone! Even if it is a police interview. Their dad can watch them for a couple of hours."

We say goodbye, and Angela gives me an unexpected side hug, which I return. Then she turns and pushes the stroller up Water Street.

"We're going to talk about Mysti's murder over breakfast, aren't we?" Eric asks, opening the door.

I nod. "You might be late for your one o'clock with Angela," I joke, walking into the restaurant.

CHAPTER 22

When we return to the booth, the server is wiping the table, laying out paper placemats that double as menus, and cutlery wrapped in tiffany-blue paper napkins. Eric orders a coffee and I order a water, sad because I've maxed out my self-imposed daily two-coffee limit.

"I'll get your drinks and be right back to take your order," the server says with a smile.

We go through the motions of perusing the menu, but it's a formality. We always order the breakfast special.

"So," Eric says, reaching across the table and taking my hand. "What does Angela Duffy have that I don't?" He teases me about postponing our breakfast thirty minutes, so April and I could have coffee with Angela.

"A motive to kill Mysti," I reply, "and an alibi."

Eric arches his eyebrows with interest, but before we can continue, the server returns. He lets go of my hand and sits back while she places our drinks on the table.

A squealing baby draws my attention to the counter

where a man holds a baby over his head. He zooms the baby and makes airplane sounds. Watching the baby squeal with delight, I can't help but flashback to a few minutes ago when Eric was holding Baby Duffy. Holding a baby suits him. He'd be a wonderful father. While I'm certain I don't want more children, raising Hannah was the most satisfying, joyous part of my life. How can I deny him the opportunity to experience that? I know we have to talk about it, but I'm scared. What if I'm right? What if Eric wants kids? It would be irreconcilable. There's no compromise for something this huge. One person would get what they want, and the other would get eternal resentment. Neither of us could live with knowing the other made such a significant sacrifice. We'd have to end our relationship.

"Megan!" Eric squeezes my hand, bringing me back to the here and now. "Welcome back," he chuckles.

"How would you like your eggs?" the server asks me, her pen hovering over her order pad.

"Unfertilized!" I exclaim.

Wrinkles corrugate between her eyes, as the server looks at her pad, unsure what to write.

"Scrambled." Eric smiles at the server, then looks at me. "Right, babe? You meant scrambled?"

"Scrambled," I agree, nodding.

"What was that about?" Eric asks when the server leaves.

"Do you want to have a baby?" I blurt out.

As soon as I say it, I realize it sounds like a suggestion instead of an attempt to open a discussion. Like when someone says, *do you want to go to a movie?* They mean they want to go to a movie and want you to go with them. They aren't trying to start a discussion about the film industry.

"Do you?" he asks with expression that conveys concern, hesitation, fear, and confusion at the same time.

"It came out wrong," I say, squeezing his hand. "I mean,"—I take a deep breath and blow it out—"have recent events caused you to reconsider your position on parenthood?"

Eric squints at me with a confused grin. "You sound like Adam when you talk like that," he says, referring to my lawyer ex-husband. "Where is this coming from?" he asks.

He leans across the table and laces his fingers with mine.

"Your expression when you met Jax," I explain. "You were awestruck when you thought you might have a son."

"It shocked me to see someone I'd never met look so much like my brothers and me," he clarifies.

"Upstairs in the apartment, when Jax told us his birthday, you were disappointed when you realized he wasn't your son. Your whole demeanour got… sadder."

"Relief," Eric insists. "I was trying to hide how relieved I was. I didn't want Jax to feel bad because I was happy he wasn't mine."

What he says makes sense, and he sounds sincere, not like he's trying to protect my feelings.

"You were so disappointed about Jason's reaction to Jax. You talked about how if you were his father, you would have embraced him and made him feel welcome."

"I was disappointed in Jason, babe, not jealous of him. I felt bad for Jax because he felt rejected."

"What about your colleague's baby?" I challenge. "You were gushing over the picture she emailed you."

"When someone on the team has a baby, it's like the department gets a new family member," he explains. "I've watched her belly grow since day one. I was excited and happy for her."

"Thank goodness," I say with a sigh of relief, feeling my shoulders drop about three inches.

"So, you don't want to have a baby?" he asks, dubious. "Right?"

"No," I reply. "Why would you think that?"

"You were so sad Jax wasn't my son. I worried it gave you… ideas."

"I was sad for you, because I thought you were sad," I clarify.

Eric's turn to let out a sigh of relief.

"And the way you stared at the baby picture on my computer this morning," he says, "It's like you were daydreaming." He shrugs. "You were wistful or something."

"I was scared," I admit, "of this conversation." I squeeze his hand and look into his brown eyes. "I don't want kids."

"You do not know how relieved I am." He grins. "The way you looked at me when I was holding Mrs. Duffy's baby…"

"OK, you didn't imagine that one," I admit. "I had a

bit of a wobble when I saw you with him." I look into his eyes and will myself not to blink. "A moment of weakness. A very brief moment."

"I like our life. I want to focus on my career without worrying about balancing it with a family," Eric assures me. "Including Jax, I have five nieces and nephews. There's no risk of the Sloane bloodline going extinct. And if I ever feel an absence of children in my life, I hang out with them until it passes." He shrugs with a smile. "And if Hannah has kids, I'll be the most hands-on step-grandfather ever."

The server appears with our food, and we sit back.

"Are we good?" Eric mouths as she places the plates in front of us.

I nod, smiling and relieved.

We thank the server, and she flits to a nearby table where a diner is waving to get her attention.

"Can you tell me about Angela Duffy's motive and alibi?" he asks, reminding me of all the things I've learned today.

Starting from the selfie I took when April and I were puddle-jumping and ending with the moment Angela and I bumped into him at the door, I tell Eric about our impromptu coffee date with Angela and her baby.

"Incredible," Eric says, shaking his head. "You're the only person I know who can turn a hostile confrontation into a friendly coffee klatch. She accused you of having an affair with her husband, called you a floozy, and threatened to kill you. Half an hour later, she's hugging you goodbye after trusting you with her deepest, darkest secrets. Extracting information is your superpower." He sips his coffee. "I should hire you to work for the HLPD."

His flattering assessment makes me blush.

"Some of her behaviour can be attributed to sleep deprivation." Full, I push my plate of half-finished food toward him.

"Sleep deprivation isn't an excuse for threatening to kill you, babe." He jabs my sausages with his fork and transfers them to his plate. "Neither is accusing you of having an affair with her husband based on a quick glimpse at the park. It sounds like Mrs. Duffy isn't thinking rationally."

"And it sounds like Cole plays head games with her. You know, gaslighting her and manipulating her. I get the sense it's making her not think straight."

I'm struck by how ridiculous I sound, defending a woman who threatened to kill me and called me a floozy.

"So, let's say Cole and Mysti were having an affair," Eric muses. "Then who is Kelsi?"

"Another mistress?" I venture a guess. "I'm certain Phillip said the flowers were for Kelsi with an i. You know Phillip. He's very particular about details. He never forgets a name."

"Cole has a wife and at least two mistresses?" Eric pushes his plate aside and pulls out his notebook and pen.

"I don't know," I reply. "I'm just trying to come up with scenarios that fit the evidence."

He grins at me, his eyes full of pride.

"Did Cole leave Wilde Flowers with the pink peonies?" he asks.

"No," I shake my head, thinking back to yesterday. "Just him and the baby."

"So, Phillip must have delivered them," Eric surmises. "I'll assign an officer to contact Phillip and get the address. Whoever Kelsi is, we need to talk to her. And if Cole kills his mistresses, we have to do a wellness check on her."

"You and April don't know anyone local named Kelsi?" he asks.

I shake my head. "Neither of us knows anyone named Kelsi, period. Local or otherwise."

"I'll get to work verifying Cole's three-hour trip to buy diapers on Sunday," he comments, making notes in his notebook.

"Angela said she caught Cole speaking to his mistress—whoever she is—on the first of the month. Where was Mysti on the first?" I ask.

"Our first confirmed sighting of Mysti in Harmony Lake is on the sixth," Eric says. "I've pieced together most of her movements for the three months before her death, but there are gaps. I suspect the gaps were when she travelled between towns. She probably stayed in motels that accepted cash and laid low until she needed to make more money. The first of the month fell into a gap."

"You would've found Cole's number on Mysti's phone if they were seeing each other, right?" I ask.

"Mysti rarely used her phone," Eric reminds me. "It's a burner. For all we know, she replaced it every week." He shrugs. "We're still waiting for call records from the landline in her motel room, and the pay phone in the parking lot of the motel."

"Huh! Payphones," I say. "I thought they were obsolete. I didn't realize the Hav-a-nap still has one."

"The Hav-a-nap has one," Eric responds. "There's one at The Embassy, one near the town hall, and a couple by the waterfront."

Now that he says it, I realize he's right. It's surreal that I pass these payphones every day without being consciously aware of them.

"Mysti could've used any of those," I realize out loud. "She was in all those places."

Eric nods.

We pause our conversation while the server clears our dishes and refills Eric's coffee.

"By the way," he says, pouring cream into his mug, "Mysti's family is issuing a press release about her death today." He stirs his coffee. "Dinnertime, I think." He pulls out his phone and swipes a few times, then hands it to me across the table. "Want to read it?"

I take the phone and read the press release the family's lawyer emailed to Eric. It says, "Everley Leighton Moregard-Davenhill, 29, of Toronto, Ontario, Canada died unexpectedly while vacationing at an undisclosed location. The Moregard-Davenhill family has no further comment, as Everley's death is part of an active investigation by local authorities. The family requests that the media respect their privacy during this difficult time."

"Vacationing? She was in hiding," I comment, passing Eric's phone back to him. "At least they didn't mention Harmony Lake by name or the date she died. It'll be difficult for the media to connect Everley Moregard-Davenhill to Mysti Cally."

"Doesn't matter," he says, shaking his head. "It's not hard to find a suspicious death matching her age and description and figure it out. Lucky for us, Mysti was rich and could have vacationed anywhere on the planet. They have a large search area, but the media will figure it out and show up here sooner or later."

"Got it." I nod, acknowledging his warning.

"What else did you and April do this morning?" He sips his coffee.

"Nothing," I reply, playing coy. "We fancied an early morning walk at the pier, that's all."

"In the rain?"

"It's only misting." I mimic Eric's tone of voice and shrug when he said these exact words about taking Sophie to the dog park in the rain this morning.

Shaking his head, Eric tries but cannot suppress a laugh. "Smart aleck," he mumbles between snickers. "Let me guess..." He pretends to think hard. "The fishing pier by chance?"

"As a matter of fact…"

His phone chimes, interrupting us.

"Hmph!" he says, reading the screen. "Guess who's at the station offering to give a statement?" I shake my head, having no clue who it could be. "Boris Bickerson," Eric replies, his thumbs typing a response.

"Wow!" I say, shocked and pleased.

I guess Mr. Bickerson has a conscience, after all.

"Does his sudden cooperation have anything to do

with you and April?" he asks.

"I doubt it," I say with a chuckle. "He was *not* happy to see us this morning. If anyone convinced him to talk to the police, my money's on Mrs. Bickerson."

We pay for breakfast, and Eric walks me to Knitorious because that's where he parked. We take our time, taking advantage of a break in the rain, and I tell him about my and April's conversation with Mr. Bickerson. I put particular emphasis on the part where Mr. Bickerson's version of events corroborates Lucas's version of events, verifying that my daughter's boyfriend told the truth about how and why his fingerprints ended up all over Mysti's motel room.

Eric stops walking just before we reach Knitorious and pulls my hand, turning me toward him.

"Please don't tell Hannah, yet." His serious expression tells me now isn't the time to tell him she already knows. "Tell her after Mr. Bickerson signs his statement. In case he changes his story. It might prove Lucas told the truth about driving Mysti to the motel and checking her room on Saturday, but it doesn't prove Lucas wasn't in her room on Sunday morning. He still has no alibi for Mysti's murder."

"I'll manage Hannah's expectations," I assure him.

I wish I could make this go away for her. Hannah's too young to worry about her boyfriend being implicated in a murder. We need to solve Mysti's murder so my daughter can get on with her life, murder-free like someone her age should, and my boyfriend can get on with his life, getting to know his newfound nephew as a person instead of a person of interest.

CHAPTER 23

"IT'S WEIRD, RIGHT?" I ask Jax when Sophie drops the orange tennis ball at my feet, after I threw the blue rubber ring for her. "She ignored the blue rubber ring on purpose and brought back a ball instead. What other dog does that?"

"Isn't Sophie trained to only bring you tennis balls?" Jax asks like it's a generally accepted fact.

"What?" I ask. "Where did you hear that?"

"I just assumed," he stammers, shifting his weight uncomfortably. "I'm sure Sophie's normal." He rushes to the other side of the deck with his face focussed on his phone.

I'm the only person in Sophie's life who's worried that her bizarre new habit of fetching and retrieving anything except the toy I throw is a symptom of something serious. Can two-and-a-half-year-old dogs get dementia? Is it possible she forgets which toy she's supposed to bring back? I don't think Sophie has vision problems; she doesn't bump into things. Do corgis go through a rebellious phase? Is she trying to express her individuality?

"Mum, Eric's home," Hannah announces, closing the screen door behind her and dropping into a lounge chair with a heavy sigh. "He said he'll join us after he changes out of his work clothes."

"OK." I pick up the squeaky rubber squirrel and lob it across the yard. "Start the barbecue in about ten minutes," I instruct as I watch Sophie ignore the rubber squirrel and sniff around it. "I'm going inside to start the potatoes and make the salad."

Sophie happens upon an old, weathered green tennis ball, picks it up, and prances proudly toward the deck. I throw my hands in the air, frustrated. I give up.

The sun forced its way through the clouds about an hour ago. The air is still cooler than it should be for mid-June, but it's barbecue weather, nonetheless. When you live somewhere that gets snowfall warnings seven months of the year, you learn to broaden your definition of barbecue weather.

"Hey, handsome," I say, when Eric joins me in the kitchen.

He presses his hands on the counter on either side of me, caging me between him and the counter, and kisses me hello.

"Is Hannah all right?" he asks, looking through the window behind me. "She looks like she lost her best friend."

"Something like that," I respond, ducking under his arm to free myself from his man-made cage. "Today was

Lucas's day off. He was supposed to come for dinner. But they changed Lucas's shift because someone he works with had a baby last night. His day off is tomorrow instead of today, and Hannah is stuck with us tonight."

"I don't schedule the shifts," he says, raising his hands to his chest in a don't-shoot-me gesture. "Unless it's an emergency like last night when we needed cover for the evidence room."

"I'm calling the vet tomorrow," I tell him as I slide a tray of mini potatoes into the preheated oven. "I'm worried about Sophie's fetch issues."

"Sophie's fine." He laughs. "There's nothing wrong with her, trust me." He smirks. "She had her annual check-up last month."

No one believes me. Am I paranoid, or does everyone know something I don't?

"What are we having?" Eric asks, rubbing his washboard stomach.

"Spiducci, rosemary roasted potatoes, and Greek Salad," I reply. "Hungry?"

"Always," he replies, looking out the window at Hannah and Jax in the backyard. "I don't want them to overhear," he explains. "Mr. Bickerson gave us a signed statement."

"Yay!" I say. "Did his statement match what he told April and me?"

Eric nods. "You can tell Hannah we verified Lucas's claims about when and why he went to Mysti's motel room on Saturday."

"Excellent," I say, nodding.

"You already told her." It's a statement, not a question.

"Yes," I admit. "But I told her *before* you asked me not to," I explain, hoping to make it seem less sneaky.

"I figured," he says with a sigh. "I questioned Renée today," he informs me. "Oh! and I found out where Phillip delivered the flowers Cole bought."

"You've had a productive day!" My interest piqued, I stop dicing the tomato, put the knife down, and turn to face Eric, giving him my full attention.

"Phillip delivered the flowers to the Harbourview condominium complex," Eric discloses. "My officer knocked on the door to the unit, but no one answered. The doorman said when Phillip delivered the flowers, he called up to the condo and offered to accept them on Kelsi's behalf, but she told him to buzz Phillip up and instructed him to leave the flowers outside the door of her unit."

"So, Phillip didn't *see* Kelsi," I conclude.

"Didn't see her and didn't hear her," Eric confirms.

"The doorman said the unit Phillip delivered the flowers to is a vacation rental. It's not owner occupied. He confirmed a woman has been staying there, but his description was vague. According to him, she comes and goes from the underground parking garage, so he's only seen her twice. The camera footage from the garage is grainy, and the car associated with the condo unit has dark, tinted windows. We ran the plate, and the car is a rental. I'm waiting for the rental company to return my call. They might demand a warrant before they tell me anything."

"Who owns the rental condo?" I ask. "The owner must know who rented it."

"The doorman provided the owner's contact information. I'm waiting for him to call me back," Eric replies. "If Cole's mistress is staying in the unit, I expect he rented the unit for her, but if I'm lucky, he used her name so his wife wouldn't find out. Her last name and contact information should be on the rental application."

"Hi, Eric," Jax says as he opens the back door. "Hannah sent me to get the meat."

"Hi, J," Eric says. "I'll grab the skewers and bring them out in a minute."

"Can you ask Hannah to set the table please?" I ask Jax.

Jax nods and smiles, then returns to the back deck.

"Later?" I ask, referring to the interviews he conducted today.

"Later," Eric agrees, kissing my forehead.

He retrieves the lamb and chicken spiducci from the fridge and goes outside. I continue chopping and dicing vegetables, wondering if the new information Eric gathered today will get him any closer to arresting Mysti's killer.

While we eat, Hannah and Jax devise a plan to meet up with some of her friends for a movie in Harmony Hills. Their plan brings Hannah out of her pining-for-Lucas slump, and Jax is excited to meet people his own age. Jax informs us he has a second interview with the Harmony Lake Fire Department tomorrow, and the three of us assure him a second interview is a good sign.

"If they don't like you, they wouldn't want to see you again," Hannah reasons.

Eric and I offer to clear the table and clean the kitchen, so they won't be late for the movie.

"Drive safe," I remind Jax as he and Hannah put their shoes on. "You're carrying precious cargo."

"My driver's abstract is spotless," Jax states with such seriousness, I half expect him to produce a copy from his pocket and show it to me.

"I'm kidding," I assure him. "I'm sure you're an excellent driver."

"I'm not kidding," Eric interjects, bellowing from the kitchen. "Drive safe."

"He's kidding too," I say to Jax, his expression more fearful than amused. "It's his sense of humour. You'll get used to it."

"Jax can't tell when you're joking," I chide Eric when Hannah and Jax leave. "He's not used to your brand of sarcasm. He's freaked out enough with being a murder suspect, waiting for the DNA results, and the job interviews. Don't stress him out."

"He's fine, babe." Eric grins. "I check in with him every day to make sure he's coping."

"You're a good uncle," I say. "He's lucky he found you."

"He's lucky he found *us*," Eric corrects me, stepping away from the sink and wiping his hands on a dish towel. "It's for the best he didn't find Jason first," Eric confides. "Jason still hasn't warmed up to the idea. He hasn't asked even once how Jax is coping. When I call or text him and mention Jax, he changes the subject and says he has to go."

"Maybe the DNA results will help him," I suggest. "When will we get them?"

"Friday at the latest, according to the link the Let Me Take A Cellfie website sent to Jason and Jax," Eric replies.

At least one mystery will be solved soon.

CHAPTER 24

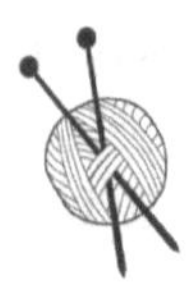

"ARE YOU WORKING TONIGHT?" I ask.

"I have to answer a few emails, but that's it," Eric replies, shrugging. "I need a night off."

"Yes, you do," I agree. We pour another glass of wine and move to the family room. Anticipating the move, Sophie's already situated on the sofa, curled up for her after-dinner nap. "You didn't correct me about Jax being stressed because he's a murder suspect. I assume if Renée placed him at the park when Mysti died, you would have told him you eliminated him."

"Your assumption is correct," he says. "No one can place Jax at the park. He may as well have no alibi."

"None of the suspects have an alibi," I say, looking for a silver lining.

I reach for the coffee table and pick up the lap blanket I'm assembling and the next square in the pile.

"Yup. We have five suspects and zero verified alibis." Eric sips his wine and puts the glass on the table, which Sophie interprets as an invitation, so she crawls onto his lap, and he automatically strokes her. "Jax, Renée, Lucas, Cole, and Mr. Bickerson." He raises a finger for each name.

"The blackmail note you found in Mysti's throat implies her killer is someone she blackmailed," I remind him. "The only suspect Mysti blackmailed was Renée Dukes."

"That doesn't mean Mysti didn't blackmail someone else," Eric points out. "It just means we don't have evidence of another blackmail scheme."

"Let's try to get into Mysti's head," I suggest, placing the lap blanket and crochet hook in my lap. "Why would she blackmail Jax?" I ask. "He just graduated from school and doesn't have the ten thousand dollars she demanded. Also, he's barely twenty-two years old. How many secrets can he have that would warrant extortion?"

"You're right about his financial situation," Eric reveals. "I looked at his bank records, and Jax couldn't have paid Mysti that much money. But his inability to pay the blackmail demand gives him a motive to kill her."

"What information could she have about him?"

Eric shrugs and picks up his wine glass. "Everyone has secrets, babe." He takes a sip.

Though they knew each other for less than forty-eight hours, Jax and Mysti shared a lot of information with each other. At least, she shared a lot of information with him—how her scam worked, that she was running away from her family, that someone was stalking her. Maybe the information Mysti shared with

Jax was part of a strategy to get Jax to share information with her. Jax said Mysti knew what questions to ask to get information. Maybe exchanging secrets was one of her strategies. Jax is young, naïve, and trusting. I could see him confiding in her if he believed she was a friend.

"What about Mr. Bickerson?" I ask. "He has no alibi and refused to talk to the police until today. Also, Adam overheard him threaten to kill Mysti."

"Adam overheard Mr. Bickerson threaten to kill *someone*," Eric clarifies. "Mr. Bickerson didn't use Mysti's name. I'm sure he meant Mysti, but I can't prove it. He admits he was in Mysti's room, and he admits he blackmailed her for the money Mrs. Bickerson spent on Mysti's... services."

"He knew Mysti's real name before anyone else in town. He knew she was rich. Do you believe he settled for blackmailing her only for the money Mrs. Bickerson paid her, or do you think he wanted more?"

"I don't know," Eric says. "The story he told you and April is consistent with the statement he gave me today. We did a thorough background check on the Bickersons and didn't find any skeletons in their closet. If Mysti blackmailed Mr. Bickerson, she did it with information we can't find."

"I think the prime suspect is Renée," I assert. "And I'm not saying that because I don't like her. She outright lied about talking to Mysti and about contacting Mysti's family. And she broke the law when she broke into Mysti's motel room and planted the GPS tracker. Also, she admits that Mysti blackmailed her for ten thousand dollars, the same amount written on the note you found in Mysti's throat."

"I agree it doesn't look good for Renée Dukes." Eric nods. "But unless I can place her at the scene of Mysti's murder, the evidence is circumstantial. And the other suspects create reasonable doubt. A murder charge wouldn't stick."

"There has to be a way to prove it." I think out loud. "Can you at least charge her with breaking into Mysti's motel room and planting the GPS tracker?"

"She could face charges for those things and blackmail," Eric replies. "She admitted she blackmailed Mysti and Mysti counter-blackmailed her. Renée's hoping if she cooperates with us, we'll reduce or eliminate any charges against her.

"Did you show Renée the picture of Mysti and Happy Hour?"

"Renée didn't recognize her," Eric replies. "The picture was taken on the ninth. Renée didn't arrive in Harmony Lake until the tenth. She wasn't tailing Mysti yet." He sighs. "But I'd really like to find this Happy Hour person and ask her some questions. I can't help but feel like she's the missing link who can help piece this puzzle together."

"I'll put Happy Hour on project status tomorrow," I offer. "If she stayed in Harmony Lake, and hung out at our local pub, someone local must have noticed her and had an interaction with her. She's not invisible."

"While you're searching for invisible people, Cole Duffy's mistress is another person I need to talk to," Eric continues. "Cole's lawyer provided a receipt for the diapers he purchased on Sunday morning, but a single purchase at the pharmacy ten minutes away from their rental cottage doesn't explain his two-and-a-half-hour absence or prevent him from killing Mysti. He admits he had a mistress but won't tell us who."

"Had a mistress?" I ask. "Past tense? Like, he had a mistress, but she died?"

"Your guess is as good as mine," Eric replies. "I'm trying to get a warrant for his cell phone records. Until then, we only have circumstantial evidence. Lucas saw Cole on the sidewalk when Mysti flagged him down on Saturday. But that doesn't mean Cole was pursuing her. His presence could've been a coincidence. Jax saw him arguing with Mysti outside her motel room on Friday, but Cole claims he was warning Mysti to leave his wife alone."

"Did Angela Duffy verify Mysti harassed her on the beach like Cole claimed?" I ask.

Eric nods. "Mrs. Duffy said Mysti approached her at the beach and offered her a free tarot card reading. Mrs. Duffy said Cole shooed Mysti away before she could take her up on it."

"Angela Duffy wanted the reading?" I clarify. "According to Cole, Angela said no. He said he intervened because Mysti wouldn't take no for an answer."

"According to Angela, she didn't say yes or no because Cole answered for her."

"Why would Mysti offer Angela a free reading?" I ask. "Free readings don't pay the motel bill."

"The free reading could be a ploy," Eric theorizes.

"Maybe Mysti used a free reading to get people hooked, then charged for subsequent readings."

"Like free samples at the grocery store." I nod.

"Prior to Harmony Lake, Cole Duffy and Mysti never crossed paths," Eric reveals. "If Mysti was Cole's mistress, their relationship started in Harmony Lake, and it evolved fast."

"What about Lucas?" I ask. "I think he's the least probable suspect. Mysti only met him once. What kind of secret could she uncover in one brief interaction? And it would be dangerous to blackmail a cop, knowing other police departments wanted to question her. Mysti was too smart to take that risk."

"She only met him once *that we know about,*" Eric corrects me. "Just because there's no evidence to support it, doesn't mean it didn't happen," he explains. "It could just mean I haven't found the evidence yet."

My face flushes with heat, and not from the wine. "Do you think Lucas was seeing Mysti?" My tone is accusatory and defensive at the same time. "And I don't mean so she could predict his future."

"No," Eric replies, rubbing the back of my neck. "I think Lucas Butler is a trustworthy guy, otherwise I wouldn't have hired him. But my personal opinion is irrelevant. My personal opinion doesn't solve murder cases, evidence does."

"How do you prove a negative?" I demand. "How do you prove something didn't happen?"

"By proving what did happen."

We're talking in circles. I'm unable to ignore my emotional attachment to the outcome, and Eric has a frustrating ability to switch off his emotions and ignore anything that isn't evidence; I call it cop mode.

I huff and sip my wine, incensed at the idea of someone betraying my daughter's trust.

"Babe, I want to eliminate Lucas as a suspect too. At least as much as Jax. But I can't let my feelings steer the investigation. Even a hint of personal bias could affect the investigation and compromise the case. It could help the killer avoid consequences."

"I know." I nod. "I understand what you're saying, I just don't like it."

Eric pulls me into him and wraps his arms around me. Something digs into my hip. I reach between me and the sofa cushion and yank out Sophie's rubber squirrel. She must've snuck it into the house when we came inside for dinner. I toss it down the hall. Sophie vaults off the sofa in pursuit of the thing. I rest my head in the crook of Eric's neck where it meets his shoulder, and he kisses the top of my head. I relax there for a moment, letting his rhythmic breathing soothe me.

"We're going to solve this case," he whispers. "We're close. I can feel it. I always get a feeling right before a case breaks open."

"You're more confident than me," I say, sitting up and finishing my wine. Sophie drops a yellow tennis ball at my feet. I want to ask her where the rubber squirrel is but say nothing.

"I have an amazing partner," he says with a wink. "We haven't met a killer yet we couldn't catch."

Is he trying to convince himself or me?

CHAPTER 25

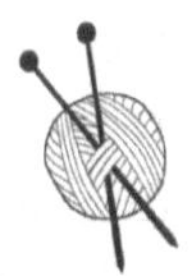

Thursday, June 17th

"Good morning, ladies," I greet Mrs. Roblin and Mrs. Vogel.

I opened the store ten minutes ago, and they're already here, settling in for a day of knitting. Sophie gets out of their way, leaping off the sofa and climbing into the sunny display window for her early morning nap, which differs from her late morning nap on her dog bed.

"Good morning, Megan!" the ladies say, almost in unison.

"Did we miss Eric?" Mrs. Roblin asks, pointing at my iced vanilla latte on the counter.

Her voice is full of disappointment.

"I'm afraid so," I confirm. "He visited before the store opened. He's busy today, so I doubt we'll see him until dinnertime."

"Oh, that's a shame," Mrs. Vogel adds. "I made date squares for him." She pulls a Tupperware container out of her knitting bag. "There's extra for young Jax too." Then she pulls out an insulated lunch bag. "In case your hobby requires us to stay over the lunch hour," she explains with a grin.

"Why don't I put them in the fridge," I offer, jerking my head toward the back room.

"Are you sure?" Mrs. Vogel asks.

"We wouldn't want to impose," Mrs. Roblin asks, producing her lunch bag from inside her knitting bag.

"It's not an imposition," I say. "I'll put them away for you. You don't have to sit here all day. I appreciate it, but I'm sure you're bored with being here by now."

"Nonsense," Mrs. Vogel says. "We love it here."

"It's so much more exciting here than the library or coffee shop where we usually knit," Mrs. Roblin says.

"Good morning," Hannah smiles at us.

"Where did you disappear to?" I ask.

"Upstairs," she replies. "Jax asked me to help him choose from a bunch of ties Eric lent him for his second interview today. He doesn't want to wear the same tie twice."

"Second interview?" Mrs. Vogel asks, her eyes narrow. "With the Harmony Lake FD?"

"That's right," I reply.

"The fire chief hasn't decided yet?" Mrs. Roblin asks, as if she expected him to decide by now.

"I guess not," I reply. "Pardon?" I ask, sure Mrs. Vogel said something.

"Nothing, dear," Mrs. Vogel smiles, unlocking her phone and tapping away on the screen.

I'm sure Mrs. Vogel mumbled something that

sounded like *I'm on it,* under her breath. Then Mrs. Roblin nodded, giving Mrs. Vogel a conspiratorial sideways glance.

I smile, collect their lunch bags and date squares, and head to the kitchenette.

This forces me to give the fridge an overdue clear-out. I open the compost bin and put it on the counter next to the fridge, then pull the garbage bin over so it's next to me. I empty the fridge, wash and disinfect the shelves, then ruthlessly toss old food, rearranging the remaining contents.

"Good Morning, Aunt Megan," Jax says behind me.

"Good morning," I say, spinning around to greet him.

"I hope it's OK to call you Aunt Megan?"

"Of course, it is!" I insist. "I like the sound of it! Congratulations, by the way," I add, hoping congratulations is an appropriate response to DNA results. "Your uncle told me the email was in your inbox when you woke up this morning."

"Do you know how to tie a tie?" he asks, holding up Eric's two-tone pink necktie.

"Isn't your interview this afternoon?" I ask, looping the tie around his neck and adjusting the length of the ends.

"Yes," Jax confirms, "but I want to get everything ready. My dad showed me how to tie a tie, then Uncle Eric showed me how to tie a tie. He tied it for me before my first interview. I just had to tighten it. Now, I can't remember how to do it."

"We've got you covered," I say, flipping one end of

the tie over the other. "This is one of my favourite ties. Eric hasn't worn it in ages since he dresses business casual most of the time now." I pull one end through a loop and make a few adjustments. "There." I tighten it but leave enough slack so Jax can get it over his head. "Did he lend you the matching pocket square, too?" I ask.

Jax nods. "Yes. Thank you," he says, inspecting the Windsor knot in the mirror by the back door. "Maybe I'll find a how-to video online and practice with another tie."

The pink tones in the tie around Jax's neck remind me of the blush-pink dress Mysti wore in the selfie with Happy Hour, which reminds me I promised to put Happy Hour's identity on project status today.

I unlock my phone and find the selfie of Mysti and Happy Hour. I copy the photo and edit the copy, cropping Mysti out of it. Then I send the photo of just Happy Hour to Hannah.

Me: Can you ask around and see if any of your friends recognize her?

Hannah: OK. Is she related to Mysti's murder? Followed by a scared face emoji.

Me: Possibly.

When I return to the store, Hannah is binding off another blanket square. This is the third day this week Hannah has knitted. In just three days, Mrs. Roblin and Mrs. Vogel have achieved something I've never been able to accomplish. They've turned my daughter into a knitter. I even noticed yarn and needles in her room when I walked past her bedroom last night.

THE FOUR OF us knit in comfortable silence—well, the three of them knit, I'm crocheting the last lap blanket with the square Hannah just finished. Hannah pulls out the yarn and needles I saw in her room. She's working on a scarf with a handwritten pattern Mrs. Roblin gave her.

"Don't tell him, Mum!" Hannah demands. "It's a surprise for Christmas. I'm making Lucas a scarf, hat, and mitts. Mrs. Roblin is helping me. They're her patterns," she says.

"He won't hear it from me," I promise.

"Good morning, Mayor Martel," Mrs. Vogel says when the door opens.

"Hello, ladies," Adam says to the all-female craft contingent. "How is everyone today?"

"What brings you to Knitorious today?" I ask, after everyone exchanges pleasantries and some light gossip.

"The postal carrier delivered your mail to Latte Da by accident." Adam drops the envelopes on the counter. "I offered to drop it off on my way to the town hall. Also, I thought I'd congratulate Jax on the email he got last night. If he's around," Adam says, not mentioning the DNA results.

"He's upstairs getting ready for a job interview," Hannah explains.

"If you hurry, you might catch him," Mrs. Roblin adds. "We're all pleased about his test results." She smiles.

How does Mrs. Roblin know about Jax's DNA test results?

"Will there be a party to give him a proper welcome?" Mrs. Vogel asks.

"We'll do something," I reply, "when Connie gets back from Europe."

"I texted him, Dad," Hannah says. "Jax says you can go upstairs if you want."

"Thanks, Princess," Adam replies.

I look at Adam and smile. "I have some mail for a few stores between here and the town hall."

"And you'd like me to drop it off on my way?" he surmises.

"Thank you, Adam! That would be great," I respond as if he offered.

Adam follows me to the harvest table, where I pick up three stacks of mail and hand them to him.

"The new postal carrier is getting better," I say, as he reads the addresses on the envelopes. "This is only the second day this week she's mixed up the mail. If she doesn't mix it up tomorrow, it'll be her best week yet."

"How do the charity knitters already know about Jax's DNA results?" Adam whispers as I walk with him toward the apartment stairs in the backroom. "I thought he just found out a few hours ago. Eric only posted it in the Modern Family group chat a few minutes ago."

The Modern family group chat is our group text thread for all the members of our non-traditional family of choice.

"I assume Hannah told them," I whisper, shrugging. "Otherwise, their influence extends beyond the borders of Harmony Lake and all the way to the Let Me Take A Cellfie labs."

"I know you're joking," Adam says with a chuckle. "But it's a scary possibility."

Adam disappears into the backroom, his feet thudding on the stairs up to the apartment.

He's right. With their extensive network of informants in every nook and cranny of this town, the charity knitters might know who Happy Hour is. And if they don't, they can probably find out faster than me.

I open the cropped photo of Happy Hour and walk over to the cozy sitting area.

"Ladies, do either of you recognize this woman?" I hand my phone to Mrs. Roblin.

She pats the top of her head, then her chest, then looks around, finally locating her reading glasses on her lap. She puts them on and examines the photo.

"I don't recognize her," Mrs. Roblin says, shaking her head. She hands the phone to Mrs. Vogel.

"Me neither," Mrs. Vogel says. "Is this related to your hobby?"

"Could be," I say. "I'm not sure. Eric needs to find her."

"Would you like us to help?" Mrs. Roblin asks.

"If it's not too much trouble," I say, smiling.

"No trouble," Mrs. Vogel insists. "Text me the photo."

"We told you we're here to help, Megan," Mrs. Roblin reminds me with a smile.

Mrs. Vogel hands the phone back to me and I text Happy Hour's photo to her. As I hit send, Adam returns from the upstairs apartment and announces he's leaving.

"Can you drop these at the library?" I drop my phone on the counter and grab the bag containing the last of the lap blankets. "Mrs. Bickerson is expecting them. The library is in the same building as the town hall," I reason, thrusting the bag toward him.

"Technically, the library is next door to the town hall," Adam corrects me. "But fine. I'll take them. What kind of mayor would I be if I refused to deliver lap blankets that will benefit sick and isolated residents?"

"Thank you," I say, smiling.

"Why do you have a picture of Kelsi on your phone?" Adam says, nodding at the photo of Happy Hour on my phone.

Kelsi? Are Happy Hour and Kelsi the same person?

"Kelsi?" I ask, making sure I didn't mishear him. "You know her?"

"Not well, but we've met. She's renting a condo in my complex. Our underground parking spots are near each other.

"Do you know her boyfriend?" I ask.

"No, but I know she wasn't happy with him last week."

"I'm listening," I say, encouraging him to continue.

"I was getting in my car to pick up my dinner order at The Embassy, and Kelsi was getting out of her car in the underground garage. She was yelling at her boyfriend on the phone."

"Did you get his name by chance?" I ask, interrupting.

"She called him several names," Adam replies. "But none of them were proper names, if you catch my drift."

"What were they fighting about?" Hannah asks, joining us at the counter.

"It sounded like he either cancelled plans with her at the last minute, or he stood her up. I'm not sure which. But it wasn't the first time, and Kelsi was fed up. She told him she never wanted to see him again. She had to yell extra loud because the reception down there is awful."

"How did you find out her name?" I ask.

"After she hung up on her boyfriend, she asked me if I was familiar with Harmony Lake. I told her I'm more familiar than most people because I'm the mayor. I introduced myself. She introduced herself."

"Did she tell you her last name?" I probe.

"No," Adam replies. "She introduced herself as Kelsi. This is her first time visiting Harmony Lake. She and her boyfriend were supposed to spend time together working on their relationship, but he was messing her around."

"Why did she ask if you were familiar with Harmony Lake?" Hannah asks.

"She wanted to know where she could *drink her cares away*, as she put it."

"Did you recommend a place?"

"The Embassy," Adam confirms. "It was happy hour that night. I told her if she hurried, she could enjoy half price drinks for two hours. I gave her directions, then just offered to drive her, since I was going there, anyway."

"You drove her to the pub?" I confirm.

"Yup. We walked in together. She thanked me for the lift, and I gave her a card for the Precious Cargo Cab company so she could get a cab home."

"Did you have a drink with her?" I ask.

"No, I went straight to the bar to pick up my fish and chips. I didn't pay attention to where Kelsi went."

"Did you see her talking to anyone when you left?" I ask. "Did she meet anyone?"

"Not that I saw," Adam recalls. "But I left right after I got my order."

"Eric might call you," I say. "Thanks for dropping off the mail and the blankets."

Adam says goodbye and leaves, weighed down with mis-delivered mail and lap blankets.

I'm taking a moment to process the information Adam just gave me when my phone rings and vibrates in my hand. Eric's name and picture flash on the screen.

"I'll be right back," I say as I walk toward the backroom.

"Hello?" I say, closing the door behind me.

"Hey, babe. You won't believe this. The owner of the rental condo got back to me. I was right, the condo was rented in Kelsi's name. Anyway, he gave me her last name and address, and I pulled her driver's license photo from the database." He pauses, then chuckles. "You'll never believe who Kelsi is."

"Happy Hour?"

"How did you know?" Eric asks, dumbfounded that I know and disappointed I ruined his surprise.

"Adam told me."

"Adam? How does he know?"

I tell him about Adam's encounter with Kelsi in the underground garage, and how it was his suggestion that Kelsi go to The Embassy for happy hour the night she met Mysti.

"I left a voicemail message for Kelsi, and I've contacted the police department in her hometown. They'll knock on her door and contact me if they locate her."

"Locate her?" I ask. "Isn't she staying at the condo?"

"She left last night," Eric informs me. "Took her belongings and left the key with the doorman."

"Oh my," I say. "Do you think she and Cole skipped town together?"

"I'm not sure," Eric admits. "Every officer in town is looking for Kelsi, Cole, and Angela. We can't locate any of them, and none of them are answering my calls and texts. I told you I had a feeling this case was about to break wide open," he reminds me. "Listen, babe. Stay safe. These people are unstable. They might feel desperate, like they have nothing to lose."

"I understand," I assure him. "You be careful too. Keep me up to date."

"I love you."

"I love you too."

I paste a smile on my face, return to the cozy sitting area, and pick up the sock I was working on before lap-blanket assembly took over my life.

"Everything OK, Megan?" Mrs. Vogel asks.

"Yes," I reply. "Nothing to worry about."

Except for the rhythmic clicking of our needles, we knit in silence, my mind cluttered with flashbacks to all the interactions I've had with people since Mysti died, including with the killer themself. How could I look someone in the eye and talk to them without seeing the evil lurking inside them?

"It's him!" Mrs. Vogel hisses when the bell above the door jingles and Lucas enters the store.

I toss a throw pillow onto Hannah's lap to hide her knitting, and Mrs. Roblin gathers the throw pillow, with the knitting concealed underneath it, and plops it into her large knitting bag.

Hannah jumps to her feet, grinning from ear to ear.

"I promised I'd take Sophie to the dog park," she announces. "Lucas is coming with me since it's his day off."

"Sophie already had a walk this morning," I remind her. "And she'll have another one at lunchtime."

"I promised," Hannah argues with a shrug.

"Why?" I ask. "Why does Eric insist that Sophie go to the dog park every single day?" Hannah and Lucas look at each other, then at me, and shrug. "A simple question no one will answer," I huff.

"So, can I take her?" Hannah asks.

"You know what?" It's a redundant question. Fed up with the dog park, I plonk my knitting on the coffee table. "I'll take Sophie to the dog park!"

I stand up and whistle for Sophie, who leaps off her

dog bed and stands at attention. When I march toward the backroom, she trots behind me.

"Ready, Soph?" I ask, attaching her leash and digging my sunglasses out of my bag. "Let's go. I can't wait to see why the dog park is so amazing."

I'm sure dogs are oblivious to sarcasm, but it makes me feel better to vent. I grab Sophie's rubber boomerang toy from the basket by the back door, and we leave.

CHAPTER 26

Our local dog park is actually two dog parks, separated by a dense thicket of trees known as the woods. One dog park is for large dogs, and the other is for small dogs. Sophie hangs out in the small-dog park. It's slow today, despite the picture-perfect June weather. Aside from Sophie, there are only two miniature schnauzers. Sophie recognizes her friends, and as soon as I detach her leash, rushes over to them. The three dogs form a butt-sniffing circle, following each other and saying hi.

"It's amazing they don't get dizzy, isn't it?" The man on the next bench chuckles, looking up from his eReader.

"Yes, it is," I agree. "You must be Salt and Pepper's dad," I say. "I'm Sophie's mum."

"Right," the man acknowledges. "Isn't it funny how, at the dog park, we cease to have our own names and are content to be known as extensions of our dogs?"

"You're right," I say. "It's the same with kids. For years, half the town knew me as Hannah's mum."

"I haven't seen you here in a while," the man says. "Sophie's dad usually brings her."

"He's working," I explain.

Salt and Pepper's dad and I exchange pleasantries and make small talk while our dogs romp and frolic in the open field. When an alarm chimes on his watch, Salt and Pepper's dad puts two fingers in his mouth and summons the twin schnauzers with a loud, shrill whistle. All three dogs respond, loping toward us.

"Hi, Salt. Hi, Pepper," I say to the dogs, petting them when they approach the bench and check me out with their noses.

Their dad attaches their leashes, tucks his eReader under his arm, and we wish each other a good day.

Sophie watches her friends leave until they're out of sight. She looks sad there's no one left to play with.

"Look, Soph!" I wave the rubber boomerang in front of her, to distract her from staring at the space in the distance where she last saw her friends. "Wanna fetch? Get the toy? Wanna get it?" I ask, shaking the boomerang and waving it around.

Once Sophie locks her gaze on the toy, I raise it above my head and behind me, then heave the thing as hard as I can across the field.

"Shoot!" I exclaim, watching the toy veer left, hurl across the field and into the woods dividing the two dog parks.

I'm not known for my killer throwing arm, so I'm surprised the thing went as far as it did. Around sixty feet is my usual maximum distance, so this is a new personal best.

I hold my breath when Sophie disappears into the woods and I lose sight of her.

"Where are you, Soph?" I mutter, worried a large dog on the other side of the trees caught her attention and lured her away.

I walk toward the woods and whistle for Sophie. Nothing. "Sophie!" I shout. Nothing. I'm about to break into a run when her head, followed by her short, long body, emerges from the underbrush.

"Phew," I sigh, then I whistle and pat my knees.

Sophie charges toward me at full throttle. She overshoots her target and circles around me before coming to a halt at my feet. She sits at attention and drops a stick at my feet, her ears perked up with pride.

I sigh. "Where's the toy, Soph?"

She looks at me, then at the stick, baffled by my lack of enthusiasm for her stellar fetching and retrieving skills.

"Did you lose the boomerang?" I ask. "Let's find it."

Sophie accompanies me as far as the edge of the open field, then sits while I venture alone into the buggy, brambly woods. It's dark in here, and a dense carpet of evergreen needles, moss, and other foliage makes the boomerang toy hard to find. I open the flashlight on my phone and use it to light my way.

"This isn't worth it," I mumble, scanning the ground for the boomerang. "Sophie has dozens of other toys." I sweep the ground with my foot as I walk, in case the toy is under something. "The boomerang isn't even one of her favourites." A sudden ripple of unease shoots up my spine, causing me to shudder and break out in goosebumps. I stop and hold my breath. Silence. I glance around, making sure I'm alone. I am. Why do I feel like I'm not? "Forget it. I'll order another one online," I convince myself, eager to get back to the open field of the dog park.

I'm about to turn around when I spot the boomerang under a nearby tree.

"Ha! Found it!" I mutter to myself with smug satisfaction.

Bending down to collect the toy, twigs crack behind me.

"Sophie?" Nothing.

If it were Sophie, she would have rushed to me when I said her name. I tell myself it's just a squirrel or a bird. Making as little noise as possible, I retrace my steps toward the dog park. Near the entrance, off the crude path, a man's hat catches my eye. I didn't notice it on my way into the woods. A black baseball-style cap with the words *Dad in charge,* in white font. It's identical to Cole Duffy's hat. Why would Cole be here? Do the Duffys have a dog? *Stop panicking, Megan!* There are probably a million hats just like it. Chances are this isn't even his hat. I should tell Eric anyway, just in case. I unlock my phone and snap a pic of the hat.

Me: Found this at the dog park. I attach the photo of the hat.

Eric: You're at the dog park? In the woods?

Me: Yes. Should I pick up the hat?

Eric: No. Don't touch it. Who's with you?

Me: Sophie.

I walk past the hat toward the opening in the trees that leads back to the small-dog park. When I emerge from the woods, Cole Duffy is standing in front of me. Sophie sits next to him.

Eric: Calling you.

"Good girl, Soph!" I say to the obedient corgi, sitting patiently and wagging her tail. "Come." She trots over to me and sits by my side.

Cole is within arm's reach of me, too close for my comfort, but if I take even one step backwards, he'll be able to push me into the woods where no one will see me. And he's too close for me to run past him and get away.

My phone trills when Eric calls. Cole snatches the phone from my hand. Sophie barks and growls.

"Give it back," I say, extending my hand for the phone.

"You first," Cole responds. "Give me back my wife."

"I don't have your wife," I hiss. Cole turns and pitches my phone into the distance. "Why would I have your wife?"

Sophie takes off, chasing after the phone, thinking Cole is playing fetch with her.

"You might not have her," Cole admits, "but you know where she is. You convinced her to take the kids and leave me."

"Angela left you?" I ask. "I'm proud of her, but I assure you, I had nothing to do with it."

"Yes, you did. She left me after she met with you for coffee yesterday. You told her to do it. You turned her against me. Just like that meddling fortune teller turned Kelsi against me."

"I did no such thing," I defend myself. "Angela and I talked for thirty minutes, and she did most of the talking. We haven't talked since. Did you follow me here?"

"I was hoping you'd lead me to my wife."

"You dropped your hat in the woods," I say, jerking my head toward the trees. "If you do anything to me, the police will know. I took a picture of the hat."

"Of course, you did." He rolls his eyes.

"What do you mean the fortune teller turned Kelsi against you?" I ask. "Is Kelsi your mistress?" Sophie returns, trotting proudly toward us with a stick in her mouth. She stops in front of me and drops the stick at my feet. "Good girl, Soph," I mutter.

"*Was,*" Cole corrects me. "Kelsi *was* my girlfriend. Mistress makes it sound wrong."

"Infidelity is wrong," I remind him, "in most circumstances."

"I love Kelsi. But we met at the wrong time. I couldn't leave my wife, but I couldn't leave Kelsi either. Do you know how hard it is to be in love with two people?"

"I don't," I answer truthfully. "But by lying to them, you took away their right to choose. Maybe Kelsi didn't want to be the other woman. And maybe Angela didn't want to be a betrayed wife."

"Duh!" he says. "That's why I didn't tell them about each other. I knew they'd both leave me, and I'd end up alone."

"Mysti told Kelsi you're married," I assume.

"They met at a local bar right after Kelsi and I had a huge argument. Kelsi told her about me and showed her a picture of us. Mysti had seen me and Angela around town and told Kelsi I have a wife and three kids."

"Kelsi left you?" I ask.

"Yup. At first," Cole admits. "But I convinced her that Angela and I were having a family vacation together for the sake of the kids. I told Kelsi the marriage was over, but Angela and I put up a united front for the kids. She wanted to believe me, but she realized I'd lied to her from the beginning. Yesterday, she stopped taking my calls. She wouldn't answer the door at the condo. I even bought her flowers. Pink peonies, her favourite. She left town last night. It's all Mysti's fault."

"It's Mysti's fault you were unfaithful and lied about it?" I ask. "Is that why you killed her? Because she ruined your… arrangement with Kelsi?"

"It wasn't enough for Mysti to ruin my relationship with Kelsi. She wanted to profit from it too."

Something agitates Sophie. Her ears twitch and something behind me in the woods gets her attention. Not wanting her to spook Cole into doing anything rash or drastic, I hold up the boomerang toy and hurl it in the direction Cole threw my phone. My arm is weaker than Cole's, so the boomerang doesn't go as far as my phone.

"Did Mysti blackmail you?" I ask. Cole looks at me with hesitation. If Mysti blackmailed him, he doesn't want to admit it. "Listen," I say, leaning toward him against my better judgement. "You aren't alone if Mysti blackmailed you. She blackmailed lots of people. Multiple police departments wanted to question her."

"Then I did the world a favour, didn't I?" Cole smirks.

Is this enough to constitute a confession?

"How did Mysti do it?" I ask. "Did she call you? Visit your rental cottage? How did she demand money from you?"

I watch Sophie run past the boomerang. She gets smaller in the distance until she stops and sniffs around.

"She slipped me a note on the beach one day," Cole admits.

"The same day she offered Angela a free tarot card reading?" I assume.

He nods. Mysti's offer of a free tarot card reading to Angela was likely to show Cole she was serious about the blackmail threat.

"I followed her back to her motel and confronted her with the note she gave me," he admits. "She told me she knew all about my relationship with Kelsi. She knew dates and times and everything. If I didn't give her ten thousand dollars in cash by Sunday, she would tell Angela. She rambled off a bunch of gibberish about karma and how I brought this on myself."

This must be the confrontation Jax interrupted between Mysti and Cole.

"Instead of paying her, you killed her?" I deduce.

"Pretty much," Cole admits. "I knocked on her motel room door on Sunday morning and told her I had the money. She told me to leave it and walk away. I told her it was on the ground outside and stepped aside so she couldn't see me from the peephole. When she opened the door, I pushed her into the motel room."

"How did you do it?" I ask.

"Let's just say she choked on her own words." He chuckles at his dark reference to shoving Mysti's handwritten blackmail note down her throat.

"You choked her?" I ask, feigning ignorance about Mysti's cause of death.

"She wouldn't stop screaming after I pushed her inside the room. I had to shut her up. I grabbed the back of her head and shoved her face into the bed. She still wouldn't stop screaming, I pushed harder to muffle the sound. She kept struggling. She was so hysterical that she couldn't hear me telling her to calm down. She kept kicking and screaming, so I pushed her head into the bed harder and harder until she stopped screaming. She stopped screaming and kicking at the same time. I let go and waited a few minutes, but she didn't wake up."

"Why didn't you call for help?" Squinting behind my sunglasses, I see Sophie in the distance, trotting toward us with something in her mouth.

"What would I say? Hello? 9-1-1? Can you send help? The girl I was smothering died." His voice oozes with sarcasm. "I panicked. I wanted to get out of there. I looked around the room for something to use to open the door. Her tarot cards were sitting on the nightstand and the death card was on top. It seemed fitting, so I crumpled it up and shoved it down her throat, along with the blackmail note she gave me."

Boom! The card and note are holdbacks. This is proof that Cole was there when Mysti died.

"Why?" I ask.

"Like I said," Cole replies with a shrug. "It seemed fitting that she should choke on her own words. When I lifted her head to shove the card and note in her mouth, there was a pink dress on the bed. Her face was pressed against it. I wrapped the dress around my hand when I opened and closed the door." He holds up his hands and wiggles his fingers. "No fingerprints, no proof." He laughs.

"Where's the dress now?" I ask.

"Tossed in a garbage bin," he says, waving away his response like it doesn't matter.

But it matters. The pink dress is the second holdback. Cole just implicated himself in Mysti's murder. If only someone else was around to hear it. Sigh.

Sophie circles us, prancing and showing off her retrieval skills with a victory lap. She stops between us and drops my cell phone on the ground between Cole and I. It rings. Eric's name and picture flash on the screen. He's persistent, I'll give him that.

"You won't need this where you're going," Cole says, bending over to retrieve my phone.

As he bends, I lift my knee with all the strength and speed I can muster.

A sharp *crack* rings out when my knee makes contact with Cole's face.

Was the crack his face or my knee?

Cole brings his hands to his face and drops to his knees in the long grass.

Pain shoots through my leg as I lunge sideways, out of Cole's reach.

"Come, Soph!" I shout. "Run!"

I bolt toward the safety and visibility of the open field. Sophie, being faster than me, is way ahead.

Behind me, I hear Cole yell after me, calling me an impolite name that rhymes with witch. I don't dare turn around. Trees and bushes rustle behind me. Is Cole escaping into the woods? No, he's chasing me, the thud of his fast footsteps grows louder and I run as fast as I can. I'm tempted to turn around to check, but convince myself to look ahead and keep going. I need a phone. I need to call the police before Cole gets me.

"Megan!"

Cole? How did he catch up to me so fast? I will myself to keep running and not turn around. I have to find help. Of all the days for the dog park to be dead! Pardon the pun.

"Megan! Stop!"

Arms encircle my waist. He's tackling me. I brace myself to hit the ground, but he hoists me into the air. With my feet dangling, I kick and flail. Screaming, I struggle to unclench his hands from my waist while trying to head butt his face with the back of my head.

"It's me," Eric breathes in my ear, bringing us to an abrupt stop.

He sounds like Eric, he smells like Eric, and he feels like Eric, but when he lowers me to the ground, I spin around to check, fearful Cole is trying to trick me.

"Where did you come from?" I ask, breathless.

"PEI originally," Eric quips, winded. I don't laugh.

"I was hiding in the bushes. A bunch of us were," Eric explains in response to my underwhelming reaction to his witty comeback. "I was sure Sophie saw me at one point," Eric says, panting. "I thought she would give us away, but you distracted her with the boomerang. Well done." His upper body heaves between breaths. "I was up the street from the dog park when you texted me the hat photo," he explains between heavy breaths. "I drove to the big-dog park and ran through the woods, hoping to sneak up on Cole. I had every officer on duty meet me here. They approached without sirens and turned their radios and phones off so Cole wouldn't hear us." He puts his hands on his knees and catches his breath. "You're faster than I expected. How can someone who hates running be so fast?"

"I guess I hate dying more than I hate running," I justify. "How much did you hear?"

"Enough," he exhales, standing up. "You did great, babe. Are you OK?" With his hands on my shoulders, he looks me over. "I was right behind you. If Cole Duffy tried anything, I would've killed him."

"I'm fine," I assure him, looking around to make sure no one heard him threaten Cole. "Are you OK?" I scan him from head to toe. "Did you get him?"

Eric stands aside, and in the distance, several uniformed officers surround Cole Duffy. He's on the ground, on his stomach, with his hands secured behind his back. His face is smeared with blood.

"I think you broke his nose," Eric says. "That crack when you kneed him was so loud, we all cringed in the bushes."

"I hope he's not too badly injured," I comment. "Will you have to charge me with assault?"

"Of course not. You did nothing wrong," Eric assures me. "The only charges I'm handing out today are to Cole Duffy. You did what was necessary to escape from a psychotic killer."

Too bad Mysti couldn't escape from him.

CHAPTER 27

SUNDAY, July 4th

"Any luck?" Eric asks when, in a huff, I drop my phone next to me on the sofa.

"No," I say, exasperated. "Jason and his wife go back to PEI tomorrow. This is our last chance to have a family dinner before they leave. Jax and Jason are having an early dinner, then Jax's going to bed early because he starts his new job tomorrow. Connie says she still has jet lag after returning from her trip, and Hannah is helping Lucas unpack before he starts a week of night shifts tomorrow."

The Harmony Lake Fire Department offered Jax a job, and he accepted. He's staying in Harmony Lake, close to his Uncle Eric. Uncle Eric is thrilled.

After he received the DNA results, Jason came to terms with having another son. He and his wife arrived in town two weeks ago. Jason and Jax have spent time getting to know each other.

Eric's brother and his wife are staying in our spare

room because our new tenants moved into the apartment above the store. Jax and Lucas. We offered Jax the apartment when he accepted the job with the HLFD, and he asked if he could find a roommate to share the rent. Lucas was still looking for an apartment in town, so it worked out perfectly. Lucas moved in a few days ago, and Hannah has devoted her free time to helping him get settled.

I pick up my phone when it dings.

April: Sorry, Megapixel, T and I have plans tonight!

"April," I inform Eric as I type a response.

Me: No worries!

"They're busy too?" he assumes. I nod. "It's fine," Eric says. "Jax said he doesn't want any fuss."

"I know," I respond. "I just want him to feel welcome and let him know we're happy he's here."

"How was brunch this morning?" Eric asks, changing the subject.

"Poor Lucas was so nervous, I thought he might throw up," I reply. "But Adam was on his best behaviour and even joked around to help Lucas relax. Hannah is happy that her dad is giving Lucas a chance."

"Let's go for a walk, then have dinner at The Embassy," Eric suggests. "Sheamus allows dogs on the patio now, so Sophie can come with us. We'll walk at the far end of the lake."

"The secluded part that the tourists don't know about?" I ask, tempted.

"That's the one," Eric replies.

"Or we could just go to the dog park," I counter. "It would be easier."

"Are you sure?" He looks hesitant, like he doesn't think it's a good idea. "I thought we'd avoid the dog park for a while. At least until your knee heals."

"My knee has healed." I lift the hem of my dress and show Eric my knee. "See? The bruise is almost gone, and it doesn't hurt at all."

I poke at the yellowish mass to prove it doesn't hurt. It hurts a little.

"I don't want you to rush it," he says. "Let's go to the lake instead. We can go to the dog park next time."

"Fine." I shrug. "But the patio might be full in this weather. We might not get a table."

"We'll get a table." Eric smirks.

"How do you know?"

"Trust me." He winks.

"If you say so," I concede and lift myself up off the sofa. "Let's go. It's not like we have a family dinner to get ready for."

"Now?" he asks, sounding unprepared.

"When were you thinking?"

"It's fine." He waves away my question. "We'll go now." He unlocks his phone and starts typing.

"Are you working? On a Sunday?" I ask, suspicious he's not telling me something.

"Loose ends," he replies without looking up from his phone.

"I thought Renée Dukes was the last loose end, and you tied that up days ago."

After the police arrested Cole Duffy for murdering

Mysti, Renée ceased cooperating with the police. Mysti's family hired a team of lawyers to represent her. Using their extensive wealth and considerable influence, they made Renée's legal problems disappear. Renée has been incommunicado ever since. Eric suspects Renée accepted a large sum of money from the Moregard-Davenhill family for her signature on a non-disclosure agreement forbidding her from talking about her involvement with the family, or with Mysti. We never found out if Mysti's fear that her family wanted to harm her was legitimate, or an overreaction to a family argument.

"Other loose ends," he mutters, still typing.

"What other loose ends?" I ask, trying to recall what is unresolved.

The police in Kelsi's hometown tracked her down the day of Cole's arrest. Cole didn't harm her. She had no clue he had killed Mysti, or that Mysti used the information Kelsi confided in her to blackmail Cole. Aside from some trust issues, she's fine.

When Angela told me over coffee that she might phone her parents, she meant it. She reached out that day and asked them to help her leave Cole. They were more than willing and arranged a rental car for their daughter. At naptime, Angela went to the police station to give a statement and answer questions. Then, she went back to the rental cottage and gave Cole a short grocery list. She knew he wouldn't return for at least a couple of hours because he'd use the opportunity to visit Kelsi. When he left, she packed their stuff and took a cab to pick up the rental car. She's staying with her parents while she figures out what will be best for her and her children going forward.

"Ready?" Eric asks, shoving his phone in his pocket.

"Ready," I say. "C'mon, Soph!"

Sophie jumps off the living room sofa and meets us at the door.

"Hang on," Eric says. "I'll grab her frisbee."

"SOPHIE WANTS you to throw the frisbee," Eric says when she drops the toy at my feet.

We're sitting on a cluster of large rocks on the shoreline. The sun is hot, and the warm lake breeze creates a vortex of curls around my face.

This end of the lake is less popular with tourists than the rest of the lake because most tourists don't know it's here. Also, it's far from the amenities of Water Street and downtown Harmony Lake, and the rocky landscape is difficult to traverse and leaves very little beach to enjoy.

"Nope," I say, shaking my head. "I don't like this game. If I throw it, she'll ignore it and bring back something else. Then I'll have to search for the frisbee and fetch it myself."

"If Sophie doesn't bring back the frisbee, I will," Eric says, tucking a few curls behind my ear. "Please just throw the frisbee." He kisses me.

"Fine." I pick up the frisbee and wave it around, getting Sophie excited for the impending pursuit. "What's this, Soph? See the frisbee? Wanna chase it?

Ready?" I bring the frisbee to my chest and flick my wrist, sending it flying along the shoreline.

In hot pursuit, Sophie follows the frisbee to its landing place, between two rocks, then sniffs around the rocks, her head and upper body disappearing then reappearing between them.

"Here she comes," Eric says, watching Sophie navigate through the rocks with her prize clenched in her mouth.

"I bet it's a stick," I say, venturing a guess at what Sophie will leave at my feet. "Or maybe a shell."

Sophie prances back to us, sits proudly at my feet, and drops a purple tennis ball.

"Good girl, Soph," Eric praises the corgi and rubs her head.

"How did you find a tennis ball way out here?" I ask, picking up and examining the ball. It's engraved. I hold it up to inspect the gold embossed letters.

"Eric & Megan," I read the top line out loud.

"Now & forever," I read the second line out loud.

Before I can process the weird coincidence that Sophie found a random tennis ball with our names engraved on it, Eric stands up, steps off the rock and takes the tennis ball from me.

Bending one knee, he kneels and opens the tennis ball. The Velcro makes a *sc-tch-tch-ch* noise as the top half of the tennis ball peels away from the bottom. It flips open like a jewellery box and inside the ball, a purple velvet lining cushions an engagement ring.

I gasp and bring my hands to my mouth.

Trembling and with a shaky voice, Eric recites a

romantic, corny, sentimental speech he prepared, bringing tears to my eyes.

"Megan Elizabeth Monroe Martel, will you marry me?"

"Yes." I jump to my feet.

Eric stands up, and I launch myself into his arms, wrapping my legs around his waist.

"Look this way and smile!"

Eric pivots us toward Hannah, who is holding up her phone. Where did she come from?

"Are you filming this, Hannah Banana?"

"Live streaming," she replies. "So everyone at The Embassy can watch."

"I'm taking still photos," April says, from behind me.

I turn my head, and April is standing a few rocks above us, her digital camera blocking her face. Cue the ugly tears.

"You planned this?" I ask Eric, straightening my legs so he can lower me to the ground.

He nods. "With a lot of help," he replies, using his thumb to wipe a tear from my cheek. "You're a hard person to surprise. Everyone is waiting for us on the patio at The Embassy."

"Everyone?" I ask. "Is this why they were busy tonight?"

"Yes," he replies with a chuckle.

"And there's nothing wrong with Sophie?" I confirm. "You trained her to only bring me a tennis ball, no matter what I throw?"

"I'll try to un-train her so you can stop fetching her

toys."

We laugh.

"Can I see the ring?" Hannah asks. She tells everyone at the Embassy that we're on our way and ends the live stream.

"Eric didn't show it to you already?" I ask, wondering how involved Hannah and April were in his plan.

"No, he said it was a surprise," Hannah replies.

"I haven't seen it either," April shouts, climbing down to our level. "Eric said we couldn't see it until he gave it to you." Eric climbs up and takes April's arm, helping her down to ground level.

After we *ooh* and *ahh* over the ring and Eric's good taste, he suggests we should head over to The Embassy.

"Let's go," I agree, then remember the frisbee. "We should find the frisbee."

"We'll find the frisbee," April offers. "You two go ahead with Sophie. Hannah and I will find the frisbee and meet you there."

"I can't believe you planned all this behind my back," I say once we're in the car.

"Everyone was in on it," he admits.

Hannah helped train Sophie by taking her to the dog park on the days Eric couldn't, to reinforce her new trick of only retrieving tennis balls. Eric booked the patio at The Embassy, and April invited everyone. Connie arranged the menu and ordered the food. Today, April had to contact everyone again to tell them to arrive at The Embassy early because I decided we should walk Sophie right away instead of later, like Eric planned. This was the flurry of texts Eric sent before we left the house, the *loose ends* he was dealing with.

Hannah arrived at the lake before us and hid the ring. Then she hid in the rocks until it was time to livestream the proposal. They chose the spot ahead of time, which is why he talked me out of going to the dog park. We stopped to sit on that rock on purpose, so when I threw the frisbee, it would land close enough to the ring for Sophie to find the purple tennis ball.

"You're stuck with me now," Eric says. "No refunds, no exchanges. Partners in crime forever."

"But maybe with a little less crime."

I unlock my phone and open the text messaging app.

"I'm sure our engagement will be murder-free," he muses. "Who are you texting?"

"My sister," I reply holding my hand in front of me and taking a photo of the ring.

I crop the photo to eliminate the car interior in the background and hit send. A few moments later, my phone dings. "She says she's thrilled for us and will call us later. Also, she and her husband are trying to get time off work to come to Harmony Lake for a visit."

"Thanks for the warning," Eric teases with a wink. "I'll enjoy the peace and quiet in the meantime."

"I know it's always exciting when my sister comes to town," I admit. "But it's not like anyone has ever died or anything."

Not yet.

A Knitorious Murder Mystery Book 9

Life Crafter Death

REAGAN DAVIS

COPYRIGHT

Sign up for Reagan Davis' email list to be notified of new releases: www.ReaganDavis.com

ISBN: 978-1-990228-03-2 (ebook)

ISBN: 978-1-990228-02-5 (print)

FOREWORD

Dear Reader,

Despite several layers of editing and proofreading, occasionally a typo or grammar mistake is so stubborn that it manages to thwart my editing efforts and camouflage itself amongst the words in the book.

If you encounter one of these obstinate typos or errors in this book, please let me know by contacting me at Hello@ReaganDavis.com.

Hopefully, together we can exterminate the annoying pests.

Thank you!

Reagan Davis

CHAPTER 1

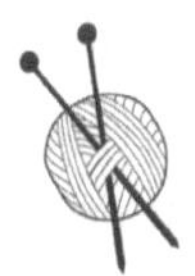

Friday, October 1st

We live ten hours apart, but I see my sister, Emmy, almost every day. Millions of people see her every day. She co-hosts the popular morning show, *Hello, today*!

"Good girl, Soph," I say as the corgi brushes past my legs and through the open door.

She propels herself off the deck and onto the frost-covered lawn, triggering the motion detector which illuminates the pre-dawn backyard with harsh, artificial light.

While Sophie does her business and conducts her first perimeter check of the day, I fix her breakfast, drop a pumpkin spice coffee pod in the coffeemaker, and turn on the TV to catch my daily glimpse of my sister.

The TV comes to life, permeating the family room and kitchen with *Hello, today!*'s snappy theme music. I retrieve my mug from the coffeemaker and savour the first glorious sip of soul-satisfying caffeine while watching the title sequence. Cast and crew member names fade in and out as my sister zooms across the TV screen, riding a Segway through the studio. Then the camera cuts to footage of her and her co-host cooking with a celebrity chef. Then another cut to footage of Emmy drinking from an oversized *Hello, today*! mug while someone touches up her hair and makeup. She and the makeup artist burst into laughter.

Hello, today! is a typical infotainment morning show. Two co-hosts and their colleagues broadcast live, cycling between news, traffic, weather, and sports updates, interspersed with lifestyle and human interest segments.

It's early, and the world is still dark and quiet, but I'm wide awake. As a reluctant morning person, I'm wired to wake up early. I envy people whose internal clocks let them sleep past dawn, but I'm not one of them. This time of year, when the days are shorter, I'm up and at 'em before the sun.

Sophie scratches at the back door, and I look away from the TV to let her in. Sophie shakes off the early morning chill, buries her face in her food dish, and devours her breakfast with enthusiasm.

"...is filling in for Miranda Monroe, who's under the weather. Feel better, Miranda!"

I spin and look at the TV when Rich Kendall—pronounced Rich Ken-doll—announces that my sister isn't at work today. Apparently, she's sick.

Miranda Monroe is my sister's given name and the name she uses professionally. Our names are almost identical, not our parents' most creative moment. They named me Megan Elizabeth Monroe, and named my sister, Miranda Elizabeth Monroe.

According to our father, when Emmy was born, sixteen-month-old me had yet to develop the necessary verbal skills to pronounce Miranda. My garbled attempt to say my baby sister's name sounded like Emmy, so that's what everyone called her. It stuck. Friends and family still call her Emmy. Despite three marriages, and three name changes, Emmy has always used her maiden name on television.

I whip my phone out of my housecoat pocket and check my text messages. Emmy always texts me when she misses work. Always. No text. I type a quick message.

Me: Are you OK? Rich said you're sick.

I hit send and stare at the screen, waiting for the three dots to appear that show my sister is typing a reply. We always reply to each other's texts right away. No dots. Hmmm.

"Good morning, Mrs. Sloane!" Eric says, shutting the front door behind him.

"Umm… we're not married yet," I remind him with a grin.

"I know. I'm practicing. I like the way it sounds."

Eric Sloane is my fiancé and chief of the Harmony Lake Police Department.

I scrunch my nose at his muskiness when he kisses me good morning.

His skin glistens and his short, dark hair is damp with sweat. He just finished a run. I can't imagine running this early—scratch that—I can't imagine running. Eric possesses a terrifying and impressive amount of self-discipline.

"Hug?" he teases, his open arms drawing attention to the sweat-soaked shirt clinging to his fat-free, well-muscled torso.

"After you have a shower," I reply, taking a step backward, just in case he's serious.

He squats to greet Sophie, who's tippy-tapping her paws on the floor at his feet, waiting for him to notice her.

"Where's Emmy?" Eric lifts his chin toward the TV, where Emmy's usual spot on the *Hello, today!* sofa is occupied by the person who provides weather updates.

"Rich said she's sick."

I check my phone again, in case my sister replied to my text, and I missed the notification.

"Is she OK?" Eric asks, squeezing his eyebrows together.

"I don't know," I reply, shaking my head. "She hasn't answered my text."

"I'm sure she's fine," Eric assures me, sensing my concern. "It's probably just a cold or something. She probably went back to bed."

"Probably," I agree.

My phone dings.

"See," Eric says, "that's her. Telling you she's fine."

I nod in acknowledgement and unlock my phone. It's a text, but not from Emmy. It's from my best friend, April.

"April," I tell Eric with a sigh. "She's asking if Emmy is OK because she's not on *Hello, today*!"

"How's their trip?" Eric asks.

April and her wife are out of town for a family wedding. They won't be back until next Friday. This is the longest April and her wife have ever left their bakery. April's wife is a talented pastry chef and together they own Artsy Tartsy, Harmony Lake's local bakery. While they're away, their pastry-chef friend is working at the bakery, staying at their house, and taking care of their cats.

"They're having a great time," I reply to Eric's question. "It helps that Marla is working at the bakery every day and texting them regular, reassuring updates."

Marla is one of my part-time employees. While April and Tamara are away, she's splitting her part-time hours between my yarn store, Knitorious, and Artsy Tartsy.

"Do you need me to help at the store today?" Eric offers.

Eric isn't working today. He's using some time off the department owes him for overtime he's worked.

"No, thanks," I reply. "You should enjoy your day off, not spend it shelving yarn and cashing out customers."

"I enjoy hanging out at Knitorious." He winks. "I have a huge crush on the owner. I can't stay away from her." With a glint of playful mischief in his brown eyes, Eric cocks one eyebrow and takes a step toward me. "Can you go in late? We could have breakfast together or something."

A familiar twinge of temptation tugs at me from

deep inside, but my overdeveloped sense of responsibility overrides my desire to play hooky.

"I can't," I say, wishing I could. "We're short-staffed with Marla helping at the bakery.

"There are plenty of odd jobs to keep me busy at home today," Eric says with a sigh. "But if you want to come home for lunch…" he winks.

"I'll do my best," I say. "And I'll give Sophie the day off to keep you company."

Sophie's ears perk up when she hears her name. She comes to work with me every day, but she'll be happy to stay home with Eric.

"I'm sure Emmy is fine," Connie insists, tucking her sleek silver bob behind her ear. "She's probably asleep, and she'll text you when she wakes up."

Connie is my other part-time employee. She was the original owner of Knitorious. I worked for her part time until she retired, then I took over the store. Connie and I are more than colleagues, we're family. Chosen family. Connie and I met when I moved to Harmony Lake almost twenty years ago. I was only twenty-one years old, new in town, lonely, and overwhelmed. My husband was an ambitious young lawyer who spent most of his time at his office in the city. My daughter, Hannah, was a baby and I was a new, anxious mother. To top it off, my own mother had recently passed away unexpectedly. I was overwhelmed. To cope, I channeled my energy into knitting while Hannah slept. One day, realizing I'd knitted through my yarn stash, I pushed Hannah's stroller into Knitorious and met Connie. She took us under her wing and filled the mother and grandmother-shaped holes in our hearts.

"I'd feel better if I knew for sure," I respond.

"Who's Emmy?" Tina asks from a sofa in the cozy sitting area, her eyes laser-focused on the stitch she's knitting.

Tina Duran is new to Harmony Lake. She moved here a few months ago, looking for a fresh start after her divorce. She works at one of the mountain resorts. Tina's also a novice knitter, and Connie has been guiding and encouraging her on her knitting journey.

"Emmy is my sister," I reply. "She hasn't returned my text, which is out of character for her."

I don't explain that Emmy is Miranda Monroe, the popular television morning show host.

Today, Tina's learning how to knit in the round by making Knitted Knockers. Every October, in honour of Breast Cancer Awareness Month, the Harmony Lake Charity Knitting Guild makes and donates Knitted Knockers. These are handmade breast prostheses for women who have undergone mastectomies or other breast procedures.

"I'm sure you'll hear from her," Tina says.

I'm about to agree with Tina when my phone dings.

"Maybe it's Emmy!" Connie suggests optimistically, reaching for my phone on the counter and handing it to me. "She probably went back to bed and just woke up."

I unlock my phone and look at the screen with a heavy sigh.

"It's April." I exhale and place the phone on the coffee table in front of me. "She sent me a funny video of a cat using dog treats to get a German Shepherd to do tricks." I smile at Connie. "If Emmy hasn't texted me by this afternoon, I'll phone her."

Tina places her knitting in her lap. "Maybe her phone died or something." She shrugs and places her knitting in her backpack, then slings her backpack over one shoulder, and stands up. "I have to go to work."

I suspect Tina is around my age, forty-one, or in her late thirties, but it's hard to tell, and it would be rude to ask. Her style of dress and the way she talks makes her seem younger, but Tina refers to movies, and music that I grew up with, which makes me think she looks younger than her actual age. Her dark hair shows no signs of grey, her brown eyes are bright, and her complexion is smooth and ageless. She has a hint of an accent that's difficult to place, but lovely to listen to. She says her accent is a combination of all the places she's lived. She was born in Brazil, but went to university in Europe. Then, after she got married, she moved around the US and Canada for her husband's job.

"I hope you hear from your sister," Tina says with a smile.

Connie and I wish her a good day, and she leaves.

"Mothballs!" Connie mutters her version of an expletive.

"What's wrong?"

"Tina left her jacket," Connie replies, pointing to the jacket draped over the back of the sofa. "That girl always leaves something behind," Connie muses, picking up the jacket and smoothing it over her arm. "I'll hang it up in the backroom."

"I'll send her a text so she knows where she left it," I offer.

According to my phone, it's almost lunchtime. I'll wait one more hour, then if I still haven't heard from Emmy, I'll phone her.

I try to focus on texting Tina, but I can't quiet the voice inside my head. It's a constant whisper warning me the reason I haven't heard from Emmy is because something is wrong. Very wrong.

CHAPTER 2

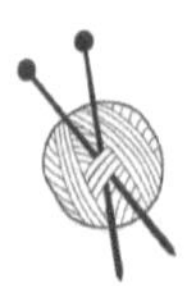

Connie is on her lunch break, and I'm washing the floor-to-ceiling display windows to distract myself from worrying about Emmy.

I flinch when the door swings open and slams against the wall with enough force to shake the yarn shelves and cause the bell to make a startling, loud crash.

"Emmy?" I blink and do a double take when my sister swoops into the store. "What are you doing here? Are you OK?" I ask, shocked to see her but relieved that she appears healthy and unharmed.

"It's over!" Emmy announces, throwing her hands into the air. "Phone Adam. I need him to represent me in the divorce!" she demands, sniffling. "Again," she adds under her breath.

Adam Martel is my ex-husband. He's also Harmony Lake's resident lawyer and our town's mayor. He represented Emmy in her first two divorces.

"What happened?" I ask, stepping out of the display window.

I close the door, making sure Emmy's dramatic entrance didn't damage it or the wall.

"Armando wants to destroy my career," she announces. "The network asked us to be contestants on the next season of *Perfect Match*. The big wigs think it will draw *Hello, today!* viewers to *Perfect Match,* and draw *Perfect Match* viewers to *Hello, today!*" She breaks into sobs. "Armando refused! Can you believe that, Sis? This is a huge career opportunity for me. Why does he hate me?" Emmy bursts into tears and sobs into a wadded-up tissue clenched in her fist.

I envelop my sister in a hug, and she collapses into my arms.

Armando Garcia is Emmy's husband. He's a professional soccer player. They've been married for three years, but I don't know Armando very well because his hectic schedule keeps him on the road most of the year. He's rarely available to accompany my sister when she visits Harmony Lake, and whenever I visit her, he's away playing soccer.

Perfect Match is a reality television show where eight B-list celebrity couples live in the *Perfect Match* house, sequestered from the outside world. Each week they face a challenge designed to test the strength of their relationship. A challenge could be something like one person being tempted by an attractive distraction, someone's former flame showing up, dealing with rumours about each other, or one person being encouraged by their housemates to keep a secret from their partner. Drama, strategic alliances, and secret relationships ensue. Each week, the home audience votes online to determine which couple failed the weekly challenge. Then, at the start of the next episode, the host reveals last week's disgraced couple and evicts them from the *Perfect Match* house. This continues until one couple remains; the last couple wins the title of *Perfect Match* and gets to return for the tournament of champions called *Perfect Match: Playing With Fire*. I don't watch the show. The concept doesn't appeal to me. Relationships are hard enough without competing to prove your love for each other in front of a prime-time audience. I understand why Armando would rather not take part.

"Did Armando say why?" I ask, leading Emmy to the cozy sitting area and helping her into an overstuffed chair.

"He says filming will interfere with soccer," Emmy snorts, rolling her eyes. "Also, *Brad*,"—Emmy sneers with contempt when she says his name—"told him appearing on the show would *devalue the Armando Garcia brand*. Whatever that means." She blows her nose. "Brad hates me!"

Brad Hendricks is Armando's agent. He negotiates Armando's sponsorship deals, media appearances, and such.

"I'm sure Brad doesn't hate you," I reassure her, having no actual insight into Brad's feelings about my sister.

"He's always hated me, and this is another way for him to sabotage my marriage." She breaks into a fresh fit of sobs. "Armando doesn't see it. He thinks Brad is his friend. If Armando had listened to me and found a new agent when we got married, I wouldn't be here right now."

"Maybe Armando doesn't want to spend the little time you have together filming a reality TV show," I suggest, trying to temper her extreme perspective while I hand her a box of tissues.

It's amazing how little time my sister and her husband spend together. Between training camp, preseason games, regular season games, postseason games, and public appearances, Armando travels over two hundred days each year. Emmy's Monday-to-Friday job on *Hello, today!* keeps her anchored to their hometown, and she devotes much of her time off to promotional appearances for worthy causes and for the network.

The bell above the door jingles—gentler this time—and Sophie appears at our feet, wagging her Corgi tail and panting. Torn between visiting me or Emmy first, Emmy wins and Sophie places her front paws on her knees.

"Hey, Soph," Emmy whispers, scratching Sophie between the ears.

"Emmy! This is a pleasant surprise," Eric says, then he looks at me. "See! I told you she was OK." He smiles at Emmy, and she looks up at him with her watery eyes and quivering chin. He looks at me again. "She's not OK, is she?"

I shake my head.

Eric places a to-go cup from Latte Da on the counter. A chocolate caramel latte, my current favourite specialty coffee from their fall menu. The chocolaty coffee aroma makes my mouth water from ten feet away.

"It's nice to see you, Eric," Emmy says, standing up and giving him a hug. "Megan, I'll be right back. I need to freshen up."

"Of course," I say, rubbing her back reassuringly. "Take your time."

Emmy tosses her bag over her shoulder and heads toward the backroom with Sophie guiding the way.

"What's going on?" Eric whispers.

"Domestic quarrel," I whisper in reply.

He nods and his mouth forms a tiny **o**.

"I told Adam I'd meet him for a round of golf later," Eric explains. "But I'll cancel if you need me."

Yes, my fiancé and my ex-husband are friends. Good friends. They golf and watch sports together. It was weird at first, but we're all used to it now. Adam and I might be divorced, but we're still family and have forged a strong friendship from the wreckage of our marriage. We're determined to keep our family intact for the sake of our daughter, and Eric supports that.

"Thank you, honey, but go. This could be your last round of the year," I say, referring to the unseasonable, summer-like weather we've enjoyed this week.

"Are you sure?" Eric looks unconvinced.

"Positive." I stand on my tippy toes and give him a kiss. Eric is almost a foot taller than me, so even when I wear heels, kissing requires some stretching on my part and some stooping on his. "Connie will be back from lunch soon, and Emmy's exhausted, so I'll probably send her home to rest. If you're golfing, the house will be quiet for her."

Persuaded to keep his golf date, Eric kisses my forehead, reminds me to call him if I need anything, and leaves. On his way out, he holds the door open for Tina as she rushes into Knitorious, breathless and flushed as if she ran here.

"Hey, Tina," I greet her with a smile. "You seem like you're in a hurry."

"Kind of." Tina nods and catches her breath. "I'm on my break and came to pick up my jacket."

"Right," I say, remembering Connie saying something about hanging Tina's jacket in the backroom. "Connie put it in the back. I'll get for you."

Tina's jacket isn't hanging on the coat rack by the back door, and at first glance, it's not in the closet. I turn on the closet light and slide the hangers over one by one.

"Aha! Found you!" I inform the jacket with a smug sense of victory when I find it squashed between two parkas that belong to the tenants who live in the apartment above the store.

"Got it," I announce, striding from the backroom to the front of the store.

Tina can't hear me because she's mesmerized by Emmy's presence. I guess Tina watches *Hello, today!* and knows who Miranda Monroe is. Emmy must've slipped past me and returned to the store while I was in the closet, searching for Tina's jacket. Tina is captivated by Emmy. Her eyes are wide, and her mouth is ajar, yet smiling.

"You're even prettier in person," Tina gushes with an awestruck expression plastered to her face.

"Thank you," Emmy smiles graciously. "You're gorgeous, by the way. Your complexion is spectacular. Tell me about your skin care regimen."

Being the true professional she is, you'd never guess Emmy is in emotional distress and just spent ten hours travelling. Her superpower is turning off Emmy Garcia and turning on Miranda Monroe with less effort than it takes to flip a light switch.

"Soap and water," Tina giggles with a shrug. "And lots of moisturizer. Especially in the cold months when the air is dry."

"It's all about the moisturizer," my sister agrees.

"Why are you in Harmony Lake?" Tina asks Emmy as I approach them at the counter. "Are you here to buy yarn? Are you a knitter?"

"Our mother taught us both how to knit," Emmy explains, jerking her head toward me. "I go through knitting phases every few years, but I'm not as dedicated as Megan."

"Miranda Monroe is your sister?" Tina asks, staring at me, dumbfounded. "The same sister you worried about this morning?"

"This is her," I confirm, smiling.

"But I thought your sister's name is Emmy?" Tina scrunches her brows together in confusion.

"Emmy is my nickname," my sister explains. "My given name is Miranda, but friends and family call me Emmy. You can call me Emmy." She flashes Tina a thousand-watt smile.

"I can?" Tina asks, mesmerized. "I'm glad you're OK, Emmy. Megan was worried."

Emmy looks at me and puts her hand on mine. "I'm sorry I didn't let you know I was coming ahead of time. It was an impromptu decision." She sighs. "I was incommunicado during the flight. I saw your texts when I landed and meant to reply from the rental car, but I couldn't get my phone to connect to the car, and it's not safe to text and drive. I told myself I'd text you when I pulled over, but I drove straight through. I didn't mean to worry you."

"You're here now," I say.

"Now that I know you're sisters, I can see the resemblance," Tina observes.

Either Tina's skills of observation are superhuman, or the resemblance she claims to see is wishful thinking. There is no resemblance and hasn't been for at least a decade. We used to have the same curly brown hair, but Emmy dyes her hair blonde now. Her colourist does an amazing job. Unless you knew her before her blonde phase, you'd never guess Emmy isn't a natural blonde. And regular Brazilian blowouts keep her curls at bay and ensure her hair is smooth, shiny, and bouncy. Growing up, we had the same fair skin, but regular appointments with a spray tanner give Emmy's complexion a year-round, sun-kissed shimmer. We both inherited our father's hazel eyes, but thanks to the miracle of tinted contact lenses, Emmy's eyes are closer to emerald green than hazel. Our body shapes have always been different. My curvy, hourglass figure is courtesy of our mother, while Emmy inherited her narrow, petite frame and delicate features from our father's side of the family. I've always been jealous of Emmy's ability to wear spaghetti straps without a bra, and I always will be.

The only physical traits Emmy and I still have in common are our height and shoe size. I suspect my sister has had some Botox because her face is suspiciously smooth for forty. She's only sixteen months younger than me, and I'm sure my forehead lines and crow's feet were well-established sixteen months ago. Compared to my sister's mannequin-like skin, my skin looks like it was made by Rand McNally.

"I wish I could stay and hang out with you all afternoon," Tina announces, throwing her jacket over her arm. "But my break is only an hour. If I don't leave now, I'll be late getting back to work."

"I'm sure we'll see each other again," Emmy assures her. "I'll be in town for a few days."

Tina leaves, and with the flip of an invisible switch, television personality Miranda Monroe disappears and my sister, Emmy Garcia takes her place.

"Emmy?" Connie drops her purse on the counter. "What a wonderful surprise." She walks toward Emmy with her arms wide. "We worried when you weren't on *Hello, today!* this morning.

"Hi, Connie." Emmy stands up, and I can tell she's fending off a fresh round of tears.

"Oh, my," Connie says when my sister, sobbing, falls into her arms, leaving an emotional puddle on the hardwood floor. "There, there, Emmy. Shhhh." Connie's blue eyes fill with the moisture of sympathetic tears.

As they sway, Connie smoothes Emmy's hair and murmurs reassuring things.

Connie is in her element. She's the most motherly woman I know, and it's never more obvious than when she unleashes her maternal instincts to comfort someone.

After they pull apart, Emmy explains to Connie that her marriage is over, and she came to Harmony Lake to process everything in a supportive, private environment. Then, worried that another fan might show up and she'll have to flip the magic switch that summons Miranda Monroe, my sister excuses herself again to freshen up.

"Why don't you take Emmy home, my dear," Connie suggests. "She's exhausted. Get her settled in your guest room, and I'll take care of the store."

"Are you sure?" I ask. "I hate to leave you on your own."

"It's not busy today. I'll be fine," Connie insists. "Emmy is distraught. She travelled ten hours for love and support."

"You're right," I admit, feeling guilty for worrying about work when my sister feels like her life is falling apart. "I'll take Emmy home."

CHAPTER 3

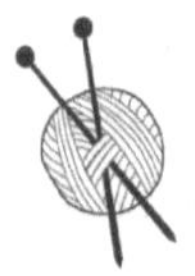

I THINK Emmy might be an emotional packer. Is emotional packing a real thing, or did I just make it up? It's like emotional eating except instead of overeating to deal with emotional upheaval, she packs everything in sight for a trip she claims is short.

For someone who says she'll only be in town for a few days, she packed enough stuff to stay forever. Considering her travel history, you'd think she'd have packing down to an efficient science. But Emmy is fragile right now, so I don't tease her about the amount of stuff she brought, or ask her how much she paid the airline for excess baggage fees. Instead, I bite my lip and help lug her collection of suitcases, rolling luggage, and overnight bags from the rental car to the guest room.

"Just a sec," I say when my phone dings in my pocket. I bring the rolling suitcase to its upright position and drop the overnight bag I'm carrying in my other hand on top of it. I slide my phone out of my pocket and look at the screen. "*Hffffftttthhhhhttttttttt!*" I suck in my breath through my clenched teeth.

"What?" Emmy asks. "Who is it?"

"Armando."

"The nerve!" She stomps her foot and drops the overnight bag and suitcase she's lugging onto the floor, narrowly missing Sophie, who's prancing around us in excited circles. "Read it to me."

Armando: Hi, Megan. Have you spoken to Emmy? We argued yesterday, and she blocked me. I just need to know she's OK.

"You blocked him?" I ask.

"I don't want to talk to him. Not yet."

"How should I respond?" I ask, dreading placing myself in the middle of their domestic dispute.

Emmy shrugs. "Don't bother." She picks up her suitcase and overnight bag and continues trudging to the guest room.

"I have to tell him something," I plead. "He's worried. And I don't want Armando to keep texting and calling me because he doesn't know where you are. What if he reports you missing or something?"

"Fine." Emmy huffs, once again dropping her suitcase and overnight bag. "But I don't want him to know I'm here."

"You do it." I thrust my phone toward her. "But I want to read it before you send it, since he thinks it's from me."

Emmy takes the phone, and after several minutes of typing, reading aloud, discussing, backspacing, and retyping she replies with:

Me: Emmy is fine. She is taking some time for herself. She'll be in touch when she's ready.

Another moment of brief deliberation, and Emmy hits send.

"There," she says, foisting the phone at me. "Done." She lets out a long, wistful sigh.

I slip the phone into my pocket, and we finish hauling her physical baggage to the guest room.

We stash the luggage out of the way because Emmy is too exhausted—physically and mentally—to deal with it now. She says she'll unpack and organize her belongings after she has a bath, something to eat, and a nap.

While Emmy soaks in a hot bath with Himalayan bath salts, Sophie and I go for a walk around the block, then I make lunch. Tomato soup and grilled cheese sandwiches, comfort food from our childhood. Our mother used to make it for us on cold winter days.

During lunch, Emmy yawns and rubs her eyes, picking at her soup and sandwich until she excuses herself for a nap.

"Eric is golfing so the house will be quiet, and no one will bother you," I tell her. "I might go back to the store. If you need me, call or text."

Emmy gives me a tight hug and tells me not to worry.

"Can Sophie stay with me?"

"That's up to Sophie," I reply.

My sister gets a glass of water, then heads to the guest room with Sophie following behind her. I'm not surprised; Sophie loves naps. The padding of feet and paws gets fainter until they disappear, and the bedroom door closes with a dull thud.

KNITORIOUS ISN'T BUSY, and Connie makes an entire Knitted Knocker while I empty the bulky yarn shelves, wash them, then re-shelve the bulky yarn.

"I hope she's still there when we get back," April says into my Airpods, disappointed about missing my sister.

"I doubt she'll stay a full week," I say. "She loves her job, and she'll miss it. But if she stays, she brought more than enough stuff with her." I explain how a reality show is the crux of my sister's disagreement with her husband, and I'm optimistic that they'll work it out. "A bit of time, rest, and a little distance will give them some perspective," I suggest.

"*Perfect Match* is our favourite show," April confesses. "We record it on the PVR so we won't miss an episode."

"Really?" I'm stunned. "You've never mentioned it before."

"It's a guilty pleasure," April says. "Watching other people's lives fall apart and judging their decisions makes me feel better about my boring, routine existence."

"Your life is neither boring nor routine."

"I know," April replies, "but compared to the couples on *Perfect Match*, it is."

"Do you vote?"

"Every week," April declares with pride. "We have the app on our phones. We vote at the end of each episode. But we're never right. The couple we vote for is never the couple that the host evicts. It's weird. Even in the online forums, masses of viewers will agree which couple should get the boot, but it's hardly ever the couple they evict. I guess the people who vote for the right couple don't post about it on social media."

"Weird," I agree, arranging yarn skeins on the newly cleaned shelf.

April tells me about her cousin's wedding dress, and the cake they made for the big day, and I'm vaguely aware of the jingle over the door behind me. When I glance at Connie, she looks at me wide-eyed. She gives her head an almost indiscernible jerk toward the counter, and by instinct, I look in that direction.

"Armando?" I ask, incredulous. I hold up my index finger, signaling to Armando that I'll be right with him. "April, I have to go. I'll call you back."

"Is that Armando?" April asks, keen for details.

"Uh-huh." I nod, even though she can't see me. "I'll call you back."

"You better! I want to know everything," April insists. "They'd be great on *Perfect Match*. They could win. Just saying."

"Bye," I say.

"Bye, Megastar."

April likes to come up with nicknames that are puns of my actual name. Today, I'm Megastar.

"Hi, Megan," Armando says.

"How did you get here so fast? We just texted an hour ago."

"I was on my way to Harmony Lake when I texted you. I was hoping Emmy might unblock me, but she didn't. Not yet."

Armando is two years younger than my sister, but he looks younger than his thirty-eight years. His skin is flawless, and he's in optimal physical shape, thanks to the trainers, coaches, and dieticians who keep him on a strict fitness and food regimen. His dark hair is styled in one of those trendy, too-much-on-top hairstyles where the top somewhat resembles a bird's nest and is longer than the sides and back. Also, Armando wears trendy active wear and footwear, provided free by sponsors who want him to be seen and photographed wearing their gear.

"Well… it's nice to see you." I smile and shrug.

"Same here." Armando advances toward me with his arms open.

I wipe my hands on my thighs and remove my Airpods. Armando and I greet each other with a double-cheek kiss and a hug.

"You remember, Connie," I say, gesturing to the chair where Connie is casting on another brown Knitted Knocker.

"Of course, I remember Connie." Grinning, Armando opens his arms. "I never forget a beautiful woman," he says, closing in on her.

She leaves her knitting on the chair and greets Armando with the standard hug and double-cheek kiss.

"Aren't you a silver-tongued devil?"

I detect a hint of sarcasm in her voice.

Connie offers to get us refreshments, and I invite Armando to take a seat in the cozy sitting area.

"Why are you here?"

"To see my wife."

"What makes you think she's here?"

"I used the find my friends app on our phones," Armando explains. "It's the only thing Emmy didn't block me from." A rolled r sneaks into the last word of his sentence.

Armando is from Ecuador, but he's lived away from Ecuador longer than he lived there. Years ago, he had elocution lessons to minimize his accent. This was at the suggestion of his agent who told him it would help him get sponsorship deals.

"If you used the find my friends app, you know Emmy isn't at Knitorious," I point out, realizing that when he texted me earlier, worried about his missing wife, he knew darn well she was at my house and that I had spoken to her. "Why didn't you go to her location? Why are you here?"

"Emmy made it clear she's not ready to see me yet," Armando says. "I don't want to upset her more. Also, I'm tired from the journey. It's best for both of us to get some rest before we talk. But I wanted to ask how she is and tell you I'm here."

I hope he doesn't expect me to breach my sister's confidence or side with him. Whether or not I agree with Emmy, she's my sister and my loyalty lies with her.

"I see," I acknowledge, staying neutral.

It's brighter than usual in the store because the windows are spotless—if I say so myself. Glancing toward the window, I'm struck by how exposed we are. There's not much blocking the view of the cozy sitting area from the sidewalk or the street,and Emmy and Armando take constant precautions to protect their privacy.

"Let's go in the back," I suggest, standing up.

Armando follows me to the back room, and we run into Connie. She's carrying a tray of tea and biscuits. Taking the tray from her, I thank her for the refreshments and tell her we'll sit in the kitchenette because there's more privacy and no windows. Smiling, she leaves us alone, closing the door that separates the store from the backroom.

Armando and I make small talk about the tea, the biscuits, then the weather. Our small talk is slow and awkward. We take turns searching for topics, with each of us struggling to keep up our respective ends of the conversation. It's obvious Armando and I don't really know each other. In fact, I think this is the first time we've been alone together. Until today, we've only seen each other at group gatherings. Aside from pleasantries about weather, Hannah, or soccer, we've never had a one-on-one conversation longer than a couple of minutes.

"Did Emmy tell you what we disagreed about?" Armando asks, addressing the elephant in the room.

"Yes."

"I would say yes if I could," Armando says, shrugging one shoulder. I assume he's referring to the *Perfect*

Match opportunity. "But I have a contract. I'm obligated to my team." He dips a biscuit in his tea, bobbing it up and down. "As far as professional soccer players go, I'm old. Over the hill. I'm one of the oldest in the league. This could be my last season. I want to go out on top. I can't afford to miss training camp or the preseason. I have to work harder than ever to stay on top of my game and keep up with the younger players."

"Did you tell this to Emmy?" I ask.

"I tried," Armando says with a sigh. "She didn't want to hear it."

"I see." I repeat my neutral, don't get involved response.

"I'm not sure how to resolve this with her."

"I don't know what to tell you," I say, shaking my head and placing my empty cup and plate on the tray. "It's not my place to get involved."

"Of course," Armando agrees. "I would never put you in the middle." Following my lead, he places his dishes on the tea tray. "But I know how much Emmy respects your opinion. She listens to you… "

I raise my hand in a stop motion, cutting him off midsentence.

"My sister knows her own mind and makes her own decisions. I would never manipulate her."

"You misunderstand. I would never ask you to." He smiles, flashing his shiny, straight, super-white teeth. Armando looks at his watch and stands up. "I should go. It's getting late."

"I'll tell Emmy you were here." I say, accompanying him to the back door.

"I expect nothing less," Armando says. "Please tell her I'm staying at the Rise & Glide Resort and Spa. I'd text her with my room number, but she blocked me."

The Rise & Glide is a ski resort in the Harmony Hills mountains. It's only twenty minutes away by car, and it's the most upscale accommodation within driving distance.

"Great choice. Rise & Glide was recently renovated. I hear the rooms are beautiful."

"I've never stayed there," Armando says. "Brad booked the suite for me. He says the online reviews and photos were good, and I trust his judgement. Also, it has a state-of-the-art fitness facility, so I can keep up with my training while I'm here."

I interpret this to mean that Armando has confided in Brad about his and Emmy's marital issues. How else would Armando explain why he needed somewhere to stay at the last minute in Harmony Lake?

After another hug and another double-cheek kiss, Armando leaves through the back door.

"Where's Armando?" Connie asks when I return to the store after cleaning up the tea and biscuit dishes.

"He went out the back."

"What did he want from you?" She crosses her arms in front of her chest and quirks an eyebrow.

"What makes you think he wanted something?"

I mean, she's not wrong, but how did Connie know Armando had an agenda?

"I've met his type before," she cautions with an air of wisdom. "They use flattery, persuasion, and charm to pull the wool over your eyes."

"Armando *is* quite charming and flattering," I agree.

"After three years of being your brother-in-law, why would he suddenly show up acting like he visits all the time?"

"I suspect he wanted me to persuade Emmy to see his side of their disagreement," I admit. "I said no and told him I won't get involved."

"Good girl." Connie lifts her chin and flashes me a proud smirk.

"Now, which shelves should I clean next?" I mutter, tapping my chin and searching my imagination for inspiration. "It's missing something, isn't it?"

"We'll decide tomorrow, my dear," Connie responds to my rhetorical question as she locks the door and turns the sign from OPEN to CLOSED.

CHAPTER 4

SATURDAY, October 2nd

It's still dark outside when I wake up surrounded by silence. I pull the covers up to my chin and hunker down, cocooning myself in the goose-down duvet and flannel sheets. Comfy, I bask in the warm silence and try to will myself back to sleep. Nope. I'm wide awake. When I close my eyes, items from my to-do list flash in my mind's eye. *Sigh.* I reach one arm outside my cocoon and stretch it across the bed, searching for Sophie. Nothing but the duvet.

"Sophie?" I ask, lifting my head off the pillow and searching the dark bed for her corgi-shaped silhouette. "Soph?" Nothing.

I wrap my pink fluffy robe around me, slip into my white fluffy slippers, and shuffle toward the coffeemaker. Someone has already made coffee. Wafts of caffeine-infused air guide my nose when I turn the corner toward the kitchen.

"Morning, Sis!" Emmy smiles from the corner of the

family room sofa. She's curled up with her feet under her butt. The afghan from the back of the sofa covers her legs, and she's leafing through a magazine. Sophie nestles into Emmy's hip, resting her head on Emmy's thigh.

"Good morning," I say. "You're up early."

"Um, excuse me?" She snorts with a chuckle. "I've been up for a while. After years of getting up for work in the middle of the night, my body doesn't remember how to sleep in."

Sophie jumps down from the sofa and trots toward me, tail wagging, to say good morning.

"I always forget," I admit, bending down to rub Sophie. "I still associate you with the teenager who refused to drag her butt out of bed before noon."

"Those days are long gone," Emmy quips, turning the page. "Sophie's been out already, but I haven't fed her."

"Thanks," I say, rummaging through the basket of coffee pods until I find one that will hit the spot: French Vanilla.

I hold up the pod and look at Emmy, wordlessly offering her a coffee. In response, she holds up her mug and smiles, indicating that she already has a coffee.

While the coffeemaker transforms the coffee pod into liquid heaven, I fix Sophie's breakfast and put it on the floor. She digs in and doesn't come up for air until her bowl is empty.

"Your fiancé went for an early morning run," Emmy advises when I join her on the sofa.

"He's weird like that," I respond, tugging the afghan until I have enough to cover the bottom of my legs.

"How's the wedding planning coming along?" my sister asks.

I shrug, swallowing a mouthful of coffee. "It isn't," I admit. "We haven't discussed it, or picked a date, or anything."

"I assumed from this pile of wedding magazines that you were in wedding-planning mode." Emmy gestures to the tall pile of glossy magazines on the coffee table.

"I didn't buy those," I confess. "People give them to me. Each magazine is a not-so-subtle hint that we have to get a wiggle on and plan our wedding."

"It sounds like you aren't in a hurry," Emmy says, closing the bridal magazine she was leafing through and tossing on top of the pile.

"I'm not," I admit. "But Eric would like to move things along." I sigh. "There's so much to plan. Even a small wedding is a lot of work."

"You could always elope like Armando and I," she suggests, grinning. "I can give you the contact information for the adorable chapel we went to in Vegas. Just choose what to wear and show up. They take care of flowers, photography, everything. They even have a package that includes wedding rings."

"It sounds tempting." I take another sip of coffee. "Is that why you eloped? Because you didn't want to plan a wedding?"

"I would've loved to plan our wedding," Emmy professes. "Eloping was Armando's idea." She breaks into a sheepish grin. "He's very romantic, you know. He wanted our wedding to be private and intimate. He said he didn't want to share me with anyone else, and he wanted us to focus on each other instead of details." She blushes as she recalls her wedding.

"I didn't realize he was so sentimental."

"He didn't even want to tell anyone we got married," she adds.

"You never told me this. Why didn't he want anyone to know?"

"He said he wanted it to be our secret. Something special that only we shared. He's a very private person, Sis. Private and romantic."

"But your marriage is public knowledge, so I assume he came around to your way of thinking?"

"We agreed to tell people, and we had a reception when we got home from our honeymoon. I think Armando would've been happier to keep it between us, but he wanted me to be happy, so we compromised." She blushes and grins again, this time looking wistfully at her wedding ring.

I remember the reception well. It was a beautiful formal event in the ballroom of a fancy hotel.

"Do you regret eloping?" I ask as Sophie leaps onto the sofa, licking her chops, and turning in circles before she lies down.

"No." Emmy shrugs. "We had the reception afterward, and a big wedding would have been awkward with his family and stuff."

"Because they're in Ecuador?"

"That and because he doesn't talk to them."

"He doesn't?" This is the first I've heard of relationship issues between Armando and his family. "Why not?"

Emmy shrugs. "It happened before Armando and I met. I don't know all the details, and Armando doesn't like to talk about it, but he said they disagreed over money. Armando's money. He said they weren't happy with how much he gave them. He got tired of fighting, cut them off financially, and they retaliated by cutting off all communication with him."

"That's awful," I sympathize. "Poor Armando."

"I know." My sister nods. "I'm literally his only family. And since his family turned his best friend against him, he doesn't have any friends from his old life either."

"His family turned his best friend against him?"

"Armando said his family tried to get his best friend to side with them about the money issue, and it destroyed their friendship. He said it was bound to happen sooner or later because their relationship became strained because his friend was jealous when Armando made the major leagues. His friend didn't get a chance to play for the majors because he had a career-ending knee injury."

"Poor guy."

My sister nods. "I think that's why Brad's friendship is so important to him. He doesn't want to lose anyone else."

"Your attitude toward Armando this morning is warmer than yesterday," I observe, wondering if reminiscing about their elopement is the reason. "Does this mean you might unblock him?"

"I already unblocked him," Emmy admits with a smirk. "Last night after you told me he visited you at Knitorious."

"You blocked his calls, you blocked him on social media, and you blocked his texts, but you didn't block him from your Find My Friends app. That was on purpose, wasn't it?"

I've been wanting to ask her this since yesterday. My sister is too strategic and too smart for such an oversight.

"Guilty." She holds her hands up in a conciliatory gesture. "I wanted to see if he'd follow me to Harmony Lake."

"Like a test?" I ask.

"Sort of," Emmy admits. Then she swats my arm. "Don't judge me."

"I'm not judging, I swear."

April might be right when she said Emmy and Armando could win *Perfect Match*.

"I spoke to him last night before bed. We're meeting today to talk."

"He's welcome to come here," I offer.

"Thanks, Sis, but I'm meeting him for breakfast in his hotel suite. The fewer people who know we're in town, the better. We don't need any speculation about our relationship while we work this out."

"Call me if you need anything," I remind her. "And you're welcome to stay here as long as you want."

THE STORE IS SO busy my brain has stopped registering the jingle of the bell over the door. It opens and closes so often, that if I looked up every time I heard it, I'd never look at anything else.

"Are you having a sale or something?" Eric asks when he and Sophie enter the store. "It's busier than usual." He hands me a chocolate caramel latte.

"Thank you for the coffee." I give him a quick kiss. "We're not having a sale," I answer his question. "It's been busy since we opened. It doesn't help that Connie and I are rushed off our feet because Marla is working at the bakery."

"And she says the bakery is just as busy as Knitorious," Connie interjects, breezing past us with a customer in tow. "Apparently all the businesses on Water Street are busier than usual today. No one knows why," Connie adds, piling skeins of peppermint pink baby yarn into her customer's arms. "It's a mystery." She shrugs.

"What are you and Sophie up to?" I ask, sorting some skeins of mislaid sock yarn.

"It was time for Sophie's walk, and she wanted to surprise you with a coffee," he explains, looking around the store at the bustle of browsing knitters.

"She's such a thoughtful dog," I say, looking at Sophie. She wags her butt, panting at me.

"I told Emmy I'd help her move her stuff to Armando's suite at Rise & Glide, but I can come back after and help," he offers. "I can work the cash register, or put stuff away, or whatever."

"That's sweet," I say. "Thank you."

"Have you spoken to Emmy?" Eric asks, following me from the shelves of sock yarn to the racks of knitting needles, so I can re-shelve some knitting needles that a customer abandoned in the sock-yarn section.

"She phoned a little while ago," I reply. "I couldn't talk because the store was too busy, but she said Armando agreed to talk to the network and his team management about *Perfect Match*. And he agreed to fire Brad and look for another agent. An agent Emmy and Armando both like. I'm glad they found a compromise."

A knitter with a sweater pattern from 1987 interrupts Eric's account of how Emmy's luggage seems to have multiplied since she arrived yesterday.

"I'm afraid this yarn company went out of business twenty-five years ago," I explain when the knitter asks if we carry the yarn used in the pattern. I direct her to the worsted weight section and tell her I'll be right over to help her find a suitable substitution. "I'm sorry, I have to get back to work," I tell Eric. "Thank you for helping Emmy. Mind your back when you lift the luggage, it's heavier than it looks." I give Sophie a quick scratch between the ears, and they leave.

CHAPTER 5

SUNDAY, October 3rd

This is my first visit to The Rise & Glide Resort since their renovations. It was renovated inside and out. The old Rise & Glide had a rustic aesthetic, reminiscent of a hunting lodge. The new, rebranded Rise & Glide Resort and Retreat is sleek and modern.

"Nice," I whisper as I enter the main lobby, greeted by calming neutral colours, clean lines, and sophisticated yet comfortable furnishings.

I could've stayed in the car and sent Emmy a text to let her know I'm here, but curiosity got the better of me.

"Megan? Is that you?"

I turn my head left, then right, searching for the source of my name.

"Deb?" I confirm when I recognize the face that matches the voice. "What are you doing here?"

"I'm the resort manager," Deb explains. "Haven't you heard? I oversaw the entire renovation." She gestures proudly around her.

"Wow." Deb and I hug. "You did an amazing job. It's beautiful."

"Thank you," Deb replies, her blushing cheeks a sharp contrast to her blonde hair with silver highlights.

Deb Kee is a modest lady, who's uncomfortable receiving compliments, even when they're well deserved. A lifetime resident of Harmony Lake, Deb recently retired from the Harmony Lake Fire Department. She is one of the many strong, pioneering women who call Harmony Lake home. Besides working in a traditionally male occupation, she was the HLFD's first ever female Firefighter of the Year. Deb Kee blazed a trail—pun intended—for the generations of female firefighters who came after her.

"I thought you retired," I say. "Connie said you were living it up in a retirement community with your rescue dogs."

Deb lets out a short, shrill whistle, and two dogs, a Miniature Pinscher and a Collie mix, trot out from behind the registration counter and stand by their owner's side.

"Retirement is overrated," Deb says while I crouch down to rub Blitz and Abby. "Besides, this isn't work, it's fun."

"I hope I have your zest for life when it's my time to retire," I comment.

"Are you here to see the ballroom?" Deb asks after some small talk and local gossip.

I shake my head. "I wasn't planning on it."

Deb asks with such confidence that I second guess

myself and wonder if I *am* supposed to see the ballroom.

"Connie said if you come by I should show you the ballroom," Deb explains. "She said if you say no, I should show you, anyway."

"Ahh." I nod. "Connie did mention it would make an ideal wedding venue."

Connie mentions the wedding a lot; I swear she thinks about it more than me.

"It would be a beautiful wedding venue, Megan. And we offer a range of wedding packages. Our event planner doesn't work Sundays, but I'd be happy to give you a quick tour, and we could look at dates if you know what time of year… "

"Thanks, Deb," I interrupt her Connie-motivated sales pitch. "But I'm here to pick up my sister. She and her husband are guests. We have a brunch date. I'd love to look at the ballroom, but Adam's expecting us. I promise to come back with Eric for a tour."

"Are you sure?" Deb asks, undeterred. "Connie said…"

"Don't worry," I assure her. "I'll tell Connie you tried. And Eric and I will meet with the event planner… soon." I smile.

Deb, Blitz, and Abby walk me to the elevator. While I wait for the door to open, Deb points out some features and special touches she insisted on during the renovation. She has my undivided attention when she tells me about the renovated spa on the sixth floor.

Deb's cell phone buzzes, and she looks at the screen. Worry lines corrugate her forehead.

"Enjoy your brunch, Megan. I have to go."

"Is everything OK?" I ask.

"Another staff member came down with that bug that's going around. She has to go home sick, and we're already understaffed."

"What kind of bug?" I wonder out loud, silently hoping there's a bottle of hand sanitizer in my purse.

"A gastrointestinal thing. The housekeeping staff call it gut rot." Deb flicks her wrist like something called gut rot is nothing more than a minor inconvenience. "At least it's happening now instead of in the middle of ski season." She shrugs.

Deb's always optimistic. Who else could find a silver lining in a gut-rot outbreak among her employees?

"Take care, Deb. I hope you don't get it."

"Don't worry about me, Megan. I have a cast-iron gut." She chuckles and rubs her belly.

"SHHH," Emmy greets me by bringing her index finger to her lips and shushing me.

I nod and pretend to zip my lips with my thumb and forefinger.

"Armando is asleep," she explains in a whisper. "He's dead to the world." She beckons me inside, then closes the door without making a sound. "Wait here," she mouths holding her index finger in the air. "I'll be right back."

I reply with a wink and a thumbs up. Emmy disappears into what I assume is the bedroom and reappears a moment later with her purse slung over her shoulder.

We exit the suite, making as little noise as possible and head toward the elevator.

"Armando needs his sleep," Emmy says in her normal tone of voice, hooking her arm through mine and pulling me close so she can speak into my ear. "We were up late last night making up," she gushes, nudging my ribs and winking. "He's exhausted!" She giggles.

"Ew," I blurt, laughing and covering my ears with my hands. "Too much information! There are some things I don't need to know."

We laugh and speed up our pace when the elevator door opens. Still giggling, we pass an employee pushing a cart with a covered tray.

"Good morning, ladies," he says with a nod when he passes us.

"Good morning," we reply in unison.

"WHATEVER IT IS, IT SMELLS AMAZING!" Emmy declares when I ask Adam what we're having for brunch.

"It's a surprise," Adam teases from the kitchen of his condo.

Adam and I have brunch every Sunday. We alternate between his condo and my house, but Adam always cooks. Our daughter, Hannah, joins us on video chat from her dorm room in Toronto. It was awkward at first, but Adam and I worked hard to come through our separation and divorce as friends. Our marriage is over, but we're still co-parents, and we'll always be family. We still love each other, but not the way spouses should. Our marriage didn't end with a dramatic bang, it fizzled slowly, over many years. We either didn't notice, or ignored the signs until it was too late. Attempts to reignite the spark were futile, and we admitted we would be happier unmarried. Our divorce isn't traditional, but it works for us, and it works for our daughter, which is all that matters.

"If you won't tell us what it is, how should I set the table?" I ask, trying to peek around him as he blocks the stove with his body. Unsuccessful, I stand on my tippy toes and try to look over his shoulder. Also unsuccessful. Instead of brunch, I get a close-up view of his salt and pepper hair.

"Set it with the standard stuff," he suggests.

"Plates or bowls?" Emmy asks. "Forks or spoons? Will we need knives? Regular knives or steak knives?" She pelts him with rapid-fire questions.

"Fine," Adam declares, defeated. "We're having Green Toad-In-The-Hole.

We scrunch up our faces in a way that lets Adam know the name isn't as appetizing as the aroma.

"I made it up," he explains with a one-shoulder shrug. "I didn't know what to call it and thought Green Toad-In-The-Hole sounded trendy." Emmy and I shake our heads. Frustrated, Adam huffs and furrows his thick brows. "I made a spinach-artichoke-cream cheese spread," he explains, and I resist my urge to dip my finger in the yummy-looking spread when he shows it to us. "Then I cut a hole in the centre of thick-slices of crusty bread and spread the cream-cheese mixture on the bread. I cracked an egg in the hole, sprinkled with grated Gruyère cheese, and baked it in the oven."

"Wow! It looks incredible, Adam," I assure him. "But it needs a better name."

His blue eyes gleam with pride at the compliment.

"Can you send me the recipe?" Emmy asks. "Armando would love this."

My ex-husband's culinary skills have come a long way since we separated. When we lived together, Adam couldn't cook anything beyond heating leftovers in the microwave—with specific instructions. And now, he's inventing restaurant-worthy recipes.

While I set the table, Emmy uses Adam's tablet to contact Hannah on video chat. Hannah doesn't know her Aunt Emmy is joining us for brunch today. Emmy's visit is as much a surprise to my daughter today as it was to me at Knitorious on Friday.

Hannah and Aunt Emmy are thrilled to see each other. They spend most of the meal talking to each other while Adam and I enjoy our Green Toad-In-The-Hole free from conversation. Though, we're able to squeeze in a short visit with our daughter before she announces she has to go and ends the video call.

"I know a great entertainment lawyer. I'll send you her contact information," Adam offers when, over a second cup of coffee, Emmy tells him about their opportunity to appear on *Perfect Match*.

"You're the only lawyer I trust, Adam," Emmy

responds. "You've handled every legal need I've ever had. I'd rather deal with you."

It's true. Adam has represented Emmy in two divorces and three real estate transactions. He drew up her will and powers of attorney, and helped negotiate her contract with *Hello, today*!

"Don't sign anything until I've looked at it," Adam counsels in his lawyer-voice.

"I know, Adam."

Emmy's tone of voice and eye-roll reminds me of our petulant teenage years when we used the same tone of voice and eye-roll with our parents.

"Promise?" Adam asks, now using his dad-voice.

"I won't sign anything until you say so." She flashes a sarcastic grin, then her phone chimes. "It's Poppy," Emmy announces, standing up. "I have to take this." She looks at Adam. "Can I step onto the balcony?"

"Of course," Adam replies. "The door's unlocked."

Poppy Prescott is Emmy's best friend and personal assistant. They've known each other since university. Emmy and Poppy complement each other's strengths and weaknesses. Poppy is an introvert who encourages Emmy to slow down and engage in occasional introspection. Emmy is an extrovert who encourages Poppy to step outside her comfort zone and interact with people more than she would without Emmy pressuring her. Poppy is a planner. She takes her time making decisions and weighs the pros and cons of her options. Emmy is impulsive and prone to acting or speaking before she thinks.

The door to the balcony closes with Emmy on the other side, and Adam leans into me.

"I'm worried, Meg."

"About Emmy?"

He nods. "She's too excited about this *Perfect Match* thing. I'm afraid she'll agree to whatever they offer, and it won't be in her best interest."

"I had the same thought," I admit.

"You know how spontaneous she is."

"Yes, I do," I agree, recalling how she spontaneously arrived on my doorstep two days ago.

"Do you think it's possible she already signed something?" Adam asks. "It would explain why she's so desperate to get Armando to agree."

"She's impulsive, Adam, but I don't think she'd sign anything without at least talking to her husband and lawyer first," I argue. "You've intervened on her behalf more than once to undo her bad decisions. I'm sure she learned from those mistakes."

Plural. More than one mistake. My sister has a habit of committing, then regretting.

"I don't know, Meg," Adam says, with an undertone of concern. "She married her first two husbands just weeks after she met them. She eloped with Armando a few months after they met and before I could draw up a prenuptial agreement. She almost signed a horrible contract with *Hello, today*!..."

"OK, Adam. I get it," I say, interrupting his verbal inventory of my sister's questionable decisions.

"She needs a babysitter." Adam arches his thick eyebrows and leans back in his chair.

"That's what Poppy does," I remind him. "She's the stabilizing voice of reason in Emmy's hectic life."

Poppy is an unsung hero. She's talked my sister off more than one proverbial ledge. I don't know what Emmy would do without her.

"I wish Mum and Dad handled their divorce more like you guys and less like World War III," Emmy comments out of nowhere when she returns from the balcony.

"Me too," I admit. "But divorce is traumatic regardless of how friendly it is. I just hope Hannah is less traumatized than we were."

"She is," Emmy reassures me. "Hannah's resilient like us." She smiles.

"Hannah will never know the pain and toxicity of parents who hate each other and can't interact with each other," Adam adds, giving my hand a quick squeeze.

Though he's not a child of divorce, Adam specialized in family law for many years and saw firsthand how divorce can bring out the worst in people. The emotions that accompany a nasty divorce can have a ripple effect throughout a family, destroying generations of relationships. Over the years, I've often heard him remind clients that *the person you marry and the person you divorce are not the same person*. It's one of the truest things I've ever heard.

"Here's hoping our family doesn't experience any more divorces," I say, hoping to shut down the topic on an optimistic note.

I stand up and start piling dishes to clear the table.

"I won't get divorced again," Emmy declares with confidence as she stands up and helps me clear the table. "I refuse. I'd rather be widowed than go through another divorce."

CHAPTER 6

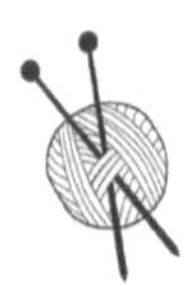

"HOW LONG ARE you staying in town?" I ask Emmy on the drive back to Rise & Glide.

"That's what I talked to Poppy about," Emmy replies. "Hannah mentioned that she's coming home for Thanksgiving next weekend. I'd like to stay and have Thanksgiving with the family. I'm not sure if Armando can stay, but Poppy is talking to the producers *at Hello, today!* to arrange for someone to cover for me next week."

In Canada, we celebrate Thanksgiving a month earlier than our American friends.

"Really?" I ask, surprised. "I can't remember the last time we had Thanksgiving together! Yay!"

"I hope Armando can stay," Emmy adds. "It would be nice for him to spend quality time with everyone. You should get to know each other better."

"I hope he can stay too," I agree. "You could stay way past Thanksgiving. You packed enough stuff to stay for at least a year," I tease.

"I wasn't thinking straight," Emmy explains, laughing. "I just grabbed whatever I saw and threw it in a bag until I ran out of bags." She bursts into a fresh fit of giggles. "Eric's eyes almost popped out of his head when he saw all my luggage. I'm sure he regretted offering to help me carry it."

"Here we are," I say, pulling into the parking lot.

"Can you come upstairs for a minute? I got swag bags for you and Hannah at that awards show I presented at last month. If I don't give them to you now, I'll forget."

"I always have time to collect swag bags," I reply, unbuckling my seatbelt.

A swag bag is a gift bag given to event attendees. My sister says they're common at awards shows. Companies fill the bags with promotional products, hoping the influential people who receive them will use the products and maybe post about them on social media, or get photographed using them. Sometimes, attendees get more than one bag, and when that happens, Emmy grabs extra for Poppy, me, or Hannah.

I leave my purse in the car and just bring my cell phone with me. As we walk from the car to the hotel, my sister pulls out her phone and starts typing.

"Just giving Armando a heads-up that we're on our way upstairs. In case he's not decent." She twitches her eyebrows at me.

At the elevator, she unlocks her phone again.

"Hmph," she says. "Armando always texts me back." She turns the screen toward me. "The message is unread. He hasn't even seen it."

"Maybe he's still sleeping," I suggest with a shrug.

"Uh-uh," Emmy says as we leave the elevator. "Armando lives a very regimented life. He eats the same food at the same time every day and adheres to a strict training routine. There's no way he's still in bed."

"Gym?" I suggest.

"Maybe," Emmy says, checking the time on her phone.

She removes the DO NOT DISTURB sign from the door handle and uses her keycard to unlock the door. I follow her into the room.

Where did the DO NOT DISTURB sign come from? I don't remember seeing it when I was here earlier, and I don't remember Emmy hanging it up when we left. Was it there, and I didn't notice it? Did Armando hang it up after we left?

"The bedroom door is still closed." I point to the closed door. "Maybe he *is* asleep. Maybe you tired him out more than you thought," I tease.

"I'll be right back," she says, ignoring my joke.

Emmy disappears behind the closed door, and I look around the renovated luxury hotel suite. The blackout curtains are closed, and the room is dark. I find a switch on the wall in the sitting area and flip it. A floor lamp next to the sofa lights up, casting a soft glow on the fixtures and furnishings. Everything looks high end. There are more plants than you'd expect in a hotel suite. Are they real or fake? It's hard to tell. I focus on a Boston fern sitting on a round end table near the balcony door. The fern could be an authentic-looking fake, or a real fern so perfect it looks fake. I rub a frond between my thumb and forefinger. It feels real, but I'm not one hundred percent convinced. I pat the soil with my finger then rub my damp finger with my thumb. The fern is real.

Tucked in behind the bushy plant, I notice the corner of a small box. I lift a few fronds out of the way for a closer look. It's an empty cigarette package. Weird. Emmy doesn't smoke, and I assume Armando doesn't smoke. Professional athletes don't smoke, do they? He didn't smell of cigarette smoke when he was at Knitorious on Friday. He hugged Connie, and if she'd picked up a whiff of cigarette smoke, she would have mentioned it after he left. I'm a non-smoker, and I'm sensitive to the specific scent of cigarette smoke. I notice it right away, often from a distance. Especially at work because I don't want it near the yarn. Second-hand smoke—and even third-hand smoke—clings. It clings to clothes, hair, pets, and yarn. No one wants to buy nicotine-infused yarn.

Maybe a previous guest left this cigarette package behind and housekeeping missed it. It would be easy to overlook; I wouldn't have noticed it if I wasn't futzing with the fern.

"Megan." My sister appears behind me like she came out of nowhere.

"What's wrong?" Her eyes are wide and blank. "Emmy?" I touch her hand. It's freezing. "Emmy, what happened?"

"Armando," her limp, cold hand points behind her. "He's not asleep, but he's not awake. He won't answer me."

Oh no! A bowling-ball-sized knot forms in my belly, and impending doom radiates throughout my body.

"No, no, no, no," I mutter under my breath as I step around my sister and lock my gaze on the ajar bedroom door.

"Armando?" I call out. "If this is a joke, it's not funny." The room is dark. I grope the wall just inside the door, find a switch, and flip it. It turns on a dim lamp on the desk in the corner of the room. Great, a lamp that creates ambience instead of actual light. I'm sure it's one of those lamps with multiple levels of brightness, but I'm not interested in figuring out how to adjust it right now. "Armando?" I call out louder than last time.

As my eyes adjust to the darkness, I'm able to make out Armando's silhouette. He's in bed, lying on his back, covered up to his mid-chest. His arms are at his sides outside the covers, and he's facing the window. He's not moving. I walk around the foot of the bed, bump into the room service cart, push it out of my way, and reach for the blackout curtains, tearing them open and squinting at the harsh, sudden invasion of daylight.

"Armando!" I shout.

His eyes are open and glassy. His jaw is slack, and cream-coloured foam coats the corners of his parted lips. He's too still.

"What's wrong with him?" Emmy charges into the room. She races around the foot of the bed, almost tripping over the room service cart, and leans over her husband. "Armando!" She taps the side of his face. No response. "He's not dead," Emmy declares, glaring at me like she's challenging me to defy her.

I pick up the receiver of the landline next to the bed and wait for the dial tone. No dial tone. Do I press 9? How do hotel phones work again? Instead of a dial tone, a man's voice comes on the line.

"Good day, Mr. Garcia. You've reached the front desk. How can I help you?"

"Er. *Ahem*." The lump in my throat blocks my words from coming out, and I clear my throat. "This isn't Mr. Garcia," I manage as I stretch over the bed and place my index and middle fingers on Armando's cool neck.

"Mrs. Garcia?"

"No," I reply, moving my fingers and hoping to feel the pulsating throb of life through Armando's body. "Mr. Garcia needs medical help."

"Ambulance?"

"Yes" I reply, still feeling around for a pulse but not finding one. "And the coroner."

CHAPTER 7

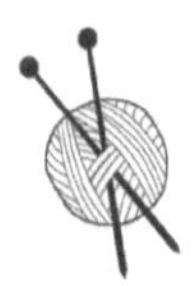

Deb Kee bursts into the room carrying a first aid kit and portable AED.

An AED, or automated external defibrillator, is a medical device that delivers a jolt of electricity through two paddles into the patient's chest to jump start the heart.

"Mr. Garcia?" Deb shouts as she rushes past Emmy and I to get to him. "Armando! Can you hear me?"

"Deb is a trained first responder," I whisper to Emmy, pulling her away from Armando so Deb can do her thing. "She knows what she's doing."

My sister and I squeeze together at the bottom of the bed. Deb isn't opening her first aid kit or rushing to use the defibrillator on Armando. She's searching his neck for a pulse, just like I did moments before. She moves her search to his exposed wrist. This isn't good.

A wave of nausea ripples from my stomach to my throat, and I'm suddenly hyper-aware of my senses. My heart pounding in my ears is the loudest thing in the room. The sunlight's glaring intensity forces me to squint. My sister's shaky hand is ice cold, and every time I inhale the smell of the food on the room-service tray next to me, it makes my stomach churn.

Sadly, I have more crime scene experience than a yarn store owner should, and I'm aware it's a no-no to touch anything unless absolutely necessary. But, thanks to the sudden and intense exaggeration of my senses, the slightest hint of the leftover food causes the Green Toad-In-The-Hole to threaten an imminent reappearance. Holding my breath, I reach for the dome-shaped cloche on the bottom shelf of the cart and use it to cover the plate of half-eaten food, then swallow hard, hoping it's enough to push the nausea down.

"Nooooooo!" Emmy shrieks and covers her mouth with her hand when Deb looks up at us, frowning and shaking her head.

"I'm sorry," Deb says softly. "The police and paramedics are on their way."

"Police?" Emmy demands. "What can the police do?"

"They have to attend all unexpected deaths," I explain.

"Death?" Emmy glares at me like I'm using a word in a foreign language. "He needs CPR!" She looks at Deb. "You know how to do CPR." Her eyes wide, she gestures toward Armando with her trembling hand. "Do it!"

Before Deb can respond to my sister's desperate plea, first responders fill the room.

"We're in the way," I whisper, tugging my sister's arm to coax her toward the door.

"I'm not leaving." Emmy yanks her arm away.

"Which one of you found him?" A uniformed police officer asks.

"Her."

"Me."

Emmy and I reply, both pointing at her.

"Oh, hi, Megan," the officer says. "Chief Sloane is on his way up."

"Thanks," I nod and attempt a small smile while trying to recall the officer's name.

By the time it occurs to me to look at the name badge on his uniform, he's leading my sister out of the bedroom. Unsure what to do, and wanting to stay out of the way, I slink out after them and join my sister on the sofa.

An authoritative, familiar voice protests the lack of light in the dim hotel suite. Eric.

A young police officer rushes to the window and combs through the pleats in the blackout curtains, searching for an opening. I stand up and wave Eric over just as the young officer opens the curtains and daylight pierces the room.

"What are you doing here?" he asks, rubbing my back. "Are you OK?" I nod. Eric scans the sofa, his gaze stopping on my sister. "Is Armando....?"

Squinting into the brightness, I nod and Eric curses under his breath. I look toward the bedroom and jerk my head. He nods and holds up an index finger.

"I'll be back," he says as he turns toward the bedroom.

The uniformed officer who accompanied my sister out of the bedroom is asking her questions. Her voice is quiet, and I can't hear her responses.

Deb is talking to a group of first responders. A police officer she's with nods and stands aside. She makes her way through the group to us.

"Let's go somewhere quieter," Deb suggests, taking my sister by the elbow. My sister opens her mouth to speak, but Deb speaks first and says, "I know you don't want to leave, but you'll be right next door."

"Megan's coming too?" Emmy asks, clenching a fistful of my rust-coloured cardigan.

"Of course," Deb replies, guiding us through the horde of moving uniforms.

Outside the room, we turn left and follow Deb down the corridor, single file, like ducklings waddling behind a mother duck, until she brings us to a stop. She swipes her keycard and holds the door while Emmy and I file past her into the vacant suite.

"Thanks, Deb." My voice hitches on her name, and I swallow an onslaught of tears.

Deb hugs me and her comforting embrace has the same intangible, maternal quality as Connie's, making it impossible to hold back the tears.

"If you need anything, text me," Deb says. I nod. She retrieves a box of tissues from the washroom and hands them to me. "Or pick up any landline and talk. The front desk knows you're here." I nod again. "I have to answer some questions for the police, but I'm not leaving the building," she reassures me. Still trying to compose myself, I nod again. "Should I tell Connie?" Deb whispers as she reaches for the door handle.

"I'll let her know," I reply. "Thank you again."

After Deb leaves, I take a deep breath and blow it out. Then I take in my surroundings. This suite is the mirror image of Armando's suite, and except for a few minor differences, the decor is identical.

I collapse onto the sofa next to my sister and put the box of tissues on her lap. She uses one to dab her teary eyes and blow her nose.

"Do you want water or anything?" I ask.

She shakes her head.

"Do you want to lie down?"

She shakes her head, then looks me in the eye.

"My husband is dead, isn't he?"

I nod.

"I'm sorry, Emmy."

"How?" she asks, pulling a fresh tissue from the box and crying into it. "How? He's young. He's healthy. There weren't any marks on him. How?"

"I don't know," I say, hugging her while she cries into my shoulder.

While my sister cries on my shoulder and I try to make sense of her husband's sudden death, my phone dings, distracting me from my morbid ruminations.

"It's Dad," I say when I look at the screen.

Emmy jolts upright and tilts my phone so she can see the screen. I haven't opened the text message yet. The notification banner on the screen reads, ***New Text Message From: Dad.***

"How did he find out?" Emmy asks, panicked. "Who told him?"

"He can't know," I say, thinking out loud. "It must be a coincidence."

"It has to be," Emmy agrees. She lifts her chin toward the screen. "Open it."

I unlock my phone and open the text message. It's a group message to me, Emmy, and Hannah.

"It's not about Armando," I say, looking at the text. "He sent us a photo of a grey-crested bird."

"Why?" Emmy asks.

I read her the text our Dad sent with the photo.

Dad: This is a Southern Lapwing, the national bird of Uruguay. He was wading in a puddle outside our window this morning.

"Uruguay?" Emmy asks. "I thought they were in Belize."

"I thought they were in Brazil," I add.

Hannah's response to the bird photo appears on the screen.

Hannah: Nice bird, Grandpa. I thought you were in Argentina? Followed by a bird emoji, a heart emoji, and the Argentinian flag emoji.

Dad: We're in Uruguay. Followed by the Uruguayan flag emoji.

"That's one mystery solved." I show Emmy our dad's text response to Hannah.

"When did Dad learn how to text photos?" Emmy wonders.

"The same day he learned how to use emojis?" I shrug.

"Do you want me to tell Dad and Zoe?" I ask.

"Not by text!" Emmy replies, appalled by the notion.

"I meant, should we phone them?"

"No." Emmy says, then she pauses while she thinks. "You know what they're like. They'll get on the next plane home. I can't deal with Zoe's chronic fussing or Dad's constant words of wisdom. And you know how he is, he'll make it about him. No, I don't want them here. Not yet."

Emmy's assessment of our dad and Zoe is pretty accurate. Our stepmum, Zoe, is a first-class fusser, even when the target of her fussing is less than enthusiastic. And our dad loves a captive audience. He thrives on being the centre of attention. I'd never say it to her face, but Emmy and our dad are similar; they're both charismatic and can command an audience.

"It would be awful if they find out from someone else," I say.

"Who would tell them?"

"Certain people have to know, Emmy. Like Armando's team, for example. And as soon as someone else knows, you can't control who they tell."

Emmy's eyes open wide and fill with panic and fear.

"People could already know." She stands up and paces in front of the sofa. "There were probably a dozen people in the other hotel room. It only takes one of them to recognize me or Armando for his death to be all over the internet. Or someone who works here might have disclosed it to someone."

"You think?" I ask, opening the web browser on my phone and typing Armando's name into the search bar.

"Well?" Emmy asks, still pacing and wringing her delicate hands. "Anything about Armando?"

"Nothing," I reply, not telling her about the article about their marital problems that I found on a gossip blog.

The article was posted early this morning. Before we found Armando's lifeless body. The headline reads, *Hello, divorce! You'll get a real kick out of this tidbit!* An obvious soccer pun and thinly veiled reference to my sister's morning show. Under the headline, the article continues:

Sources tell us a certain morning show co-host kicked her sporty husband off the marital pitch. Does she suspect foul play, or is their perfect match less perfect than everyone thinks? She said, Goodbye, work! and ran away from the game for a timeout with her family. He must be a soccer for her because he followed her. Will she decide he's a keeper or kick him to the curb?

The article doesn't mention Emmy and Armando by name, but the tacky soccer puns and implied references to Emmy's morning show make it obvious who the article is about. There's even a reference to the *Perfect Match* reality show, which is top secret until the network reveals the contestants. Who tipped them off? Only a handful of people know Emmy is in Harmony Lake, and even fewer know Armando followed her. Could the source be someone local? Someone I know or someone who works at the resort?

Luckily, the short, poorly written story hasn't been picked up by a more reputable website with a larger audience.

There's no need to share this with Emmy and cause her more distress, but I quickly copy the website address and text it to Eric. If Armando's death turns into a murder investigation, he might want to question the source of this nasty article.

"Let's phone Dad and Zoe," Emmy suggests. "Together. If I fall apart and can't talk, I'll need your help."

Before we phone them, we text Dad and Zoe and ask if they're available to talk. We don't want to break such shocking news to them while they're on a guided tour, or somewhere remote without the amenities they might need if one of them goes into shock, or reacts worse than expected.

CHAPTER 8

AFTER A TEARFUL, heartbreaking conversation with Dad and Zoe, we hang up. They took the news better than we expected but wanted to catch the next flight home. We dissuaded them by assuring them there won't be a funeral until after the coroner releases Armando's body. Emmy promised to call them every day, and we both promised to keep them up to date on the coroner's findings.

"I want to tell Poppy," Emmy says. "She's my best friend, and as my PA she'll arrange my bereavement leave with the network."

"Good idea," I agree.

"And I have to tell Brad Hendricks," she declares. "He'll know who to inform. Which sports people need to know. But I don't have my phone. I left it in my purse. In the other room."

I like that we're referring to the hotel room where Armando died as *the other hotel room*, or *the other room*.

The euphemisms are less distressing than *Armando's hotel room*, or *Armando's room.*

Someone knocks on the door, and I gesture for Emmy to sit down.

"Here." I thrust my phone toward her and stand up to answer the door. "Use my phone as long as you need. I'll use the landline to call April and Connie."

"Thanks, but I can't," she explains. "I store everyone's phone numbers in my phone. I don't have them memorized."

I peer through the peephole, and as if by divine intervention, Eric is standing in the hall, holding Emmy's purse.

"Your timing is perfect," I say when I open the door.

Eric kisses my forehead, and I step aside so he can come inside.

"I'm sorry I didn't get here sooner," he says. "The coroner arrived, and I couldn't get away. Are you OK?"

I nod.

"What did the coroner say?" Emmy jumps off the sofa and wrings her hands in front of her.

"He said he'll know more after the autopsy," Eric replies. "But there are no obvious signs of trauma or foul play."

Signs. When Eric says the word *signs,* I have a mental flashback to the DO NOT DISTURB sign Emmy removed from the door when we returned from brunch. I have to mention it to Eric, but not in front of Emmy. She has enough to deal with. The last thing she needs is me suggesting someone else was in Armando's room while we were at brunch.

"Does that mean Armando died of natural causes?" Emmy asks, her eyes pleading for the answer to be yes.

"It means we don't know for sure yet, but there's no reason to suspect it wasn't natural causes."

One of Eric's superpowers is answering a question without actually answering a question. It's frustrating as heck, and it's my least favourite superpower.

"Is my phone in there?" Emmy asks, pointing to her purse in Eric's hand.

"Yes." Eric looks at the purse in his hand like he's shocked it's there. "I had to go through it, but everything is in there," he says, handing her the designer handbag.

"Thank you." Emmy takes the purse and opens it, scans the contents, gives it a shake, then scans again, and pulls out her cell phone before closing it. "I need to notify Brad. Then I need to tell Poppy. Is it OK if I go in the next room?"

"Do you want me to come?" I offer.

"No, I'll be fine this time." She forces her mouth into a weak smile.

"I need to talk to you when you're finished," Eric says.

Emmy nods, then retreats to the bedroom, closing the door behind her.

"This time?" Eric asks, taking my hand and leading me to the sofa. "Who did Emmy already notify?"

"Dad and Zoe," I reply, then I tell him everything that happened, starting with when I arrived at Rise & Glide to pick up Emmy for brunch, and ending with his impeccable timing delivering Emmy's purse. I also mention the DO NOT DISTURB SIGN that was hanging on the door when we returned to the hotel.

"I'll have an officer take an inventory of the DO NOT DISTURB signs in Armando's room, and take them into evidence," Eric says, typing on his phone. "If there's only one sign, whoever hung it was in the room. And those signs are glossy, they hold fingerprints well."

"Also," I add, "I touched something in the bedroom."

I explain to Eric about my nausea and magnified senses, and that I touched the cloche because if I didn't cover the food on the room service cart, I would have thrown up.

"Are you feeling better now?" he asks, concerned.

"Yes," I assure him. "Physically, I'm fine. The situation overwhelmed me, and I freaked out."

Eric pulls me into him, and I rest my head and hand on his chest while he strokes my hair. I take a few deep breaths, and repeat the words, *heavy shoulders, long arms* in my head.

Heavy shoulders, long arms is a mantra I learned in a yoga class almost twenty years ago. It helps release the tension in my neck and shoulders.

"How are you emotionally?" Eric asks. "Do you need anything?"

"It's weird," I reply. "Armando was my brother-in-law, but we didn't know each other. They've been together for three years, but I've only met him a handful of times. I know our neighbours and even our postal carrier better than I knew Armando. I'm upset for Emmy, but not as upset as I'd expect, if that makes sense."

"Could be shock," Eric suggests. "Sometimes we suppress our feelings so we can function for someone else. You're taking care of Emmy right now. Maybe you'll have more feelings when she doesn't need you as much."

"Maybe," I agree but doubting it.

"Can I ask you a few questions about this morning?" Eric asks.

"Of course," I reply, sitting upright. "For Emmy's sake, I'll do whatever it takes to help get this over with."

"Was the food cart there when you picked up Emmy this morning?" Eric asks.

"I don't know." I shrug, shaking my head. "I didn't go into the bedroom when I picked her up. I was inside the suite for less than a minute. Emmy was ready when I arrived. She went into the bedroom to get her purse, then we left. The bedroom door was closed."

"So, you didn't *see* or *hear* Armando when you picked up Emmy?"

"That's right," I confirm. "Emmy said he was asleep." I tell him Emmy's joke about Armando being extra tired because they were up late *making up*. Recollecting the conversation reminds me of the resort employee we encountered. "He was pushing a room service cart down the hall. He said good morning to us. Maybe he was delivering the cart to Armando's room."

"Maybe," Eric says, making a note in his notebook. "I'm waiting for Deb to get me the access history to the room. The time when you picked up Emmy falls into the time window of when the coroner's estimates Armando died."

"The coroner thinks Armando could have died *before* Emmy and I left for brunch?" I ask, incredulous. "Eric, I think my sister would have noticed if her husband was dead."

He looks at me and places a hand on my knee. "The bedroom was dark, babe. You said she was in denial when he didn't talk to her. Deb said she was in denial and wanted her to attempt resuscitation."

He's right, but I just can't believe my sister could attend brunch and be her normal cheerful self, when she knew, even on a subconscious level, that her husband was dead.

"Does that happen?" I ask. "Do people fool themselves like that?"

"It could be an honest mistake. If he was dead, and I'm not saying he was, she might not have realized. She could have believed he was asleep. The room was pitch black."

"If the cart we saw in the hallway went to Armando's room, he couldn't have died before we left for brunch. If the food arrived after Emmy and I left, Armando was alive when I picked up my sister. He had to be."

"Because the food was partially eaten," Eric says, completing my thought. "He would've gotten out of bed, eaten, then returned to bed."

"Exactly! When you get the access records, we'll know who delivered the food to Armando and when they delivered it."

"And the coroner will confirm whether Armando ate the food on the tray, and approximately what time he ate it," Eric adds. "We took the food as evidence, in case it contributed to Armando's death."

Eric's phone rings. While he answers it, I crack open the bedroom door and peek inside. Emmy is sitting on the bed with her phone to her ear, used tissues piled into a small mountain on her lap. I step inside and close the door behind me.

"You OK?" I mouth when she looks at me.

Still holding the phone to her ear, she presses her lips into a tight line and nods.

"Do you need anything?" I ask silently, exaggerating each word so she can read my lips.

She shakes her head.

"I'm right outside," I whisper.

She nods again and mouths, "Thank you."

I leave the bedroom and return to the sitting area where Eric is ending his phone call.

"What's wrong?" I ask, when I see how tense his facial muscles are.

"Does Emmy smoke?"

"No."

"Was Armando a smoker?"

"Not that I'm aware of," I reply. "I meant to ask Emmy, but it didn't come up."

"Why would you ask Emmy if Armando was a smoker?"

"Same reason as you. The empty cigarette package

under the fern." I point to this hotel suite's almost-identical fern on an almost-identical round end table.

"There's a pack of cigarettes under the fern in Armando's room?" Eric asks, studying me with narrowed eyes.

I nod. "It was there when Emmy found Armando's body. Isn't that why you're asking if Armando smoked? Because of the cigarette packaging?"

"No," Eric replies. "I'm asking because we just found nicotine patches in Emmy's luggage."

"Why would Emmy have nicotine patches?"

What aren't you telling me, Emmy?

I sit on the sofa drumming my fingers and wishing I hadn't left my knitting in the car. I could use it right now to focus my worrying mind and occupy my idle hands. How will my sister explain the cigarette package in her hotel suite? And the nicotine patches in her luggage?

Eric is on the phone with an officer in Armando's suite, instructing them to confirm the cigarette package is still under the fern fronds and to collect it as evidence.

"Was it there?" I ask when he ends the call.

He nods. "Forensics will process it. They also found a few discarded cigarette butts in a bowl on the balcony. With any luck, they'll find DNA and fingerprints."

"I'm glad the package was still there."

"What package?" Emmy asks, emerging from the bedroom.

Her eyes are puffier and redder than before.

I look at Eric for guidance, and he gives me a discreet nod.

"The cigarette package near the fern in the other hotel room," I explain. "Did Armando smoke?"

If her answer is yes, this could open up some smoking-related, not-murder theories for how Armando died.

"No," Emmy says, bewildered. "What brand were they?"

"I'm not sure," I reply, wondering why the brand is relevant. "The room was kind of dark, and I'm not familiar with the different cigarette brands. The box was mostly white, if that helps."

"I've never seen Armando smoke, but he told me once that when he was younger—long before we met—he was a social smoker. When he went to clubs and stuff."

"I bet his trainers didn't like that," I comment.

"They didn't," Emmy concurs. "That's why he quit. He was afraid it would affect his performance on the pitch."

"Is it possible he started again?" Eric asks.

Panic flashes in Emmy's eyes, and she gasps, bringing her hand to her mouth.

"Oh my god! I killed my husband!"

CHAPTER 9

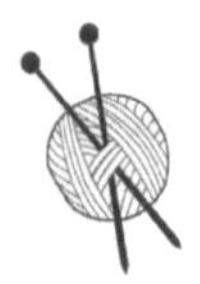

I RUSH OVER to Emmy and slap my hand over her mouth.

Alarmed and confused, she digs her fingers between my hand and her face and tries to wrench my hand away. I push her hand down, and she stops struggling. She looks at me, terrified. What's wrong with her eyes? Why do they look like that? *Focus, Megan.*

"Don't say another word!" I command. "Emmy, I mean it. Don't talk."

I look at her, searching for agreement. She nods, and the muscles around her eyes relax. Scrutinizing her expression, I realize why her eyes look strange.

"I'm going to remove my hand. Say nothing." She nods again. I remove my hand, and my sister locks eyes with me. "Repeat after me," I instruct. "I want my lawyer."

Emmy opens her mouth to protest, or question me, or something, but I shoot her a stern glare that lets her know, in no uncertain terms, I'm dead serious. Pardon the pun.

"I want my lawyer," Emmy mumbles, our gazes still locked.

"Tell him," I whisper, pointing at Eric.

The confusion that clouds her face is replaced by comprehension, and Emmy turns to Eric, straightening her spine.

"I won't say anything else or answer questions without my lawyer present."

"Understood," Eric replies.

I blow out a sigh of relief.

"You're missing a contact lens," I say to Emmy, pointing to her left eye, which is its natural hazel colour. Her right eye is still the emerald green I've grown accustomed to. "You must have cried it out."

"I should take out the other one," she says. "I'll be right back."

"Why did you muzzle her like that?" Eric asks after the bedroom door closes.

"Because you're a cop," I reply. "You already suspect Armando died before Emmy left the hotel this morning. Which means if Armando was murdered, you think Emmy is a suspect. I had to stop her before she said something else self-incriminating in front of you."

He looks at me speechless, and his eyes are sad, like a wounded animal.

"Honey, I'm sorry." I take his hand. "You know what Emmy is like. Sometimes she speaks before she thinks. Like a minute ago when she accused herself of killing Armando."

"You mean when she *confessed* to killing Armando," he corrects me.

"It wasn't a confession, Eric, and you know it. It was a spontaneous outburst from an overwhelmed, traumatized widow, who's trying to survive the worst day of her life."

"You're good," he says with a chuckle, "but I can't pretend she didn't say it."

"I know." I nod. "That's why I stopped her before she said something else."

I unlock my phone and open the messaging app, my thumbs darting back and forth across the keyboard.

Me: Emmy needs a lawyer. It's urgent.

"Who are you texting?" Eric asks.

"Emmy's lawyer," I reply, hitting send.

"Adam?" he asks. "You're inviting your ex-husband to this family crisis and freezing me out?" The pain in his voice makes my heart ache.

"Honey, I'm sorry. But you're a cop," I reiterate. "And I'm not inviting my ex-husband, I'm contacting my sister's lawyer. They just happen to be the same person."

"I'm your fiancé and Emmy's future brother-in-law," Eric reminds me, his voice sad and quiet.

"You're also the chief of police," I counter. "In this situation, how can you be both?" I ask rhetorically. "I'm sorry, Eric. My sister is having the worst day of her life, and she needs me right now. I have to protect her."

My phone dings.

Adam: Where?

"Adam?" Eric asks.

"Uh-huh." I nod, typing a response to Adam.

Me: Rise & Glide. Room 808.

Adam: On my way. Try to keep her quiet until I get there.

Adam gets it. He knows Emmy needs guidance and support from a voice of reason.

"I can't believe how swollen and blotchy my eyes are," Emmy says, using one hand to feel her way out of the bedroom, while her other hand presses a cold, damp washcloth against her eyes. "Eric," she says, facing the wrong direction.

"Over here, Emmy," he responds.

Following the sound of his voice, she turns her head and almost faces him.

"May I go back to the other room?" she asks. "I need my hemorrhoid cream." She turns away from me. "Megan, do you know if I remembered to pack my hemorrhoid cream? Did you see it when I stayed at your place?"

I shake my head out of habit, then realize she can't see me because she's facing away from me, and the washcloth is covering her eyes.

"I don't know," I say.

"The other room is a crime scene until the coroner determines how Armando died," Eric explains. "I can't let anyone access it."

"Can someone bring me the hemorrhoid cream?"

"I'm afraid not," Eric replies.

"There might be ice in the ice bucket," I suggest.

"You could make an ice pack. Maybe you should lie down and rest your eyes."

Emmy nods. "I don't want to leave until the swelling goes down. What if someone takes my picture and posts it online?"

Emmy gropes her way back to the bedroom and closes the door behind her.

"What was that about?" Eric asks.

"Because of her job, Emmy is vigilant about her appearance when she's out in public," I reply. "I don't blame her. I wouldn't want my photo posted online if I were crying, and I'm not a public figure."

"No, I mean the hemorrhoid cream," Eric clarifies. "Why does she want hemorrhoid cream for her eyes?"

"It reduces swelling," I explain.

"Eww," Eric cringes, scrunching his nose.

"She doesn't use it anywhere else," I assure him. "And if she did, each body part would have a separate tube."

"That makes sense," he says, less repulsed by the idea of using cream intended for one body part on another. "Listen, babe, I'm sorry I got defensive when you stopped your sister from talking, and when you texted Adam for her. I overreacted. I want to support you and Emmy, not investigate the situation. The coroner hasn't declared Armando's death a murder yet..."

"Hold that thought," I say, interrupting Eric's apology when someone knocks on the door.

Adam must have been nearby when I texted him,

otherwise he just set a land speed record getting here from his condo.

"I'll go," Eric says when I motion to stand up.

While Eric answers the door, I reflect on what he said. He said, *the coroner hasn't declared Armando's death a murder yet.* Yet. He might not want to admit it, but Eric thinks Armando was murdered, and he expects the coroner to reach the same conclusion.

Whoever knocked on the door, it isn't Adam. But his voice is familiar. I've heard it before but can't place it. It's probably a police officer from the other hotel room.

Frustrated that I can't connect the familiar voice to its owner, I stand up and crane my neck to see who it is.

"Brad?"

"Megan?"

"What are you doing here?"

"Emmy called and told me about Armando. I came to see her."

Eric moves aside, permitting Brad access to the hotel suite. As soon as he's within six feet of me, I smell it. Cigarettes. Either Brad is a smoker, or he was just with someone who smokes.

"Emmy told you what room we're in?"

"No, I asked the front desk. The hotel knows Armando and I arrived together. I booked both suites in my name. I'm staying down the hall."

"Armando didn't mention that you're in town too."

I think back to Friday when Armando visited me at Knitorious. He said Brad booked his suite, but I don't remember him saying anything about Brad accompanying him to Harmony Lake.

"I tagged along for moral support," Brad explains. "Armando was pretty worried. He and Emmy had a huge argument. Armando thought she was serious when she threatened to divorce him. I came with him in case his attempt to win her back didn't go well."

"It's nice to see you again," I say. "I'm sorry it's under such awful circumstances."

"Same here," Brad says, then we share an awkward hug that convinces me Brad is a smoker. "You look great, by the way. Divorce agrees with you."

"Thank you?" I'm not sure how to respond to his odd compliment. "You met Eric at the door, I presume?"

I gesture to Eric, who extends his hand for Brad to shake.

"Yeah, you said you're the police chief?" Brad asks, shaking hands with Eric. "Why is the police chief here if Armando died in his sleep?"

Emmy told Brad that Armando died in his sleep? But we don't know if that's true. I guess she had to tell him something when he asked.

"We attend all unexpected deaths," Eric explains.

"And we're engaged," I add. "Eric is my fiancé."

"Oh." Shocked, Brad looks from me to Eric, back to me, then at my engagement ring. "Armando never mentioned it. Congratulations."

"Thanks," Eric and I respond.

Aside from Emmy and Armando's reception after they eloped, I've only met Brad twice before today. He's a sports agent and former athlete. He looks like a former athlete. Not that all former athlete's look the same, but if you drew a caricature of a former athlete, I'm betting it would resemble Brad. He looks like a middle-aged version of every jock I went to school with. He's tall, fit, has perfect posture, short hair, perfect teeth, and a deep voice. This is our third encounter, and the third time I've seen him wear a collared golf shirt and khaki golf pants.

"Emmy was so upset she could barely talk when she called me," Brad says. "I didn't want to make it worse, so I didn't ask her anything. But I need to know. What happened? How could Armando die in his sleep? I was with him yesterday, and he looked great. There was nothing wrong with him."

"He died in bed," I clarify. "We don't know if he died in his sleep."

"What do we know?" Brad asks, looking back and forth between me and Eric.

"We're waiting for the coroner to establish how Armando died. In the meantime, we treat it like a crime scene," Eric says.

"A crime scene?" Brad asks, awestruck. "Armando was a strong, fit guy. If he saw it coming, he would've put up a fight. Did he put up a fight?"

"Have a seat, Brad," Eric urges. "I need to ask you a few questions."

"Armando was with Emmy most of yesterday and all night. If something happened to him, she either did it or knows who did," Brad accuses.

"Whoa!" I say, offended on my sister's behalf.

"What's going on out here?" Emmy says from the bedroom doorway. "Brad? What are you doing here?"

"Looking for answers," Brad replies. "You called and told me my best friend died but didn't give me any details or an explanation. I need to know what happened to Armando."

"I wasn't keeping anything from you, Brad. I don't have any details or an explanation." Emmy's eyes well up with fresh tears. "We don't know yet how he died."

"C'mon, Emmy," Brad chortles. "You were alone with him all night. Tell us what happened. What did you do?"

"Hey!" Eric positions himself in front of Brad, blocking his view of Emmy. "Enough! Let's talk at the station."

"Are you serious?" Brad asks. "Why are you taking me to the station? Take her. She's the one hiding something."

"Let's go." Eric escorts Brad to the door, and they leave.

"I see why you think Brad doesn't like you," I say to my sister when we're alone.

"He doesn't even try to hide it," Emmy responds.

"You haven't eaten since brunch. That was hours ago. You should eat something."

"I won't be able to keep it down, Sis." She looks at me. "Do you think Armando is still in the other room?"

I shake my head. "The body usually leaves with the coroner. Anyway, if Armando is there, they won't let you see him."

"I know," Emmy says. "I don't want to leave the hotel before him. I don't want him to be alone. Is that weird?"

"No, it's not weird. Nothing you feel right now is weird." I squeeze her hand. "Adam is on his way, as your lawyer. After you talk to him, I'll ask Eric if I can take you home."

"And you'll make sure Armando leaves first?"

I nod.

CHAPTER 10

EMMY and I sit in exhausted silence, waiting for Adam to arrive when her phone rings.

"It's the head of the network," she says, looking at her phone screen.

"You don't have to answer it," I remind her.

"No, I'll take it," she decides, then puts the phone to her ear and does a decent impersonation of a cheerful hello.

I only overhear some of their conversation before Emmy disappears into the bedroom and closes the door, but it sounds like the caller is offering condolences on behalf of the network that airs *Hello, today!*. They must have heard about Armando's death from Poppy. News of Armando's death is reaching more and more people, and I'm worried the unavoidable onslaught of attention will overwhelm Emmy.

While Emmy is on the phone with the network executive, I call April and Connie to tell them what happened. I don't want my best friends to hear it through the rumour mill.

"We can be home by tonight if we pack and leave now," April says.

She's shuffling things in the background. Is she already packing?

"No," I insist. "Stay with your family. Armando's death is a reminder that anything can happen at any time. You should spend as much time enjoying your family as possible. Emmy won't want Armando's death to cast a shadow over your cousin's wedding celebration. Please stay. You'll be home on Friday, anyway."

It takes some more convincing, but April agrees to stay put. I agree to contact her right away if I change my mind and want her to come home.

Connie, who's amazing in a crisis, jumps into action and is on her way to my house to pick up Sophie. It's a relief to stop worrying about Sophie's routine of scheduled walks and meals.

"I have to go, Connie. I think Adam's here."

A second knock on the door. With the phone to my ear, I open it and beckon Adam inside.

"Keep me up to date," Connie instructs. "I'm just pulling into your driveway. Don't worry about Sophie. We'll keep her as long as you need."

I thank Connie, and we end the call.

"What's going on, Meg?" Adam demands. "The elevators won't stop on this floor without a special key, and there are police officers in the stairwell, preventing people from accessing the eighth floor."

"How did you get up here?"

"I texted Eric, and he sent a cop to accompany me."

"I didn't know any of that was happening," I tell him. "Emmy and I haven't left this hotel suite since we left your place after brunch."

"Why?"

I guide Adam to the seating area, and we sit down.

"Armando's dead."

"What? How? When?"

"I don't know," I reply, frustrated by the lack of answers.

I tell Adam everything that has happened since Emmy and I left his condo after brunch, then I wait while he considers what he just heard.

"Did you tell Hannah?" he asks after he processes the deluge of facts and details I flooded him with.

"Not yet. I want to talk to her without rushing. I thought I'd call her when Emmy goes to sleep."

"I'd like to be there," Adam says.

"Of course," I agree. "I assumed you would."

"Poor Emmy!" Adam says with a heavy sigh. "Where is she?"

"In the bedroom talking on the phone. First the network phoned her, then Poppy phoned her again. She's overwhelmed, Adam. She's functioning, but I don't know if the reality has hit her yet, if that makes sense."

Adam nods. "Can I do anything? Other than as her lawyer. As family. What can I do?"

"I don't know." I shrug.

"I knew I heard voices," Emmy says when she opens the bedroom door.

"Emmy, I'm so sorry to hear about Armando."

Adam stands up, and Emmy crumples into his arms, sobbing.

While Emmy soaks Adam's chest with tears, I search the bedroom and both washrooms for more tissues. Nothing. We've used them all. I pick up the landline and request more tissues from the front desk, then bring Emmy a roll of toilet paper to dry her tears. For whatever reason, the toilet paper amuses her, and she goes from tears of grief to tears of laughter. Emotions are weird.

By the time Emmy composes herself, Deb Kee restocks the suite with several boxes of tissues and encourages us to eat by bringing us refreshments. She took it upon herself to bring us coffee, tea, juice, a fruit platter, a cheese and cracker tray, and a variety of finger sandwiches.

"Just have a bite," I coax Emmy. "One cracker? A piece of cheese? One strawberry?"

Emmy crinkles her nose and shakes her head. She pushes away the plate I made her.

"I can't. Maybe later."

"OK," I say, returning the plate to the room service cart. "You have to drink some water, though." I nudge the glass toward her.

"Fine," she agrees to shut me up.

With all the crying, I'm worried Emmy will get dehydrated if she doesn't drink enough. None of us have an appetite. Food seems so complicated and unappealing right now.

"When you're ready, Emmy, I need you to tell me everything," Adam says.

Emmy nods, then tells Adam what she remembers since we left him after brunch. Her version of events is almost identical to mine. Under the circumstances, her recollection is more lucid and detailed than I expect. She also tells us some intimate details about her relationship with Armando that I wasn't aware of until now. After her disclosure, I understand why my sister accused herself of killing Armando when Eric and I asked her about the cigarette package we found in the other hotel room.

Emmy's mouth and throat are dry after all the talking, and she drinks an entire glass of water. Success! As I refill her glass, someone knocks on the door.

"It's Eric," I say, peeping through the peephole.

Eric walks over to Emmy and hands her a small bag from the local pharmacy.

"Hemorrhoid cream," he says. "I wasn't sure which brand to get. There are a few different ones."

"Thank you, that's thoughtful. Something Armando would do," Emmy says, standing up to hug him. "I'll be right back." She excuses herself and disappears into the bedroom with the pharmacy bag.

I'm dying to ask Eric what Brad said at the station. But Emmy will be back any second, and I'm not sure he can talk about it in front of Emmy's lawyer.

"Do you think she can handle a few questions?" Eric asks, looking back and forth from me to Adam.

"She wants to cooperate," Adam says in his lawyer voice. "If she can't cope, I'll end the interview."

Eric nods and sits down.

I go into the bedroom to check on Emmy. She's in the washroom, assessing her eyes in the mirror.

"Do you still want to talk to Eric?" I ask.

She nods, looking at me in the mirror. "I want to help. I want the coroner to determine that Armando died of natural causes, and I want Eric to close the file."

We return from the bedroom, and Adam shoots Emmy a look. She nods, then he nods.

"Emmy, tell Eric everything you told me," Adam says.

"All of it?" Emmy asks, shifting uncomfortably next to me on the sofa.

"All of it," Adam confirms.

While Eric jots down notes in his notebook, Emmy tells him everything that happened from the time she woke up this morning until he brought her purse from the other hotel room to this one.

Eric asks Emmy some clarifying questions about her version of events, and so far, Emmy is holding herself together, and the interview is going well.

"Was the room service cart in the room when you left for brunch?" Eric asks.

"No," Emmy replies. "It wasn't there. And my husband was alive. We said good morning. I kissed him goodbye before I left, and he kissed me back."

This means Armando was alive when we left for brunch. He was alive to open the door for the food, and he was alive to eat it. I knew Emmy didn't kill him.

"Who hung the DO NOT DISTURB sign on the door?"

Taken aback, Emmy looks to the side and small creases fight through the Botox and appear between her eyes.

"I don't know," she replies. "Now that you mention it, I remember taking the DO NOT DISTURB sign off the door, but I don't remember Armando hanging it up. We never use the DO NOT DISTURB sign in hotels because we always decline housekeeping when we check in."

Eric nods and makes notes in his notebook.

"Do you want to tell me anything else?" he asks.

Emmy looks at Adam, and he nods.

"There's one more thing." Emmy takes a deep breath and pulls herself to her full seated height.

"Brace yourself," I whisper to Eric with my eyebrows raised.

Panic flashes across his face as he tries to guess what kind of intimate information he should prepare himself to hear about his future sister-in-law.

"Armando travels a lot." Emmy begins by providing some background information that gives important context to the rest of her story. "Like, a lot. He's away—he was away—more than half the year, and I can't travel with him because my job keeps me at home from Monday to Friday, and I do appearances on weekends. Anyway," Emmy refocuses, "when Armando and I were in the same bed, I had this… thing... I would do to him."

Eric shifts in his chair and swallows hard. I try not to smile at his discomfort.

"I'm listening," he says, then inhales deeply and blows it out.

"When we went to bed, I would wait for Armando to fall asleep. It never took long, Armando is—was—a great sleeper. Then, I would very carefully stick a nicotine patch on him. In the morning, I'd wake up before him—also easy since my body is used to waking up at 4 a.m. every day for work—and carefully remove the patch without waking him. I'd hide the patch by wrapping it in toilet paper and placing it at the bottom of the garbage pail." Emmy shrugs. "He was none the wiser."

Eric looks at me, confused.

"Is this another strange beauty trick like the hemorrhoid cream?"

"No," I reply. "It's a trick, but not the beauty kind."

"It had nothing to do with beauty," Emmy explains. "After a few nights of sleeping with the nicotine patch, Armando became... dependent on them.

"You mean addicted," Eric corrects her. "Did Armando know you were drugging him with nicotine while he slept?"

"Of course not," Emmy replies. "That would defeat the purpose."

"What purpose?" Eric asks, squeezing his brows together. "Why would you drug your husband without his consent?"

"When he'd go back on the road, he'd have trouble sleeping. Armando didn't know it was because of nicotine withdrawal. He thought he couldn't sleep without me." She looks down at her hands and wrings them in her lap. "It made him miss me when we were apart," she adds, still staring at her wringing hands and avoiding eye contact with Eric.

"And when Megan found the cigarette package, you assumed it was Armando's, and you panicked," Eric deduces. "It's dangerous to use a nicotine patch and smoke. It can cause heart problems. You thought the patch and your manipulative scheme killed him."

Emmy nods then launches into a fresh round of sobs and fights to collect herself so she can continue.

"It seemed harmless when I did it," Emmy explains between sobs. "It didn't occur to me that Armando was a former smoker, and the patches might give him cravings. Also, Brad smokes, so besides the patches, Armando was inhaling secondhand smoke from Brad. When you guys asked me about the cigarette package, I panicked. What if Armando started smoking again to satisfy his nicotine cravings? What if he was smoking in secret and didn't tell me? I put a nicotine patch on him last night, Eric. If my husband died of a heart attack, it's my fault."

CHAPTER 11

EMMY AND I CAN LEAVE. Finally. It's only been one afternoon, but it feels like we've been trapped in this luxury hotel suite for weeks. I can't wait to change into comfy clothes and relax in my not-luxurious-but-comfortable home. But Emmy refuses to leave. Her eyes are still swollen, and her sunglasses are in the other hotel room.

"Take mine," I insist, thrusting them toward her. "I have a backup pair in the car."

"It's not just the sunglasses, sis. I don't have any of my stuff. I can't change my clothes or even have a shower."

Emmy crosses her arms in front of her and huffs. I sympathize. She's lost her husband, and everything she owns is down the hall yet inaccessible to her. I'd hate to be in her position.

"You can borrow anything I own. Anything at all. We'll get you settled at home, then make a list of what you need, and I'll get it."

I'm sure Connie will stay with Emmy while I pick up provisions.

"I'm doing everything I can to get you access to your belongings as soon as possible," Eric promises.

"Where's Armando?" Emmy asks, looking at Eric with pleading, desperate eyes.

"He's at the morgue," Eric explains. "The coroner will conduct a post-mortem, then release the body. When the coroner releases Armando's body, you can arrange for whichever funeral home you choose to pick him up."

Judging by the expression on Emmy's face, this information overwhelms her.

"Not today," I assure her. "You don't have to decide yet. It'll be a few days at least."

"Good," Emmy mumbles. "I don't know any funeral homes."

"Emmy, this is all standard procedure," Adam adds, using his reassuring, non-lawyer voice. "In fact, Eric has made a few exceptions for you. He should have separated you and Meg until after you were both questioned. But he let you stay together. Alone. Without a police chaperone."

Emmy nods, crying silently.

Adam's right. Eric broke the rules for us. And if Armando was murdered, this special treatment could compromise the case. His career and reputation could be on the line. Guilt washes over me for not once considering the fine line Eric has to walk between being an excellent investigator and a supportive fiancé and future brother-in-law.

"I'll walk you out," I say to Adam.

"I'll get someone to bring you the elevator," Eric adds. "It won't stop on this floor without a key."

"It's fine," Adam says. "I'll take the stairs. It'll be good for me," he chuckles and rubs his flat stomach.

He's trying to lighten the mood. Adam is as lean today as he was the day we met when I was eighteen, and he knows it. He's proud and often brags about his superpower of eating whatever he wants and still fitting into clothes he wore twenty years ago.

"Thank you for... for... everything," I say to Adam as we walk to the door that leads to the staircase. "I don't know what we would've done without you today. Emmy listens to you more than anyone else."

"You don't have to thank me, Meg. I love Emmy like a sister. I'd do anything for either of you." He stops walking, so I stop. He turns to me. "I'll do anything to help. I know I wasn't always there for you. I might have let you down in marriage, but I won't let you down in divorce."

"Ditto," I blurt out, welling up with tears. "I'm sorry," I say, apologizing for my emotional collapse. "It's been a long, horrible day."

"You're doing great," Adam says, hugging me. "Emmy will be fine. Eventually. Until then, everyone wants to help."

I wipe my eyes and resume walking to the stairs.

"We should tell Hannah soon," Adam says. "Before she hears it from someone else."

"I know," I agree as we stop at the door to the stairwell and smile at the police officer standing guard.

"Meet me at the house. Let yourself in. I'll get Emmy settled, then we'll call Hannah."

The drive home is quiet. Emmy cries silent tears and stares out the window, watching the world pass.

"It was nice of Deb to let us leave through the delivery entrance," I say to break the silence.

"Yes, it was," Emmy agrees. "She was great. I'll have to send her a thank you gift and a note."

"I'll take care of it," I offer, relieved to do something useful.

When she heard about Emmy's concern that someone might recognize or photograph her leaving the hotel, Deb sprang into action and drove my car around to the delivery entrance behind the kitchen. Then, assuring us there would be no video surveillance cameras, she led us down the hall, to the room next door to the room where Armando died. Though it looked like just another hotel room door, it led to a maze of employee-only service hallways. Deb navigated us through them and escorted us downstairs on a service elevator. We slipped out of the hotel and into my waiting car unseen by anyone aside from a handful of kitchen employees, delivery people, and employees who were having their break outside near the delivery dock. Deb assured us all staff members sign a confidentiality agreement as a condition of employment. Any employee who discloses information about Emmy or Armando would lose their job.

"Whose car is that?" I ask, pulling over on the street outside my house. "I recognize Adam's car, but I don't recognize the other one."

"It's Poppy's rental car," Emmy says, unbuckling her seatbelt.

"Poppy? Didn't you talk to her on the phone earlier? How did she get to Harmony Lake so fast?"

"She got here this morning," Emmy explains. "I phoned her yesterday to tell her Armando and I were working things out. I told her I plan to stay in town until after Thanksgiving, so I could have Thanksgiving with my family. Poppy and I always have Thanksgiving together. I didn't want to leave her on her own, so I invited her to come to Harmony Lake for Thanksgiving too. I hope you don't mind."

"Of course, I don't mind," I insist. "The more the merrier." I wince as soon as my ears hear the insensitive comment my mouth blurts out. "I don't mean Thanksgiving will be merry. I mean, I haven't seen Poppy in ages. Also, you need your best friend right now, so I'm glad she's here for you."

It's quite a coincidence that Poppy is already in town when Emmy needs her more than ever. And she showed up for Thanksgiving a week early? On such brief notice? Did Poppy arrive in town before or after Armando died? My intuition tells me Poppy's timing is more than a coincidence.

"Emmy!"

Poppy and Emmy throw their arms around each other and cry into each other's shoulders.

"Hi, Poppy," I say. "We're glad you're here."

"Where else would I be?" Poppy asks, freeing up an arm to fold me into a group hug with her and Emmy. "I can't believe it. I'm still in shock."

"We're all in shock," Emmy mutters, pulling away from our embrace. "I need to freshen up."

"Use anything of mine you want," I insist, spying Adam waiting in the living room. "Poppy, can you help Emmy get settled and find whatever she needs? Adam and I need to call Hannah."

"Of course," Poppy replies, draping a protective arm around Emmy's shoulder.

"Emmy knows where everything is," I say. "If you need me, just shout."

Nodding, Poppy guides my sister toward the bedrooms, mumbling comforting words as they go.

"She was in the driveway when I got here," Adam explains, referring to Poppy.

"Thank you for letting her in."

"I sent Hannah a text while the three of you were hugging," Adam continues. "I asked if she could talk. She knows something's up. I told her we want to talk to her together."

"OK." I nod in agreement, dreading the conversation we're about to have with our daughter.

"How's Emmy?" I ask when Poppy appears in the kitchen alone.

"Better than I expected," Poppy replies. "She showered and put on your white pajamas. I laid with her until she fell asleep."

"Thank you," I say, hugging Poppy and squeezing her tight. "I can't believe how good your timing is. You appeared in my driveway right when Emmy needs you most."

"It's not a coincidence," Poppy says, taking a seat at the kitchen table. "I left for Harmony Lake yesterday when Emmy told me Brad was here. I figured he'd try to cause trouble, and Emmy might need me. I travelled all night. When I got here early this morning, I was exhausted, so I checked into that little motel off the highway. When I woke up, I phoned Emmy to let her know I was here. She was at brunch with you and Adam. She said she'd call me after you dropped her off at the hotel. Next thing I know, she called and told me Armando was dead. I couldn't believe it. He was fine when she left, then dead when she got back. How does that happen?"

Poppy asks the same question we're all asking.

I offer Poppy a coffee, and she accepts. Even though it's late in the day, I decide to join her and take out two pods of hazelnut cream. Time has no meaning today; we're all doing whatever it takes to get through each torturous moment.

"Why did you follow Brad here?"

"I don't trust Brad Hendricks as far as I can throw him," Poppy reveals. "He hates Emmy. She wanted Armando to fire Brad and sign with a better agent. I'm sure he came to Harmony Lake with Armando to stop them from working things out."

"Because if Emmy and Armando worked it out, it would mean Brad would lose a client," I conclude.

"Exactly," Poppy concurs.

"Brad told me he tagged along to offer Armando moral support."

"Ha!" Poppy blurts, her chestnut brown ponytail bouncing. Then, she smiles for the first time today, and her single dimple winks at me. "The only person Brad Hendricks wants to support is himself. He knows Emmy was serious about leaving Armando. If Armando didn't agree to fire Brad and sign with another agent, she was out."

I wonder if Brad knows Armando agreed to fire him to save his marriage?

"Emmy can't access her belongings for a few days," I explain. "I told her I'd get whatever necessities she needs until then."

"I can make a list for you," Poppy offers. "I know which brands to get, and which stores sell them, and everything."

I place a pen and some paper in front of Poppy.

"That would be awesome. Thank you, Poppy. Can you stay with Emmy while I get everything on the list? I don't want to leave her alone."

"Why don't I go?" Poppy suggests. "It'll be easier. I know what to get. And I know what to substitute if necessary."

"Thank you." I force a tight smile. "You know my sister better than I do."

"She's my best friend and my boss," Poppy chuckles.

"Is knowing what toiletries she prefers a best-friend duty or a PA duty?"

"Both," she replies without looking up from the list she's making.

"Is part of your job as Emmy's PA to monitor the internet for posts and stories about her?"

"Yes," Poppy replies, putting down the pen and looking at me. "I have alerts set up with her name and nickname. I get a notification whenever a new link mentions her."

"Did you see this?" I unlock my phone and open the web browser, then find the gossip site's implied post about Emmy and Armando's marriage, and hand my phone to Poppy.

"I haven't seen it," Poppy confirms, shaking her head. "I didn't get a notification because the post doesn't mention her name. It's a low blow, but Emmy's used to gossip sites writing crap about her. Sadly, it comes with the territory when you're on TV." She hands the phone back to me. "Did Emmy see this?"

"I don't think so," I reply. "I'll tell her how I found the post by accident while searching for information about Armando because Emmy's worried someone might have leaked his death."

"Can you send me the link?" Poppy asks. "I'll use the contact link at the bottom of the page to contact them and ask them to remove it. I don't know if they will, but I can ask."

"I'm sure the police will ask them to remove it too," I comment, texting the link to Poppy.

"Police?" Poppy asks, concerned. "Why do the

police care? Gossip sites post fake stories about celebrities all the time."

"But this isn't fake," I point out. "Whoever tipped off the gossip site has inside information about Emmy and Armando's marriage and their whereabouts. There's even a reference to *Perfect Match*. If someone murdered Armando, the police will want to know who wrote this and why."

"Murder?" Poppy's brown eyes are wide. "Emmy said Armando died in bed."

"He did," I confirm. "But *how* he died is still a mystery. The police have to treat it like a crime until the coroner confirms otherwise."

"Oh. I didn't know." Poppy's face droops. "Poor Emmy." She looks at me. "She's waiting to find out if someone murdered her husband."

CHAPTER 12

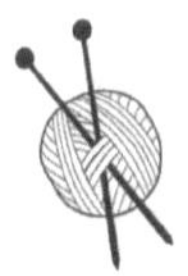

"Do you think someone killed Armando?" April's voice asks in my Airpods as I ease my car into the garage.

Since Adam left in his car to go home, and Poppy left in her car to get Emmy's necessities, I can move my car off the street. I pull it into the garage, so the driveway will be available for Eric and whoever else might need to park at our house today.

"I don't know," I admit. "But I think Eric suspects murder."

"Why?" April asks.

"A slip of the tongue," I reply. "He said the coroner hasn't determined if it's murder *yet*. As in, he expects the coroner will determine that Armando was murdered."

"I hate to say it, but my first thought was murder too."

"Me too," I admit with a sigh. "How else do you

justify a young, healthy person dying suddenly with no signs of trauma and no evidence of an accident?"

"I hope we're wrong," April says. "I hope Armando died of natural causes."

While April and I discuss how strange it feels to hope for a specific cause of death, another unfamiliar car pulls into the driveway.

"Who's this?" I wonder out loud.

"Who's who?" April asks. "Is someone there? I can't see, remember? I'm four hours away at my aunt's house."

The car's occupant gets out, sees me in the garage, and waves. His upper body disappears inside the car, and he re-emerges with flowers.

"Hi, Rich," I call out, waving over my head.

"Rich Kendall?" April whispers in my ear as if he can hear her.

"Yup," I whisper. "In the flesh."

"Holy guacamole, Megapop, did your sister's friends and coworkers charter a bus to follow her to Harmony Lake? Rich is the third person to follow her."

"Fourth," I correct her. "Armando, Brad, Poppy, and now Rich. It's strange. I have to go. I'll call you back."

I tap my Airpod to end the call and join Rich on the driveway, giving him a hug.

"Megan," Rich says, smiling, yet still sad. "It's lovely to see you again. Too bad it has to be under such sad circumstances."

Obviously, Rich has heard about Armando.

"Yes, it's been an awful day," I agree. "Let's talk inside."

On Emmy's behalf, I thank Rich for the flowers and take them from him.

"Flowers seem like such a trite offering for such a significant shock, but I didn't know what else to do." Rich smooths his sandy blond hair, ensuring his side part is tidy and tugs the sleeves of his pullover, exposing blond-haired forearms. "I was hoping to see Emmy," Rich says, easing himself onto the living room sofa. "Is she here?"

"She's asleep," I reply. "I'd rather not wake her." I place the flowers on the coffee table and straighten a few blooms that shifted in transit.

"Of course," Rich agrees. "Let her rest."

"Does Emmy know you're in town?"

"I don't think so," Rich confesses. "*I* didn't know I was coming. It was a spontaneous decision."

"A flight followed by a long drive was spontaneous?" I ask.

Rich chuckles but ignores my question.

"I got here last night, checked into my room, and lost my nerve. I was going to leave town today, and Emmy would've never known I was here. But when Poppy called and told me about Armando, I couldn't leave."

"What do you mean, you lost your nerve? Why did you come to Harmony Lake?"

"I know what happened between Emmy and Armando," Rich divulges. "I know the network offered them a spot on *Perfect Match*."

This doesn't answer my question. What did Rich plan to do before he lost his nerve?

"Did Emmy confide in you?" I ask.

Besides having crazy-good chemistry on screen, Emmy and Rich are friends off screen too. But I didn't know Emmy confides in him about her marriage.

I've always suspected Rich is in love with Emmy, or at least has a crush on her. I've never mentioned it to her, and I don't know if I'm right. I have nothing to base my suspicion on other than the way he looks at her. Rich Kendall looks at my sister the same way I look at a skein of half-price cashmere yarn in my favourite colour. Also, in a crowded room, every time I'd glance at Rich, I'd catch him watching Emmy with the same smitten expression Eric has when I catch him watching me in a crowded room.

"Of course, she told me," Rich replies. "We're friends. Friends tell each other things. Also, Emmy's appearance on *Perfect Match* would impact me. I'd either be without a co-host on *Hello, today!* or the network would have to arrange a roster of rotating co-hosts."

"Right," I say. "I didn't think of that."

"Emmy was so excited, she couldn't wait to tell me. When Armando said no, she was devastated. Their marriage wasn't easy. They hardly ever saw each other. And when they were together, she didn't fit into his disciplined life. Sometimes Emmy felt like she was an inconvenience Armando had to fit in between the demands of his team and his health regime."

"Wow," I say, shocked.

I offer Rich a refreshment, and he accepts a glass of water. I excuse myself, go to the kitchen to get his water, and process the revelation Rich just told me about Emmy's marriage.

This is the first I've heard that Emmy and Armando were anything besides happy. If what Rich says is true, why didn't Emmy share it with me?

"*Perfect Match* was the only thing Emmy ever asked Armando to do for her," Rich continues when I hand him a glass of water. "And when he said no, she was hurt. When Emmy didn't show up for work on Friday, I worried. Everyone worried. She didn't call or text anyone. We didn't know where she was. Thankfully, we found out she was here. Emmy's never run off like that, Megan. That's when I knew their relationship issues were serious. I worried about my friend and came here to support her. By the time I got here, she and Armando had worked it out. Emmy didn't need my support anymore. I planned to go home today without her ever knowing I was here."

"Rich?" Emmy appears in the doorway between the hall and the living room. "What are you doing here?"

While Emmy and Rich hug and he offers his condolences, I excuse myself and leave the room to give them some privacy.

I wasn't expecting a steady flow of visitors and condolence calls, and our fridge isn't up to the task. After rummaging through the fridge, freezer, and pantry, I find the fixings for a plate of cheese and crackers, two kinds of grapes, and hummus with mini pitas. I plate everything and gather napkins and small plates while the microwave thaws out some cookies from Artsy Tartsy I found in the freezer.

"Look, Emmy, your favourite cookies! Chocolate cherry oatmeal cookies from Artsy Tartsy."

"Not right now, thank you." She forces a small smile. "Maybe later."

"You have to eat something," I say with a sigh.

"You must keep your strength up," Rich reminds her. "Share a cookie with me. You always go on about this wonderful bakery in Harmony Lake. Now I get to see what the fuss is about."

Rich breaks a cookie in half, and puts half on a plate he hands to Emmy, and half on a plate he places on his lap.

"Fine. I'll try," Emmy concedes.

"Thank you," I mouth to Rich from behind Emmy's back.

He smiles and bites into his half of the cookie.

It takes about fifteen minutes for Emmy to finish her half of the cookie, but she does it. She even drinks some apple-spice tea I made for her.

"Poppy!" I jump up when, struggling, Poppy opens the front door. "Let me help you with those."

"Thank you, Megan," she replies, dropping an armful of shopping bags on the floor in the hallway. "The rest is in the car."

I slip on my shoes and go outside to Poppy's open trunk.

"I'm glad I got you alone," Poppy hisses, coming up behind me. "There's been a development."

"What happened?" I drop the bags I'm collecting back in the trunk and spin around to face Poppy.

"Armando's soccer team is issuing a statement

about his death," Poppy replies. "Brad's office sent me a text while I was shopping. They're releasing the statement overnight."

"It will be all over the news when we wake up tomorrow," I say, finishing Poppy's thought.

"And *Hello, today!* is working on a tribute to Armando. They plan to air it tomorrow morning."

"We have to prepare Emmy," I say.

Poppy and I empty the trunk and schlep the rest of the bags into the house.

Poppy and Rich greet each other, neither seeming shocked by the other's presence.

I observe them from a distance as I move the bags out of the hallway. I can understand Rich not being shocked to see Poppy since it makes sense for Emmy's best friend to rush to her side, but why isn't Poppy shocked to see Rich? Did she know he was coming? Or, maybe like me, Poppy suspects Rich is in love with Emmy, and expected him to show up in Harmony Lake.

How can I prepare my grieving sister for the surge of attention when Armando's team releases their press release about his death? And, if Emmy is on bereavement leave, and Rich is in Harmony Lake, who will host the show tomorrow?

Rich announces that he has to leave, and Emmy walks him to the door. They hug, and he says the usual platitudes about being there for her if she needs anything.

"I'll walk you to your car," I offer, holding the door for Rich.

"Thank you for visiting, and for convincing Emmy to eat something."

"It was only half a cookie," Rich reminds me with a chuckle.

"But it's half a cookie more than she would've eaten if you didn't persuade her," I say as he presses the button on the key chain that unlocks the car. "I hear the show plans to air a tribute to Armando tomorrow," I say. "Poppy and I will warn Emmy. In case she asks, who's hosting the show tomorrow? Emmy's on bereavement leave, and you're in Harmony Lake."

"Thanks to the miracle of satellite technology, I'll host on location from Harmony Lake," Rich explains. "Our producer, Sonia Chang came to Harmony Lake with me, and the network dispatched a film crew to join us when they heard about Armando."

This makes the knot in my stomach tighten. It feels predatory that the network's response to Armando's death was to send a film crew to the location.

"You don't expect Emmy to co-host with you, right?" I gasp. "She can't work the day after her husband died."

"Of course not. We'll do an on-air tribute to Armando, but Emmy won't be there. I'll broadcast live from locations close to Harmony Lake. I'll do fewer segments than usual, and the folks at our satellite stations will do more segments than usual. It'll be fine," Rich assures me, like the show is my biggest concern.

I don't give two hoots about the show. Emmy is my biggest concern, followed by the rest of my family, friends, and neighbours.

CHAPTER 13

Monday, October 4th

Before leaving the sanctuary of my bedroom, I sit on the bed, cross my legs, and take a few deep breaths. I had hoped a shower and clean clothes would give me a fresh perspective, help make sense of Armando's death, and make my sister's grief less painful to watch. It didn't. The situation is still horrible, and we still don't know how Armando died. The only difference is I'm cleaner and smell better. In hindsight, it was a lot to expect from a fifteen-minute shower and a clean outfit.

"How was your night?" Eric asks, entering the bedroom and closing the door behind him.

"I slept with Emmy," I reply. "I should say, I stayed with Emmy. There wasn't much sleep."

"I figured," Eric replies, kissing my forehead and sitting across from me on the bed. "I got home late, and you weren't in bed, so I assumed you were with Emmy. I heard you get up a few times, but I didn't want to interrupt."

"Where is Emmy?" I ask.

"She fell asleep on the sofa in the family room," Eric replies. "I covered her with a blanket, and Sophie is with her."

"Thank you for looking after her while I showered," I say, rubbing the back of his hand. "Did she eat or drink anything before she fell asleep?"

"I warmed up some of the soup Connie dropped off yesterday. Emmy had a few spoonfuls, and she picked at a fresh orange-cranberry croissant from Artsy Tartsy."

"April was here?" I ask. "She promised she would stay with her family and finish her trip."

"April wasn't here," Eric assures me. "She sent Phillip to the bakery. He dropped off the croissants along with a ton of other pastries and more flowers."

Phillip Wilde is my next-door neighbour at home and work. He owns Wilde Flowers, the florist shop beside Knitorious.

"Good," I say. "I'm glad she didn't rush home."

"Wait until you see how much food we have. Our kitchen has more food than most restaurants. And the flowers! We have more flowers in the house than Phillip has at Wilde Flowers!"

I'm sure Eric is exaggerating about the amount of food and flowers, but between the homemade chicken noodle soup Connie dropped off last night when she brought Sophie home, the pastries from April, and the various casserole dishes and other comfort food from friends and neighbours, our fridge went from almost empty to overflowing. Most of the food arrived last night. Armando's death became public after midnight, but thanks to Harmony Lake's over-achieving rumour mill, our friends and neighbours had a head start.

"There's a list," I remark with no context. "I'll show you how to use it."

"A list?" Eric asks, like he didn't hear me. "You'll show me how to use a list?"

I nod. "For the food. When someone drops off something, we have to add it to the list. Who it's from, what they brought, and what their dish looks like. Also, we have to label their dish. To make sure we thank everyone and return the correct dishes to the correct people."

"OK." Eric says. He leans against the headboard of the bed, and I lean into him, listening to the rhythmic beating of his heart. "How was Hannah when you told her about Armando?"

"She wanted to come home and be with her Auntie Emmy," I reply. "But picking up Hannah is a nine-hour round trip. I can't leave Emmy that long. Adam doesn't want to be that far away if Emmy needs a lawyer, and Hannah's boyfriend can't pick her up until Thursday."

"I'll pick up Hannah tomorrow if the coroner declares Armando's death accidental or natural causes," Eric offers.

He said *if*. Another clue that Eric thinks Armando was murdered.

"You think Armando was murdered, don't you?"

"I don't know," Eric replies. "I just know Armando's death doesn't make sense unless he had an underlying medical condition. And team doctors monitored his health constantly, so it's hard to believe they wouldn't uncover a life-threatening condition before now. I think we should hope for the best and expect the worst."

"When will you hear from the coroner?"

"His preliminary findings should be available this morning," Eric replies. "He did the autopsy yesterday."

"The coroner hates working on weekends," I point out. "How did you convince him to do an autopsy on a Sunday?"

"I reminded him the public interest in this case means every move we make will be scrutinized."

"Thank you." I stretch to give him a kiss, then rest my head on his chest again, letting the steady rhythm of his heart soothe me.

I know Eric doesn't care whether the coroner gets scrutinized for not doing the autopsy right away; he cares about my sister and her need to know how and why her husband died.

"Emmy wants to watch the *Hello, today!* tribute to Armando," Eric says, interrupting my ability to hear the reliable and reassuring thump of his heartbeat. "But I didn't think you'd want to wake her up, so I set the PVR to record it."

"Good idea," I agree. "Poppy said the network will send Emmy a copy of the tribute later today, but if it's on the PVR, she can watch it as often as she wants until they send it."

"How was your conversation with Brad Hendricks?" I ask.

"He's intense," Eric says. "Is he always that uptight,

or is it because of Armando's death? The man is wound tighter than a two-dollar watch."

"I don't know him well enough to have an opinion," I respond. "I've only met him a few times. Emmy doesn't like him though, and it's obvious he doesn't like her. Did he admit he left the cigarette package in Armando's room?"

"Yes, he did." Eric stretches his neck and looks down at me. "How did you figure that out?"

"Lucky guess." I shrug. "Brad smelled like cigarette smoke when I hugged him yesterday. I figured he was in Armando's room, smoked on the balcony, and left the empty package behind."

"Well done, babe. Maybe you should be the investigator."

"And you'll look after Emmy?"

"On second thought, I'll investigate. You comfort your sister." He sighs. "Brad admits the cigarette package was his, and the brand we found in Armando's room matches the brand that Brad had in his pocket when I took him to the station. Forensics will confirm it when they process the package, and the butts we found on the balcony."

"How long will that take?"

"Later today or tomorrow at the latest," Eric replies. "Brad said he was in Armando's room on Saturday morning, before Emmy arrived. He said they had breakfast from room service, then went to the gym together. Brad claimed he hasn't been in Armando's room since. According to Brad, Armando texted him on Saturday afternoon to tell him Emmy was moving into his hotel suite, and they were working out their issues. He says that was the last communication he had with Armando."

"Was Brad disappointed they got back together?"

"He wasn't happy about it."

"He said that?" I ask, incredulous as I push myself off Eric's chest and into a sitting position. "What kind of person hopes his best friend's marriage falls apart?"

"According to Brad, it's not that he *doesn't like* Emmy, it's that she distracted Armando. In Brad's opinion, Armando was a better soccer player before Emmy came along."

"Emmy wanted Armando to fire Brad and sign with a different agent."

"Brad said he's a highly sought-after agent. He has a long waiting list of athletes who want to sign with him. He claims Armando never mentioned firing him or signing with someone else. Brad is very proud of the fact that no client has ever fired him. Ever. He even mentions it in his bio on his company's website."

"Did Brad have a key to Armando's room? Does he have an alibi for yesterday morning?"

"Why would Brad Hendricks have a key to Armando's room?" Eric asks.

"Because he booked the room. The reservation was in Brad's name."

"I'll ask the hotel if they issued Brad a key to both rooms," Eric says, unlocking his phone and tapping on the screen. "As for his alibi, Brad says he was in the gym on the second floor all of Sunday morning. I'm waiting for the hotel to send the access records for Brad's room and the gym to confirm his alibi."

If Emmy is telling the truth, and Armando planned to switch agents for the sake of their marriage, Brad's perfect record would be tarnished. He wouldn't be able to brag about never being fired. His company would have to update his bio on their website. Would Brad Hendricks murder his best friend to save his reputation?

Stop thinking like that, Megan. There's no proof Armando was murdered.

Yet.

CHAPTER 14

"Do you want to watch Armando's *Hello, today!* tribute and montage?" Emmy asks, queuing the PVR.

"Yes," I say.

I join her and Sophie on the sofa, stealing some of the blanket.

Before Emmy presses play, Eric's phone rings, and he glances at the screen.

"I want to watch the montage, but it's the coroner," he says, holding up his phone.

"Take it!" Emmy commands, sweeping him out of the room with a flick of her wrist. "You can watch it later. The coroner is more important."

With a nod, Eric puts the phone to his ear and disappears down the hall.

The wordless montage and tribute to Armando is heartbreaking. He was so young and healthy and full of life. Video clips and still photos fade in and out, accompanied by music.

"Do you recognize the song?" Emmy asks. "It's the first song we ever danced to."

"I remember," I say, dabbing my tears with the edge of the blanket.

Snippets of Armando's life with Emmy, footage of him on the soccer pitch, and Armando's appearances at media and charity events dance across the screen. The song ends with a close-up of Armando and Emmy, arm-in-arm on a red carpet, smiling, then it fades to a photo of Armando in his team uniform, grinning with his arms crossed in front of his chest, resting his foot on a soccer ball. His name and dates of birth and death appear across the bottom of the screen.

We watch the tribute twice. The second time, Emmy pauses each image and video clip to explain where and when it happened.

It's a beautiful tribute, but it seems incomplete. Aside from Armando, Emmy, and his teammates, there are no other people. No family, no friends, and besides soccer photos and footage, nothing before he met Emmy.

"I'll be right back," Emmy says, crying. She throws the blanket off of her legs. "I just need a minute alone."

Before I can offer to leave instead, she's gone, and the door to the guest room closes with a thud.

"Where's Emmy?" Eric asks when he returns from his phone call.

"She'll be right back," I reply. "She needed a minute alone." I lift the blanket and tap the sofa seat. "Do you want to watch the tribute?"

"Later," Eric replies, joining me under the blanket. "How was it?"

"Sad," I respond. "And kind of lonely."

"Lonely?"

I explain to Eric how the montage focused on Armando's professional soccer career and his life with Emmy, but nothing else.

"There were no friends, no baby pictures, and no family photos. It's like Armando didn't exist professionally until he made the major leagues, and he didn't exist personally until he met Emmy. Doesn't that seem strange to you?"

"It's possible the network couldn't include those photos or video clips without permission from the people in them," Eric reasons. "Armando died yesterday, and they had the tribute ready to air early this morning. Maybe they didn't have enough time to get permission."

"You could be right," I concur.

"And Armando was a professional athlete," Eric adds. "Soccer was his biggest focus since he was a little kid. Maybe his only friends were teammates and other soccer people. He spent all his time practicing, working out, and travelling to games."

"And Emmy said Armando didn't communicate with his family, so if they have all his baby pictures and stuff, it would've been difficult to get them. Speaking of Armando's family, did someone notify them?"

"Emmy was Armando's next of kin, and she already knows. I don't have a duty to notify anyone else."

"What about his family in Ecuador?" I ask. "I know

they didn't communicate, but they'd want to know he died, wouldn't they?"

"Brad told Emmy he'd take care of it. I didn't ask him for details. But now that Armando's death is a murder investigation, I'll contact Brad and ask him specifics about Armando's family history."

"What?"

I jolt to an upright position and perfect my posture.

Sophie bounds into the room and jumps on the sofa. The padding of Emmy's bare feet on the hardwood floor grows louder as she gets closer to the family room.

"How did my husband die?" Emmy asks Eric from the doorway to the kitchen.

"PULMONARY ASPIRATION INDUCED ASPHYXIATION," Emmy mutters to herself like she's memorizing a new-to-her foreign phrase.

She stares into the distance, contemplating the tongue-twisting medical term. It's quite a mouthful. I pull the blanket higher, covering us almost to the shoulders. Annoyed that I interrupted her nap, Sophie moves from our laps to the sofa cushion next to me with a sigh.

"Pulmonary means it relates to the lungs, right? My husband had a problem with his lungs?"

"The contents of Armando's stomach went down his windpipe and into his lungs, preventing him from breathing," Eric explains. "Asphyxiation means oxygen deprivation, and aspiration refers to inhaling a foreign substance."

Emmy nods, and a glint of comprehension flashes in her eyes.

"He choked on vomit."

"Yes," Eric confirms.

"Gut rot," I say, flashing back to my conversation with Deb Kee in the hotel lobby.

"I'm sorry?" Eric tilts his ear toward me.

"The reason Armando vomited," I explain, giving Emmy's hand a hopeful squeeze under the blanket. "Deb said the resort was short staffed because of a stomach bug making its way through the employees. They nicknamed it gut rot. Maybe the gut rot jumped from employees to guests, and Armando caught it."

"I'll mention it to the coroner," Eric says, making a note. "But it doesn't fit his findings."

"If Armando choked on vomit, there was something in his stomach," Emmy declares, connecting the dots of her husband's death. "Since room service delivered the food *after* we left, it proves Armando died *after* Megan and I went to brunch. He was alive when I left."

"Makes sense," I concur.

"There was food in Armando's stomach, food from the tray in the room. And you're right, room service delivered the food after you left, but..."

"This means Armando didn't die because I put a nicotine patch on his back while he slept, right?" Emmy asks, interrupting Eric's explanation.

The relief in her voice is palpable, and her eyes swell with fresh tears, but unlike the rest of the tears she's cried since yesterday, these are tears of relief. Relief that her hair-brained nicotine scheme didn't kill her husband.

Eric takes in a deep breath and rubs the back of his neck, then exhales.

"It's unlikely, but it's not that simple," he says.

"Did the nicotine patch make him throw up?" Emmy asks.

"No, a combination of Rohypnol and Fentanyl did."

"What?" Emmy and I demand, in stereo.

"The coroner found both drugs in Armando's system," Eric says, looking at Emmy. "Did Armando use recreational drugs?"

"No! Of course not!"

"I didn't think so, but I had to ask," Eric asserts.

"Do people take Rohypnol recreationally?" I ask, wondering why someone would want to knock Armando unconscious.

"You'd be surprised," Eric says, nodding.

Eric explains that Rohypnol is a date rape drug. It's tasteless and renders the victim unconscious. They often wake up with no memory of what happened while they were under its influence. Fentanyl is a strong opioid painkiller. Even a tiny amount can cause death. A combination sounds like a cocktail for murder. This doesn't strike me as an accidental overdose.

"Armando had regular drug testing," Emmy adds. "His team outsources drug testing to a third party. The tests are blind. The players' names aren't associated with their samples, so no one can alter them. Armando passed every drug test he ever had. And he was vehemently anti-drug. He wouldn't even take aspirin for a headache."

Yet she drugged him with nicotine, anyway. Oh, Emmy.

"If Armando didn't drug himself..."

"Someone else drugged him." I finish Eric's sentence. "But not Emmy!" I add. "The evidence proves he was awake when we left."

"In theory, Armando could have been drugged right before you left," Eric asserts. "He could have answered the door, eaten, then feeling the effects of the drugs, gone back to bed thinking he was ill."

"He could've been drugged right *after* we left too," I chime in. "Same scenario, but with someone other than Emmy as the killer."

"Both options are feasible until we rule out one of them."

"How did the drugs get into his system?" Emmy asks. "Did the coroner find injection marks?"

"We're waiting for forensics to process the food, and for results of some toxicology tests, but the coroner suspects Armando ingested it. Someone contaminated his food or drink." Eric shrugs. "But he hasn't ruled out that someone could have..."

"Laced his nicotine patch?" Emmy deduces.

"We found the discarded patch in the trash can, just like you said. Forensics is testing it to make sure it doesn't contain anything it shouldn't. They're testing the unused patches too. The results should come back today."

"This makes no sense," I plead to Eric. "You always

say follow the evidence, but the evidence doesn't point to Emmy. If she dosed Armando with a lethal combination of drugs, she wouldn't discard the used patch in the room, then tell you. And if the drugs were in the patch, Armando would have been dead or too drugged to answer the door and eat."

"Right now, Emmy, you're the only person we know had access to Armando to drug him, and you have a history of drugging him without his consent."

"And I made that stupid remark to Adam and Megan at brunch," Emmy says, slapping her palm against her forehead and shaking her head. "I'm not saying anything else without my lawyer."

Emmy reaches out of the blanket and unlocks her phone and taps the screen. I presume she's texting Adam.

What remark did she make to Adam and me at brunch? *Think, Megan, think!* So much happened yesterday that everything before we found Armando's body is a blur. What self-incriminating thing did Emmy say?

I'm replaying the events of yesterday morning in my mind when my phone dings, interrupting me just as I mentally relive Emmy and I getting in the car to go to Adam's condo.

"A text from Hannah," I tell Emmy. "She's asking how you are. She didn't text you in case you're sleeping."

"I'll text her in a minute," Emmy responds. "She reminds me so much of you, Sis."

That's it! I remember! Emmy just came back inside

from talking to Poppy on the balcony. We were talking about how divorce affects families, and she said Hannah is resilient like us. Then I commented, I hope none of us gets divorced again, and she said, *I'd rather be a widow than go through another divorce.*

If she didn't bring it up, I wouldn't have remembered. Now that I remember, I have to tell Eric. It would be wrong not to.

Eric's phone rings, and he excuses himself to take the call.

"Why did you mention it in front of Eric?" I hiss, nudging her ribs.

"Mention what?" Emmy hisses back.

"The thing you said at brunch. You incriminated yourself. You should've talked to Adam before you mentioned it to Eric."

"I assumed you or Adam already told him what I said."

"I forgot about it until you mentioned it. And I don't know if Adam remembers either."

"I didn't mean it the way it sounded. I didn't mean I'd kill Armando before I'd divorce him, but considering everything that's happened, it sounds… like..."

Emmy pauses, searching for the right word.

The word she's searching for is motive. It sounds like a motive.

CHAPTER 15

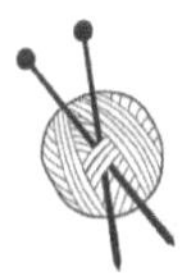

SOPHIE SNIFFS a different spot on the same tree she's been sniffing for three minutes. This is fine with me because I'm in no hurry to get home. We can extend this walk forever, and it would suit me just fine. It's better than watching grief slowly strangle the life out of Emmy and ignoring the unspoken tension between me and Eric because he's investigating my sister for murder.

"Where's Emmy now?" April asks through my Airpods after I tell her about Armando's cause of death and Emmy's position at the top of Eric's suspect list.

"At home," I reply. "Poppy is with her. Eric went to work. Later today, we're going to Adam's office so Eric can ask Emmy more questions. Poppy offered to stay at the house and answer the door while we're gone. I showed her how to update the list when someone drops off food."

"It's a good thing Knitorious is closed on Mondays," April says. "What will you do tomorrow?"

"I'll only work half a day, and Poppy will stay with Emmy."

Ready to move along to the next tree, Sophie trots ahead of me until she reaches the full length of her leash.

"I'm sure Eric knows Emmy didn't kill Armando," April assures me.

"Eric, the future-brother-in-law might know, but Eric the cop needs evidence."

"Did Poppy get the gossip website to delete the post about Emmy and Armando?"

"I don't know," I admit. "I forgot about that stupid post."

"Want me to check if it's still there?" April asks.

"You're already checking, aren't you?"

"Maybe. It depends. Do you *want* me to check?"

"Do it."

"Already done. I opened the website while we argued about it. Do you want the good news or the bad news?"

"Good news," I reply. "I don't think I can handle more bad news."

"They deleted the post."

"Good job, Poppy!" I sigh. "What's the bad news."

"There's a new post about Emmy. Should I read it to you?"

"Yes, please. And can you send me the link?"

The headline is, *Soccer Star's Life Ends in Sudden Death.*

I scoff at the author's flippant use of a soccer pun for such a serious subject.

Sudden death is the term used when the next goal ends the game and determines the outcome. The article below the insensitive headline reads: *Everyone's favourite morning television host is saying, Goodbye, love! after her husband died under mysterious circumstances at an undisclosed location. Our thoughts and prayers are with the grieving widow who lost her perfect match this morning. The soccer widow is grieving in private, at a harmonious lakeside location, under the watchful eye of her sister, a notorious yarn wrangler with a reputation for getting tangled up in murder investigations. According to our sources, the widow's long-suffering co-host raced to her side with impure intentions, hoping after everything is dead and buried, she'll look at him and say Hello, number four!*

"That's horrible!" I shout, picking up speed because I want to get home and erase this cruel, toxic excuse for gossip from the virtual universe. "I want to know who wrote it and who tipped them off."

"All the blog posts on this website have something in common," April observes. "They're about people associated, either directly or indirectly, with the network that airs *Hello, today!* Most of the posts are about the celebrities who appeared on *Perfect Match*."

"Are you suggesting the network, or the people who work on *Perfect Match* run the blog?" I ask. "As a promotional platform for their shows and stars?"

"I don't know," April replies. "But whoever leaked this... this... trash, has inside information. The timestamp at the bottom of the article is yesterday afternoon."

"They posted it before Armando's death was

announced," I say, putting it all together. "And they referred to me, Knitorious, Harmony Lake, and that I've helped Eric with his previous enquiries. It could be someone local. A friend or neighbour."

"And they hinted Emmy lost her chance to be on *Perfect Match* when Armando died. They even made a dig about Armando being her third husband," April points out.

"They know Rich Kendall is in town and hinted that he has feelings for her. Something I've long suspected."

Who would know all this information? Are multiple people working together? The article says, *according to our sources.* Plural. Maybe they're getting information from multiple people.

"What if the person or people behind these disgusting posts killed Armando?" April asks.

"Then I look forward to exposing them for the murdering scum they are."

ROUNDING THE CORNER TOWARD HOME, Sophie and I walk so fast I almost break into a run. Almost. I can't wait to show Poppy the article and get her to do whatever she does to get it removed. With any luck, she can get the website to delete it before Emmy finds out about it.

"Rich," I wheeze when I spot his car in the driveway.

I stop to catch my breath and pull myself together, so I don't charge into the house like an out-of-shape hysterical person. I open the link April sent and take screenshots of the article, in case whoever posted it deletes it. Then I text the link to Eric, asking if he found out who's behind these posts. He texts me back saying the cyber unit is looking into it. He said something about IP addresses, but I'm not as technically inclined as he gives me credit for.

I compose myself, take one more deep breath, and proceed home.

"Hi, everyone," I say, bending at the knees to detach Sophie's leash.

We exchange greetings, and I join everyone in the living room while Sophie trots to her water bowl in the kitchen.

"Megan, I don't think you've met Sonia Chang," Emmy says, gesturing at the familiar woman in the armchair. "Sonia is our executive producer."

"We haven't met," I say to Sonia. "But I'm a huge fan of your work." I extend my hand, and when Sonia shakes it, I'm a little star-struck.

"It's lovely to meet you, Megan. I'm sorry for your family's loss."

Before becoming the executive producer for *Hello, today!* Sonia Chang was a respected investigative journalist. Her exposés on human rights issues, political scandals, and corporate agendas helped topple governments, CEOs, and other powerful people who used their wealth and influence to exploit the vulnerable masses.

Sonia sits in one armchair, and Poppy sits in the other. Rich sits next to Emmy on the loveseat, and I take a seat on the sofa. Sophie sits at my feet, dripping water from her chin to the floor and still panting from our walk around the neighbourhood.

A tray of pastries and fixings for coffee and tea crowd the coffee table. Someone assumed the role of hostess in my absence.

Emmy, Poppy, Rich, and Sonia are discussing work stuff. I smile and nod politely, pretending to follow along.

Emmy is quiet and distracted. Her face is heavy with exhaustion. She's physically in the same room as us, but mentally she's somewhere else.

Rich doesn't take his eyes off Emmy. He leans in and mutters something close to her ear, causing the corners of her mouth to curl into a brief, weak smile. No matter who is talking, Rich remains fixated on Emmy. Every so often, he gives her knee a reassuring tap or rubs the top of her hand. He loves her; it's so obvious, it's almost tangible.

Poppy is her usual self and attentive to everyone in the room. Is she oblivious to Rich's infatuation with Emmy or ignoring it? I get the sense she's accustomed to it.

Sonia Chang oozes quiet confidence. Her posture is perfect yet relaxed. Her delicate features and perfectly coiffed, conservative chin-length bob contrast with her rabble-rousing reputation. She looks too small and quiet to lead a revolt against the powers-that-be and expose corruption. She shoots the occasional sideways glance at Rich, and I detect a flash of contempt in her expression when she catches him rubbing Emmy's arm. Is the contempt aimed at Rich, Emmy, or both of them?

"Can I get you a drink, Megan?" Poppy asks, interrupting my people watching.

I figured she was the stand-in hostess.

"No, thank you, Poppy. I'll get it. Can I get anyone else a drink?" I smile at the shaking heads and polite smiles. "I'll refresh the tea while I'm in the kitchen." I collect the teapot from the coffee table and disappear into the kitchen.

As I plug in the kettle, a rustling behind me catches my attention.

"Those are beautiful," I comment on the large arrangement of fresh-cut flowers wrapped in kraft paper and tied with black twine.

"They're from Sonia and Rich," Poppy says, sniffing the bouquet.

"Are Sonia and Rich a couple?" I ask, thinking that if they are, Sonia's contemptuous glare at Rich doting on Emmy is justified.

"No," Poppy replies with a giggle. "They definitely are not a couple."

The way she says it makes me think there's more to their story. Rich and Sonia must have a history.

"You said the flowers are from both of them, so I wasn't sure."

"They delivered them on behalf of the *Hello, today!* cast and crew," Poppy clarifies.

"Ahh," I say. "Emmy doesn't mention Sonia often. Did I pick up on some tension between either Sonia and Rich or Sonia and Emmy? Is there anything I should know about?"

"Sonia isn't Emmy's biggest fan," Poppy whispers,

sidling up next to me as I fill the teapot with kettle water. "I think Sonia is jealous of the attention Rich gives Emmy. Rich and Sonia have known each other a long time. Sonia was the target of Rich's attention until Emmy started working at *Hello, today!*."

"I see."

Sophie bounds past us and scratches at the back door. I open the door, then put the lid on the teapot.

"Emmy and I couldn't find a vase…"

I forgot Poppy is still carrying the flowers.

"I'll take care of it, Poppy. Just put them on the table." I gesture to the kitchen table. "Thank you for taking care of everyone. I wouldn't have left you alone if I knew people were coming over."

"Don't worry about it." Poppy dismisses my comment with a flick of her wrist. "Did you have a nice walk?"

"It was nice to get out of the house," I admit. "I don't know how you convinced that website to delete the story about Emmy and Armando, but can you do it again?"

Panic flashes across Poppy's face.

"I forgot to contact them. If they took down the post, it wasn't because of me, but I'm glad it's gone. I'm sorry I forgot to deal with it when I got back to the motel last night."

"Don't worry about it," I assure her. "Yesterday was a nightmare. Are you sure you won't reconsider and stay here instead of the motel?"

"I'm fine at the motel," Poppy insists. "And it's only a short drive to see Emmy." Poppy squints like she just remembered something. "You said you want me to contact the website *again*? Did they post another article?"

I nod. "A horrible post about Armando's death."

"Send me the link."

I unlock my phone and send the link to Poppy.

"Eric is looking into it. With any luck, he'll convince them to take it down before Emmy finds out it exists."

"I hope so," Poppy agrees, nodding. "Does Eric know who's behind it?"

"Not yet. The cyber unit is looking into it. He wants to find the mystery blogger and talk to them about Armando's murder."

"He thinks the murderer is the source of the information?" Her eyes are wide, and her mouth hangs open.

"I don't know."

"Does Eric think he'll find the blogger?" Poppy asks.

"He seems confident," I reply, picking up the teapot. "He said something about tracing the blogger's IP address. And he said they might be able to identify the device the blogger used."

"Device?" Poppy asks. "You mean the type of computer they used?"

"Or phone, or tablet, or whatever." I shrug. "I'll drop off the fresh tea, then deal with the flowers."

"Let me take that," Poppy says, reaching for the teapot.

"Thank you," I say, relinquishing it to her. "I'll pop these flowers in a vase and join you in a few minutes."

CHAPTER 16

THE TALL, rectangular crystal vase is heavier than I remember. It came with a floral arrangement someone sent me when my mum died. I used it again about ten years ago when Adam's law firm sent flowers to the house after his grandmother died. Now, I'm using it to arrange flowers in honour of Armando's death. It's a death vase. It only sees the light of day when someone dies.

"Would you mind if I help with those?" Sonia Chang asks, her warm brown eyes smiling as she points to the bouquet I just laid on the counter next to the kitchen sink.

"You'd be doing me a favour," I reply. "I wasn't blessed with a green thumb or an eye for floral arranging."

"I love flowers," Sonia says, taking over the unwrapping of the bouquet. "My parents owned a florist shop. I've been creating floral arrangements since I was a little girl."

"Be my guest," I say, stepping away from the counter.

As I step back from the counter and Sonia steps forward to take my place, I detect a faint scent of cigarette smoke. Behind her, I lean in and inhale. Does Sonia smoke? My nose says she does. The evidence is subtle but undeniable. I don't know why I'm shocked, but I am. For whatever reason, I just assumed she didn't. I guess everyone has a guilty pleasure; mine is expensive yarn, and Sonia Chang's is smoking.

Sonia shows me the proper way to trim a stem and how to ensure the angle is correct, then delegates stem trimming to me. She'll arrange them in the vase. I trim each stem over the kitchen sink and pass the flower to Sonia, who nestles it in the vase.

"I'm a huge fan of your investigative journalism work," I say, trying not to sound like a journalism groupie. "Do you mind if I ask why you left investigative journalism to produce a television morning show?" Sonia sighs, and I fear I've crossed a line. "I understand if it's none of my business. Please don't feel obliged to tell me."

I pass her a white lily and pick up a sprig of Italian ruscus.

"Love," Sonia replies with breathless nostalgia. "When the network offered Rich the co-host position at *Hello, today!* he broke up with me. He said our schedules were incompatible. Rich had a fixed, Monday-to-Friday schedule, and I flew around the world on assignment. Sometimes for weeks at a time."

"I didn't know you and Rich were together." I hand her a stem of bells of Ireland.

"*Were,*" she echoes. "We *were* together. I took the producer job so we could stay together. Rich promised me a life of domestic bliss. He promised me kids, dogs, and a cozy suburban life, so I took the producer job and pivoted *my* life to accommodate *his* career."

"What happened?" I ask, cutting another lily.

"He fell in love with Emmy and dumped me."

"I'm sorry, Sonia," I say, handing her the lily. "When did this happen?"

"When the network hired your sister to fill the co-host position on *Hello, today!*" she replies, stabbing the lily into the centre of the arrangement. "I auditioned for the co-host job, but I didn't get it."

She jabs another sprig of Irish bells into the vase, her floral arranging becoming increasingly aggressive the more she talks about her relationship with Rich and the sacrifices she made for him.

"Wow," I say, stunned that the network wouldn't want a journalist of Sonia's calibre to host their flagship morning show.

"They said viewers would always associate me with the intense, investigative reports they knew me for," Sonia continues. "They said viewers wouldn't accept me as a fun, bubbly, morning show host. Emmy got the co-host spot, and I got to keep my job as executive producer." She stabs a white rose into the arrangement. "If I'd gotten the job, Miranda Monroe would never have entered our lives, and Rich and I would still be together," she says, using Emmy's professional name and fussing combatively with the flowers in the vase. "We'd probably be at home right now in our cozy suburban house, playing with our golden retriever and making lunch for our kids." She flashes me a strained smile.

Could Sonia Chang hate my sister enough to kill Armando? There's no doubt Sonia is smart enough to frame Emmy for the crime, and she arrived in Harmony Lake before Armando died. Maybe Sonia killed Armando to make Emmy as miserable as Sonia was when Rich left her. Maybe Sonia wanted to give Emmy a taste of her own medicine. Or maybe she hoped the network would fire Emmy because of the negative publicity, thereby eliminating her from the show and from Rich's life.

"Listen, Megan, your sister should get a lawyer," Sonia says in a gentle voice, like she's telling me bad news and is sad she's the messenger.

I'm tempted to tell her Emmy already has a lawyer, but I don't.

"Why would you say that?" I ask.

"Because I think it's possible Emmy found out something about Armando. Something big. Something that made her angry enough to kill him."

I open my mouth to ask Sonia what she's talking about when Emmy and Rich come into the kitchen.

"Such beautiful flowers," Emmy says, admiring the flowers in the vase. "Can I help arrange them?"

"Sonia and I will take care of it," I insist, trimming another white rose.

"Let us do this for you," Sonia adds, sounding

almost friendly toward Emmy.

"I thought it would be good for Emmy to get some fresh air," Rich says, guiding Emmy toward the back door with his hand on the small of her back.

"Good idea," I agree. "Sophie's already out there waiting for you."

"When Poppy gets off the phone, can you tell her we're on the back deck?" Emmy asks.

"Will do."

With Rich and Emmy outside, I check the living room for Poppy. I'd rather not have any eavesdroppers overhear my conversation with Sonia. I spot Poppy through the living room window. She's standing on the driveway, squinting into the sun, with her phone to her ear.

"What did you mean when you said Emmy found out something about Armando?" I ask Sonia while trimming another stalk of Irish bells, thankful there are only a few untrimmed stems left. "They argued about a reality TV show," I hiss, handing her the trimmed foliage.

"I know," Sonia acknowledges. "The producer of *Perfect Match* is a close friend of mine. I'm the person who suggested to him that Emmy and Armando would be good contestants. And I know Brad spun a yarn about reality TV reducing the value of Armando's brand, but there's another reason Armando didn't want to take part in the show." She stops fussing with the blooms and looks me in the eye. "Emmy wasn't Armando's first wife. He was married to someone else before he married your sister."

"OK." I shrug, relieved Sonia didn't drop a huge bombshell of controversy on me. "So was Emmy. Even if Armando didn't tell her about his first marriage, she'd get over it." I shrug again. "At our age, everyone has a past. Emmy was married twice before she married Armando."

"Your sister's prior marriages ended in divorce," Sonia explains. "Armando's didn't."

I gasp and bring my hand to my mouth.

"Oh my! Armando's first wife died? He was a widower?"

Sonia shakes her head.

"The first Mrs. Garcia is alive and well in Baña, Ecuador. They never divorced."

"Annulment?" I suggest, hoping Sonia will nod in agreement.

"No annulment, no divorce, no death. In the eyes of the law, Armando was married to his first wife when he died."

If this is true, Emmy isn't Armando's widow. His real widow is in Ecuador.

"You're mistaken," I insist, shaking my head and dropping the shears in the sink.

"I'm not." Sonia's voice and demeanor exude an abundance of confidence and a hint of smugness. "I wish I was."

Hmph. Somehow, I doubt that.

"Why were you investigating Armando in the first place?"

"Someone contacted me with an anonymous tip. The tip was about something else, but when I started looking into it, my investigation led me to Armando's first wife."

"What was the tip about?"

"Corruption in major league sports." Sonia waves her hand and shakes her head as if it doesn't matter. "Major league sports is full of corruption, but it's hard to prove. The power and money are concentrated in such a small number of stakeholders," she explains, getting off track. "Anyway, I couldn't prove the tipster's allegation."

"What was the allegation?"

"It's irrelevant, Megan. Nothing came of it. What I just told you about Armando's real wife is what's important."

"Do you have proof?"

"I was an investigative reporter, remember? I know how to confirm a story and double-check the facts."

I disappear from the kitchen and reappear seconds later, holding out Adam's business card.

"Can you send the proof to this lawyer?" I ask.

"Sure," Sonia replies, taking the card and reading it. "But I also have to send it to the police. I'm sure being the future wife of a police chief, you understand." Sonia smiles and her eyes glisten with the same contempt as when she watched Rich comfort Emmy in the living room.

"Totally," I say, handing her Eric's card with my other hand. "Here's the police chief's contact information." I smile. "Thanks for filling me in, Sonia."

And giving the police another motive for Emmy to kill her husband.

CHAPTER 17

***Me:* Sonia Chang is sending you alleged proof that Armando was a bigamist.**

***Adam:* Does Emmy know about this?**

***Me:* No.**

***Adam:* Don't tell her until I verify it.**

I reply with a thumbs-up emoji.

"Where is everyone?" Poppy asks.

Distracted by Armando's potential bigamy, I didn't hear her come in.

"Back deck," I say, then look up from my phone. "Is everything OK? You were out there for a while."

"Everything is fine." Poppy smiles. "Yesterday when I picked up Emmy's essential items, I couldn't find a specific product Emmy uses daily. I substituted with another brand, and Emmy got upset. She went on about her life being hard enough without worrying about her skin reacting to a different moisturizer. She lectured me about her very sensitive skin and how it breaks out if she changes her skin care routine. And when she eventually faces the world, all eyes will be on her, and she doesn't want the headlines to focus on her skin. You know how she is."

"Oh," I say awkwardly. "I'm sorry, Poppy. Emmy isn't herself right now. She's in shock and…"

Poppy raises her hand like a girl scout to stop me from talking.

"I understand, Megan. But Emmy would react like that even if her husband didn't die. It is what it is." She shrugs. "You don't see it. You live far away and don't interact with her every day."

"Umm…" I'm not sure how to respond to Poppy's rant, but I feel like I should defend Emmy, especially since she's in no state to defend herself right now.

"Anyway," Poppy continues, "I called the manufacturer to ask where the closest seller is in this neck of the woods, and they just called me back."

"Oh. I'll get it. Tell me what and where it is."

"No need. When they heard who it was for, they offered to send Emmy free samples by overnight courier. One of the many perks of Miranda Monroe's charmed life." Poppy shrugs. "Her nighttime moisturizer should arrive on your doorstep sometime tomorrow."

Charmed life? Has Poppy forgotten that my sister, her best friend, was widowed yesterday?

I guess Armando's death is taking a toll on everyone, not just Emmy. It seems Poppy is straining under the pressure of all the demands that come with being Emmy's PA and best friend. I've never heard Poppy say anything critical about Emmy before. Since it's a one-off, I'll attribute her rant to stress and let it go.

I turn my attention back to my phone.

Me: Can we talk?

Eric: Of course. Work or personal?

How do I answer that? In this case, his work is my personal.

Me: Yes.

Eric: Do you want me to call you?

Me: In person?

Eric: Where?

WHEN I ARRIVE AT KNITORIOUS, Eric is already there, sitting on the sofa in the cozy sitting area. There's a to-go cup from Latte Da on the coffee table. I know without asking it's a chocolate caramel latte for me.

"It's not like you to drink coffee past noon," I say, joining him on the sofa and kissing him hello.

"It's for you," he says. "But I think you already knew that."

"I had a hunch," I admit. "The super-hot, local police chief likes to surprise me with coffee."

"It's probably just his excuse to see you during the day."

"He doesn't need an excuse," I say, then give him another kiss before I crack the lid on my chocolate caramel latte and take the first glorious sip. "Thank you for meeting me here. It's the only place I could think of where no one would interrupt us."

"How's your day?" he asks, massaging the back of my neck.

"Longer than a marathon," I reply, leaning into his touch. "Yours?"

"Busier than a moth in a yarn store," Eric replies with a muffled chuckle.

"Not funny," I say, laughing and gesturing to yarn store we're sitting in.

"How's Emmy?"

"Tired. Rich and Sonia came over to visit her. Then she went for a nap. Poppy is staying with her until I get home."

"Listen babe, I've been thinking," Eric says. I pivot my hips so I'm facing him. He moves his hand from my neck to my knee. "Maybe someone else should investigate Armando's murder."

"Who? You're the only murder investigator the HLPD has."

"I can borrow someone from another town. You were right yesterday. Maybe I can't be both a cop and a fiancé. Being there for you and our family takes priority over investigating a murder."

Taken aback by his proposition, I'm not sure what to say.

"Who would investigate it?"

"I'm not sure." Eric shrugs. "I'd find the best investigator around. Someone thorough with an excellent reputation."

"*You're* the best investigator around," I remind him. "*You're* thorough and have an excellent reputation. Do you want to recuse yourself?"

"I want to do what's best for us. I don't want to blur the line between work and home, and I don't want my job to interfere with our relationship."

"If our relationship wasn't a factor, if this investigation didn't cause tension between us, would you want to recuse yourself?"

"No," Eric admits.

"Do you think Emmy killed Armando?"

"No. But right now she's our number one suspect and investigating Armando's murder means investigating your sister."

"I trust you," I say. "I don't know if I'd trust another investigator. You'll follow every lead, and you're open-minded about all the possibilities. I know you'll do whatever it takes to uncover the truth. You won't just charge my sister with murder because you can force the evidence to fit."

"You don't want me to step back, do you?"

"Only if it's what you want."

"How about this? We'll take it day by day. If the line between work and home gets too blurry, or the investigation causes stress in our relationship, I'll step back."

Eric's phone dings and vibrates in his pocket, but he ignores it. I recognize the sound; it's an email notification.

I nod and say, "Good compromise."

He kisses my forehead.

"Now, can I talk to you as a cop for a minute, Chief Sloane?"

Eric sighs. "What's up?"

"There's something I didn't tell you yesterday. I

didn't mean to leave it out. I forgot about it until Emmy jogged my memory this morning."

"The brunch conversation Emmy alluded to earlier?"

I nod and take a deep breath. "She didn't mean it. I don't know how she meant it, but she didn't mean it the way it sounded," I say, laying the groundwork for my sister's incriminating statement. "It's not even evidence. It's probably irrelevant, but not telling you feels like lying."

"Just tell me already." He smiles and takes my hand.

I relive the conversation at brunch yesterday and include Emmy's comment about preferring to be a widow over a three-time divorcée.

"If she had just killed her husband with a lethal overdose of drugs, she wouldn't have risked saying it. Emmy's impulsive, not stupid."

"Thank you for telling me," Eric says, without acknowledging whether the self-incriminating statement will impact the evidence against Emmy. His phone buzzes again, and he ignores it again. "I got an email from Sonia Chang a little while ago."

"I know," I say, nodding. "She sent the same information to Adam. Do you think it's true?"

"I'm not sure," Eric replies. "I assigned an officer to verify it. For Emmy's sake, I hope it's not true."

"Because it gives her a motive to kill Armando?"

"Because it will break her heart," he replies.

"Yup," I agree. "Sonia hates Emmy. She has her own reasons to kill Armando."

"I'm listening."

Eric sits upright and produces his small notebook and pen.

"Sonia and Rich were a couple. He dumped Sonia because he fell in love with Emmy."

"Wouldn't that give her a motive to kill Emmy, not Armando?"

"Killing Armando makes Emmy suffer. An eye for an eye. Sonia lost Rich, and Emmy lost Armando."

Eric nods. "I'll look into it."

"Sonia said she discovered Armando's first wife by accident, while she was investigating an unrelated tip. If the unrelated tip led her to Armando, he might have another secret Emmy doesn't know about."

"Did Sonia tell you what the unrelated tip was about?"

"Something about corruption in sports. She wouldn't talk about it, just said she couldn't prove it, and it was irrelevant. Also, I think Sonia might be a smoker."

"Did you observe her smoking?"

"No, but she was beside me at the kitchen sink for several minutes, and she smelled of cigarette smoke. It was faint, but it was nicotine."

"I'll question Sonia." He unlocks his phone, types a quick message, then returns the phone to his pocket. "I'm still waiting for the forensics results on the cigarette package and butts we found. If they don't match Brad, we'll run them against Sonia."

"This gives Rich a motive too," I point out. "If he believed Armando was the only obstacle between him and a happy ever after with Emmy, maybe he removed the obstacle. He was in town before Armando died, and he's already visited Emmy twice since yesterday. It's like he's inserting himself into her life and trying to be her primary support person while she grieves. There's something territorial about it, like when Sophie pees on every tree we walk past."

Eric's phone dings and buzzes again. More email notifications. Are they forensic reports for Armando's case? Part of me wants him to check, and part of me doesn't want to know. I try to put Eric's inbox out of my mind.

"Did you figure out who published the nasty blog posts about Emmy and Armando?" I ask.

"No, but it's not someone local."

"How do you know they aren't local if you don't know who did it?"

"The first post, the one about Armando following Emmy to Harmony Lake, originated from a coffee shop a few blocks from Emmy and Armando's house. The second post, the one about Armando's death, originated from Latte Da."

"That's only a few stores away from Knitorious," I say, shocked. "The mystery blogger followed Emmy to Harmony Lake?"

"That's my conclusion. It can't be Armando, because the second post appeared after he died, but it could be Rich, Sonia, Poppy, or any of the crew who arrived in town yesterday. Has Emmy been to Latte Da?"

"No!" I snap, offended by the suggestion that my sister would reveal intimate details of her life in such a disrespectful manner. "Except for when I walked

Sophie earlier, and now, Emmy and I have been together every minute since we found Armando's body. We haven't been near Latte Da!"

"I'm sorry, babe. I have to ask."

"What about Brad?" I ask, ignoring Eric's apology and keen to change the subject.

"He's still a person of interest. We haven't ruled him out."

"Brad had a lot to lose if Armando fired him," I say. "It would be a blow to his reputation and his ego. He was Armando's confidant. He could be the mystery blogger and Armando's killer."

"I know," Eric replies. "We're investigating all the suspects, not just Emmy."

"There must be a way to determine who followed Emmy to Harmony Lake and visited Latte Da when the mystery blogger posted the article."

"We interviewed the employees who worked at Latte Da yesterday. We showed them photos of the *Hello, today!* cast and crew. They didn't recognize anyone. Well, they recognized Emmy and Rich from seeing them on TV, but they didn't recognize anyone from the coffee shop. They assured us they'll keep their eyes peeled and notify us if any of them visit Latte Da. They'll note the date and time."

"Speaking of employees," I say, "have you interviewed the hotel employees who were working when Armando died?"

"Most," Eric replies. "The guy who delivered Armando's breakfast caught that gut rot bug and called in sick today. I hope to interview him tomorrow."

"I should get back to Emmy," I say, standing up.

"And I should get back to the office," Eric responds, also standing up. "I need to go through my inbox before I interview Emmy."

A knot forms in my stomach when I wonder if the forensics reports in Eric's inbox eliminate or further implicate Emmy as Armando's murderer.

CHAPTER 18

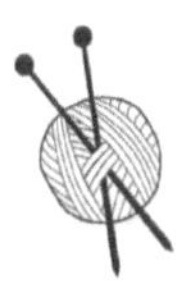

"Do you know Rich Kendall is in love with you?" I ask Emmy on the short drive to Adam's law office.

"He told me a long time ago," Emmy replies with no hint of surprise. "I've made it clear to him I don't feel the same way."

With Armando out of the picture, maybe Rich hopes Emmy will reconsider her feelings for him.

"You never mentioned it to me."

"Why would I?" Emmy shrugs. "It's irrelevant. Did Rich tell you he's in love with me?"

"No, I could tell by the way he looks at you," I reply, not revealing that Sonia later confirmed my hunch. "Did anything ever happen between you and Rich?"

"Gawd no!" Emmy chuckles for the first time since Armando died. "I love Armando. I would never cheat on my husband. Besides, it would be unprofessional to have a relationship with someone I work with."

I shift the car into park and turn off the engine.

"We're early," I say. "Shall we sit here for a few minutes?"

"Uh-uh." Emmy shakes her head and looks with determination at the renovated, large Victorian house. "I want to get this over with. I have nothing to hide. I didn't kill my husband, but maybe I have information that will help Eric figure out who did."

"We'll find Armando's killer," I assure her. "The murdering scumbag who did this won't get away with it. I won't rest until they're behind bars."

"Not much," Emmy replies when Eric asks her what she knows about Armando's family. "Armando stopped communicating with his family before I met him. I think his parents live in Ecuador. He said his mum was from Brazil or Belize or something. He had an older... sister? I think?" Emmy says, unsure whether Armando had a sister or whether she was older than him. "I think she emigrated. Armando never talked about his family, and if I asked him about them, he'd change the subject," she says, justifying her lack of information about the family she married into. "He had a best friend who was like a brother, but I don't know his name. They stopped talking because his friend didn't make the major leagues and was jealous when Armando did. His friend had a career-ending knee injury." Emmy huffs, exasperated. "You should ask Brad," she says, clearly frustrated by how little she knows about her husband's past.

"Brad knew Armando longer than me, and I think he knows more about his family."

"Do you know why Armando stopped communicating with his family?" Eric asks.

"Money," Emmy replies. "Armando said they were unhappy with how much money he gave them. He refused to increase the amount he sent them, and they cut him off completely."

"When did they cut him off completely?" Eric asks.

Emmy shurgs and shakes her head. "Sometime before we met."

Could one of Armando's estranged family members have orchestrated his murder? Maybe when Armando stopped sending money, they decided he was expendable. Or maybe they hoped they'd inherit his money.

"Did you hang the DO NOT DISTURB sign on the hotel room door?" Eric asks.

"No," Emmy says, shaking her head. "Someone hung it up after Megan and I left for brunch. I made a mental note to ask Armando about it when I removed it. But I forgot because I found my husband's dead body."

"We only found one DO NOT DISTURB sign in the hotel suite," Eric says, "so it's probable the sign you removed from the door handle was the sign from inside the room. We found your fingerprints on it."

"Because I removed it from the door handle," Emmy reminds him, irritated. "I told you that."

"But your fingerprints were the only ones on the sign."

"Whoever hung it up either wiped off their fingerprints, or wore gloves." Emmy shrugs.

"Can you think of anyone who would want to hurt Armando?" Eric asks.

"A crazed fan or someone who was jealous of him, maybe," Emmy theorizes. "Armando was amazing. He was the complete package. He donated his time and money to underprivileged kids. He visited children's hospitals. He was smart, funny, gorgeous, talented..." Emmy's words fade, and her eyes swell with tears.

"Can you think of anyone specific who might have killed Armando?" Eric clarifies.

Emmy nods.

"After our argument about *Perfect Match,* Armando agreed to fire Brad and find a new agent. One who's more open-minded and doesn't hate me. If Armando told him, Brad could have freaked out and killed him. Brad's ego would never accept being fired or Armando choosing me over him. Brad and Armando are close friends, but I'm not sure how close they'd be if Armando wasn't Brad's client."

"I need a list of everyone who entered the hotel room."

Eric hovers his pen above the paper, ready for names.

"No one. Not while I was there," Emmy replies to Eric's question. "I mean, room service delivered food, but otherwise it was just me and Armando."

"I have the access records for Armando's room," Eric says, flipping through the binder that lays open across his lap. "The door was unlocked six times between when Armando checked in, and when you found him."

"Do you know who unlocked the door six times?" I ask.

Eric opens the binder rings and removes a sheet of paper.

"Armando entered the room after checking in on Friday," Eric read. "Armando entered the room again after visiting the gym that evening. On Saturday, housekeeping entered the room while Armando and Brad were at the gym. Armando returned from the gym. Armando returned later the same day from the pool. Yesterday, Emmy returned to the room after brunch with Megan."

"Hold up," Emmy straightens her spine. "Did you say housekeeping entered the room?"

Eric nods. "Housekeeping entered the room Saturday morning while Armando and Brad were at the gym."

"That's not possible," Emmy says. "Armando declined housekeeping. He always declined housekeeping when he checked into a hotel." She turns to me. "He usually only stayed in one town for a night or two, and he'd rather not have anyone in the room, so he specifically declined housekeeping services."

"Maybe Armando forgot to decline housekeeping this time? Or he requested something and housekeeping brought it to the room?" I suggest. "Like extra towels or pillows, or something."

"That's the only possible explanation," Emmy concedes.

"I'll ask Deb Kee if there's a record of Armando declining housekeeping services or contacting the front desk to get something delivered to his room," Eric says, making a note on the page he just read from.

"Also, Armando eats six times per day. Shouldn't there be a record of room service delivering his food?" Emmy asks. "Someone opened the door to bring the food inside."

"There's only a digital record if a keycard unlocked the door," Eric explains.

"When someone enters the room from the outside," Adam clarifies.

"Right," Eric says. "If Armando opened the door from inside, there wouldn't be a record. Room service employees do not have keycards. Armando had to let them in. He opened the door from inside when room service delivered his food. This is also why there's no digital record of Brad entering the room, Emmy entering the room when she arrived on Saturday, or Megan entering the room when she picked you up for brunch yesterday."

"Because Armando let Brad and I in, and I let Megan in," Emmy concludes. Then she looks at me. "Do you know what this means?"

The killer was someone Armando knew and trusted. He let them in.

CHAPTER 19

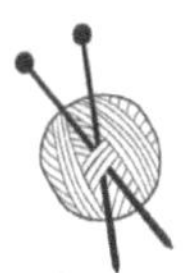

TUESDAY, October 5th

The world is wet and grey. The cloudy skies are so dark, the streetlights on Water Street keep flickering on and off even though it's daytime.

"If Armando never divorced his first wife, it explains why he pressured Emmy to elope and skip a big wedding," April says into my Airpods. "He didn't want the attention a big wedding would attract."

"And it explains why he tried to convince Emmy to keep their marriage a secret," I add. "I don't want it to be true, but my instincts tell me it is," I admit.

"Sonia is an experienced investigative journalist," April adds. "She wouldn't tell you unless she had proof to back it up."

"Did I tell you our theory that the mystery blogger is someone who followed Emmy to Harmony Lake?"

"No!" April retorts. "Who is it?"

I tell April that Eric doesn't know who the mystery

blogger is, but he knows where they posted their vile content from.

"I have a hunch it might be Brad," I admit.

"Why?"

"Because he was Armando's confidant, and he knows all the information the blogger alluded to in the posts. Also, the posts were more critical of Emmy than Armando, and Brad is open about his dislike for her."

"Interesting," April says. "I went to the website, and the second blog post was gone. Someone deleted it."

"Good," I scoff.

"Why would they delete the posts about Emmy and Armando, but leave the other posts up?"

"Who knows?" I reply. "Maybe they had an attack of conscience."

While I sweep the floor and replenish a few barren shelves, April updates me on her visit with her family and her cousin's wedding celebration. Like all family events, her cousin's wedding isn't without its share of family drama. But I can't help but feel a twinge of jealousy because April's family drama revolves around the bride's ex-boyfriend attending the nuptials as her best friend's plus one. I'd rather deal with a nuisance ex than a murder investigation any day.

"I think the only thing Emmy ate yesterday was an orange-cranberry croissant from Artsy Tartsy. She's eaten very little since Armando died. I'm afraid if her appetite doesn't improve, she'll get sick," I say after thanking April for sending boxes of fresh pastries to the house yesterday.

The store doesn't open for another ten minutes, but Tina knocks on the window to get my attention.

"Hi!" I shout and wave, even though she can't hear me from the sidewalk.

"Hi?" April asks confused. "Is someone there?"

"Tina," I reply. "It's raining again. I should let her in."

It's been raining off and on all morning. Ten-to-fifteen-minute increments of hard rain, then nothing. Mother nature can't make up her mind.

April and I end our call. I unlock the door and flip the sign from CLOSED to OPEN.

"Hi, Megan," Tina says, taking off her raincoat and laying it on the counter. "How's Emmy doing?"

"Under the circumstances, she's doing as well as you'd expect," I reply.

"Please give her my condolences," Tina says. "Her husband's death shocked everyone at Rise & Glide."

"I forgot you work there," I say. "Did you work on Sunday?"

"I was supposed to," Tina replies, "but I caught that stomach bug that's going around."

"Gut rot," I say with a knowing nod. "How are you feeling?"

"It's a fast and furious bug," Tina informs me. "You feel like you're going to die for twenty-four hours, then it stops." She shrugs, then panic flashes across her face, and she covers her mouth with her hand. "I'm sorry! I shouldn't have said that. About feeling like dying."

"It's fine," I chuckle, waving away her comment. "I know what you meant."

"I finished two Knitted Knockers since I was here on Friday." Tina reaches into her backpack, pulls out a plastic bag and hands it to me. "I dropped a stitch on one of them," she cautions. "I tried to fix it like Connie showed me, but it looks a bit wonky."

"I'm sure it's fine," I assure her. "Connie or I will look at it. If we can fix it, we will." I stash the bag under the counter. "Thank you for using your knitting superpower for good. Sadly, the demand for Knitted Knockers exceeds the supply."

"I could've made a third one except I ran out of yarn," Tina says.

I gesture to the yarn display Connie and I set up for Breast Cancer Awareness Month.

"Everything on these shelves is buy-one-get-one-free until the end of the month."

"I bet Emmy is excited to get back to work," Tina comments as she digs through skeins of yarn.

"She hasn't mentioned work yet. I'm sure she'll go back when she's ready."

"Oh," Tina says, her face clouded with confusion. "Her glam squad is checking in later today. And I overheard someone say Emmy is working tomorrow."

What happened to the confidentiality agreement hotel employees sign? The one that says they could lose their jobs if they discuss guests outside of work?

"Who said that?" I ask, hoping it's just speculation.

"The Sonia woman talked about it in the dining room last night. She said Emmy's glam squad is due in Harmony Lake today. Two people. Hair and make-up. I checked, and the network made two reservations for today."

"What else did Sonia say?"

"She said the ratings for yesterday's show and the tribute to Emmy's husband were through the roof, and she wants to capitalize on it by doing a segment with Emmy."

Speechless, my mouth is agape. The more I learn about Sonia, the more I dislike her. I'm a fan of her work as an investigative journalist, but I'm not a fan of her as a person.

"I'm sorry," Tina says. "I assumed you knew."

"Sonia talked to you about the show's ratings and Emmy's glam squad?"

"No," Tina chuckles. "She was talking to her dinner companion."

"Who did she have dinner with?"

"Rich Kendall."

"Would you like me to wind these for you?" I ask, ringing up four skeins of yarn for Tina. Tina checks her watch and considers my offer. "You can wait, or you can leave them and come back later."

"It's fine," Tina says with a smile. "I like winding yarn, and I have to skedaddle, or I'll be late for work."

"Connie will be here any minute. She'll be sorry she missed you." I bag Tina's yarn and thank her again for her Knitted Knocker donation. "And thank you for telling me about Emmy's glam squad and her potential return to *Hello, today!*" I say, handing Tina the bag.

"I'm not supposed to talk about guests," Tina

admits. "I'd appreciate it if you didn't tell anyone it was me who told you."

"I'll never reveal my source," I promise.

"I love Harmony Lake. I'm glad I took the job at Rise & Glide and moved here. You and Connie have made me feel welcome. I like Emmy and feel bad for what she's going through, so if I overhear anything else, I'll break the rules and tell you."

"I appreciate it, Tina, but you shouldn't risk getting in trouble or losing your job."

"I want to help," Tina insists. "I've heard about your sleuthing history. You and Chief Sloane have a perfect record for solving crimes. I want to help keep your record perfect."

"That's sweet, but you shouldn't put yourself or your job on the line..."

The bell over the door brings an abrupt end to our conversation.

"It finally stopped raining!" Phillip announces from behind a large floral arrangement of fall-coloured asters, chrysanthemums, and marigolds.

Who are they from? Where will I put them? Our house is full of condolence flowers and food. We're out of empty surfaces.

Tina rushes over to hold the door for him, and he places the vase on the coffee table in the cozy sitting area.

"Gotta go," Tina quips with a wave as the door closes behind her.

"They're gorgeous," I tell Phillip. "Who are they from?"

There's no visible card in the arrangement.

"They're from your future groom," Phillip replies, fussing with the flowers and reorganizing a few blooms. "It's your October bouquet."

Our very first date was to a local fundraiser that included a silent auction. One of the silent auction items was a year's supply of monthly floral arrangements from Wilde Flowers. Eric had the winning bid. When the first year of floral arrangements expired, Eric renewed it for a second year as an anniversary gift. We're nearing the end of my second year of flower deliveries.

"Thank you," I say. "How did you find time to create this masterpiece? You've been so busy with condolence flowers."

"I'm a professional florist, sweetie! We're super-heroes without capes." We laugh. "I delivered them here because I figured you might be out of space at home."

"You figured right," I confirm.

"And I thought you could use something pretty to cheer you up since your brother-in-law died."

"Thank you, Phillip."

While Phillip and I hug, it occurs to me that this is the first time I've seen him since Saturday. Because we're next-door neighbours, I take for granted that we see each other almost every day.

"How's Emmy?" Phillip asks.

"As well as you'd expect under the circumstances," I reply with my standard response.

"How's Eric feeling?" Phillip asks in a hushed tone.

The concerned tone in his voice worries me. He's asking like there's something wrong with Eric that he's not supposed to know about.

"Fine?" I reply, confused.

"Witch hazel," Phillip whispers with a wink. "Trust me. It worked wonders for my mother."

I'm about to ask why he thinks Eric needs witch hazel and what Phillip's mother used it for when the bell over the door jingles and Connie strides into the store.

"Hello, my dear." She hugs me tight and plants a kiss on my cheek. "Hello, Phillip." They give each other a side hug and exchange air kisses. "Where's Sophie?" Connie asks, marveling at the corgi-free space around her ankles, where Sophie usually waits in eager anticipation for Connie to greet her.

"At home with Emmy and Poppy," I reply. "Emmy likes to have her around."

Connie admires my October floral arrangement and compliments Phillip on his creative mastery, then takes off her jacket.

"I'll be right back," Connie says as she heads toward the back room to hang up her coat. "Oh my!" she declares, stopping at the counter. "Tina was here, wasn't she?" She holds up the jacket that Tina left draped across the counter. "I'll hang it in the back. She must go through so many jackets at the rate she leaves them behind," Connie chuckles on her way to the back room.

"I'll text Tina and let her know she left it here," I call after her.

"I should get back to the shop," Phillip says with a

sigh. "I have to fill an order and deliver it to the most unworthy recipient ever!"

"Who?" I ask, wondering who Phillip has deemed unworthy of his floral artistry.

"I can't even!"

He rolls his eyes and waves his hand in front of his face with a dramatic flourish.

"Yes, you can," I encourage.

"Fine. It's that horrible Sonia woman your sister works with."

Who ordered flowers for Sonia Chang? And what did she do to make Phillip deem her unworthy?

CHAPTER 20

"WHO ORDERED FLOWERS FOR SONIA?"

"Sonia Chang?" Connie asks, returning from the back room.

I nod and update her on what she missed while she was hanging up jackets.

"It's a corporate order from the Hendricks Agency," Phillip replies.

The Hendricks Agency is Brad's agency. Why would Brad buy Sonia flowers?

"Did they give you a message to write on the card?" I ask.

"Yes." He arches one eyebrow.

"What's the message?"

"Do you regret it yet? B."

Regret what? How vague and cryptic.

"That's it? That's the entire message?" I ask.

Phillip nods.

"I don't care if she won a Pulitzer Prize for Investigative Reporting, Sonia Chang is not a nice person,"

Phillip declares, crossing his arms in front of his chest.

"You've met her?" Connie asks.

"Yesterday," Phillip replies with a huff. "She came into Wilde Flowers with Rich Kendall to get flowers for Emmy."

"The flowers were beautiful, by the way," I interject. "The white and cream blooms with dark green foliage were…" I pinch my thumb and forefinger together and make a chef's kiss. "And I loved the presentation in kraft paper with black twine. Very trendy."

"Do NOT give me credit for that floral arrangement!" Phillip says, giving his foot a dramatic little stomp. "I didn't make it!"

"Who made it?" Connie asks. "Noah?"

Noah is Phillip's apprentice.

"No!" Phillip replies. "Sonia made it."

"You offer self-serve floral arrangements?" I ask, unaware Phillip offered this option.

"No!" Phillip shakes his head. "But that didn't stop Sonia Chang. She said she knew what she wanted. She walked around my shop and went INSIDE my floral cooler." He crosses his arms in front of him. "No one goes inside my floral cooler. She helped herself to whatever she wanted and acted like she owned the place. While she was collecting and arranging MY flowers, SHE gave ME tips for creating bouquets and took it upon herself to FIX arrangements I'd already made."

"Oh my," Connie says, gripping her pearls and shaking her head.

I'm not sure if the "Oh my" is in response to Sonia's

behaviour, Phillip's distress because of Sonia's behaviour, or both.

"Her parents owned a florist shop when she was growing up," I add, hoping some context might help soothe Phillip's hurt feelings.

"I know," Phillip responds. "She told me. She also told me my floral cooler was the wrong temperature, my arrangements were out of proportion, and she gave me a lesson in symmetry."

"Phillip, your floral arrangements are beautiful. Your proportions and symmetry are always perfect," I assure him, even though I'm not sure exactly what proportion and symmetry mean in the context of floral design.

"I know," Phillip concedes with less frustration and offense. "But it was hard to listen to her without defending myself."

"Why on earth didn't you defend yourself?" Connie asks.

"Because she's Sonia freaking Chang! The Pulitzer Prize-winning investigative reporter." He clears his throat. "I can barely say my own name in front of her. She's intimidating."

He's right, she is. Without saying a word, Sonia's mere silent presence can invoke an attack of self doubt. She's made of spectacular achievements and righteous confidence.

"There, there, Phillip," Connie comforts him and rubs his back. "Sonia will leave town in a few days. In the meantime, if you don't want to fill the order for her floral arrangement, don't. Let the Hendricks Agency find another florist to fill the order."

"And give her the satisfaction of intimidating me?" Phillip thrusts his chin into the air. "Never! I will create the most beautiful, proportioned, symmetrical floral arrangement the world has ever seen."

"You go, Phillip!

"Yes, you will!"

Connie and I cheer him on in unison as he leaves Knitorious.

"Wow," I say. "What do you think about that?"

"I think Phillip Wilde is the most talented florist I've ever met, regardless of Sonia Chang's opinion," Connie replies.

"I agree with you," I say. "Phillip is right about Sonia's tendency to take over. At my house, she insisted on arranging the flowers in a vase. She showed me the correct way to trim the stems and supervised while I did it. Her unapologetic assertiveness is one of the qualities that makes her so good at investigative journalism and television production."

"For someone as successful and controlling as Sonia Chang, it must've been difficult to accept that Rich fell in love with someone else, particularly someone Sonia regards as less accomplished than her." Connie makes a good point.

Could Sonia have intended to kill Emmy, but killed Armando instead? Or did Sonia kill Armando, then disclose his bigamy to give Emmy a motive for his murder? Not only would Sonia eliminate Emmy from *Hello, today!* and Rich Kendall's life, she would get accolades for uncovering Armando's bigamy and Emmy's motive.

"Why would Brad Hendricks send flowers to Sonia?" I wonder aloud. "Are they an item?"

"Who knows, my dear?" Connie shrugs. "But if they are, Sonia doesn't have a type, she has a spectrum. Brad and Rich are as different as two men can be."

She's right. Brad is intense and tenacious. He radiates competitiveness and ambition, and built his agency from scratch. Rich, on the other hand, is laid back and reactive. Thanks to his first-class private education, he's well-spoken and well-connected. He secured his audition for *Hello, today!* because he went to school with the son of the guy who runs the network.

Every instinct I have is tingling; something is going on between Brad and Sonia, and it goes deeper than dinner and flowers. If Armando's agent was dating Emmy's producer, Emmy would have told me. Whatever their situation is, it's a secret.

"Did you text Tina, my dear?" Connie asks, bringing me back to the here and now.

"Not yet," I reply. "I'll do it now."

I pull out my phone and send Tina a quick text.

While I have the text app open, I should text Adam. Maybe, as Emmy's lawyer, he can advise her not to return to work or give interviews while the police are investigating Armando's murder. My thumbs hover over the keyboard as I decide what to type. The bell over the door jingles.

"Hello, Megan."

"Hi, Mrs. Roblin. How are you?"

We go through the now-familiar exchange of pleasantries. She asks me how Emmy is, I answer, and she asks me to pass along condolences on her behalf. While we banter, I abandon the unfinished text message to Adam, lock my phone, and slide it under the counter.

Mrs. Roblin is a member of Harmony Lake's Charity Knitting Guild, a collective of local knitters who use knitting to benefit worthy causes. The Charity Knitters, as we call them, are the driving force behind this month's Knitted Knocker campaign.

"How's Eric's problem?" Mrs. Roblin whispers, leaning over the counter.

I lean too, and we meet halfway, our foreheads only inches apart.

"Eric's problem?" I ask, confused. Then I remember the comment Phillip made about witch hazel, and I wonder if Mrs. Roblin is referring to the same thing. "I don't know what problem you mean, Mrs. Roblin."

Does Eric have a problem I don't know about?

"You know," Mrs. Roblin urges in a whisper. "His problem?" She winks and turns sideways, arching her back so her butt sticks out, then glances at it over her shoulder.

Why is she showing me her backside?

"I'm sorry, I don't know what you're talking about," I admit with a shrug.

Mrs. Roblin reaches into her large knitting bag and pulls out a blue, ring-shaped memory foam pillow. She slides it to me across the counter. Why is she offering me a hemorrhoid pillow?

"I was going to take it to the police station, but I

thought this would be more discreet. And I was coming here anyway, so it's more convenient."

"A hemorrhoid pillow?"

Mrs. Roblin replies with an understanding nod.

I squeeze my eyes shut tight when I realize what's happening. Word has gotten around about the hemorrhoid ointment Eric purchased on Sunday for Emmy's eyes.

"This is very thoughtful, Mrs. Roblin, but Eric doesn't need it." I nudge the doughnut-shaped cushion toward her. "He purchased the ointment for someone else." I smile.

"I see." Mrs. Roblin smiles at me again. "Perhaps *you* would like to borrow the pillow, Megan?" She slides it toward me again. "Keep it as long as necessary. I don't need it." She taps the cushion with her fingertips.

"The ointment wasn't for me, either," I explain, bumping the pillow toward her. "It was for my sister." Mrs. Roblin slides the pillow toward me again and opens her mouth to speak. I put my hand on the pillow and stop it mid-slide before it crosses the halfway point between us. "For her eyes," I add before she can offer the hemorrhoid pillow to Emmy.

"Her eyes?" Mrs. Roblin asks, flabbergasted.

I explain to Mrs. Roblin how people—TV people in particular, according to Emmy—sometimes use hemorrhoid cream to reduce swelling. Like when your eyes are swollen from crying because your husband died.

Excited about this potential new use for hemorrhoid

cream, Mrs. Roblin asks me if it would help her swollen ankles.

"I doubt it," I caution, hating to dampen her enthusiasm. "You should ask a medical professional before you apply it anywhere other than what the tube recommends."

"I'll go straight to the pharmacy after my shift and ask the pharmacist," Mrs. Roblin announces with glee.

"Your shift?" I ask.

"Yes, my shift," she reiterates. "I didn't just stop in to drop off the pillow. I'm here to help Connie watch the store so you can take care of your grieving sister and pursue your *hobby.*" Mrs. Roblin opens her mouth and gives me an exaggerated wink.

My *hobby* is how The Charity Knitters refer to my propensity for sleuthing. They have taken it upon themselves to encourage and support my hobby because its inline with their aim of ensuring Harmony Lake remains the cozy, tight-knit, safe community we all know and love.

"I told her not to come in today, Verna, but she wouldn't listen," Connie chimes in, addressing Mrs. Roblin by her first name. "I told Megan the store would be fine without her, but she insisted on working today."

"We're short-staffed," I justify. "Marla is working at Artsy Tartsy until April gets back from…"

"Nonsense," Mrs. Roblin interrupts, joining me behind the counter and bumping me out of the way with her hip when she bends over to stuff her large knitting bag under the counter. "You're not short staffed. I'm here. Connie ran this store for almost forty years before you took over, Megan. I'm sure she can manage a few more days."

Mrs. Roblin flashes me a smile so sweet she might melt if she stepped outside in the rain.

There's no point fighting it, I'm overruled.

"Well, I was only working a half-day anyway, so I guess I can leave early."

It's not like I have a choice. I'm outnumbered, and they know when they join forces, I can't win.

"Take tomorrow off, too, my dear," Connie says, rubbing my arm. "Take care of Emmy."

"And every day after that until you finish your *hobby*," Mrs. Roblin adds with another indiscreet wink.

I collect my jacket and bag, then retrieve my phone from under the counter and text Adam.

Me: Can we meet? It's about Emmy.

Adam: I was going to text you the same thing. Can you come to my office?

Me: Law office or town hall?

Adam: Town Hall in forty-five minutes?

Me: I'll be there.

Harmony Lake Town Hall is a short walk from Knitorious. It would take longer to drive there and find parking than to walk. Also, it's not raining right now, and I can use some fresh air to clear my muddled thoughts.

I thank Connie and Mrs. Roblin for looking after Knitorious and remind them to call or text me if they need anything. Then, I leave through the front door and turn left, toward Latté Da. I have time to kill—pardon the pun—so I may as well get a chocolate caramel latté and savour it on my walk to the mayor's office.

As I approach Latté Da, a familiar, athletic figure lights a cigarette on the sidewalk outside the coffee shop. Brad Hendricks. Why is he at Latté Da? Is he satisfying a craving for the best coffee in the world, or is he posting his latest anti-Emmy blog post?

CHAPTER 21

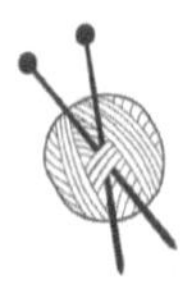

"MEGAN!" Brad smiles.

"Brad!" I smile. "What brings you to the best coffee shop in the world?"

"This is my office today," he replies, holding his cigarette at arm's length and hugging me with his free arm. "I need to answer emails and stuff. The hotel is great, but their coffee is *meh*. I need good coffee, and I can work anywhere there's Wi-Fi."

The cigarette smoke ghosts a blue trail toward me, biting my nose and throat when I inhale.

"Smoke break?" I ask, nodding toward his cigarette.

"Yup. I reward myself with regular breaks. My laptop is inside." He jerks his thumb behind him. "How's Emmy doing?"

"Not great," I reply. "But she's strong. She'll be OK."

"How are you doing? You found him. That must be hard to deal with."

"It is. But I'll be OK too. I have a lot of support," I reply. "How are you?"

"I have to stop myself from texting him about ten times a day," Brad says, his voice thick with emotion. "I have to take calls, and answer emails, and act like everything is normal, and my best friend didn't die two days ago."

"I'm sorry for your loss," I say.

"Ditto."

"I was just talking about you this morning," I say, changing the subject.

"Good things I hope?" Brad gives me a wink and a sideways grin.

"My neighbour, the florist, was filling an order for The Hendricks Agency," I say, watching Brad's face for a reaction. Nothing.

"I guess what they say about small town gossip is true," Brad chortles, taking a drag off his cigarette and exhaling a cloud of white smoke.

"We're more tight-knit than you city-folk are used to," I say, playing along. "Which lucky lady will receive one of Phillip's gorgeous floral arrangements?"

"It's not what you think," Brach chuckles. "A client and his wife had a baby."

He's lying with a straight face while looking me in the eye. No fidgeting, no sweating. He takes another drag of his cigarette without breaking eye contact.

"I thought they might be for someone special." I smile.

"Megan, if you're asking if I'm available, the answer is yes." Brad puts his hands on the wall behind me, trapping me, then narrows his eyes and brings his face closer until we're almost nose-to-nose. He reeks of stale cigarettes and coffee. "I thought you were wrapped up tight in Chief Sloane's long arm of the law," he says in a low, husky voice. "But I'll be in town for a few more days if you want to get together."

He's uncomfortably close. Being pinned between his ego and the wall is making me claustrophobic. Brad moves his hand to bring his cigarette to his mouth, and I duck out of his man-made cage, retreating to a safe distance. He turns to face me, leaning his back against the wall and flicking cigarette ash onto the sidewalk.

"No, thanks," I sneer. "I don't mess around, and you're not my type."

"It was a joke, Megan!" Brad's awkward laugh doesn't conceal his wounded pride. "I was kidding." He exaggerates his words and shrugs with his hands facing the sky. "But for real, Chief Sloane is a lucky man. I apologize if you thought I was serious. To be honest, I haven't been myself since Armando died."

He drops his cigarette butt on the sidewalk. "The police are still at the hotel, and Sloane keeps asking me questions. The same questions over and over. It's making me paranoid. He acts like he doesn't believe me, and he's trying to catch me in a lie."

He rubs the ball of his foot on the cigarette butt.

"*Will* he catch you in a lie?" I ask.

"Of course not," Brad retorts, bending down to pick up the flattened cigarette butt and lobbing it into a nearby trash can. "Anyway, I lawyered up. Your fiancé can't question me anymore unless my lawyer is present."

"Then why are you paranoid?"

"I returned to my room around the time Armando died," Brad reveals. "The keycard keeps a record every time I unlock the door. Eric kept asking if I saw anyone or anything strange near Armando's room when I entered my room."

"Did you?"

"No," Brad shrugs. "I turned right off the elevator. Armando's room is left. I didn't look left. I saw nothing."

"Where were you before you returned to your room?" I ask.

"Gym," Brad replies. "But there's no proof. Another guest used his keycard to unlock the door and held it open for me." He shoves his hands in his pants pockets. "My lawyer says my alibi is weak."

"The guest who let you in can confirm it," I suggest.

"I used the weight room, and he used the sauna. We didn't see each other again."

"And because you didn't need your keycard to *leave* the gym, you can't prove how long you were there," I deduce.

"Right," Brad says. "And there aren't a lot of security cameras at the hotel. Which, ironically, was one reason I booked it. Privacy was important to Armando, and he didn't like hotels that record his every move."

"Armando was your best friend," I say, summoning my most sympathetic voice. "I'm sure if you had *any* information, *any at all*, you'd tell the police. Because you want to find your best friend's killer just as much as they do, right?"

"Yeah,"—Brad shrugs one shoulder—"of course I

would. But they don't need to know *everything*. Like they don't need to know about something that won't help them. Like small insignificant stuff that has nothing to do with Armando's death."

I get the sense Brad didn't tell the police the whole truth about the morning Armando died.

"Sometimes, information that seems insignificant is important. Eric says they solve cases all the time because of a small, seemingly insignificant tip." I pause. Brad's eyes dart left and right like a trapped animal looking for an escape route. "What's insignificant to you could be the key to putting Armando's killer behind bars."

"Megan, if I tell you something, will you tell me if you think it's significant?"

"Of course. Armando was my brother-in-law. I want justice for him as much as you."

"The night before he died, I texted Armando about going to the gym in the morning. He didn't text me back. I wasn't surprised. Emmy was there, and I figured he was taking time away from his phone." Perspiration beads on Brad's forehead. "The next morning, when Armando still hadn't replied to my text, I left for the gym without him. While I was waiting for the elevator, I heard a knock. Someone from room service was knocking on Armando's door. The door to Armando's room opened just as I stepped onto the elevator."

"Did you see Armando open the door?" I ask.

"No, but the lady who delivered the food said, 'Good morning, Mr. Garcia,' and I heard Armando say, 'Good morning' as the elevator door closed."

Didn't Eric say the room service employee who delivered Armando's food was a man?

"You heard a woman's voice, then Armando's voice," I confirm.

"Right."

"Would you recognize her if you saw her again?"

"I think so," Brad replies with a one-shoulder shrug.

"Why didn't you tell the police?"

"Because of what happened next," Brad looks at his feet, embarrassed. "After the gym, I returned to my room and had a shower. Then I texted Armando again. He read the text but didn't reply. He left me on read, Megan. My best friend left me on read!"

According to my twenty-year-old daughter, Hannah, leaving someone *on read* is rude and a major breach of online etiquette. *On read* means you read the text message but didn't reply.

"You thought Armando was ignoring you?"

"It's the only logical conclusion, right?!" Brad smiles, and his face relaxes with relief.

He interprets my question as validation of his frustration, not as the confirmation of fact that I intended it to be.

If Brad's ego is as fragile as it is enormous, being ignored by Armando would have angered and offended him. Was Brad angry and offended enough to kill Armando?

"What did you do about it?" I ask. "You didn't let Armando ignore you and not *do* anything, right?"

I continue to sympathize, hoping Brad will continue to confide more details.

"I went to his room again," Brad replies, vindicated.

"You were inside Armando's hotel room on Sunday morning?" I ask, trying to hide my shock.

"No." Brad replies. "I knocked, but Armando didn't answer the door." He shifts his weight from one foot to the other, and beads of sweat form on his upper lip. "I knocked again and shouted, 'Hey buddy! It's me. Open the door.'"

"Did Armando open the door?"

Brad shakes his head, and his dark eyes fill with moisture.

"I should've kept knocking," Brad says, then swallows hard. "I shouldn't have left. Maybe if I forced him to answer, Armando would still be alive. But I was mad. I thought he was ignoring me. I thought he and Emmy were in there laughing at me. I stomped down the hall to my room."

"I don't think Armando was ignoring you," I say. "Emmy wasn't there, she was at brunch with me. It's possible, when you knocked, Armando was already dead."

"He wasn't dead, Megan," Brad says matter-of-factly. "He read my text message a few minutes before."

"Maybe he was debilitated and unable to answer the door," I suggest.

"Then why did he open it to hang the DO NOT DISTURB sign?"

"You saw Armando open the door and hang the sign?"

"No, I was walking back to my room when I heard a door open and close. I knew it was Armando's door. I stomped back to Armando's room, and he'd hung the DO NOT DISTURB sign on the door."

"And it wasn't there before?" I confirm.

Brad shakes his head.

"The sign was still swinging."

A shiver runs along my spine when I imagine Armando's killer's hand hanging the DO NOT DISTURB sign on his door.

CHAPTER 22

ADAM FLARES his nostrils and twitches his nose.

"Meg, have you been smoking?" he asks, closing his office door and pausing on the way to his desk to sniff around me.

"You know I don't smoke," I reply. "Brad Hendricks smokes, and I was just with him."

"What were you doing with *Brad Hendricks*?" Adam asks, pronouncing Brad's name with a scornful inflection.

"Getting lied to," I respond, laying my jacket over the back of the chair in the mayor's office.

"Be careful around him, Meg. He's a lech."

Adam sits behind his desk and leans back, resting his ankle on his opposite knee and swiveling his chair in lazy semicircles.

"You've only met him twice. How do you know he's a lech?"

"Remember Emmy and Armando's reception? Brad asked me if I knew you and if you were single." Adam rolls his eyes. "Even after I told him I was your husband, he kept looking at you like your dress was filet mignon."

"You never told me that," I say.

"I forgot about it until I saw him at Latté Da earlier."

"Anyway," I say, directing the conversation to the reason for our meeting. "Rumour has it, Emmy is returning to work tomorrow. A segment for *Hello, today!* because they want to capitalize on the increased viewership Monday's show had."

Adam sighs. "It's not a good idea, Meg. Emmy shouldn't make any public statements or answer questions. Armando's death is an active murder investigation. She could say something to implicate herself."

"I know. That's why I'm here," I say. "I'm hoping that, as her lawyer, you'll help me convince her it's a bad idea." I shake my head and huff. "I can't believe they'd exploit Emmy's grief to increase their ratings."

"Emmy knows the score," Adam asserts. "She's grieving, Meg, but your sister is smart, and she's been in the industry a long time. She knows they want to increase ratings and lure new viewers to the show. If Emmy agreed to do it, she knows what she agreed to. It's not in her best interest, and I'll tell her that, but she's not as naïve as you think."

"But she's grieving, and maybe she's not thinking straight. Someone has to look out for her. And by someone, I mean us. I'm her sister, and you're her lawyer."

"Speaking of looking out for Emmy," Adam segues, opening a file folder on his desk. "Sonia told you the truth. Armando Garcia was already married when he married Emmy. There's no record of his first marriage ending in divorce, death, or annulment. He was still married to the first Mrs. Garcia when he died."

"This will break Emmy's heart, Adam," I say, on the verge of tears.

"There's more," he says, stone-faced. "The first Mrs. Garcia has three children, and Armando's name is on the birth certificates as their father."

"Armando had kids?"

I'm gobsmacked. My mouth hangs ajar, speechless.

"The youngest is three years old."

"How is that possible?" I demand. "Armando hasn't returned to Ecuador since he left fifteen years ago." I pause while a thought occurs to me. "Unless she comes here..."

Adam raises his hands off his desk, then lowers them again in a calm-down gesture, interrupting my train of thought.

"We won't mention the kids yet," he says. "We should tell Emmy about Armando's first wife, but I don't think we should mention the potential kids. Just because his name is on the birth certificates, doesn't mean he's the biological father."

"What about the rest of Armando's family?"

"Nothing as exciting," Adam replies, flipping through the pages in the open file folder. "His parents live in Ecuador. They previously lived in Brazil and Columbia. Emmy was right about Armando having a sister. Her name is Cristina Garcia. She emigrated years ago. I couldn't find anything else about her. She probably got married and changed her last name. And the best friend Emmy mentioned, who was like a brother to Armando, kind of *was* Armando's brother. His name is Mateo Cruz. Mateo's parents died in a single-vehicle car accident when he was eleven. Mateo was the only survivor. The Cruz family and the Garcia family were friends, and Armando's parents became Mateo's legal guardians. I haven't found any information about Mateo Cruz's life after the Garcias became his legal guardians."

"Anything else?" I ask. "I'd like to get the shock over with at once."

Hello, world! Guess who's making a comeback?

Rumour has it our favourite mourning show host is plotting a comeback this week. We knew she'd come out from under the mountain of casserole dishes and condolence flowers, eventually. Her smitten co-host is thrilled. He can't wait to have her on the sofa again! Meanwhile, the grieving widow's crafty sister has been knotty! She and a certain sports agent got up close and personal outside a trendy café. Was he whispering sweet nothings in her ear or just blowing smoke? Was she needling him for information about a certain soccer player's last kick at the ball?

"Ugggggghhhh," I groan, when April finishes reading the disgraceful drivel. "The double entendres are horrendous!"

"I know, right?!" April agrees. "I cringed when I read it."

"When was it posted?" I ask.

"A few minutes ago," April replies. "I subscribed to the stupid blog, so I'll get notified whenever they publish a new post."

"Can you send me the link?"

I'm in the car, on my way home from Adam's office. April called me to tell me about the mystery blogger's latest post.

"What were you and Brad doing outside Latté Da?" April asks. "The blog implies you and Brad were... cozy."

I tell April about Brad pinning me against the wall.

"The mystery blogger misinterpreted the situation," I add.

"What a creep!" April exclaims.

I'm not sure if she means Brad or the mystery blogger, but the descriptor applies to both.

"Brad must be the mystery blogger," I surmise. "Who else could it be?"

"How would Brad Hendricks know about Emmy returning to work?" April asks.

"Sonia!"

I tell April about the flower order for Sonia from Brad's agency.

"Talk about strange bedfellows," she says. "If Brad and Sonia are an item, why did he make you an indecent proposal?"

So many questions, so few answers.

"WHERE'S POPPY?" I ask, crouching down to greet Sophie.

"She went to Harmony Hills to get a new phone. She destroyed hers."

"What happened to it?"

"She was doing my laundry and somehow dropped her phone in the load of darks," Emmy says, sitting sideways with her knees slung over the arm of the chair, leafing through a bridal magazine. "She spent all morning searching for it. I found it when I helped her fold the laundry."

"You let Poppy do your laundry?" I ask, wondering if laundry is a PA task or a best friend task.

"I don't *let* her do it. She wants to do it." Emmy shrugs. "She just *does* it. Poppy's always auditing my life, searching for things to fix. Today she fixed my laundry situation." She raises her index finger. "Technically, she did *your* laundry since I've been wearing your clothes since Sunday."

Emmy closes the magazine and adds it to the pile on the floor next to the chair.

"The closest phone store is in Harmony Hills," I say.

"She knows," Emmy says. "She looked it up on my phone. The good news is, Poppy's phone was insured. She gets an identical replacement, and it won't cost her anything."

Reaching for Sophie's leash, I spy a familiar to-go cup on the kitchen counter. "Did you go out today?"

"I sat in the car while Poppy ran into Latté Da," Emmy replies. "Their pumpkin spice is addictive."

I'm glad Emmy left the house and drank something without being nagged into submission.

"Adam's coming over. He wants to talk to you. I texted you, but you didn't reply." I say, attaching Sophie's leash.

"Sorry," Emmy says. "I gave Poppy my phone to ease her anxiety about not having one. And I didn't want her to drive all the way to Harmony Hills without one."

"Poppy knows the password to unlock your phone?"

"Sometimes Poppy needs to access my phone for work," Emmy explains, picking up the pile of magazines.

"I'm taking Sophie for a walk before Adam gets here."

Eric's car pulls into the driveway as Sophie and I step outside. We wait for him at the top of the driveway. Sophie tippy-taps her front paws, excited to greet him. Me too, Sophie, me too.

"Hey, handsome."

"Want some company?" Eric asks, getting out of his car.

We meander down the street hand-in-hand, stopping at trees, fire hydrants, and wherever else Sophie's nose dictates.

"How's your day?" I ask.

"Weird," Eric says, rubbing the back of his neck. "People keep asking how I'm feeling. They look at me like they pity me. Two people suggested I try witch hazel, and a third asked me if I've had a bath with

Epsom salts. I told them I didn't know what they were talking about, but they just smiled and nodded. The desk sergeant switched chairs with me because his chair is softer and better for my problem. What problem? Babe, I don't know what they're talking about."

"They're talking about your heinie, honey," I say, giving it a discreet tap.

I explain to Eric how word spread about the hemorrhoid cream he purchased for Emmy.

He doubles over laughing so hard he grabs his stomach because it hurts.

"I bought three tubes!" He says between fits of laughter. "I didn't know what brand to get." He wipes tears from his eyes. "Everyone must think my hemorrhoid situation is pretty serious."

"Connie and Mrs. Roblin know the truth," I tell him. "I assured them your derriere is perfect. Word should spread through the rest of the town by tonight."

"I guess my backside being the *butt* of local gossip is a hazard of living in a small, tight-knit community." His amusement at his own pun triggers a laughter aftershock.

Eric's butt pun reminds me of today's blog post.

"There's another blog post," I say.

"I know," Eric responds. "You talked to Brad Hendricks."

"Yes," I confirm. "But it wasn't as intimate as the blog post suggests."

I tell Eric about my interaction with Brad, including the part where he trapped me between him and the wall.

"Did any part of him touch any part of you?" Eric asks, his jaw clenching and unclenching.

"No," I assure him. "He only trapped me for a few seconds. The blogger just had perfect timing."

"I need to show Brad a photo lineup of employees who worked at Rise & Glide on Sunday. With any luck, he'll recognize the woman he saw delivering food to Armando's room. While he's there, I'll pin him against a wall and talk to him about personal space and respect."

"I don't know if I believe his story," I say. "Lying comes easy to Brad. When he lied about the flowers he ordered for Sonia, he didn't fidget, blink, twitch, or break eye contact. If I didn't know for a fact that the flowers were for Sonia, I would've believed his lie."

"The cigarette package we found in Armando's room and the butts on the balcony belong to Brad," Eric says. "Forensics confirmed Brad's DNA was the only DNA present on them."

"DNA doesn't prove *when* Brad was in Armando's room," I point out. "He admits he was there on Saturday, but no one noticed the cigarette butts or empty cigarette pack until Sunday. We only have Brad's word for when he was inside the room. And he's already lied at least once."

"Deb confirmed that Armando declined housekeeping services when he checked in, and there's no record of him requesting anything that housekeeping would have delivered to his room."

"Then why did housekeeping enter his room on Saturday morning?" I ask.

"I've interviewed the housekeeping employees, and they deny being in his room."

"Great, another mystery to solve."

"We know how the drugs got into Armando's system," Eric says.

"How?"

"The killer drugged the food on the room service cart."

"Does that mean you suspect the employee who delivered the food? Or whoever prepared the food?"

"I wish it were that easy," Eric says with a sigh. "Armando followed a strict eating plan that required him to eat specific foods at specific times. He gave a copy to the hotel when he checked in on Friday. The chef posted it on the kitchen wall. Some items on Armando's eating plan aren't foods the hotel typically stocks. They brought in food just for him. They segregated it, labelled with his name and room number. Anyone who had access to the kitchen had access to the food. They'd know which food was Armando's and even when each item would be prepared and delivered to him."

I flashback to when Deb escorted Emmy and me out of the hotel through the delivery entrance.

"The delivery entrance is by the kitchen," I say. "When we left the hotel on Sunday, Deb took Emmy and I to the delivery entrance. The kitchen is right there. The punch clock is right there. Employees were coming and going from their shifts, and employees who were on their breaks were socializing just outside the delivery entrance. Anyone could have accessed Armando's food."

"Even someone who doesn't work there, like delivery people," Eric adds. "And when the weather is nicc, they leave the door open for fresh air."

"This eliminates Emmy as a suspect, right?"

"The food arrived after you and Emmy left for brunch. Since Emmy didn't have access to the food to tamper with it, she can't be the murderer."

"That's amazing!" I stand on my tippy toes, throw my arms around his neck, and give him a kiss. "I'm so relieved. We can tell Emmy, right? As soon as we get home?"

"Absolutely!"

"This might make it easier for Emmy to hear the news about Armando's first wife," I hope aloud.

"The cyber unit found the source of the second blog post."

"The one posted on Sunday?" I ask. "About Armando's death?"

"It was posted from Emmy's phone."

I sigh and nod, unsurprised.

"Of course, it was," I mutter, rolling my eyes and shaking my head.

"Babe, are you sure Emmy didn't go to Latté Da on Sunday? She didn't have to go inside. She could've picked up the Wi-Fi signal from the parking lot or the sidewalk."

"I can guarantee Emmy wasn't anywhere near Latté Da on Sunday, but I can't say the same about her phone."

CHAPTER 23

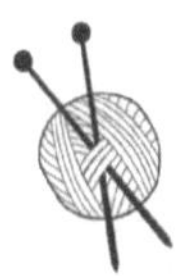

"It's a silent montage," Emmy pleads. "I won't even wear a mic. The camera crew will get footage of me looking forlorn. They'll edit the footage so it captures the essence of my grief. Now that Eric has eliminated me as a suspect, I don't have to worry about incriminating myself."

"They're using you to increase ratings," Adam points out.

"And I'm using them to counteract the negative publicity I've gotten since Armando died."

"What negative publicity?" Adam asks.

"I'll text you links," Eric replies, referring to the gossip blog.

"That gossip blog makes me seem like a merry widow, and when the media covers Armando's death, they use photos of Armando and I smiling and laughing. The world needs to see that I'm a real person and my grief is real."

"You know about the gossip blog?" I ask.

"*You* know about the gossip blog?" Emmy retorts.

"I found it by accident on Sunday. How did you find out?"

"People told me," Emmy replies with a shrug.

"You weren't supposed to find out," I say. "We didn't want you to stress about it."

"We?" Emmy asks.

"Poppy and April and me," I reply. "April monitors the blog and tells me about new posts. Poppy offered to contact the blog and ask them to remove the posts."

Emmy chuckles. "Poppy didn't contact them, did she?"

"She forgot," I reply. "The last few days have been overwhelming. I'm not surprised she forgot. But they deleted the posts, anyway. How do you know Poppy didn't contact them?"

"Poppy is the most non-confrontational person I know," Emmy replies. "She doesn't even send back food at a restaurant when they give her the wrong order. Sending a cease-and-desist letter would be way outside her comfort zone. The blog deleted the posts because *I* contacted them."

"There's something else we need to talk to you about," I say. "Did you and Armando ever talk about your previous marriages?"

"Of course," Emmy replies. "He knew about both of my previous marriages."

"How about Armando?" Adam asks. "Was he ever married before you?"

"No," Emmy insists. "He was too focused on his career to have a serious relationship."

"Armando was married to someone else before he married you," I state.

"Who told you this lie?" Emmy demands, crossing her arms in front of her chest and arranging her legs in an aristocratic leg cross.

She bounces her foot in the air.

"Sonia Chang," I reply.

"Lies!" Emmy rolls her eyes, bouncing her foot harder and faster. "Sonia hates me. She's been trying to get rid of me since the day they hired me."

"She has proof."

"Fake!"

"I verified it, Emmy," Adam adds. "It's true."

"I verified it too," Eric says. "As part of the investigation. Adam and I came to the same conclusion as Sonia."

"Fine!" Emmy shrugs one shoulder. "So what? Armando was divorced and didn't tell me. Big deal. It changes nothing."

"He wasn't divorced," I say. "Armando was still married to his first wife when he died."

Emmy lets out a gasp like someone punched her in the gut. She looks from me to Adam to Eric, searching for a hint of doubt. We're all steadfast and certain.

"Sonia must love this," she scoffs. "I bet that smug, arrogant witch couldn't wait to tell you."

Emmy's face flushes with angry heat.

"It's not about her, Emmy," Eric says.

"Why was Sonia looking into Armando's past, anyway?" Emmy asks.

"She said she was following an unrelated tip, and somehow it led to him. She wouldn't elaborate," I say.

"There was no other tip," Emmy concludes with a huff. "I bet she looked for something scandalous in my past, but my life's an open book. When she couldn't find anything to destroy me, she went after Armando. No wonder she won a Pulitzer." Emmy scoffs. "Show me the proof."

I watch Adam pass the file folder on his lap to Emmy, hoping he removed the birth certificates.

As Emmy flips through the pages, inspecting each one, her demeanour weakens from hostile denial to broken sadness.

"You guys know his sister's name, his best friend's name, his parents' names… you know Armando better after three days than I did after three years." She closes the file and drops it on the coffee table. "My husband was a stranger."

"This doesn't change how you felt about each other," Eric reminds her. "It doesn't change that Armando loved you and you love him."

"I'm not even his widow, a woman in South America is." Emmy swallows hard, choking back tears, and dabbing her eyes with the cuff of her—my—half-button chambray shirt. "There's no way I'm doing the grief montage for *Hello, to*day!" She shakes her head with angry determination. "Not anymore. Where's my phone?" Emmy scans the room for her phone.

"Poppy has it," I remind her.

"I need it," Emmy says. "I need to call them and tell them I won't be filming tomorrow. The contact information is in my phone. I need Poppy to bring back my phone."

"I'll pick it up for you," I offer.

It's time to confront the non-confrontational Poppy and shove her outside her comfort zone.

ROOM 204... 206... 208. I take a deep breath and remind myself to stay calm. Heavy shoulders, long arms. One more deep breath. I knock on the door.

"Hey, Megan!"

I force a smile.

"Hi, Poppy."

She stands aside so I can enter the small motel room.

"Where's Emmy?"

"At home."

"Who's with her?"

Poppy's forehead corrugates with worry. Is her concern authentic? Since learning Poppy Prescott isn't who I thought she was, I'm not sure if anything she says or does is genuine.

"Eric," I reply. "Emmy needs her phone. I'm here to pick it up."

"Sure thing," Poppy says, unplugging Emmy's phone from the nightstand between the two double beds. "Tell her I said thank you."

She extends the phone toward me.

"Did you publish the blog post when you were at Latté Da with Emmy or when you went to get your new phone?" I ask, snatching the phone from Poppy's hand.

"W-what blog post?"

"Today's blog post," I specify. "I get why you're confused since you post so many. This was your third one since Saturday, right?"

"What are you talking about?" Poppy screws up her face in confusion and lets out a nervous half-laugh.

"You're the mystery blogger."

"What?" Poppy asks, her brown eyes wide. "Why would you think that?"

"Where should I start?" I jab my fists into my hips and jut out my neck with righteous indignation. "The mystery blogger followed Emmy to Harmony Lake. You followed Emmy to Harmony Lake. The first blog post, about Emmy and Armando's marital problems, was published at a coffee shop near Emmy's house before you left for Harmony Lake. The second post, about Armando's death, was published at Latté Da using Emmy's phone. Except Emmy wasn't anywhere near Latté Da on Sunday. But her phone was."

"How did Emmy's phone go to Latté Da without her?" Poppy asks.

"You took it," I reply. "You stayed with Emmy in the guest room until she fell asleep. Then, when you left to pick up her essentials, you took her phone with you. You returned it when you got back. You used Emmy's phone to frame her as the mystery blogger. When I told you about the first blog post, you pretended not to know about it. But your eyes filled with fear when I told you the police were looking into it. Then, when we discussed the second blog post, you asked me if the police would be able to find the blogger's location *and* device. You panicked when I told you they might locate the device. You panicked so much that you destroyed your phone and replaced it with an identical one." I point to Poppy's phone on the nightstand. "You put your phone in the laundry and told Emmy you lost it. You were planning to tell Emmy you found your phone when you got the new, identical replacement. But Emmy thwarted your plan when she found your old phone in the laundry. If your plan had worked, when the police traced the blog to your phone, you would've tried to deny it by giving them your new phone and claiming you couldn't be the blogger. Today, you published another blog post from Latté Da using Emmy's phone, ensuring the finger of suspicion would point at her instead of you."

"I wasn't at Latté Da today," Poppy insists. "I was at your house with Emmy. Then I went to Harmony Hills to get a new phone."

"Yes, you were. Emmy waited in the car while you went in. The cup from her pumpkin spice coffee is still in the kitchen. You saw Brad and I on the sidewalk outside."

"Does Emmy know?" Poppy asks, defeated and lowering herself to sit on the edge of the bed.

"I don't know. I think she might," I reply. "I suspected it was you when she told me you knew her password, but something she said made me certain."

"What did she say?"

"She said you're the most non-confrontational person she knows," I say, quoting Emmy. "It made me realize the blogger is a coward. Only a coward would say such hateful, cruel things and hide behind the anonymity of the internet. The other people I suspected are too direct and opinionated to hide their hate behind an anonymous blog post. They prefer to hate Emmy honestly and in the open."

"Please don't tell her," Poppy pleads, pressing her palms together.

"Why did you do it?" I ask, ignoring her plea. "Do you hate Emmy?"

"I love Emmy. She's my best friend," Poppy explains. "But sometimes I get… frustrated at how entitled she is and how much adoration she gets. Don't tell me you don't see it, Megan. Like after Armando died, Emmy worried about what people would say about her puffy eyes. She freaked out when I couldn't find the right brand of moisturizer because she doesn't want her skin to breakout while she's in mourning. She had a gorgeous husband who worshipped her, but she played head games with him and made him chase her across the country to prove it. Men trip over themselves to get any attention from her. Rich Kendall has been in love with her for years, and his constant attention annoys her. Big companies rush products to your house with overnight delivery just so she'll keep using their stuff. It's like the world revolves around her, and she expects it to."

"She didn't deserve the vitriol you posted about her, Poppy. Or to be framed for it."

"I know. You're right."

"What about the other posts? The non-Emmy posts. Did you write those too?"

Poppy nods. "Do you know what my superpower is?"

"Bad puns?"

"My other superpower," she chuckles. "Invisibility. People don't notice me. I blend into the background. People talk like I'm not in the room. It doesn't occur to them that I'm listening. And even when they notice me, it's a matter of time before they get used to my presence and act like I'm not there. I hear a lot of stuff, Megan. A LOT. I need to put it somewhere. Do something with it. The gossip blog is my outlet. I leave the other posts, but I delete the posts about Emmy because I love her. I posted them when I was angry or frustrated, but when the feeling passed, I deleted them."

"Not because she sent you a cease-and-desist email?"

"I get those all the time." Poppy flicks her wrist. "I ignore them."

This explains why, as April pointed out, the blog focuses on people related to the network that airs *Hello, today!* and the cast members of *Perfect Match.* Poppy works there. She's in the building every day.

"Do the police know I'm the mystery blogger?"

"I asked Eric to let me talk to you first. I can't make any promises, but I'll ask him to consider this a private matter if you help me."

"Anything."

"First, delete today's blog post about Emmy."

"Already done," Poppy says. "I deleted it about an hour ago. And I promise I won't write anymore gossip posts about Emmy."

"Next, what's the deal with Brad Hendricks and Sonia Chang?"

"They dated for a while on the down low," Poppy replies. "I got the feeling Brad was more into Sonia than Sonia was into him. I think she used him for his physical attributes, if you know what I mean, and hoped he would make Rich jealous. It didn't work. Rich only has eyes for Emmy.

"Past tense? They aren't together anymore?"

"Sonia ended it about two weeks ago. Brad didn't take it well. He even showed up at the station to see her. Sonia didn't like that. She told him if he came to the station again, she'd get security to escort him out. She hates attention unless it's attention for how good she is at her job. Sonia is always secretive, but for the past couple of weeks, she's been more secretive than usual. I noticed she started carrying a second phone and disappears when it rings."

"Does Sonia smoke?" I ask.

"No. Definitely not. Sonia's a health nut. Her entire life is a practice in control and discipline. She follows a strict diet and exercise plan and says smoking is pollution for the body."

Sonia had a faint aroma of cigarette smoke when she was at my house on Monday and said she knew what Brad said about *Perfect Match* devaluing the Armando Garcia brand. He made that comment to Armando on Thursday. How did Sonia hear about it? Emmy didn't tell her. It had to be Brad. If Sonia hates smoking, why was she dating him? Is Brad her source? Did he tell her about Armando's first wife? Did Sonia date Brad to use him for information about Emmy and Armando?

"WHERE'S EMMY?" I ask Eric, who's hunched over the coffee table typing on his laptop, surrounded by papers.

"Bathtub," he replies. "She said you're out of Himalayan bath salts."

"Because she uses them every day," I grumble, dropping my tired self onto the sofa next to him.

"How did it go with Poppy?" Eric asks, leaning back.

"As we expected," I reply, then tell him about our illuminating conversation.

"At least we can cross one mystery off the list," Eric says. "Do you think Poppy killed Armando?"

"No," I say, shaking my head. "What motive would she have?"

Sophie jumps up and nestles between us.

"What motive did she have for the blog posts?" Eric asks, answering my question with another question.

"Frustration. Jealousy. But I don't think she's frustrated or jealous enough to kill Armando. Her goal with the blog is to vent, not to hurt anyone. That's why she doesn't use names, and that's why she deleted the posts about Emmy. Poppy promised she wouldn't write anymore anti-Emmy blog posts."

"Will you tell Emmy that Poppy is the mystery blogger?"

"I think so." I nod. "I suspect she knows, but I'll tell her, anyway."

"Do you think it'll ruin their friendship, babe?"

I shrug. "That's up to them."

"Did you learn anything else?"

"Sonia and Brad were dating. I don't know how long they were together, but it was hush-hush, and she ended it two weeks ago."

The coroner's report is open on Eric's laptop.

"Do you know where the killer got the Rohypnol and the Fentanyl?" I ask.

"They're common street drugs," Eric replies. "The killer could've gotten them anywhere. But they had to get them in advance. And plan how and when to contaminate Armando's food. This is a premeditated murder, not a crime of opportunity. The killer had to arrange everything ahead of time."

"Revenge," I suggest, eyeing the coroner's report. "The killer–or killers–had time to let their anger fester and plot their revenge."

"We released the crime scene," Eric says. "Emmy can pick up her stuff whenever she wants."

"Did you tell Emmy already?"

Eric nods. "She wants to go in the morning. Let me know if you need help. I have to go to Rise & Glide anyway to interview employees."

"Did you interview the person who delivered Armando's food?"

"He's still sick," Eric replies. "Deb said he got dehydrated and needed IV fluids."

"I guess gut rot isn't as fast as Tina says it is."

"Tina?" Eric asks. "The knitter?"

"She had gut rot on Sunday and Monday. She said it was an intense twenty-four-hour bug."

"Tina works at Rise & Glide?" Eric asks. "I don't remember seeing anyone named Tina on the employee list," Eric says, leaning forward and picking up a file folder. He scans the first page, then the second. "No Tina."

"She said she left before we found Armando's body. Maybe she's not on the list because she left early."

"If that's the case, this list is incomplete and there are more employees to interview." Eric exhales a tired sigh. "I need to interview every employee who worked between Friday and Sunday. Not just employees who worked on Sunday."

"Sorry, honey."

"I'll ask Deb about it in the morning," Eric says, making a note inside the file folder.

"May I look at the coroner's report?"

"Go ahead," Eric says, handing me his laptop.

"It says here that Armando previously fractured his clavicle and previously fractured his distal radius," I comment. "Emmy never mentioned it."

"The coroner estimates the fractures were over twenty years old. They've long since healed," Eric says, scrolling through the report. "It says here,"—Eric points to the screen—"that the previous fractures are not relevant to the cause of death."

"It also says the coroner estimates the fractures happened at the same time. How did Armando break his collarbone and his wrist at the same time?"

"The coroner said the older the fracture, the harder it is to pinpoint the exact timeframe," Eric explains. "The coroner's time frame is an estimate. But he was close. According to the medical history his team doctors gave me, Armando told them he fell out of a tree and broke his collarbone at age ten, and fell off a bike and broke his wrist at age twelve."

"Armando was lucky he didn't break something that impacted his soccer career like his friend Mateo's career-ending knee injury," I say.

No wonder Mateo was jealous when Armando made the major leagues and he didn't.

CHAPTER 24

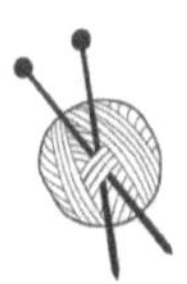

WEDNESDAY, October 5th

"Hi, Deb," I call out, approaching her from behind.

"Hello, Megan!" Deb excuses herself from the landscaper she's talking to and walks toward us with Blitz and Abby leading the way. She gives me a hug. "If you're looking for Eric, he's not here yet. I'm expecting him in about an hour."

"Actually, we're looking for you," I say, handing her a bouquet. "We wanted to thank you for everything you did on Sunday."

"Oh, my." Deb blushes, taking the flowers. "You shouldn't have. I didn't do anything. I wish I could've done more."

"You helped us through a horrible situation," I insist. "You took care of Emmy and me when we were in shock."

Emmy thanks Deb and gives her a hug. They both tear up and apologize to each other for the awful events of the previous Sunday that were neither woman's fault.

"Thank you! I'll go straight inside and put them in my office."

"We'll walk in with you," I say. "We're collecting Emmy's things from Room 814."

"I'll send a porter to help you," Deb offers.

"Thanks," I reply, squinting into the morning sun. "Is Tina working? She left her jacket at Knitorious yesterday, and I brought it with me."

"She's coming in late," Deb explains. "I don't know if you heard, but one of our employees got the gut rot real bad. He had to go to the hospital. Well, Tina is visiting him today and taking him a thermos of soup. I told her she could come in late. You can leave her jacket with me. I'll be sure she gets it."

"I'll go get it," Emmy offers.

I hand Emmy the car keys and tell her Tina's jacket is in the backseat.

"Tina has nominated herself as Gary's caregiver," Deb continues.

"Gary?"

"The employee who got the gut rot real bad."

"Right."

"I think she feels responsible for him since she saved his life."

"Tina saved Gary's life?" I ask. "How?"

"She found him and got him to the hospital. He was dehydrated and needed IV fluids," Deb explains. "Gary lives alone, and Tina lives nearby. She stopped by to check on him. She said he was weak and pale and confused. She took him to the hospital. He's home now, but he's still sick, and she's taken it upon herself to check on him every day."

"Tina's very thoughtful," I agree. "I hope Gary makes a full recovery and returns to work soon."

"YOU DON'T HAVE to go in," I say, looking at the numbers on the door and bracing myself to return to the scene of the crime. "You can wait in the car. I'll get everything and meet you there."

"I'm doing it," Emmy says, staring at the door handle like she's trying to open it with telepathy.

I've offered to collect her things at least half a dozen times since last night, but Emmy wants to be here. "Ready?"

"Ready."

Emmy swipes the card and opens the door. The room is bright with daylight, unlike last time we were here. I'm flooded by emotions when I step inside. Somehow it feels like a different room and the same room, all at once. It feels like we found Armando's dead body forever ago, and also like it was yesterday. Housekeeping was here. They made the bed, cleaned the washrooms, fluffed the sofa cushions, and opened the curtains. There's no room service cart. There's no sign that someone died here. You'd never guess a murder happened here, or this room was the epicentre of a murder investigation.

When the porter knocks on the door, I open it. He props the door open and wheels the luggage cart inside.

"Would you mind waiting in the hall?" Emmy asks. "We'll bring the luggage to you in the hall."

"Sure," he says. "Whatever you like. Shout if you need me."

The porter wheels the cart back into the hall and stands next to it.

"Thank you," I say to him and smile.

"I don't want anyone else in here," Emmy says.

In silence, we collect Emmy's things, stuff them in random bags, zip up each bag as it becomes full, and take them to the porter in the hallway. He arranges the bags on the cart like he's playing an oversize game of Jenga.

"Just one more minute." I hand the last overnight bag to the porter, then return to the room and find Emmy. "That's it," I say. "Everything is on the luggage cart."

Emmy nods and sits on the edge of the bed.

"Do you want a few minutes alone?"

Emmy nods.

"I'll be in the hall." I pick up the keycard from the dresser. "I'm taking the keycard."

I close the door behind me and join the porter in the hall. We make small talk. He avoided the gut rot and says the scourge seems to be over because no one—except Gary—called in sick today. We run out of things to talk about and wait in bored silence until Emmy leaves the room.

"Ready?"

"Ready."

We turn toward the elevator and a door at the other end of the hall opens. Brad Hendricks and Sonia Chang emerge from the room. Together. They look at us and freeze like we caught them with their pants down.

"You have got to be kidding me," Emmy whispers when she sees her two biggest haters.

We exchange awkward waves with the unlikely couple.

"Did you like your flowers, Sonia?" I call down the hall. "Brad has great taste in florists, eh?"

I smile and give Brad a nod.

They stand glued to their spots by the door to Brad's room while Emmy and I follow the porter and the luggage cart onto the elevator.

"Flowers?" Emmy asks when the elevator door closes. I tell her about my conversations yesterday with Phillip and Brad. "Poppy didn't tell you Brad and Sonia were a couple?"

"I devote as little time and energy as possible to Brad and Sonia," Emmy says, dismissing them. "They're a perfect match. I hope they make each other miserable."

THE PORTER LOADS the luggage into my compact SUV, and Emmy follows me home in her rental car, which had been at the hotel since she joined Armando there on Saturday.

One by one, Emmy and I remove the bags from my

car and carry them into the house with Sophie following us back and forth.

As I reach into the car for another suitcase, Sophie barks and snarls, causing me to bolt upright and search for the source of her warning.

"What do you want?" I ask. "How do you know where I live?"

"You're on the Hendrick's Agency Christmas card list," Brad replies.

"I'd like you to remove me from your Christmas card list," I say, crossing my arms in front of my chest.

"Can I come inside and talk to you for a minute?"

"No. You can talk on the driveway."

"Ugh!" Emmy groans as she appears behind me. "What do you want, Brad?" She lets the screen door close behind her.

"Hi, Emmy," Brad says. "Listen, I owe you an apology. I'm sorry I accused you of murdering Armando, and for the other things I said to you on Sunday. Armando would've killed me for talking to you like that. I'm sorry."

"You knew, didn't you?" Emmy asks, ramming her hands into her hips.

"Knew what?" Brad asks.

"You knew Armando was a bigamist." She shifts her weight and leans toward him menacingly. "Didn't you?!"

"It's not that simple, Emmy," Brad replies as Emmy's frustrated moan drowns out the end of his sentence. "Armando was a complicated guy. But he loved you. He told me you're the only woman he ever loved."

This is the nicest thing I've heard Brad say. Ever. And he sounds sincere.

"Is that what you came to say?" Emmy asks. "You said it. You can leave now."

"I need to talk to Megan about something," he says.

Emmy marches to the car and wrestles a rolling suitcase out of the back seat.

"I'll be in the house," she announces, marching to the door. "Call me when *he's* gone, and I'll come back."

Emmy opens the door, follows the corgi into the house, and slams the door behind her.

"What do you want, Brad?"

"I want to apologize for yesterday."

"You'll have to be more specific."

"I'm sorry if my joke made you uncomfortable. I was kidding, but maybe I took it too far."

I assume he's referring to his offer to get together, but I feign ignorance.

"Are you referring to the lie you told me?"

"I didn't lie to you."

"Yes, you did."

"No, I didn't."

"You just did it again."

"Did what?" He laughs.

"Lied to me."

"What did I lie about?"

"You told me you bought flowers for your client who had a baby. I know for a fact they were for Sonia Chang."

"I was protecting my privacy." He shrugs. "It wasn't a lie."

"It wasn't the truth." I mimic his shrug. "Anyway, I heard Sonia dumped you. Why was she in your hotel room this morning?"

"Where do you get your information?" Brad chuckles and shakes his head. "What can I say? Sonia can't help herself." He smacks his hands against his broad chest. "Women get weak in my presence. Weak in the knees." He winks. "Are you feeling weak, Megan?"

"The only part of me that feels weak in your presence is my stomach. You make me sick," I scoff. "Why do you do that?"

"Do what?"

"As soon as you show a glimpse of humanity, you erase it by regressing into a narcissistic, predatory creep."

"Fine," Brad concedes. "I lied about the flowers. Sonia and I dated for a while, but she dumped me. She said the same thing as you. She said I have the emotional maturity of a carrot, and she can't be with someone who won't let themselves be vulnerable."

"Wow. Sonia and I agree on something," I sneer. "What about the message you sent with the flowers? What did, *do you regret it yet* mean? What would Sonia regret?"

"Dumping me," Brad replies like it's the only obvious answer. "I told her she'd regret it. She says she doesn't, but her visit to my hotel room this morning says otherwise, am I right?"

"If you say so." I sigh and roll my eyes.

"I want you to know I'm not Sonia's source. I didn't tell her anything about Armando's past, and I didn't confirm anything when she asked me. It's possible she gleaned something vague from overhearing my half of conversations with Armando, but whatever information she told you about him, she uncovered without my help."

"She didn't coax Armando's secrets from you during pillow talk?" I suggest.

"No. I'd never betray my best friend like that," Brad insists. "The flowers were the only thing I lied about yesterday, I swear. Everything else I said was true."

"I don't know if I believe you," I admit. "You're an effortless liar."

"Why would I lie about my best friend ignoring me? Why would I lie about walking away from his room when staying might have saved his life?"

"Because it's better than admitting you killed him?"

"You think *I* killed Armando?" Brad shouts, then looks around to make sure no one overheard him. "Why would I kill my best friend?"

"Because Armando was planning to fire you and sign with a new agent," I reply. "Your reputation for never being fired, and your bank account, would take a hit."

"Armando would never fire me," Brad says with confidence. "Trust me."

"He told Emmy he would."

"He said that to keep her sweet," Brad says. "Look, Armando was at the end of his career. He had one, maybe two seasons left, tops. It wouldn't be worth his while to fire me and sign with someone else. He'd have to pay me a lot of money to break his contract, and most agents don't want a client that close to retirement. Also, I was Armando's best friend. I know his secrets. He trusted me. He needed me."

What Brad says makes sense. On Friday, Armando said he was at the end of his career and wanted to go out on top.

"Secretsss?" I ask. "Plural? Armando had more secrets? Are his other secrets related to the bigamy?"

Does Brad know if Armando had children? Does he know the truth about the birth certificates Adam uncovered?

"I shouldn't have said anything," Brad says.

"Emmy has a right to know," I protest. "Did Armando keep other secrets from her?"

"I can't… Look… Armando…" He sighs. "I can't say anything else until I talk to my lawyer."

"Armando is dead. Who are you trying to protect?"

I'm confident the only person Brad wants to protect, ever, is himself.

"I'll say this." Brad takes a deep breath and lets it out. "Armando wasn't the soccer player everyone thought he was."

"WHAT DID HE WANT?" Emmy asks after Brad leaves.

"I'm not sure, to be honest." I collapse on the living room sofa. Sophie jumps on the chair next to me and monitors the front yard through the window. "He apologized for being a jerk yesterday, then he was a jerk again. He admitted he and Sonia are in a situationship. He swears he didn't tell Sonia about Armando's first wife, but won't admit he knew Armando was a bigamist. He insists he didn't kill Armando."

"Of course, he does," Emmy replies. "Since Eric eliminated me as a suspect, Brad knows the police are closing in on him, and he's scared. Do you believe him?"

"Which part?"

Emmy shrugs. "Any of it?"

"I don't know," I admit. "Brad's a convincing liar. He clearly knows more than he admits. I get the sense he wants to talk, but his loyalty to Armando is stronger than his desire to unburden himself and do the right thing."

"My makeup bag and the bag with my electronics are still in the car. I'm going to get them. I'll be right back," Emmy says, slipping her feet into her shoes.

She disappears through the front door. I take a deep breath and contemplate what Brad said and didn't say, yesterday and today. I'm trying to find order in the chaos when Emmy comes back inside.

"They aren't there!" She throws her hands in frustration.

"Your makeup bag and electronics aren't in the car?" Emmy nods. "I remember you saying, *I'm taking my makeup bag and electronics to the porter.*"

Emmy nods. "Right after I said that, I saw my phone charger next to the bed. I put the bags on the washroom counter and left them there."

"It's understandable," I say. "You had a lot on your mind. I bet they're still where you left them."

"I'll ask Poppy to pick them up for me," Emmy says, reaching for her phone.

"We're taking a break from Poppy today, remember? It was your idea," I remind her. "I'm not ready to see her yet. I'll pick up your stuff."

"I'll come with you," Emmy says.

CHAPTER 25

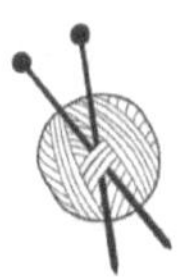

On the drive to Rise & Glide, Emmy admits she suspected Poppy was the mystery blogger.

"I don't make Poppy's life easy, Sis."

"That doesn't give her the right to libel you," I say. "Poppy needs to find a healthier way to cope with her frustrations."

"We have a complicated relationship," Emmy says. "Our boundaries are blurrier than a foggy night."

"Just give me one day to be mad at her. You can resume normal dysfunction tomorrow."

My phone rings through the Bluetooth speaker of the car, and Eric's name and photo flash across the screen on the dashboard.

"Hey, handsome!"

"Hey, handsome!" Emmy echoes beside me.

"Hey, babe. Hey, Emmy. How's everyone's day?"

"OK." I pause. "Brad just left."

"Hendricks?"

"Uh-huh."

"He was in our house?"

"I sent him away, but Megan let him stay," Emmy interjects.

"No. We talked on the driveway."

"What did he want?"

"He apologized to Emmy, he apologized to me, then he befuddled me with doublespeak."

"The nerve of that guy showing up at the house! I'm meeting with him and his lawyer today. I'll warn him never to get within a hundred feet of you again. Hopefully, he'll recognize the person who delivered the drugged food to Armando and pick them out of a photo lineup."

"He knew about the bigamy."

"Did he admit he knew?"

"He wouldn't say he didn't know."

"He knew," Emmy adds.

"We just missed each other at Rise & Glide this morning. Did you get Emmy's stuff?"

"We did. It's all good. How are the interviews going?"

"Good. The only person missing from the employee list is Tina. Deb says Tina probably forgot to punch in. I'm at the office now, but as soon as Deb sends me copies of Tina and Gary's personnel files, I'll question Gary at his house, then head back to Rise & Glide to question Tina. She hadn't arrived for work yet when I left."

"Oh," I say, concerned about Eric picking up the gut rot virus at Gary's house and bringing it home. "Please be careful. Keep your distance and touch nothing."

WHEN WE PULL into the hotel parking lot, Rich Kendall, Sonia Chang, and other *Hello, today!* crew members are getting out of their cars.

"Do you mind if I pop over and compliment them on today's show?" Emmy asks.

"Take your time," I reply. "I'll call April back."

Emmy bolts out of the car to talk to her co-workers, and I call April and catch her up on everything that happened since we spoke yesterday. Our conversation is shorter than normal, because April has a lunch date with her parents, but she assures me she's keeping a close eye on the gossip blog, and there are no new posts.

I get out of the car to join Emmy, and the thud of the car door closing gets Rich Kendall's attention. He looks at me and waves with a smile.

"Hi, Rich." I wave.

He jogs over to me.

"Hi, Megan." Rich beams. "How are you?"

"I'm OK," I reply. "Good show this morning. The on-location segments you're doing in nearby towns are great. It's nice to see you outside of the studio, wearing something other than a suit."

"We're enjoying them too," Rich replies. "And the ratings have increased every day this week, so the viewers agree. How's Emmy doing?" He jerks his head toward the group of co-workers Emmy is with. "She puts on such a brave face."

"Emmy is resilient," I say, neither confirming nor denying how Emmy is coping.

"If there's anything I can do, please ask, Megan. I'm always available, and I'd do anything for Emmy. Anything at all to ease her pain."

"It would ease Emmy's pain to know who killed Armando and see them behind bars," I say.

"I would help if I could. If only I knew for certain…"

Rich's voice trails off before he finishes his sentence.

"If only you knew what for certain?" I ask, sensing he wants to disclose something. "You don't have to be certain, Rich. The police will determine the certainty of whatever information you have."

"I don't have any information," Rich says, chuckling and shaking his head.

"Rich, did you kill Armando?"

"No!" he insists. He glances around to see who else might be in earshot of our conversation. "I would never"—he snaps—"I love Emmy! I would never hurt her."

"Even if it meant Armando would be out of Emmy's life?" I ask. "And you could step in to help her through her grief?"

"That's twisted!" Rich decries. "Yes, I love Emmy. But if I'm ever lucky enough that she might reciprocate those feelings, I want it to be genuine. I don't want her to love me because she's confused and lonely in the wake of her husband's death."

"That's good to hear," I respond. "Emmy values your friendship, and she needs her friends more than ever. If you have any insight or thoughts about who killed Armando and why, it would help Emmy deal with his death and move on."

"I didn't kill Armando," Rich says with a sigh. "But I'm afraid if it weren't for me, he might still be alive."

"What do you mean?"

"I think I might have brought Armando's killer to Harmony Lake with me."

"Didn't you travel to Harmony Lake with Sonia Chang?" I ask, trying to recall the order in which the caravan of travelers arrived.

"Yes," Rich confirms. "Sonia is ambitious. When she wants something, she pursues it with relentless persistence."

"Do you think she's ambitious enough to commit murder?" I whisper.

"She can be frightening when she wants something." Rich nods.

"Why would Sonia kill Armando?"

"Sonia still has feelings for me," Rich explains. "She's jealous of the close friendship and working relationship Emmy and I share." He smiles. "Admit it, Emmy and I have great on-screen chemistry."

He clears his throat. "Also, Sonia and Emmy were both short-listed for the co-host job on *Hello today!*, but the network offered it to Emmy. Sonia's not used to losing. She never got over it. I'm afraid Sonia sees Emmy as the obstacle between her and her dream man and dream job."

"Wouldn't it make more sense for Sonia to kill Emmy instead of Armando?" I argue. "Emmy's death would leave an empty spot in your heart and on the *Hello, today!* sofa."

"I suspect Armando was collateral damage," he suggests. "When Sonia and I checked into the hotel, we saw your fiancé helping Emmy carry her luggage. They didn't see us."

"You and Sonia knew Emmy was in Armando's room the night before he died," I conclude.

Rich nods. "And I wonder if Sonia poisoned the wrong person's food."

Rich might be onto something. Through Brad, Sonia could find out Armando's room number. And if Brad told her he was planning to go to the gym with Armando on Sunday morning, she might have assumed Emmy was in the room alone, and the room service delivery was for her.

"Just let me grab my purse, and we can go inside," Emmy shouts, approaching the passenger side of the car.

Rich says a hasty goodbye, then jogs to catch up to his co-workers at the front door of the hotel.

Emmy opens the back door, slings her designer purse over her shoulder, and holds up a small wallet.

"I found this on the floor in the back seat," she says, handing me a red, faux-leather, compact wallet.

It has the same dimensions as a credit card, but fatter. I unzip the wraparound zipper and the wallet opens like an accordion, revealing about a dozen credit card slots. There's nowhere to keep coins or bills.

"Is it yours?" I ask.

Emmy shakes her head.

"Then whose is it? It's not mine."

I wrack my brain trying to remember who, aside from Emmy, was in my car and might've dropped their wallet. Deb Kee comes out of the hotel, intercepting us just as we reach the door. I zip the wallet shut and clutch it in my hand.

"You're back," Deb says with a smile. "What can I do for you?"

"I left two bags and a charging cord in room 814," Emmy explains. "My brain is a sieve right now," she chuckles. "May I get them?"

"Of course," Deb says. "If you'd like, someone can retrieve them, and you can relax in the lounge."

"Thank you, Deb, but I'd rather get them myself." Emmy says. "I'm worried I left something else behind, and I haven't realized it's missing yet. Checking the room once more will ease my mind."

"You'll need a keycard." Deb raises her index finger. "I'll be right back."

Deb disappears, then reappears minutes later, and hands Emmy a keycard.

On the elevator, I unzip the mystery wallet again. It's familiar. I've seen it before, but I can't place it. No one aside from Emmy has been in my car for days. Whoever owns the wallet is probably searching for it high and low, or they've already gone through the hassle of cancelling all their cards.

"Pull out a card." Emmy waggles her eyebrows at the wallet.

I slide a random card out of a slot. It's the back of a driver's license. I turn it over, and the photo that fills the left side of the card draws my focus. Emmy inspects the driver's license over my shoulder.

"Tina!" I say, looking at her photo and wondering how her driver's license ended up in my backseat. Then it hits me. "It must have fallen out of her jacket in my backseat this morning. I'll text her and let her know I have it."

I slide Tina's driver's license back into its slot.

"Read the name!" Emmy's voice is quick, and she struggles to swallow like she has a lump in her throat.

"What's wrong?" I ask.

Emmy's eyes are full of panic; her breaths are shallow and fast.

I flip the card over and read the name on Tina's driver's license.

Cristina Garcia Duran.

My heart pounds in my ears and my throat. I blink and read the name again, to be sure.

Emmy and I lock eyes.

Tina Duran, the knitter, is Cristina Garcia Duran, Armando's sister?

CHAPTER 26

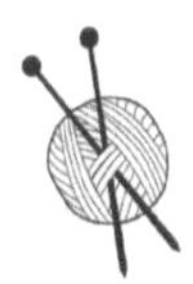

The elevator door opens, but Emmy doesn't move. She's frozen. I grab her arm and yank her off the elevator. We hook arms and race-walk to room 814.

"Maybe Cristina Garcia Duran is a common name," I suggest when we're alone inside the room.

"This isn't a coincidence," Emmy says, shaking her head.

We sit on the sofa and, one by one, remove each card from the wallet and read the name. They all say Cristina Duran except for her government issued ID, which says Cristina Garcia Duran.

"What's this?" Emmy asks, unfolding a receipt that's wrapped around a card. "A receipt from a pharmacy in Harmony Hills." She hands it to me.

"It's a receipt for syrup of ipecac." I look at Emmy. "Why would Tina buy syrup of ipecac?"

"Megan!" Emmy slaps her hand across her mouth and tears fill her eyes. "Armando choked on vomit!

What if he threw up because Tina gave him syrup of ipecac?"

"The coroner's report didn't mention syrup of ipecac," I respond. "If Tina is Armando's sister, why didn't she tell us when she met you on Friday?"

"Did she know I was your sister before Friday?" Emmy asks.

"I didn't tell her, but someone else could have," I reply. "Even if Tina knew we're sisters, she couldn't have known you'd show up in Harmony Lake on Friday. No one knew until you got here."

"But it's a logical assumption that I'd show up eventually," Emmy reasons. "It's also a logical assumption that my husband would accompany me." She pauses and collects her thoughts. "I mention you on the show sometimes. I never use your name or mention Harmony Lake, but maybe over the years I gave away enough non-identifying information for Tina to find you."

"You think Tina moved to Harmony Lake and learned to knit so she could befriend me and lie in wait for you to bring Armando here?"

It's too far-fetched to be true, right? It's preposterous… isn't it?

"What other explanation is there?" Emmy asks. "What's the date on the receipt?"

I scan the bottom of the receipt.

"Friday October 1st. Just after 8 p.m."

"The day I arrived."

"And a few hours after Armando checked into the hotel where Tina works."

"I didn't realize she works here," Emmy says, shaking her head. "The Tina I met at Knitorious on Friday is the same Tina you and Eric were talking about on the phone, and the same Tina whose jacket you gave to Deb this morning."

"The same person." I nod. "I know her as Tina Duran. She's recently divorced and came to Harmony Lake to build a new life."

"And take care of some unfinished business."

"Who said that?" Emmy demands.

"Tina?" I say, stunned when, out of nowhere, she appears in the bedroom doorway.

"I overheard Emmy ask Deb if she could come up to the room," Tina explains. "I sneaked in and waited for you. I couldn't believe my eyes when I walked into Knitorious on Friday and you were standing behind the counter, Emmy. I'd waited so long for that moment. Then, your husband checked into the hotel where I work. It was too perfect. I couldn't have planned it better. I even borrowed a keycard from housekeeping and also sneaked in on Saturday morning to be sure it was him."

"You're Armando's sister?" Emmy asks, inspecting Tina with narrowed eyes.

I'm inspecting Tina too. Looking for a family resemblance between her and Armando. There's none.

"Armando Garcia is my brother," Tina confirms.

"Why did you kill your brother?" I ask.

"My brother isn't dead," Tina corrects me. "My brother, Armando Garcia, is alive and well in Ecuador.

He lives with his wife and their three children. He works as a bus driver. Armando has a happy life."

My phone rings and Eric's name and photo flash across the screen.

"I should answer it," I say. "If I don't, he'll worry. And he knows where we are."

"If you want to know why I killed your husband, don't let Megan answer," Tina says to Emmy, then she opens her mouth to reveal a lozenge clenched between her front teeth. "It's a fentanyl lozenge. I just took two Rohypnol tablets. I only have about fifteen minutes left."

"Spit it out!" I beg, as my phone stops ringing and Emmy's phone rings.

"Uh-uh," Tina says. "I didn't mean to kill him. His death was an accident. I can't live with myself, and I'm going to die the same way he did."

Emmy declines Eric's call, and moments later, we both receive a text message from him.

Eric: Tina delivered the food. She might be Armando's sister. Trying to locate her. Are you safe?

"I'll reply to Eric's text and throw him off your scent," Emmy says to Tina as her thumbs fly back and forth across her phone screen.

"If you didn't mean to kill him, why did you give him a lethal cocktail of drugs?" I ask.

"He should've passed out. I was going to take inappropriate photos of him, use the photos to blackmail him, then sell them to the media and ruin his life," Tina explains.

"You were going to take inappropriate photos of

your brother?" Emmy asks, placing her phone face down on the table in front of her. "Ewww."

My phone dings with the text reply Emmy sent to Eric and I.

Emmy: We're safe. Room 814. Don't come in until we shout for you. Bring Naloxone and an ambulance.

"I told you," Tina says, leaning against the door frame, "he wasn't my brother."

"Was the man you killed Mateo Cruz?" I ask? "Armando's best friend?"

"Former best friend," Tina corrects me. "How did you know?"

"I suspected, but I didn't know," I admit. "When Adam verified Sonia's claim that Armando was married, he also uncovered birth certificates for Armando's children. But Armando hasn't been to Ecuador since he signed his major league contract. He also found the legal guardianship papers showing that your parents became Mateo's legal guardians after Mateo's parents died, but he didn't find any trace of Mateo after that. Then, Armando's medical history included a broken collarbone, and a broken wrist. Both around the same age.

"Mateo was the sole survivor of a fatal car accident that killed his parents. When the coroner estimated the injuries occurred together, I wondered if they were from the accident. Armando made up stories to explain the healed fractures because he knew they might show up on CT scans or MRIs, and the team doctors would ask about them. And earlier today, Brad made a cryptic comment about Armando not being the soccer player everyone thought he was."

"You're good," Tina chortles.

Are her eyes getting heavy, or am I imagining it?

"I was married to Mateo Cruz?" Emmy asks. "Why did he use your brother's name?"

"He had no choice," Tina says. "It was a big mess, but Mateo used it to his advantage. Armando and Mateo were best friends and teammates. They played the same position. Years ago, their team travelled to a tournament, and when they arrived at their destination, the equipment manager realized some bags didn't make it onto the team bus. Almost half the team didn't have uniforms. Armando couldn't play in the tournament, but he went with them to cheer them on."

"Why couldn't Armando play?" Emmy asks.

"He had to rest his knee for a few weeks."

"Our-Armando told Emmy that Mateo suffered a career-ending knee injury," I say. "But it was your-Armando who injured his knee?"

"Yes," Tina confirms. "My brother Armando, the one who's alive and well, had a knee infection, and the doctor drained fluid that accumulated. It was not a career-ending injury. He was good as new after four weeks of rest. Mateo, the man I killed and who you knew as Armando, never injured his knee."

"What happened next?" Emmy asks.

"Soccer has pretty strict rules. Every player has to wear a uniform, *their own* uniform. The team couldn't get the missing uniforms in time, so they played with fewer players than normal. With fewer players to substitute, it was going to be a tough tournament."

"Did they have to forfeit the tournament?" I ask.

"That wasn't an option. The team would have to pay a fine, and the spectators would demand refunds. They had to play. Even though he couldn't play, Armando's jersey was among the ones that made it onto the bus. The coach and the team manager decided Mateo would wear Armando's uniform and play as Armando. They were similar height and had similar hair colours, and they were out of town where fewer people would recognize them. Unbeknownst to anyone, major league scouts were in the stands."

"The scouts thought they were watching Armando Garcia play soccer, but they were watching Mateo Cruz play soccer in Armando's jersey," I surmise.

"Exactly." Tina disappears into the bedroom and returns to the doorway seconds later with the chair from the desk. She sits down and fights a yawn. "The scouts were so impressed that they offered Mateo, who they knew as Armando, a major league opportunity."

"Why didn't Armando tell the scouts that the player who impressed them was actually Mateo?" Emmy asks.

"It would have been an enormous scandal," Tina explains. "Mateo wasn't the only player the scouts signed at the tournament. A scandal like that would've put all the major league contracts from the tournament in jeopardy. It would have destroyed careers and teams."

The irony makes me shake my head. The infection and draining procedure on real-Armando's knee might have healed as good as new, but his knee still ended his career. If not for the infected knee, Armando would have worn his own jersey and played in that tournament.

"The people in charge convinced Mateo to go along with it and pretend to be Armando Garcia?" I ask.

"They convinced both Armando and Mateo. And Mateo promised to share his major league earnings with my brother. He promised to send half of his earnings to Armando."

"Did Mateo honour the agreement?" Emmy asks.

"Yes," Tina replies, slouching forward and propping up her head with her hand. "Until he met Brad."

"I knew Brad had to be involved," Emmy hisses. "What did he do?"

"When your-Armando signed with Brad, his income increased because he earned income from sponsorship deals. But he only sent home half of his soccer earnings. He kept the rest of the earnings for himself. He insisted he earned the sponsorship money on his own, so he should keep it. My family disagreed. We believed that the sponsorship money too was possible only because he was pretending to be Armando. The argument escalated and got ugly. We threatened to expose his true identity."

"Why didn't you expose the scheme?" I ask.

"Because we feared the other people affected might harm us. Brad travelled to visit my family. He told the local government about our threat. Soccer is important to the local economy. The scandal would have destroyed so many people. They pressured my family to stay quiet. Brad offered my family a lump sum of money for signing something, promising never to disclose the scandal. The local officials pressured us to take it."

"You came to Harmony Lake, and bided your time, hoping Mateo-pretending-to-be-Armando would show up so you could blackmail him with dirty pictures, then sell the dirty pictures, and get the money you believe he owes your family," I surmise.

"I followed his soccer career like a rabid fan," Tina explains. "And when he married Emmy, I tuned into *Hello, today!* every day." She looks at Emmy. "Whenever you mentioned anything about your personal life, I wrote it down. Eventually, I pieced together that your sister lives in Harmony Lake and owns a business. My marriage was over. I had no reason to stay where I was, so I moved here. It didn't take long to find a recently engaged, forty-ish business owner whose daughter was away at university."

Tina looks at me. "I like you, Megan. You're my friend. You made me feel welcome, and you introduced me to other friends. I almost got cold feet and didn't go through with it. But I went through with it, and it went wrong. So wrong," Tina says, crying. "Instead of falling asleep, Mateo collapsed. I struggled to get him into bed, then he started twitching and shaking. He had a seizure or something. Brad sent a text, then showed up at the door, knocking and shouting. I watched through the peephole until Brad left, then I hung the DO NOT DISTURB sign on the door in case he came back, or someone else showed up. When I returned to his bedside, he was dead. I don't know what happened. I tried to make him look peaceful. Like he was sleeping."

"He threw up," I explain. "Armando's body tried to purge his stomach contents, but he was unconscious and on his back. He choked to death."

"Didn't Armando—I mean, Mateo—recognize you when he answered the door?" Emmy asks.

Tina shakes her head. "He had no clue who I was." She forces herself to sit upright and blinks rapidly a few times. "We hadn't seen each other in over twenty years. I've lived abroad most of that time. I look and sound different now."

Sensing that Tina is running out of time, I try to move her confession along.

"Deb said Gary delivered the food to Armando. How did you intercept him?"

"I almost didn't," Tina admits. "The kitchen is always busy. There was no opportunity to drug the food. When my co-workers started getting the stomach flu, it gave me an idea. I put ipecac in Gary's water bottle. He's one of those people who tracks his fluid intake every day. I knew it was his job to deliver Mateo's first meal on Sunday. I figured when the ipecac made him sick, everyone would assume he caught the stomach flu that's going around, and I would make sure I was nearby to take over Gary's duties. But Gary didn't get sick. Well not right away. I thought it didn't work, but I stayed close to him anyway, just in case. I waited in the service hall."

Tina jerks her thumb behind her, toward the door to the

service hall which is next door. "I was there when Megan picked you up for brunch. I knew Armando was alone in the room. Gary rolled the cart to room 814, then ran next door, and threw up all over the floor in the service hall. I reported Gary's illness to Deb, then took over his duties. I told Deb that Gary threw up *after* he delivered the food to room 814. I mixed the crushed-up drugs in Armando's food in the hallway, then knocked on the door. He wanted to eat in the bedroom, so I rolled the cart in there. Then I pretended to leave. But I didn't leave, I waited just inside the door. I ran in when I heard him collapse."

"You knew Gary would mention that he didn't finish the food delivery before he got sick, and that you were in the service hallway when he threw up, so you kept feeding him ipecac to prevent him from coming to work or answering questions for the police. You weren't taking soup to Gary because you're a kind person, you were lacing the soup with syrup of ipecac to keep him sick."

"He almost died too," Tina admits with silent tears streaming down her face. Her breaths are shallow and laboured. "That's when I knew I couldn't live with what I'd done. I knew I needed to confess and kill myself. I was going to write a letter, but I wanted to apologize in person." She looks at Emmy. "I'm so sorry, Emmy."

Tina collapses. Her head rolls back, forcing her jaw open, and her limp body slides out of the chair and onto the floor. Her head hits the wooden seat of the chair on her way down.

Is Tina breathing? Is she dead? Emmy grabs my hand and pulls me off the sofa.

"Now! Eric!" Emmy screams, clutching my hand and leaping over Tina's feet to get to the door.

Emmy opens the door, and we almost crash into two paramedics rushing to rescue Tina.

I resolve never to enter room 814 again.

CHAPTER 27

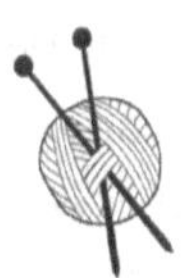

TUESDAY, October 19th

Eric sweeps into Knitorious and, with a victorious grin, slaps the list on the counter.

"That's it!" he declares, dusting his hands together. "Every Tupperware dish, casserole dish, and thank-you card, delivered."

"Thank you, honey." I kiss him, then he sinks into the sofa in the cozy sitting area, with a triumphant sigh and Sophie at his side.

We got home on Saturday from Armando's funeral. I continue to refer to him as Armando, because that's how we knew him.

But it took us until today to organize dishes, sign thank-you cards, and drop off everything to friends and neighbours.

The coroner released Armando's body the day after Tina's confession. Poppy helped Emmy arrange for a funeral home near Emmy to pick him up in Harmony Lake and transport him. So far, the truth about Armando's identity, that he was Mateo Cruz pretending to be Armando Garcia, is still a secret. The real Garcia family doesn't want any negative attention from Tina's actions, so they allowed us to call him Armando at the service.

Emmy still feels violated by her husband's lie, but she's relieved he wasn't a bigamist, and that he truly loved her and only her. That being said, Emmy doesn't want to profit from Armando's death. She offered to give his estate to the real Garcia family, but they don't want it either. Together, Emmy and the Garcia family decided Armando's legacy will fund a soccer scholarship for underprivileged youth and provide soccer fields and equipment to underprivileged communities.

"Any update on Tina?" I ask, joining Eric on the sofa and picking up the Knitted Knocker I was working on before he arrived with his victory list.

On a positive note, The Charity Knitters are on track to have their most successful Knitted Knocker campaign ever. Thanks to Rich Kendall mentioning their campaign on *Hello, today!*, knitters from nearby towns have been making Knitted Knockers and dropping them off at Knitorious. There's a huge bin of them on the harvest table in the middle of the store.

"She's out of the hospital, and they transferred her to jail, but she's still under the care of a mental health team," Eric replies. "Tina knows Emmy recorded her confession, and she told her lawyer she'll plead guilty and accept the consequences of her actions."

Eric figured out Tina Duran and Cristina Garcia Duran were the same person when he received her personnel file from Deb. When he checked the employee list the night before, he looked for someone named Tina. He didn't know her last name, or that Tina is a short form of Cristina. Turns out she was on the list the entire time.

After Emmy texted Eric from the hotel room, to tell him not to come in until she shouted for him, she opened the voice recording app on her phone and recorded Tina's confession. Tina will face charges for Armando's murder and for poisoning her coworker. Gary has made a full physical recovery and returned to work at Rise & Glide.

"If only Brad Hendricks would accept—or even acknowledge—the consequences of his actions," I gripe.

Brad denies convincing the Garcia family to accept a lump sum payment and sign a nondisclosure agreement about Armando's true identity. Despite the police tracking down his travel history, and proving that he was near the Garcia family when they received their lump sum payment, Brad insists he was on vacation, and the timing was a coincidence. With no one willing to say otherwise, Brad won't face consequences for his part in perpetuating Armando's lie. The injustice infuriates me, but I believe what comes around goes around, and Brad will receive his comeuppance sooner or later.

"At least he cooperated with the murder investigation," Eric reminds me. "After Tina confessed, Brad picked her out of a photo lineup as the person he saw knocking on Armando's hotel room door the morning he died. Gary told us Tina was in the service hallway when he threw up, but he couldn't place her with Armando's food. Only Brad could do that."

"Good morning!" Connie sings as she breezes through the front door. "Did you watch *Hello, today!* this morning?"

Sophie leaps off the sofa to greet her.

"We did," I reply. "The show is even better with the new producer. And the on-the-road episodes are my favourite!"

Yesterday was Emmy's first day back at work since Armando died. While she was on bereavement leave, Sonia Chang resigned from the network, and the new producer hopes to capitalize on the success of the on-location episodes in Harmony Lake by taking the show on location one week per month. To start, they're visiting hometowns of the cast and crew.

"Mine too!" Connie agrees. "This week they're visiting Rich Kendall's hometown, and it looks like such a cozy, sweet community. And the atmosphere on the show is much more relaxed without Sonia. The banter between Rich and Emmy is even more entertaining than usual."

While Tina was confessing to Emmy and I in room 814, Sonia Chang was emailing the head honcho of the network. She tendered her resignation, effective that day. Less than forty-eight hours later, she sat in the anchor seat at a rival network and aired an in-depth exposé about corruption in reality television. She specifically unveiled behind-the-scenes corruption at *Perfect Match*. According to Sonia Chang, and the proof she uncovered, the outcome of *Perfect Match* was predetermined, and viewer votes were meaningless.

To say April was upset is an understatement. Her

favourite reality TV show was fake. She swears she'll never trust reality TV again.

The network paid contestants hush money to follow a script and keep quiet about the predetermined outcome. As a result, *Perfect Match* was cancelled, several people associated with the show lost their jobs, and the previous seasons' celebrity contestants lost a lot of angry fans. Some even lost their jobs on other shows.

I have a theory about Sonia Chang's investigation into *Perfect Match.* I suspect Sonia discovered the corruption at *Perfect Match* from her friend, who is a producer on the show. She recommended Emmy and Armando as contestants on the next season of *Perfect Match,* so they would be in the crossfire when the show imploded because of her exposé. To increase the impact of her comeback story, she would've exposed Armando's alleged bigamy. Little did Sonia know, if she'd kept digging when she found the real Mrs. Garcia, she would've exposed an even bigger case of corruption: Armando's true identity. Emmy and Armando's marriage probably wouldn't have survived the public probing, and Emmy would've lost her job and reputation for sure. Sonia would've gotten revenge against Emmy for taking the job on *Hello, today!* and Rich Kendall's heart, and Sonia would've re-established herself as the queen of investigative reporting. Armando's murder thwarted Sonia's plan. She jumped ship to another network and aired her investigative report sooner than planned.

"Did you guys read Poppy's new blog post?" April

asks, her voice competing with the jingle of the bell over the door.

Her abrupt entrance startles Sophie, who jumps to attention.

"No," I reply, my heart sinking into my stomach. "Is it another anti-Emmy post?"

So far, Poppy has remained true to her word and hasn't posted anymore anti-Emmy blog posts since I confronted her about being the mystery blogger. Emmy and Poppy talked it out, and Poppy admitted that being Emmy's best friend and assistant was too much. Poppy resigned as Emmy's assistant but kept her status as Emmy's best friend. In fact, Poppy had to hire an assistant for herself after her recent overnight success.

Following the *Perfect Match* fiasco, Poppy's little-known, anonymous gossip blog got a lot of attention from readers who found it while searching online for information about *Perfect Match* and the show's previous contestants. The blog became so popular so fast that Poppy now runs it full time. She sells advertising space for obscene amounts of money, and instead of relying on her invisibility superpower to learn tidbits of gossip about B- and C-list celebrities, she gets tips from all over the world about A-list celebrities. According to Poppy, the tipsters are often celebrities themselves, looking for publicity or trying to control how they're portrayed in the media.

"I think Poppy is too busy to post about Emmy," April teases. "But listen to this. *For Stitcher, For Poorer, In Stitchness and in Health.* I think the headline is a nod to you Megnificent." April clears her throat and continues,

"Wedding bells will ring this Christmas for a certain A-list celebrity actor, who's returning to the scene of the crime to put a ring on it. The alliterative actor will say her vows surrounded by love and harmony. Lake on one side and mountains on the other, the celebrity couple booked every room, cabin, and cottage in between, so their nuptials will be cozy and paparazzi-free."

"Someone is getting married?" I venture a guess. "Someone who's first and last initials are the same… someone who visited Harmony Lake before…"

"It's Jules Janssen!" April blurts out before she explodes from waiting for me to piece it together.

"Jules Janssen is getting married in Harmony Lake?" I ask. "To whom?"

"The co-star she fell in love with. You know, that handsome guy. The tall one?" April raises her hand above her head to show me what tall means. "He's handsome and sultry. He has that hair." She musses the top of her long blonde hair, then pushes my shoulder. "You know who I mean."

I don't know who she means.

"Oh! *Him*!" Connie agrees, snapping her fingers and nodding. "I know who you mean. He has that voice and does the thing with his eyebrows." She does a weird thing with her eyebrows.

"Yes!" April points at Connie. "Him. He's the guy Jules Janssen is marrying in Harmony Lake at Christmastime."

"It's just a rumour," I point out. "It's a gossip blog. And Poppy didn't mention any names."

"When is Poppy's blog ever wrong?" April challenges.

"She's right, my dear," Connie agrees. "Poppy's blog hasn't been wrong yet."

"Think about all the A-list celebrities walking up and down Water Street, in and out of our stores," April remarks, absorbed in the fantasy.

My phone and April's phone chime in unison. It's a text from the WSBA—the Water Street Business Association.

"See, I told you it's true," April says smugly, then shows Connie the text.

"What?" Eric asks.

"Jules Janssen just booked every room at Rise & Glide, King of the Hill, and the Hav-a-nap motel," I reply.

"I'm surprised she wants to come back here," Eric comments.

"Jules said Harmony Lake was beautiful," I recall out loud. "She even talked to Adam about filming here."

"Last time she came to town, she ended up in the middle of a murder investigation," Eric says. "Why would she want to get married in a town where she was once a murder suspect?"

"There's no such thing as bad publicity?" Connie suggests with a shrug.

"I'm sure it'll be fine," April retorts. "People don't die at weddings."

I hope not.

IN STITCHNESS AND IN HEALTH

Love is in the air when Harmony Lake hosts the celebrity wedding of the century.

But, when the famous bride and groom back out at the last minute, there might not be a wedding.

The big day seems even less likely when the wedding planner is murdered and the blaring of police sirens replaces the ringing of wedding bells.

Can I figure out who tied the knot around the wedding planner's neck? I vow to unravel the clues and find the killer before the big day.

ALSO BY REAGAN DAVIS

Knit One Murder Two

Killer Cables

Murder & Merino

Twisted Stitches

Son of a Stitch

Crime Skein

Rest In Fleece

Life Crafter Death

In Stitchness and in Health

Neigbourhood Swatch: A Knitorious Cozy Mystery Short Story

Sign up for Reagan Davis' email list to be notified of new releases and special offers: www.ReaganDavis.com Follow Reagan Davis on Amazon

Follow Reagan Davis on Facebook and Instagram

ABOUT THE AUTHOR

Reagan Davis doesn't really exist. She is a pen name for the real author who lives in the suburbs of Toronto with her husband, two kids, and a menagerie of pets. When she's not planning the perfect murder, she enjoys knitting, reading, eating too much chocolate, and drinking too much Diet Coke. The author is an established knitwear designer who regularly publishes individual patterns and is a contributor to many knitting books and magazines. I'd tell you her real name, but then I'd have to kill you. (Just kidding! Sort of.)

http://www.ReaganDavis.com/

Made in United States
Troutdale, OR
10/11/2024